LITTLE JACK

Hell's Handlers Book 6

Lilly Atlas

Other books by Lilly Atlas

No Prisoners MC
Hook: A No Prisoners Novella
Striker
Jester
Acer
Lucky
Snake

Trident Ink
Escapades

Hell's Handlers MC
Zach
Maverick
Jigsaw
Copper
Rocket
Little Jack

Join Lilly's mailing list for a **FREE** No
Prisoners short story.
www.lillyatlas.com

Holly Lane has spent her life under the crushing thumbs of her cop father and controlling mother. Now, well into her twenties, she's finally getting a fresh start and moving into her own apartment. Breaking away from her parents should be easy, but how can Holly begrudge their overprotective nature when their other daughter was murdered by an outlaw biker years ago?

With his brand-spankin' new patch, Little Jack has a satisfying life in the Hell's Handlers MC. Sure, the town's new sheriff is messing with his club, but it's nothing they can't handle. Life only gets better when LJ's dream woman walks out of his fantasies and into the vacant apartment next to his. Holly is sweet as sugar, curvy in ways that make LJ's mouth water, and the woman can bake like no other. Personal demons keep LJ from chasing a long-term relationship with any woman, but that doesn't mean he can't have a little fun with his hot new neighbor.

Holly is pretty sure life is finally on the right track when she meets LJ on her first day in town. Incredibly tall, bearded, tattooed, and strong enough to unload her car without breaking a sweat, her new neighbor just might be perfect.

With outrageous chemistry and a genuine liking for each other, Holly and LJ seem destined for an explosive encounter until a tornado rolls through their budding relationship in the form of Holly's father. As the new town sheriff, her father only has one item on his agenda: eliminate the Hell's Handlers MC.

LITTLE JACK

Lilly Atlas

PROLOGUE

Staring at her own face on a corpse in a coffin topped the list as the most surreal experience of Holly's twelve years. So bizarre, the shock overrode her grief. A truth she wouldn't have thought possible when she woke up that morning, eyes swollen and tear stains on her pillow. Or when she finally fell asleep the night before, with a crater in her heart.

But it was true. Holly was so stunned by the sight before her, she forgot to be sad.

She closed her eyes and softly counted aloud to ten. Tightening her grip on the edge of the unforgiving wooden pew, she opened her eyes only to find herself gazing at her own image once again. Her shoulders sagged as all the air left her body and the hole in her heart seemed to grow in size. As it had at least a hundred times over the past two weeks, the exercise proved futile.

Reality hadn't changed.

Holly still had a front-row seat to exactly what she would have looked like had she died instead of her twin. Her best friend. Her other half. The person she loved most. And the sentiment was mutual.

Or it had been mutual. Now, Holly was left loving Joy just as much, but not having that love returned. Because Joy was gone.

"Joy," she choked out on a sob as pain once again exploded its way through her body. She hadn't thought anything could hurt more than that time she'd cracked a rib trying to catch a baseball her older brother threw to her. Instead of catching it with her mitt, the ball slammed into her body. This made that experience seem like getting hit with a cotton ball.

Some funeral worker had wound Joy's hair into two long, tight braids that lay over her shoulders and ran halfway down her torso. Her favorite hairstyle. Both their favorites. Neither wanted the hassle of dealing with long hair, but their mother insisted they not cut it. Braids at least kept the too-long locks from being totally annoying. Other than wearing far more makeup than Joy would have been allowed or would have wanted in life, she looked like herself, but peaceful. As though she were sleeping. But Joy never slept on her back. She was a stomach sleeper all the way. Not Holly, she much preferred to sleep on her back. Like a corpse, Joy used to tease. Now the sentiment had new meaning, and Holly would probably never sleep that way again.

Though nearly impossible to tell apart by sight, their personalities couldn't have been more different. Joy was outgoing, brave, rebellious, and so much fun to be around. The embodiment of her name. Holly was far more introverted. Happy to spend her free time in the kitchen baking instead of out causing trouble. "Holly and Joy," their mom always said. "Two different cookies shaped from the same cookie cutter." That's right, born on Christmas Eve, her parents named their identical twin girls Holly and Joy.

A fact that used to make Holly gag, but now that Joy was gone both literally and figuratively, she'd give anything to hear someone chuckle over their names.

"Could have been worse," Joy had always liked to say when Holly complained about the cheesiness of their names. "If we were boys, we might be Frosty and Rudolf. Or they coulda called us Jingle and Belle." The ridiculous argument always led to them trying to one-up each other, thinking of the most outrageous Christmas themed names their parents could have dreamed up.

"Fuck," Holly whispered as a sharp pang pierced her already battered heart. Thankfully, her parents were out by the funeral home's exit, seeing off the last of the mourners, so no one was around to hear her swear. Mamma Lane didn't abide by her pre-teen daughters cussing. Nothing pissed her off more.

"I'm so sorry, Joy," Holly whispered. "I should have gone with you. Maybe if we'd both been there—" She shuddered, unable to finish that sentence as guilt once again swamped. Even though it'd been a constant emotion over the past few weeks, the crushing feeling still killed her. The logical side of her knew that had she been with Joy that day, there could be two coffins side by side at the front of the room. But the part that loved her sister beyond reason blamed herself for not saving Joy.

Maybe whoever kidnapped, and eventually murdered half of Holly's heart would have been deterred by the prospect of going after two kids instead of just one. Or maybe she could have fought off the attacker while Joy ran for help. Or maybe she could have done...something, *anything* to prevent sitting in a room with her sister's corpse. The maybes and what-ifs had torn her apart over the past few weeks and probably would for the rest of her life.

How was she supposed to go on without Joy? They'd been so excited to turn thirteen in a few months. Ready to enter their teen years as a unit. They often spoke about going to college together, someday getting an apartment in Tampa, and eventually marrying another set of twins. Together forever.

Now it was all over. Gone in an instant.

Holly felt so lost and alone. Constantly cold as though all the warmth had faded from her life with Joy's death.

And the added sense of responsibility was overwhelming. How she spent the remainder of her life just became twice as important as it had been only two weeks ago. Now, she was no longer living for herself, but for two. And she refused to let Joy down by living half a life.

"I promise, Joy-Joy," she whispered to the lifeless body in the shiny black coffin with a silky yellow interior—Joy's favorite color. Bright and cheery. Just like her twin's personality. "I promise I will live every day to the max. For you."

Silence was the only response, of course, because dead bodies didn't speak, no matter how hard Holly wished otherwise. With a thousand-pound weight resting on her chest, Holly finally stood and walked toward the coffin. She'd been waiting for a private moment away from all the pitying gazes. All four of her limbs seemed to grow heavy as though she was slogging through thick mud.

When she reached the coffin, Holly dug half of the Best Friend's necklace out of her pocket. It was one of those hearts split down the middle with best on one side and friends on the other. A trinket they'd purchased a few years ago with their allowance money. Though they'd never taken it off in life, Holly's mother hadn't wanted Joy to wear it today. She thought it not classy enough.

But there was no way Holly would allow that coffin to be put in the ground without Joy's half of the necklace. Afraid to disturb the peace Joy's body seemed to have found, she didn't clasp it around her sister's neck but hid it under her palm instead. Then she held onto the charm of her own necklace as she let the tears fall. "Goodbye, J-Joy," she said, then pressed a kiss to her sister's forehead. "I'll wear this for the rest of my life."

"Holly? Holly, where are you?" Her father's panicked voice sounded from the hallway outside the visitation room.

She should call out. Alert him to where she was. The poor man had just lost a child in the most traumatic of ways, but all of a sudden, exhaustion hit so hard, she couldn't summon the energy to shout back.

"Holly?" Pounding footsteps drew closer until they came to a stop somewhere behind her in the visitation room. "Jesus, Holly. What's wrong with you? Do you have any idea how worried your mother was when we couldn't find you?"

As she turned away from the coffin, Holly used every last bit of her fledgling strength to bite her tongue. For the past two hours, family, friends, and what seemed like a thousand police officers from around the state had paraded in and out of the memorial service.

For her dead twin sister.

Throughout the entire ritual, Holly sat with her butt rooted to the very seat she now returned to. She didn't cry, didn't speak with any of the guests, didn't move a muscle. Just stared at her sister. Most mourners seemed to understand without words that she needed this time to be with her sister. So where did her parents think she would be?

This should have been the very first place they looked before anyone even edged toward worry. She was trying, really trying to remember their grief was just as consuming as hers, but they'd changed over the past two weeks. They'd changed when Holly needed them most, and it was so hard to deal with the loss of Joy and the change in her parents at the same time.

"Been right here the whole time, Dad," Holly said as her father approached. He sat, leaving an empty seat between them. No hug, not even so much as a pat on the back for comfort. That wasn't her father's style. All he had to offer was a burning desire to punish whoever it was that took Joy from them.

"Well, your mother was scared shitless. You should have let her know you planned to stay in here." His eyes narrowed, and the expression of near disgust wasn't lost on her. As though he couldn't stand to look at her face now that the other half of her was missing.

Welcome to the club.

Holly sunk her teeth into her lower lip so hard she made herself jump. "Just been sittin' here. Haven't moved."

He grunted. It wasn't often she saw him in his police uniform these days. Not since he'd been promoted to detective and wore civilian clothes ninety-five percent of the time. Today, he looked so official in the crisply pressed navy-blue uniform. With the same blonde hair she and Joy shared along with those blue eyes, she and her twin were clearly their father's daughters.

"Come on," he said, voice thick with regret as he stared at the lifeless body of his child. "Y-your mother's waiting in the car. She wants to get to the cemetery before everyone else. After that, everyone is coming to the house. Gonna be a long afternoon." Holly couldn't help but notice the trembling in his hands and the agony written all across his face.

More socializing. All Holly wanted to do was curl up with Joy's childhood stuffed giraffe and hide under the covers for the next week. But instead, she had to spend the day schmoozing people who pitied her.

Holly rose and started for the exit. Each step felt like she was leaving her sister behind and the urge to turn back, run to Joy, and hold on with everything she had was nearly impossible to resist.

"Hol?" her dad called out.

She turned to see him still staring at Joy, silent tears on his cheeks. Her heart softened. She knew she'd been difficult over the past two weeks. Angry at them, angry at herself, angry at the whole world.

"When we get home, you stay inside the house. Preferably within sight of your mother or I the entire time, you hear?"

A sense of foreboding overtook her as she stared at her father's sunken eyes and haggard face. The man seemed to have aged ten years in the past seventeen days since Joy had been kidnapped. Everything was about to change. Her life was in the midst of a dramatic shift. The transformation went beyond learning how to live without her best friend. Ever since Joy had been abducted, her parents acted as though Holly would also vanish at any point in time. She was watched like a hawk.

Questioned every time she left the room about where she was going, who she was going with, when she'd been back. Hell, she couldn't even go to the bathroom without an interrogation about her plans.

This would become her life moving forward. She could sense her parent's obsession with her whereabouts wasn't a passing neurosis due to recent circumstances. No, Joy's death had altered the way her family functioned from here on out.

Holly was about to enter her teenage years, and they wouldn't be anything like she'd expected.

As she stepped outside, her father at her back, Holly squinted and lifted a hand to shield her eyes from the harsh glare of the afternoon Florida sun. Didn't make any sense how the sun could shine so bright and beautiful while she suffered from such intense darkness and heartache on the inside.

A rumble from somewhere to her left had her father tensing in an instant. As the noise grew, she had the urge to cover her ears. Holly's jaw dropped as ten giant motorcycles rolled down the street, stopping in front of the funeral home.

"Fuck," her father bit out. With a crushing grip, he snagged her arm and dragged her behind his body. Holly gaped in shock as his hand fell to the gun resting at his hip.

"Dad!" she whisper-yelled. "They're not going to do—"

"Quiet, Holly! You have no idea what these men are capable of. They killed your sister, for Christ's sake."

A stare-down ensued between the president of the local motorcycle club and her father. To Holly's frightened mind, the standoff seemed to last for hours.

Joy's kidnapper, and ultimately her murderer, hadn't been identified as of yet. Holly didn't have a clue what evidence the detectives were working with, but her father was one hundred percent convinced the MC was to blame. More than to blame, he believed they were directly responsible. Or so she'd overheard when she'd been unable to sleep and snuck into the kitchen for a late-night snack. He'd hated the gang since as far back as Holly could remember, and now made it his mission to see every one of them behind bars for Joy's murder.

Holly wasn't so sure. About six months ago she'd had a run-in with the president of the MC. Curly was his name. He'd helped her when she'd gotten herself in a sticky situation, something she'd never told her father. That was until the lead detective on Joy's case questioned her about the day Joy went missing. He'd flat out asked if she'd ever had any interaction with someone from the MC and she'd been unable to lie. It was hard to imagine the man who'd saved her bacon kidnapping and murdering her sister. He'd actually been kind, calling her Little Miss and helping her despite knowing full well who her father was.

But what did she know?

Holly peeked around her father's side. Her gaze met Curly's. The old man gave her a sympathetic smile and a nod. "Little Miss," he mouthed.

"What the fuck?" her dad growled. "Keep your fucking eyes off my kid."

Curly made a production of skirting his gaze.

Some of the remaining mourners lingered as they got into their cars, watching the scene with nervous curiosity.

"I'm coming for you, assholes. Enjoy your freedom while you've still got it because one day real soon you're gonna miss it."

"Dad," she tried again. "I really don't think it was them."

"Holly, I said be quiet. Get behind me. I don't want their filthy fucking eyes on you." He pushed her out of sight.

The next thing she knew, the doors opened behind her, and two men emerged wheeling the now closed casket containing her sister's body out of the funeral home. Holly gasped and covered her mouth with her hand.

Oblivious to the tension, the undertakers wheeled the casket down the ramp and to a waiting hearse. Her father's body tensed.

All the bikers revved their engines at once. Holly resisted the urge to cover her ears as the sound rose to deafening.

"Fucking disrespectful animals," her dad mumbled as the last bike tore off behind the group.

While he'd seen it as a disturbance of the peace and quiet, Holly had viewed the simultaneous bike-rev as a sign of respect. A little tribute to Joy, biker style.

"They'll pay for what they did to your sister, Holly. If it takes my last dying breath, I'll make all those fucking bikers pay."

Holly swallowed as she watched the bikes fade into the distance. It felt symbolic. Her old life disappearing, leaving behind something unfamiliar and ominous.

CHAPTER ONE

LJ stuffed his size-fourteen feet into the running shoes he'd worn long past their prime. Yeah, those suckers needed replacing before he ground his knees or ankles to dust, but they were like a longtime lover. Comfortable, familiar, a perfect fit.

Or so he'd heard. He sure as hell didn't have any experience with long-term relationships, but word on the street made them sound like old, beat-up shoes. He chuckled to himself. Maybe that analogy was why he hadn't held on to a woman longer than a few months. Most of them probably wouldn't appreciate the comparison to stinky old footwear.

Okay, that was bullshit. He knew the real reason he shied from commitment but preferred to blame it on something more straightforward.

After hydrating the fuck outta himself all day to make up for hours spent pouring a different kind of liquid down his gullet the night before, LJ resigned himself to the one hangover cure that worked every time. Running. It sucked balls while he was at it, but pounding the pavement for a good ten miles sweat out whatever toxins were making him feel like shit. So, at five in the evening, he finally dragged his sluggish ass off the couch and got ready to run.

Only perk that came from hitting the bottle as hard as he had the previous night was a deep, dreamless sleep. A rare feat. However, choosing that route was a slippery slope with only one of two endings. Alcoholics Anonymous or swallowing his gun. Since neither outcome sounded desirable, LJ kept a tight handle on the amount of alcohol he typically consumed.

But last night had been a special occasion. A celebration quite a long time coming.

As he stepped outside, LJ slid his Oakley's over his nose, but not before the sun singed his throbbing brain straight through his eye sockets. "Last time I fuckin' drink ever again," he muttered, as he jogged past the empty second-floor apartment next to his. His limbs moved like they were made of wood instead of flesh and bone. Picking up the pace, he turned the corner only to narrowly avoid taking out a woman carrying a box twice her size. "Whoa, shit," he shouted as he dodged right.

Whoever she was, she yelped and staggered back, unbalanced by the heft of the box.

LJ lunged forward, snatching the heavy load from her with one arm as he used the other to steady her by her shoulder.

"Holy crap, you're huge. And you just saved my life," she said, panting with a hand pressed to her heaving chest.

LJ chuckled as he set the box on the concrete walkway. "Since I was the one who almost took you out, I'm pretty sure the save doesn't count."

"Oh, it counts," she argued, voice full of sass. "And I'm pretty sure I'm the one to blame since I got all cocky and decided to haul the biggest box in the trunk."

With another chuckle he straightened, faced her, and—*fuck me* —his dick punched against his running shorts in an instant.

"I'm Holly," she said, a sweet smile playing on those pouty, unglossed lips as she stuck out her hand.

Holly. A sweet name to go with that sugary smile. God, she was...lush was the only word that came to mind. On the shorter side—well at least compared to him—curvy as fuck, with tits he'd kill to bury his face between, the woman was just his type. He hadn't been lucky enough to catch a glimpse of her ass yet, but he bet it was round and jiggled as she walked. Jesus Christ, he could get lost for days in all that softness.

"Um, okay," she said, as she started to draw her arm back.

"Shit, sorry!" he grabbed her hand and didn't let go. "Zoned out for a second. My brain's a little slow today due to some poor choices last night. I'm LJ. You moving in?" The smoothness of her skin didn't escape him for one second. Especially the way her silky fingers curled around his larger and much rougher palm. Despite the soft feel, her grip was solid.

She smiled, and it lit her up, all glowy and shit. God, she was so fucking adorable, with her honey-blonde hair pulled back in a loose, low ponytail. Perfect complement to those round, ocean blue eyes he could drown in. And, apparently, she'd turned him into a poetic pussy.

"I am! Apartment 2A."

Well, well, well. This could get interesting. Hopefully, he could keep his dick under control and not scare her away by being rock hard every time they came in contact. "You're right next to me. Welcome to the complex. That place has been sitting empty for about six months. Ever since the murder-suicide that took place in there. Crazy couple. Used to fight all the time. He finally offed her, and himself a few minutes later."

Her smile flipped upside down in an instant as the color drained from her face. "Murder?" she croaked, eyes bugging. "Suicide?"

Aw, fuck. He was an ass. Sometimes, he forgot not everyone had the crass sense of humor he'd gotten used to tossing out around his MC brothers. "Uh, no, sorry. I was just teasing you. Sounded much funnier in my head." He shrugged.

Holly's mouth opened and closed a few times.

Well, there went any opportunity of sucking on her nipples or seeing exactly what that body looked like without the tattered T-shirt and yoga pants.

For a woman to be rocking a sloppy ponytail, no makeup, and scruffy clothes and still make his dick hard as a pipe...that said something.

Him and his stupid fucking mouth.

Holly's head dropped back, and she let out a melodic laugh that did absolutely nothing to squelch his hard-on. "So that's how you're gonna be, huh?"

Or maybe not so stupid...

His grin had to be huge as fuck with the way it was stretching his cheeks. Damn, she was gonna be a fun neighbor. Especially if she ever let him between those thick thighs. "You doing this by yourself?" he asked, pointing to the box between them.

Holly rolled her baby blues. "No. Not exactly. My dad and brother are coming out in the morning to help me unload the U-Haul. I wasn't supposed to get in until tomorrow, but I wanted a few hours to get acclimated to the place before my overbearing family descends." She shrugged and looked away. "You know how it is."

Uh, no, he did not. His family wouldn't spit on him if he were on fire. "I'll take your word for it."

That had her head snapping back in his direction as she gave him an openly curious look.

He bent down and hoisted the box up to his shoulder. "Lead the way, pretty girl."

Her eyes widened. "Damn, you make that look easy. Where'd you get all those muscles? I could use a few."

The laugh he belted out had her giggling alongside him. "I'll give you the website."

"Seriously," she said with a shake of her head. "You do not have to do this. Carrying big boxes sucks. Save yourself and finish your run. Although running sucks just as bad." Her face scrunched as though running truly offended her.

Jesus, if she didn't stop saying the word suck, she just might find herself on her knees preparing to do just that. "Eh, no biggie," he said, exaggerating the flex of his admittedly sizable biceps. "Gotta let these puppies out to play every now and again, or they'll get bored and run away." He gestured for her to head down the hallway first.

She snorted as she led him to her apartment door. Ahh, there was the ass view. Just as he'd imagined. Plump, round, and so fucking squeezable his palms itched.

Oblivious to his stare and his boner, or at least polite enough to pretend she was oblivious, she held the door open for him. As soon as he stepped through, something warm nudged straight into his crotch. "What the fuck?"

He set the box down and found the biggest dog he'd ever encountered getting up close and personal with his junk. "Shit," he said with a laugh as he reached down to scratch the jet-black beast behind his ears. "Had you warned me you had such a huge boyfriend, I'd have toned down the flirting."

Holly, who'd made it to the kitchen by this point spun on her heel and darted back toward them. "I'm so sorry! Biscuit, get over here. Leave LJ alone. I'm so sorry," she said again. "I thought he was asleep in my room, or I would have warned you about him. He's a total whore." She tried in vain to wrestle the humungous hound away from LJ's family jewels.

"No worries." LJ squatted down which at least got the dog away from the danger zone. It was like the hairy guy could smell his arousal or something. Some kind of primitive man to beast bond. "He's a handsome guy. What is he?"

"A mountain mastiff," she answered. "Worst guard dog in existence, as you can see, but thankfully he's big enough he tends to intimidate on sight."

LJ watched her as she scratched the dog behind his ears. The big baby rolled to his back, presenting his long stomach for a good rub. LJ obliged at once.

"How'd you know he was a boy?" She asked as her hand joined his on Biscuit's belly.

"For real?" he asked with a laugh. "Come one, look at that thing. It's kinda hard to miss." He pointed toward the large schlong sticking up proudly between the dog's hind legs. "We've got a few things in common."

Holly's mouth dropped open, then she snickered. "I see you're gonna keep me on my toes."

"I'll take you any way I can get you. On your toes, your back, right up against that wall." LJ winked. "Come on, let's grab some more of your shit before it gets dark."

Her face turned an adorable shade of pink. "Um, thanks, LJ. Hopefully, I can repay the favor someday soon."

Uh, yeah, he could think of at least twenty ways she could repay the favor, and all involved her being naked and moaning his name. Since he assumed he'd come on strong enough for the first meet, he kept those thoughts to himself.

"Biscuit, go to your bed," she ordered. The giant dog obeyed at once, loping over to a substantial oval dog bed in the center of the bare living room.

"Biscuit?" Poor guy.

She blushed even harder as she nodded.

For the next thirty minutes, they worked in relative silence as they unloaded her Jetta. LJ made sure to let her lead the way up the steps each trip, so he had a prime view of that stellar ass.

"That's it, right?" She asked as he deposited a box marked "Baking Shiz" onto the small kitchen island. It'd been the heaviest box by far. And not the only one with a baking label. The woman must like to bake. Second to the possibility of headboard-banging sex, this could be the best thing about having her as a neighbor.

"Yes, ma'am," he quipped.

She shot him a look over her shoulder as she opened her refrigerator. "Ma'am? I'm twenty-four, LJ, not sure I qualify as a ma'am." She removed two bottles of Yingling and a small Tupperware case, then made her way back to the island.

Huh, look at that. "Hey, we're almost the same age! I'm twenty-five, and I was in the military for four years, so all females are ma'am to me."

She handed him a bottle, then fished through her purse for her keychain, which she also tossed to him.

"Uhhh…"

With a laugh, she snatched the keys back. "Sorry, forgot we just met or something. Here." She handed the keychain back, this time holding out the bottle opener attached to a key ring.

Instant bottle opener? Another check in this girl's pro column.

"Ahh, I'm with you now, pretty girl." He popped the cap on his beer, then did the same to hers. "Thanks," he said after taking a sip. "This hits the spot." So much for never drinking again. All it took was one sweet smile and two big tits to have him going back on his word.

"Yes, it does." She peeled the Tupperware open. "Want one?"

Before he even had a chance to peek in the container, a sugary, strawberry smell hit his senses and he nearly groaned. "Holy shit, what the hell is that?" he asked peering down at what looked like a cupcake but with gooey strawberries on top instead of frosting.

"They're mini vanilla cheesecakes with a strawberry glaze."

If she said anything after glaze, LJ completely missed it. He was too busy staring at the delicious-looking confection. As if on autopilot, he snagged one of the treats and took a taste, devouring half the cheesecake in one bite.

This time, he did groan, loud, as the fantastic flavor of strawberry combined with a zing of something tart, maybe lemon, mixed with creamy vanilla goodness flooded his taste buds. "Holy fucking shit," he said, mouth full. Didn't even matter how much of a pig he came across as. He shoved the rest of the cheesecake in his mouth and reached for another.

"Please," Holly said, pushing the container toward him with sparkling eyes. "Help yourself to as many as you'd like."

She stood, watching his face, lower lip tucked between her teeth. The seductive pose drew him away from his snack. All he could think about was sinking his own teeth into that plump lip and seeing if her eyes darkened to a stormy sea or remained Caribbean calm.

"Do you like it?"

Was she nervous? Standing there abusing her lip and drumming her fingers on the counter.

"Like it? Shit woman, this is the best thing I've eaten in ages. Where'd you buy these?"

There she went getting all pink again. Damn, the blush was just too cute. LJ had never been one to go for the innocent type, hell, he was an outlaw biker for fuck's sake. Not to mention other parts of his past and present that didn't attract innocent girls. Those types of women did not come with the territory, but this one had a wholesome air of purity around her that was drawing him in.

"I made it," she said in a near whisper.

"No shit?"

She laughed. "No shit. I'm a pastry chef."

Oh man. A sexy neighbor who carried a bottle opener, had some sass to her, looked like sex in clothes, and was a pastry chef. He was seriously fucked. "You opening a bakery in town or anything?"

Her phone buzzed from the counter, and she grabbed it, firing off a quick text with a frown.

"Sorry." She rolled her eyes. "Overprotective parents checking to make sure I'm not in a ditch somewhere." Holly sighed. "Anyway, opening a bakery is my goal, eventually. I don't have the capital for it right now, but I've been building an online business. Custom cakes, desserts for events, things like that. But even that's getting tricky."

"How come?"

"Well," she chuckled and gave him a sheepish smile. "I'm sure you're not interested in talking about my work issues. I've probably kept you long enough. Thank you for your help."

She went to place the lid on the Tupperware, but he caught her wrist before she completed the task. God, that soft skin...if it

17

was that smooth on her arm, he couldn't imagine the satin he'd discover under her clothing.

Her gaze shot to his and they stared at each other for a few seconds before he said. "I wouldn't ask if I didn't want to know. Once you get to know me, you'll find out I'm not one to waste my time on bullshit I don't care about. Okay?"

"Uh, okay." She blinked and stared at his hand on her arm. The one where his thumb was stroking her skin.

"So tell me about it."

"Well, the problem is two-fold. First, this kitchen is too small to keep up with my orders. And second, it can be hard to get a license for a home bakery if you own a dog. Unless you can prove the dog will never be in the cooking space."

As if he knew he was the topic of conversation, Biscuit wandered over and nudged LJ's hand. LJ obliged the handsome guy with a good scratch behind his ears.

Holly rolled her eyes. "And as you can see, keeping him away from this space is not gonna happen."

The second he stopped rubbing, Biscuit whined and nudged his hand again. "So what are you gonna do?" He went for a third little cheesecake and Holly just fucking beamed.

"I used my parent's kitchen for an online business before moving here, so I have a little saved up. I'll probably rent time from a commercial kitchen. Sometimes churches rent out time in their kitchens, or restaurants that close earlier let bakers rent time and space after hours. That kind of thing."

The wheels in LJ's head started to turn. "Well, pretty girl, I better get going. Gotta double my run now to make up for all this sugar."

"Yeah, I'm never gonna apologize for that. In fact, living next to me, you're pretty much doomed to become my guinea pig."

"Sugar, you can experiment on me anytime."

Her eyes widened; the double meaning not lost on her.

Chuckling to himself, LJ leaned forward and pressed a kiss to her cheek as he swiped a cheesecake for the road. "See ya around, sugar. Thanks for the sweets."

"Oh, uh, of course." She blinked and raised a hand to her red cheek. Biscuit trotted after him to the door. As he opened it to leave, Holly seemed to snap out of her trance. "Thanks for the muscle!" she called out.

Once he was outside and away from all the sugary goodness —both the dessert and the woman—LJ fished his phone out of the zip pocket in his running shorts. "Hey, Z," he said after his club's enforcer picked up on the third ring.

"LJ! Hey, brother, glad to hear your voice. We were wondering if you survived the night." Zach said. There was a loud clanking in the background. Zach must be at work. He owned the local gym in town and did some seriously great business.

"I'm still kicking...barely."

Zach laughed. "How many women did you wake up with this morning?"

That would be none. Because he never woke up with a woman. In order for them to wake up in his bed or vice versa, he'd have to fall asleep with them, and there was no way in hell that was happening. One disaster on that front was enough to last him a lifetime.

"Hey, Z, Toni around? I had something to run by her."

The laugh that came from Zach was slightly evil. "Damn, must have been quite a night if you won't even talk about it. But yeah, Toni is here, helping out at the front desk. Everything all right?"

Protective didn't come close to describing Zach. Of course, he wouldn't let LJ talk to his woman before ensuring the topic of conversation wouldn't upset her in any way. "You bet. Just had an idea for her."

"You got it, brother. Hang on a sec."

Brother. Damn, that word sounded so good. LJ had been a prospect for way longer than the usual timeframe. One emergency after another with the club had kept him from being patched in when he should have. But as of last night, that was all in the past. He was officially a fully-patched member of the Hell's Handlers Motorcycle Club.

"Hey, LJ, what can I do for you?" Toni came on the line.

"Hey, hon. Listen, I have this new neighbor…"

CHAPTER TWO

"You meet your next-door neighbor?"

"Huh?" Holly faced her dad. "What did you say?" She dropped the box she'd been hauling on the floor of her bedroom.

"Need me to talk to him? Check him out?" Her father rested his arm on a stack of boxes all marked *Clothes*.

"Dad, what are you talking about?"

"Here, sweetie," Holly's mom, Cynthia, handed her a tall glass of ice water. She had some residual back problems from an old injury, so she'd been relegated to opening kitchen boxes and washing the dusty dishes.

"Thanks, mom," Holly said as she grabbed the glass from her gray-haired mother. Cynthia had recently decided to stop dying her hair and embrace all that fifty-seven was doing to her head. Looked good on her. Elegant.

Her dad, on the other hand, still had a full head of light hair in the exact same neatly parted style she could always remember him wearing it. "I saw a big guy jogging down from the apartment next to you as we pulled in this morning. And you keep looking at the door every time we go up or down the stairs. Figured you were nervous about living next to him."

With a sigh, Holly rolled her eyes. She wasn't sure if she was more annoyed with her Dad for assuming every male in the universe was out to harm her or disappointed that LJ had left without so much as a hello.

Geez, listen to her. It's not like they were actually friends. They'd only been in each other's presence an hour or so. Much more of this thinking and she'd be creeping up on psycho territory.

"Dad, don't you dare 'check him out," she said, crooking her fingers air-quote style. "Please. I do not want to be known as the girl in the apartment complex with the meddling cop father. I met my neighbor yesterday. He's a very nice guy who helped me carry a bunch of heavy boxes. End of story."

Her dad frowned, and her mother looked seconds from crying as she worried her bottom lip and ran the dishtowel over one plate again and again.

Shoulda kept my big mouth shut.

"Honey," her mom whispered, clutching the dish to her chest like a life preserver. "You can't be letting strange boys into your apartment. It's so dangerous. You know what could happen."

"I'm checking him out," her dad said. He pulled the notepad he always carried out of his back pocket. Habit of a former detective. Now, as sheriff of a small town, he could probably lose the pad, but Holly didn't see that happening anytime soon. "What'd you say his name was?"

"I didn't." She folded her arms across her chest. Here they went with the same conversation they'd been having for years. Twelve years to be exact. It was as though in her parents' eyes, her development had frozen solid the day her sister disappeared. She was forever an immature pre-teen in their minds. Doomed to need mom and dad to save her from herself and all the poor choices she was one step away from making. "And he's not a boy, Mom. He's a twenty-five-year-old man like I'm a twenty-four-year-old woman."

Just as she was working up a real mad, a tear spilled from the corner of her mother's eye and rolled down her wrinkling face. And like every time before it, Holly's resolve wavered. How could she begrudge the woman her overprotective nature when her child had been kidnapped and murdered?

She couldn't. End of story.

Holly was their last link to the daughter they'd lost. An exact replica and a daily reminder of their pain and devastation. For years, that knowledge had messed with her head. Okay, it still messed with her head despite all the protests of being a grown woman. Her parents treated her as though she might be snatched out from under them at any point. And it never changed no matter how old she got. There was a time when Holly had considered moving across the country to break the cycle, but she couldn't do it. Couldn't leave them to worry themselves sick over her wellbeing.

Where her parents were concerned, she was admittedly weak. The guilt of causing them fear and sleepless nights was too much to handle, so she allowed them far too much control over her life so they would have some semblance of peace. Hence why a twenty-four-year-old woman followed her parents from the suburbs of Tampa to a little town in the mountains of Tennessee. Though, she had put her foot down on living with them. She may be a pushover where they were concerned, but she had a limit to her tolerance, and living with them was it.

They'd engaged in an epic showdown complete with hysterics from her mom, statistics of raped and murdered women from her dad, and snickers from her older brother who worked SWAT out of Knoxville.

"Him being a man makes it worse, honey," her mother said, laying a soft hand on her daughter's arm. "We just worry about you because we love you so much. If anything were to happen —" Her mother brought her closed fist to her mouth to smother a sob.

"Mom," Holly said as she wrapped her arms around her mother. "I'm fine. Dad just added about ten deadbolts to my door. I'm on the second floor. I have pepper spray in my purse. The parking lot is well lit. My neighbor is very nice. I have Biscuit. You guys are exactly three point four miles away, and I have a direct in with local law enforcement." She drew back and looked her mother straight in the eye before giving her father the same attention. "I'm safe, I'm happy, and I'm excited to start this new chapter in my life. Okay?"

Her mom sniffed. "All right." Then she walked over to Holly's dad who wrapped her in a gentle hug. "You'll check him out, right, Doug?"

"Of course, Cyn."

Holly ground her molars together. Why did she bother? It wasn't as though they cared one single bit about her wants and needs. Especially when it came to the need for independence. It wasn't easy, but Holly forced herself to remember a lack of trust in her wasn't what fostered this behavior, but the trauma of actually having a daughter stolen from them in the worst way.

And once again, Holly caved. Didn't stand up for herself. Let her parents walk all over her.

"Hey, think this is the last one. Where do you want this bitch?" her brother yelled from the front door.

"Daniel, language!" her mother said as she frowned at Holly's older brother.

With a laugh, Holly called out, "What's it say on the box?"

"Kitchen. Big surprise."

"Hmm, I know you aren't the smartest guy out there, but I'm pretty sure even you can figure this one out, big bro."

"Holly Elizabeth!" It was her turn to be scolded, but she'd take it, because it broke the tension of moments ago.

"What?" she asked her mother with an innocent expression. Cynthia shook her head and walked out of the kitchen, followed closely by Doug. Probably off to plot the FBI investigation of her poor neighbor. Pretty much killed any chance of seeing the guy without his clothes on.

Holly sighed. So much for that fantasy coming to life. He'd been so yummy. Super tall and bulging with enormous muscles all over. The bald head and close-cropped beard did crazy things to her insides. As did all those delicious tattoos.

Danny lumbered into her bite-sized kitchen and set the box on the stove. "You're funny, Hol. Just because we don't live in the same house doesn't mean I can't put frogs in your bed still." He grabbed the stretchy headband she'd donned to keep any stray hairs at bay and snapped it against her scalp.

"Ouch! You're such a bully," Holly said as she elbowed him in the gut.

Of course, that landed her in a headlock which was how their parents found them a few seconds later.

"Daniel, seriously? You're a decorated police officer. Don't you think you should be a little more mature?"

Holly almost laughed. The stories he'd regaled her with about the guys on his SWAT team were anything but mature. With six years on her, they'd had a love-hate relationship growing up. She and Joy would gang up on him, though he always managed to best the duo. Once Joy was killed, that all changed, and they'd grown much closer. Though she didn't see him nearly as often as she'd like, they remained tight but never stopped giving each other shit. It was just part of their dynamic.

"Sorry, Mom," he said as he rolled his eyes in Holly's direction.

She just snickered.

"Okay, Holly," Cynthia said, voice all business. "Keep putting us to work. What should I unpack next?"

Danny shot her a look that screamed "Please, no more!" which was pretty much the same way Holly felt. It was about four in the afternoon and they'd been working since seven. Enough was enough. Not only of lugging boxes but also of time spent with the parents.

"You know what?" Holly said with a smile as she gently encircled an arm around her mother's shoulders. They were the same height, but the similarities ended there. Slight, almost waif-like, Cynthia was far more delicate than her daughter. She always had her light pink glasses on, which was the only pop of color the woman ever wore. Everything she owned was black, white, or gray. It'd gotten so bad, Holly could barely stand to wear something if it wasn't radiating color to offset the monochromatic mother she'd grown up staring at. Well, once Joy had died anyway. "I'm beat. Thinking I'm gonna order a pizza and zone out on Netflix since Danny got the TV all set up."

Her mother adjusted her glasses. "Would you like us to stick around? I'd hate for you to be lonely or nervous all by yourself."

"We'd be happy to stay for a while, Holly Berry," her dad said, using the atrocious nickname she'd garnered as a child.

Were they kidding? She was *dying* for some alone time.

"I'll stick around," Danny said once again reaching for her headband. This time she was ready and slapped his hand away. "Dad, why don't you take mom to that Italian place you told me you've been meaning to check out? You guys have only been here a few weeks, you need to scope out the good joints for Hol." He winked at her.

Sometimes Danny was the best brother a girl could ask for.

"Hmm, what do you say Cyn? Care to accompany the town's sheriff on a date?" He held out his arm for his wife.

"I'd be delighted," her mom replied, curling her arm around her husband's as she lovingly gazed at him. For all her parent's faults, they genuinely loved each other. Many relationships fell to pieces after suffering the loss of a child. Not her parents. They drew comfort and strength from each other instead of turning against one another.

"Well, all right," Danny said with a cheesy grin. "You two crazy kids get on out of here." As though he were a cattle dog, he herded her parents toward the door.

"Bye, Holly," her mother called out.

"Bye, guys!" she said around a laugh. "Have fun. And thank you!"

"Keep your doors locked!" her father yelled. "Stay away from the neighbor until I check him out. Maybe you should send Danny over—"

"Yeah, okay, we'll do that. Buh-bye." Danny practically shut the door in their parents' faces. "Shit, they're like ten sets of parents in one, aren't they?" he said with his back resting against the door.

"Seriously." Holly ran a hand through her hair, pulling out the rubber band. As her hair fell around her shoulders, she grimaced. "Ugh, I'm so sweaty and gross. Here." She tossed Danny a pizza delivery menu she'd found tucked under the windshield wiper of her car that morning. "Order whatever you want while I take a shower. My treat."

The menu fluttered to the floor not even halfway to her brother. With a snort, he moved to retrieve it. "Nice throw there, slick. And, fuck yeah, you're paying. I drove my ass all the way out here on my day off only to be used as slave labor."

"Ha," Holly said as she started for the bathroom. "Sorry you had to drive a whole fifty minutes there, bro." She flipped him off. "Credit card is in my wallet."

His bark of laughter had her smiling. "Feels fucking good to swear now that the 'rents are gone, huh?"

"Sure as fuck does." She wasn't a huge swearer but being forbidden to do it always made her want to run her mouth like a sailor.

Danny laughed again, and as she slipped into her room, she heard him ordering an extra-large pie with the works.

Twenty-five minutes later, Holly strolled out of her bedroom, hair clean and dry just as Danny was shutting the door while balancing a giant pizza box and a smaller Styrofoam box she assumed was garlic knots. "You got any beer?" he asked as he placed the box on her mini kitchen island.

"Sure do. It's in the fridge." The smell of piping hot pizza-goodness hit her nose before she'd even stepped into the kitchen. "Oh man, that smells amazing. My mouth is watering." As she spoke, her stomach let out a loud rumble. "And my stomach is growling, apparently." She grabbed a slice from the box, not bothering with a plate, and took a giant bite. "Mmmm," she moaned with her mouth full.

"You're such a lady," Danny said as he returned with two beers.

"Damn straight," she said, around the bite.

"Oh here, the pizza guy handed this to me. Said it was taped to your door." Danny flicked an envelope across the island.

After swallowing her pizza and washing it down with an icy swig of beer, she peeled the envelop open. Inside was a small slip of paper.

Toni – 387-555-8757. Owns the diner in town. They close at 2pm. She's a friend. – LJ

The words were scrawled in a masculine chicken scratch.

A mix of emotions ran through Holly. Gratitude and happiness at the fact LJ had gone out of his way to think of her and inquire about a place for her to rent kitchen space. Unfortunately, those positive vibes were chased away by a completely irrational jealousy of whoever this Toni woman was. Girlfriend? Fiancé? Fuck buddy?

She'd enjoyed the time spent with LJ yesterday, and had been excited by the prospect of living next door to a single and sexy man. But, of course, he'd have a woman in his life. He was giant-tall, bearded, mouth-wateringly muscled and—she read the note again—clearly sweet. She'd probably have to witness a parade of women coming and going from the apartment next to hers. The thought made the pizza turn over in her stomach.

"You frown at that paper any harder, and it might sprout legs so it can run away from you."

Holly jumped. Crap, she'd forgotten she wasn't alone. From across the island, Danny watched her with concern. "Everything okay?"

With a smile for her big brother, she shrugged off the unwarranted jealousy and nodded. "Yes, better than okay, actually. I've got my first lead on a possible rental kitchen, courtesy of my new neighbor," she said as she waved the paper in Danny's face

"From your neighbor, huh?" He reached for a second slice. "That's the second time you've mentioned him. Is he cuuute?" he asked as though he were a high school girl instead of a thirty-year-old SWAT officer.

But of course, since he'd hit the nail on the head, Holly's face flamed, which only caused him to crack up. "Oh, my God, look at your red face. I think someone has a crush! That's so adorable."

"Shut up!" She balled up her napkin and shot it across the island. It hit Danny square in the face, which had her dissolving in giggles.

Once they'd calmed and resumed eating, Danny grew serious. "Glad you decided to move out here with Mom and Dad. I know it was a hard decision and that they need to mellow as far as you're concerned, but I'm thrilled to have you close again."

Holly's throat constricted, making it difficult to swallow. "Thanks, Dan."

He gave her a smile. "I'm gonna help you out as far as they're concerned. Get them to back off and start seeing you as an adult. It's more than just them being overprotective, isn't it?"

Holly nodded as she felt the telltale prickle of tears in her eyes. "Yeah, it's a little unhealthy. On both our parts. Their constant need to know where I am, what I'm doing, and who I'm with, and my always giving them what they ask for." She shrugged. "If circumstances were different..." If Joy hadn't been murdered...

"Yeah, I get it. I'm on your side, Hol."

"Thanks, Danny."

Holly fingered the note again. Meddlesome parents aside, the pieces of her life were beginning to fall into place. She'd have to think of something to bake for LJ. As a thank-you, of course, not a means to worm her way over to his apartment.

CHAPTER THREE

Five a.m. was way too fucking early to be driving to work. For Christ's sake, the goddammed sun hadn't even shown its face. As the primary project manager for one of his club brother's construction companies, he often worked long-ass days, but this was pushing it. He'd been working with Rocket for the past few years, even before prospecting with the club. In fact, Rocket was the one who introduced him to the Handlers and encouraged him to prospect. A fellow veteran with his own set of demons, Rocket had boasted the sense of brotherhood in the MC rivaled that of the military, and so far, he'd been right.

Even though it was ass-crack of dawn early, LJ couldn't blame the fatigue on the hour. He'd been up since three when the familiar nightmare tossed him out of bed and onto his unforgiving wooden floor. The details were fuzzy, but he'd woken drenched in sweat and tangled in blankets on the floor with a bitch of a bruise on his hip.

Nothing new, but a damned shit way to start what was going to be a demanding workweek.

At the moment, LJ had four major projects running concurrently. Made for never-ending grueling days, but he found the work satisfying as hell. Not to mention the constant activity kept his mind occupied, and that was always a positive. His first destination of the day consisted of storm damage repairs on a multi-million-dollar home high in the mountains. The job was a rush because the owners were hosting a wedding in a few weeks. Once he'd checked on that site, he planned to pop in on the other three and make sure the crews were on task. Combine those chores with church scheduled for eight that evening and LJ would be hauling his tired self home with just enough time to catch a few Z's before starting all over again.

Vat of coffee in hand, he opened his front door and nearly stomped on a sizable white bakery box with his clown-size work boot. Written in a flowy script across the lid were the words *Thank You* followed by a smiley face. Man, if the contents of that box were half as delicious as Holly's cheesecake, he'd be doing her favors every chance he got.

Hopefully, a few of those favors would be of the sexual variety. Ever since meeting her, he hadn't been able to scrub the image of her curvy as fuck body from his mind. Especially not once he'd jerked himself to completion over a fantasy of that soft body naked and spread out for him on his bed.

LJ lifted the box and opened it to find an assortment of giant cookies. Immediately, the scent of chocolate and fresh-baked goodness tickled his senses and he inhaled a deeper hit. Some of the cookies were clearly chocolate chip, some smelled like peanut butter, others deep dark chocolate, and then... snickerdoodles. Oh man, somehow the sugar goddess next door knew his weakness. Cinnamon and sugar.

Hell fucking yes.

Was five in the morning too early to gorge on cookies?

Fuck no, it wasn't.

After stuffing an entire cookie into his mouth, he moaned. God, that woman could bake. The box was filled to the brim. After devouring a few more, he carried what remained in the box to his work truck. Holly had made so many cookies, he could bring the container to church that evening and still have plenty to binge on. Sharing the goods might help kick her business off the ground because if there was one thing he knew about his brothers, they liked to eat. Especially if the food came from a pretty woman.

Though he just might leave out how smokin' hot Holly was. None of those assholes needed that information.

Midway through a sweaty day, LJ tossed his hard hat in the bed of his truck before guzzling water straight from the gallon jug. With the bandana he wore under the protective helmet, he wiped his sweaty head. One job site down, three to go.

"Heading out, boss?" Gary, one of the electricians he frequently contracted asked, opening his own large bottle of water.

"Yeah, man. Gotta head over to the bank job. We hit a snag with the plumbing." LJ rolled his eyes. This was the second time in a month his plumber had called with some bullshit issue he should have been able to solve. Might be time to look for a new one. "Kinda hate to leave though. Been loving working on this place."

"Tell me about it," the shorter man said as he wiped his mouth. Gary's long black hair was braided down his back, sticking out from the hard hat he hadn't bothered to remove. "Always nice to work with an unlimited budget."

"Seriousl—" The loud blare of multiple sirens had both men's heads whipping around.

"What the fuck?" Gary muttered as three cop cars came tearing up the extended driveway in full showboat mode. Lights, sirens, screeching breaks, the works.

"No fucking clue," LJ returned, but the intense churning in his gut let him know this was gonna fuck up his day but good. "Oh, fuck," he said as the door to the lead car opened and out stepped —or stomped—Sheriff's Deputy Richard Schwartz, the biggest douche nozzle LJ had ever had the displeasure to meet.

As though he had the authority of God, Schwartz marched his way over to where LJ and Gary stood with four other officers trailing behind him. Schwartz stopped about two feet from LJ.

The gleeful smirk on his smug fucking face was as much a show of power as his hand resting on the butt of his gun.

"Dick," LJ said, working to school his own smirk.

Schwartz's face turned red, and he scowled so hard he was a risk of facial injury. Guy must not be much of a poker player.

"You in charge here?" Schwartz was about six-foot with sandy hair and an overall pretty-boy look. Think boy band meets country bumpkin. He took his job as deputy sheriff in the small town of Townsend way too seriously and was one of the few cops the Handlers' had never been able to bend to their will. Thankfully, the sheriff kept him in line ninety-nine percent of the time. Looked like today was going to be the one percent Sheriff Coleman couldn't control.

"Sure am. You want a tour? See how the other half lives? Can't imagine you'll ever make it to this type of life on a cop's salary."

Eyes narrowed, Schwartz snorted. "You're the hired help. Pretty sure dirty fucking bikers aren't snapping up all the mansions."

Well, he had a point there. LJ certainly didn't have the moola to own a ten-bedroom monstrosity, but he was pretty fucking satisfied with his life. With a frustrated sigh, he said, "The fuck you want, Dicky? I got too much shit to do to be standing around waiting to see if you're gonna ask me on a date or if you just wanna suck me off."

Red darkened Schwartz's cheeks, and his blue eyes practically shot sparks. Looked like the guy was about three seconds from losing his shit, and wouldn't LJ love the fuck outta that? Twenty witnesses were all able to vouch that the deputy made the first move. Damn, it'd be fucking sweet. But instead, Schwartz shook off his pissed off expression and half of his mouth curved up into a shitty grin. "Got a call in about some concerning things going on out here."

"Concerning things?" LJ asked with a grunt. "Oh boy, Dicky. You've really got me shaking now."

"Operating without proper permits, not adhering to safety protocols," Schwartz said as he pointed to LJ's bare head.

LJ couldn't help but laugh. "First off, I'm well out of the bounds of the work zone. And second, who the fuck calls the cops over a hard hat issue? Nice try, Dicky. What else you got?"

"Hiring undocumented workers."

Well shit. That one could shut down work for days. All of the men working for Rocket had their papers in order but hauling them all in to verify would eat up precious time he didn't have to spare.

"Seriously? What the fuck does the local sheriff's office care about the citizenship of my employees? You ain't ICE, Dicky. What's the matter? You bored? Need some action? Donut shop not carrying your favorite flavor today?"

Gary coughed in a failed attempt to disguise a laugh. When Schwartz's gaze shifted to the electrician, Gary said. "Seriously, deputy, none of the things you mentioned are police matters. Besides, I've worked with LJ for years and he runs a tight fucking ship. Can't say I've ever seen so much as a loose board to trip over."

Standing behind their superior like well-trained dogs, the rest of the officers shifted as though uneasy with the direction of this conversation. They should be uncomfortable. Most likely, they were led to believe this little power play was a legit matter instead of a bullshit call. Some kind of weird show of strength that made no sense. And it needed to end. LJ had places to be.

"How about this?" he said. "I'll have Rocket give Sheriff Coleman a call." They can work out whatever shit needs to be addressed. Sound good?" Coleman wouldn't risk the bank he made off the MC over a few imaginary safety violations or unjustified concerns over the citizens of Rocket's company. Schwartz was already on thin ice with his boss if rumors were to be believed. The unspoken threat to Schwartz's job had LJ flying high for about two seconds. Until a genuine smile curled Schwartz's lips and he rocked back on his heels.

"You know what? You do that, Jack. You go right ahead and do that." Then the arrogant bastard laughed as he spun on his heel and started for his cruiser. "Have a feeling I'll be seeing you around soon, Jack."

"What the hell was that load of horseshit?" Gary asked as the two men watched the officers drive off.

"Fuck if I know," LJ said. He rubbed a hand across his bald head. "But I don't have time to deal with it now. I'll bring it up to Rocket and Cop at church tonight. I need to roll."

"All right man. Have a good one." Gary stuck his hand out, and LJ gave it a quick shake before sliding into his truck.

After powering through a challenging fourteen-hour day, LJ dragged his exhausted and grimy ass through the clubhouse and into the chapel. Tonight was his first official church since patching in and, damn, did it feel good to finally be included in the closed-door meetings.

Just as he stepped into the chapel, Maverick's furious voice rang out. "It's complete and utter bullshit, Copper."

LJ blinked as the room fell silent. A few of the guys were still filtering in, but everyone stopped and stared at Maverick. Ninety-nine-point nine percent of the time, Maverick was a laid-back jokester. Every other word out of the man's mouth was rife with innuendo and snark. To hear him pissed as fuck was unusual, to say the least.

"What's up with him?" LJ whispered to Rocket as he slipped into a seat on his boss's right.

Without taking his gaze off the scene unfolding, Rocket shook his head. "Not sure. Mav followed Copper in here, ranting and raving. Don't know what happened but the guy is fucked off."

Huh.

"I hear you, Mav," Copper said. "Settle down, and we'll discuss it." He glanced around the room. "Everyone in?"

"We're all here," Viper, the club's VP said from Copper's right.

"All right, Mav start it off." Copper waved toward his road captain while taking his seat.

After cracking his knuckles, Maverick blew out a breath. "Got pulled over by that fucking cocksucker, Schwartz, on my way over here."

Zach's brows drew down. "Which one is he?" Z was the club's enforcer, and not at all a fan of the local authorities.

"Sheriff's deputy. That douche with the fancy fucking haircut. Looks like an overgrown frat boy. Think he's maybe late twenties. Walks like there's a stick up his ass," Mav said, his mouth twisting like he'd eaten something rotten.

Nodding along, Zach held up his hand. "Enough said. I hate that fucker."

They weren't the only ones.

"He pulled me over for going sixty-six in a fifty-five."

"Seriously?" Zach said. "Thought Coleman had him on a tight leash?"

Copper grunted. "Always has. Can't remember the last time one of us got written up for speeding."

Coleman had been the town's sheriff for a good twenty years. The club had a great relationship with the man. He looked the other way on the club's loan sharking, gambling, and any other less than legal undertakings the Handlers might get involved with. In return, Copper kept the MC away from running drugs, guns, or girls. In fact, the club worked to keep the town free of those activities in general. And of course, they greased the old timer's pockets.

Generously.

Everyone was a winner.

Except Schwartz who'd fought the sheriff at every step of the way, constantly wanting up the MC's ass.

LJ cleared his throat. "I had a run-in with Dicky today, too."

"Fuck me," Mav muttered.

"What happened?" Copper asked, shooting Maverick a *shut it* glare.

LJ regaled the room with the events of earlier. With each word he spoke, Rocket coiled tighter until he was practically vibrating with anger next to LJ. He'd worked damn hard to grow his contracting business, and any threat to it couldn't be seen as anything but personal.

"Shit." Screw, a newer member who'd prospected alongside LJ for part of his time piped up. The two had become close during the months they'd spent taking shit from the patched brothers. "I got a speeding ticket from Schwartz last night too." He leaned back in his chair, rubbing one hand over his clenched fist. "Looks like we may be fucked, boys. And not in the way I normally like. You all know Coleman's got pancreatic cancer. Came on fast and furious. Town board just voted in this new guy to fill the remaining three years on Coleman's term. Schwartz was positively fuckin' giddy as he told me how his new boss's first order of business was us."

Copper frowned. "Coleman assured me his replacement wouldn't be an issue for us," he said as he stared Screw down.

"Don't know anything about that, prez. Just relaying what Schwartz told me. He seemed pretty fucking certain this guy was not a friendly."

The entire room fell eerily quiet until Copper finally said, "Fuck," in a soft voice. He turned his piercing gaze on Screw. "He give you any more information?"

Shaking his head, Screw said, "No, just that he's got a new boss whose number one goal is to tear us a new asshole."

Copper let out a growl then leaned back in his chair, stroking his bearded chin. Every man in the club knew to give him a moment while he was thinking through shit. "Okay," he said after a few minutes. "Shell was planning to head to the station in a few days. We need bodies for the charity run next month. Usually, Coleman is all about that. I'm gonna send her in there, have her make nice with the new sheriff. We'll see what happens when she brings up the club and who her ol' man is."

Mav started to laugh, a mischievous gleam in his eyes. The smartass could never stay mad for long. "You're gonna owe her a damn good fuck for sending her to the wolves, Prez."

Copper narrowed his eyes at Mav. "First of all, I always fuck my woman right." A few men snickered while others whistled and whooped.

Despite the initial seriousness of the meeting, LJ couldn't keep the grin off his face. He'd been waiting to be included in this shit for so long. Felt incredible to finally be one of the brothers.

"And you forget, that woman manages Copper without even trying," Zach said. "A hard-ass sheriff will be a piece of cake. She'll have him eating out of her palm in no time."

"His mouth better not get anywhere near her, not even her fucking hand," Copper muttered. "But yeah, she'll handle him just fine."

Still smirking, Mav lifted his hands in surrender. "You know her better than anyone."

"You're fucking right, I do. Now, it's LJ's first church. Welcome, brother. This has been a long time coming," Copper said with nod.

As the rest of the guys nodded and offered their welcoming words, LJ ran a finger over the bandage on his left arm. The spot where the Hell's Handlers official brand was healing. "Thanks."

"Whatcha got there, LJ?" Mav asked with a raised eyebrow. "Your mommy send you with some treats for your first scout meeting?"

Beside him, Rocket coughed to hide his laugh. LJ didn't mind. He was used to their ribbing for one, and so fucking glad to be there they could roast him all night long for all he cared. "Nah," he said. "Got a new neighbor who's a pastry chef. Helped her out with something, so she left this at my door."

"Helped her out, huh?" Mav said as he reached across the table and opened the box. "You help her by loaning her your dick?"

I wish.

"No, asshole, carried some shit into her apartment. Not all of us are fucking pigs."

With a mock hurt gasp, Mav bit into a peanut butter cookie. His eyes rolled toward the ceiling. "Holy fuck," he said. "I don't care where you got these or what you had to do to get them, you need to get more. For me. Hundreds more. These are the shit." He jammed the rest of the cookie into his mouth and let out a muffled groan as he reached for another.

That one sound was all it took for the rest of the vultures to descend on the box. Cops forgotten, within minutes, only crumbs remained and every man in the room was alternately munching and groaning.

"Shit," Mav said when he'd finally polished off his third cookie. "Someone should record this. There's gotta be cookie porn out there somewhere. With all this moaning and shit, we could make a lot of money. Anyone wanna take their shirt off?"

LJ ground his teeth together. The thought of another man being even partially naked while eating Holly's baked goods had him feeling somewhat murderous.

Shit. Clearly, he needed sleep. And probably to get laid. It'd been a good two months, and he was losing his mind if he was worried about his brothers being clothed while eating cookies.

CHAPTER FOUR

"Holly! What a nice surprise. How are you, dear?"

Holly smiled at the older woman who practically screamed grandmother. Apparently, she'd been running the front desk at the sheriff's station since she was in her early twenties, nearly fifty years ago. Holly had only met her one other time, but the woman was just the welcoming type who felt comfortable from the first introduction.

"I'm doing well, Mrs. B, how about yourself?"

"Now, what did I tell you about calling me Marjorie?" She asked with a scowl that didn't even come close to making her look anything but kind. With tight white curls that only came from weekly visits to the salon, and soft wrinkles around her mouth and eyes, not to mention the crystal dish of Werther's atop her desk, Marjorie Beasley could have played a sitcom grandmother.

"You told me Mrs. B was your husband's cranky mother, and you refused to be called anything but Marjorie."

"That's right, dear." She folded her veiny hands on top of her desk. "What is that amazing smell?"

"Oh, I almost forgot," Holly said with a laugh. "Brought you guys a little pick-me-up to get you through the afternoon." She set the bakery box on the desk in front of Marjorie.

Those warm brown eyes narrowed at the same time they sparkled. "Don't you mean you brought something to put this entire office in a sugar coma so crimes can be committed all over town?"

Holly mock gasped. "Marjorie," she said, pressing a hand to her heart. "How could you even think I'd have any motive other than to bring the fine officers of Townsend happiness?" She threw in a wink.

It was Marjorie's turn to laugh and Holly found it was a wonderful sound full of happiness.

"Well, whatever your plan, I thank you on behalf of the department for the sugar and calories."

"You're very welcome," Holly said with a small curtsey.

"I'm guessing you aren't just here to sugar me up?"

"My dad asked me to stop by this afternoon. Something he wants to run by me, apparently. He in?"

"He's here, dear. I haven't actually seen him since I returned from lunch. He might have someone in his office, but he always lets me know if he shouldn't be disturbed and he hasn't said anything yet, so feel free to poke your head in and see what he's up to."

"Thank you, Marjorie. I appreciate it."

"My pleasure, dear."

Holly wandered down the long corridor to the door at the end of the hallway. Her father hadn't claimed the prior sheriff's office close to the entrance but chose one much farther away for reasons she didn't comprehend.

When she reached the closed almond-colored door with her father's name placard, she knocked twice.

"Enter," came a terse reply that had Holly rolling her eyes.

She opened the door. "Really, Dad? Could you sound any less invitin—? Oh, I'm sorry. I didn't know you were in a meeting." Seated in the chair opposite her father's desk was a tiny woman with curly blonde hair and a friendly smile.

"No, it's totally fine," the woman said as she waved Holly in. "This is nothing personal or private. Interrupt away."

Holly looked to her dad, who just shrugged. "Fine by me," he said.

"Well, if neither of you cares, I'll sit and hang until you're done," Holly said, indicating the empty seat next to the woman.

"Absolutely. I won't be more than a few minutes. I'm Shell, by the way." She held out a hand with short, unpolished, but neatly shaped nails.

"Holly." She shook the offered hand and gave the woman a quick once over. By the smooth skin and youthful appearance, Holly guessed them to be within a few years of each other in age. Shell wore denim cutoffs and a fitted olive-green T-shirt. No jewelry or makeup even seemed to be present.

Low maintenance.

Holly's kinda girl.

"So what is it that I can help you with, Miss Ward?" Holly's father broke in, his voice flat.

Holly frowned. What was with him today?

Shell either didn't notice or didn't care. "Shell, please," she said with a sweet smile. "I'm here to talk to you about a fundraiser I'm organizing. It's something my group has been running annually for the past five years or so, and Sheriff Coleman has always lent us deputies to manage crowds, direct traffic, and such. I wanted to see if we could count on you to continue that tradition this year?"

Holly's lips twitched. Shell was good. She knew just how to demand what she wanted while making it sound like an innocent request.

"And what kind of event is this?" Her father asked, folding his arms on his desk.

Shell smiled. "It's a motorcycle poker run to raise money for an anti-bullying campaign."

Uh-oh.

"It's been a very well attended event for the past year. Bikers come from all over to participate, and we've raised quite a bit of money in recent years. Last year my ol' man was able to donate about ten thousand dollars to the local children's hospital." She said that last part with a note of pride in her voice. "We choose a different organization each year, but they typically support children or women."

Her father didn't so much as crack a smile. Whatever came next, it wasn't going to be pleasant. "Um, Dad," Holly broke in. Who the hell knew what she'd say when he acknowledged her, but she had to diffuse the sudden tension somehow.

But he never so much as glanced in her direction. Voice hard as steel, he leveled a gaze on Shell that had Holly's gut clenching. "And who might your *ol' man* be?" The words sounded like he couldn't stand the feel of them on his tongue.

With all the confidence of someone who wasn't facing a pissed off sheriff, Shell looked Holly's father straight in the eye. "My ol' man is Copper, the president of the Hell's Handlers Motorcycle Club."

For about three seconds, the room fell so silent, Holly could almost hear the Cliff bar she'd scarfed for lunch digesting in her stomach. Then her father chuckled. The annoying sound morphed into full-on laughter before long.

A hot flush of shame washed over Holly. Oh, how she wished she'd returned to the lobby to wait until her father was free. Beside her, Shell sat, calm as she'd been the entire time though her eyes weren't quite as soft as before. The blue had darkened with irritation.

"Man, that's some funny shit," her father said as his laughter died down. "Bikers raising money for an anti-bullying campaign. No, Miss Ward, this office will not be participating in that farce. Nor will we have anything to do with the motorcycle club unless it involves locking the members behind bars for as many days as I can possibly manage. But you can bet your ass my officers will be there writing citations if one of you so much as crosses the speed limit or tosses a bottle on the ground."

Shell gasped. Her eyes were so wide, they looked like they'd been drawn by a cartoonist.

"Dad…" Holly started.

"Will that be all, Miss Ward?"

With a sigh, Shell stood, shoulders straight and head held high. "I guess so. Thank you for your time." She nodded at Holly before walking to the door.

"Miss Ward," Holly's dad called out as her hand landed on the doorknob.

"Yes?" She turned halfway.

"Sheriff Coleman may have looked the other way, hell, he may have colluded with the criminals you associate with, but he's no longer in this office. I am. And I'm not so easily swayed from the law I swore to uphold. You seem like a nice kid. I'd hate to see you caught up in the inevitable fallout when my office dismantles the club. It's not too late to walk away, but it will be soon."

"Dad, Jesus," Holly muttered. She stared at his stern face like she'd never seen him before. He'd basically just threatened the woman who came asking for help to raise money for a fantastic cause. Holly would be lying if she said living with a man who hated bikers above all hadn't colored her opinion of them. Over the years, she'd grown to distrust her memory of the afternoon a biker president helped her out of a hot spot. Especially after irrefutable evidence came to light. She'd been wrong. Dead wrong. Curly, the MC president of her hometown club, was in fact the man who killed her sister and he now spent the rest of his days behind bars.

Despite the evidence and conviction, something about the whole outcome of her sister's investigation never sat right with Holly. But then, she'd been twelve, naïve, and basing her entire opinion on one encounter with a man. Since the trial, she'd formed her own fear of the biker world, letting her father's opinion sour her view of an entire subculture. It'd been easier that way. Easier to deal with the devastation of Joy's death if she had someone to blame. Easier to live with her father if she bought into his hatred rather than fight against it. Easier to give in to the parents who'd lost so much and demanded Holly's safety at all times.

Easier not to form her own opinions, rock the boat, or risk hurting people who'd already been hurt so badly.

But today's behavior? This blatant prejudice based solely on who someone associated with twisted Holly's gut in knots.

With her hand still on the door, Shell turned and looked Doug straight in the eye. "I'm not a kid, Sheriff. I'm a fully-grown adult. In fact, I have a kid. And I've been through things that would turn the rest of your hair gray."

Holly bit her lip to keep from smirking as her father's eyes narrowed.

"You're new around here and clearly have a false idea of who and what the Handlers are, so I'll do you a favor and clue you in. Those men do more for this town than anyone else. They keep the citizens far safer than this office ever has." She stepped forward and held her hand out, crossing her wrists in front of her. "If you'd like to carry through on that threat, you might as well do it now because there isn't anything in the world that will make me walk away from my family."

When her father's handcuffs remained hooked to his belt, Shell turned and strode from the room head held high. Holly had the insane urge to applaud. As the door closed behind Shell, Holly whipped her head around. "Dad! What the hell was that?"

Her father speared her with his cop look as she and her siblings used to call it. It was the no-nonsense, don't mess with me glare he claimed to use during interrogations. Fortunately for her, the look lost its power somewhere after her eighteenth year. "Police business, Holly. Stay out of it."

She scoffed and rolled her eyes. "Seriously? You just performed that *police business* right in front of me, and now I'm supposed to butt out? Dad? She was a sweet woman asking you to help direct traffic for an incredible cause and you acted like a total jerk."

Her father slammed his closed fists down on the top of his desk, making his coffee mug and Holly jump. "No!" he yelled. "I acted like a sheriff telling a criminal I'm not going to jump in their pocket like the last man in my position did."

"Do you really think she's a criminal?"

"I think she associates with a group of outlaw bikers I'm making it my mission to disband. Before the year is out, every one of those bikers will be held accountable for their actions. Now, I tried to give her a chance to see reason, but if she won't, I can't take responsibility for what happens to her."

The strength it took to clench her teeth and avoid spitting out angry words had Holly's jaw aching. How, even after all these years, was it possible for her father to be so blind in his hatred? As Shell said, he didn't know a damn thing about the Hell's Handlers. All he had was a festering hatred over a decade in the making. And now he had tunnel vision and a mission to destroy any man who wore leather and so much as glanced at a Harley. Nothing about his behavior was professional. All her father saw in every biker was the man who killed his child.

And that's what kept Holly from speaking her true mind again and again. It's what had her eventually believing his rhetoric that all bikers were murderers and rapists. But seeing his behavior today, she had to wonder if she'd made a mistake in never challenging his opinion.

As traumatizing as it had been to lose her sister, losing a child had to be worse. No matter how she disagreed with her parent's handling of the situation, she couldn't fully condemn them because she knew they'd suffered and continued to suffer every day since her sister went missing.

"Look, Dad, I'm here because you wanted to talk to me about something."

"Oh, yes!" He smiled, seeming to shake himself out of his disgust. "I have someone I want you to meet." Still grinning, he pulled out his phone and tapped what she assumed was a quick text.

"Uh, okay. Who am I meeting?"

There was a rap at the door.

"Come on in, Richard," her dad called out.

Once again, the door opened, and this time a man she guessed was in his early thirties strode in. He was fairly tall with light brown hair, styled so perfectly it looked like it'd stay in shape through a hurricane. His trim body was clothed in the tan sheriff's deputy uniform issued by the town.

"Holly, this is Deputy Richard Schwartz. Deputy, this is who I was telling you about, my daughter, Holly."

"Well, Doug, she certainly is as pretty as you described. Hello there." He held out a hand for her.

Oh, Jesus. A set-up? Really? Holly cast a side-eyed glance at her father before holding her hand out. The sheriff was positively beaming which pretty much guaranteed Holly wanted nothing to do with this guy. Her idea of a suitable date and her father's were worlds apart.

"It's uh, nice to meet you." She slipped her hand into Richard's larger one. Immediately, he closed his palm and held her tight. For the first time since the deputy stepped in the room, she shifted her focus to his face. Deep blue eyes bore into hers and a grin that could only be described as smug tilted his lips.

"I've heard a lot about you. Been looking forward to this moment for the past few weeks."

This moment? They were having a moment? And why had he heard of her but not the other way around?

"Guess what?" he said, still holding her hand as he slid into the seat Shell had vacated.

Holly cleared her throat. "What?"

"We are going out tomorrow night."

She blinked? Did the man just order her on a date? Arrogant asshole. "I'm sorry?" she said.

"Yeah, honey, I told Richard you were new in town and didn't have any plans tomorrow night. He jumped right in and offered to take you to dinner. Isn't that great?"

Uh, no?

She actually did have plans tomorrow night. She planned to work on a few new recipes before her meeting with the owner of the diner LJ had recommended. Showing up to an interview of sorts with a box of deliciousness was never a bad idea. And she wanted some new and exciting creations to offer.

But one look at her father's hopeful gaze and Holly fell into a pattern over a decade in the making. The one where she couldn't say no to her parents because she couldn't bear to bring them any further sadness or heartache than they'd already suffered.

"Sure is. What time were you thinking, Richard?"

He flashed her a conceited victory smile she wanted to smack off his face. But that meant she'd have to touch him and had no desire to do so. Though the ass still had a firm grip on her hand. In fact, he was now stroking a thumb over her wrist.

What was this guy's deal?

"I'm working until seven-thirty. How about I pick you up at eight?"

No way, no how did she want to be stuck in a car with this guy at the end of the night, dependent on him to return her home without demanding a kiss or worse. Granted, she might be overreacting to the situation, but the whole thing felt like a slimy set-up she wanted no part of. Hell, the moment she walked out the door, her dad and Deputy Richard would probably high-five and share a glass of scotch to celebrate a plan well executed.

"How about you get my number from my dad and text me the address of where to meet you. That'll save you some time."

For the first time since he walked in the room, some of the wind seemed to leech out of Richard's sails. "I don't know…"

"Please?" She asked with a smile. "I'm trying to learn my way around town, and I find it helpful to drive everywhere."

Lame.

"Well, I guess I can approve of that."

Seriously?

God, now she was going to have to let down her father's subordinate at the end of the night. Nothing awkward about that.

"Great." Holly stood, tugging her hand out of Richard's grasp. "Then I'm going to head out. Lots to do this afternoon. Nice to meet you, Richard."

As he went to reach for her hand again, she stuck it in her pocket and backed toward the door. "Bye, Dad."

"Bye, Holly."

Before either man could comment further, Holly slipped out of the room.

Not for the first time in the few days since she'd moved to Townsend, she wondered if she'd made a mistake. The grip her parents had on her life was clearly unhealthy, and it was time to start setting some boundaries.

But how was she supposed to tell the two people who already lost one daughter that the remaining one didn't need them nearly as much as they wished she did?

CHAPTER FIVE

LJ stepped out of his apartment into the cooling evening air at the same moment Holly emerged from her place. Also in that instant, his cock filled to rock hard because…holy hell, the woman was on a mission to make all men in a ten-mile radius hard as stone tonight.

"Oh, hey," she said. Those blue eyes lit, and a smile appeared on her shiny red lips. Red like someone had glossed a fuckin' apple. They looked delicious as fuck. "Fancy meeting you here."

"Christ woman, you look like sex on legs."

The most adorable blush tinged her cheeks, nearly matching them to those lips, and her hands worked at smoothing imaginary wrinkles on her fitted black dress. Her outfit was simple, no flaunting of cleavage, no sparkles or other shit he'd seen women wear around the clubhouse, but it hugged her curves.

Hugged. Her. Curves.

Enough said.

The woman was *bam, bam, bam* hour-glass perfection.

And that rack was sent straight from heaven.

Or maybe had been gifted to her from hell. A little trick of the devil to torture the poor, slobbering, Y-chromosomes of the world. The dress might not have been revealing, but it was snug enough to inspire some off-the-charts erotic fantasies of peeling it from her delectable body inch by luscious inch.

"Thank you," she squeaked.

LJ stared, raking his gaze over her again and again. He couldn't stop eye-fucking her from every angle possible. Only when his perusal reached her face, did he notice she was watching him with a raised eyebrow and a tilted head. "Shit, sorry, did you say something?"

A small laugh bubbled from her. "Not gonna lie, I'm pretty pleased with the reaction to this dress so far. And to think, I almost wore jeans. All you missed was me asking how your day was going."

"Better now, sugar. Much better now. And I'm pretty sure I'd have had the same reaction to that ass if you were wearing jeans." If he wasn't mistaken, her gaze flicked briefly to the bulge in his pants before returning to his face.

That's right, that's exactly the reaction I was talking about.

A thought occurred that had him frowning. "You got a hot date?"

As she shifted her weight on some very sexy and very spiky heeled ankle boot thingies, Holly rolled her eyes. "I have a date, yes. Not so sure about the hot part."

LJ leaned against the wall space between their apartment doors and crossed his arms over his chest. "Now, I'm intrigued." And not at all ready to beat the fuck outta whoever came to collect her.

Right.

Her thin laugh was more of the nervous variety this time. "It was a set-up." Holly grimaced. "By my dad."

"Oh, man." He couldn't help but laugh.

"Yeah, pretty high on the pitiful-o-meter. Apparently, he told this guy who works for him that I'm new to town and too lame to have weekend plans yet. Not sure if the guy felt like he *had* to ask me out or what, but here I am." She shrugged. "Least I got to see your tongue hanging out of your mouth, huh?" she said with a wink.

LJ threw back his head and let out a laugh. This girl was a trip. As well as serious eye candy. "Amen, sugar. Guess I owe your pops a thank-you right about now."

She let out a feminine grunt. "Let's not go that far."

"What time is this guy picking you up? Want me to meet him? Growl a little?" Maybe tear off his balls so using them was out of the question that night?

Smoothing a hand over her perfectly smooth blonde locks, she said, "Thanks for the offer to play big brother, but I'm meeting him at a restaurant."

"Seriously?" What kind of man didn't pick up his woman for a date? And more importantly, why did she assume there was something brotherly about his offer?

"Yes, this way I'm not stuck with him at the end of the date. You know, in case it sucks. I won't have to have any awkward no-I-don't-want-a-kiss-at-the-door conversations." She tapped the side of her head. "Not just air swirling around in here."

Damn, she was funny, smart, sexy as fuck, and baked like a dream. His cock was fully charged and ready to go. Full being the key word. He stepped closer—using the move to spread his legs and relieve some of the tension in his pants—until he was only inches from her, and she had to tilt her head back to see his face. She wasn't a tiny woman, and he fucking loved that, but she was short enough, he'd have to bend way the fuck down to taste those juicy lips.

Holly's breathing hitched before kicking up to a light pant, making her suckable tits rise and fall in a rapid clip. Goddamn, he wanted those beauties in his mouth.

"How about this," he said, staring down at her. "You go on your shitty date with the loser tonight. And tomorrow night I'll take you to a party. You can meet some people, kick back, and I promise to tell you again just how fucking gorgeous I think you are."

Holly's eyes widened, and her jaw dropped. "Um, yeah, uh, wow. That sounds fun. I'd like that."

He chuckled when she took one step back as though needing him out of her personal space to engage her brain.

"Perfect," he said. "It's a date."

"What should I wear?"

"It's casual. Jeans are good. I want the opportunity to see that ass wrapped in denim. Plus, we'll take my bike."

"Bike?"

The loud and familiar rumble of motorcycle pipes flooded the parking lot then cut off at the same moment Holly's gaze dropped to his chest. For the first time since they emerged from their apartments, she seemed to notice what he was wearing.

"Oh, shit," she muttered on an exhale before gnawing the lipstick off her bottom lip.

"Yo, LJ, get your giant ass down here, brother. Hey! That the sexy neighbor girl you were telling me about? The one with the tits and ass? Hey, sexy neighbor!"

Goddamnit.

Screw was clearly visible through the slats of the second-floor railing. The mouthy motherfucker sat astride his Fat Boy next to Maverick and Thunder, one of the MC's newer prospects.

As LJ opened his mouth to tell Screw to fuck off, the heavy pounding of feet approaching from the staircase had both him and Holly turning.

"Oh, shit," she said at full volume this time as a furious man in uniform stormed straight toward him.

He wore a badge indicating he was the new town sheriff. LJ had wondered what the fucker looked like. Now he knew. He looked like a rabid animal out for blood.

"What the...I didn't do shit." LJ said as the sheriff drew closer.

Holly stepped between him and the charging law enforcement officer, hands on her hips. LJ grabbed her waist with the intention of hauling her behind him until she said, "Dad, stop!" in a deadly, but low command that had him freezing in his tracks.

Dad?

Dad?

Fucking Dad?

Oh for fuck's sake…

"Holly, are you okay? Get out of the way, honey." There was genuine panic in the sheriff's voice. What the hell did he think LJ was going to do to her?

"Dad—"

"Did he threaten you? Touch you? Scare you?"

"Dad—"

"Get your fucking hands off my daughter unless you'd like to spend the night in jail." His voice was as quiet as Holly's had been, probably to keep LJ's nosey brothers in the parking lot from hearing, but no less lethal than a raging shout.

"What the fuck?" Maverick's pissed off voice floated up from the parking lot. Great, that guy was already over the top pissed at the sheriff's office. He did not need any fuel on his fire. Especially when the sheriff seemed all too willing to toss their asses behind bars.

"Dad!" Holly screamed this time. The biting sound seemed to snap the sheriff out of whatever fury-induced trance he'd fallen into. His gaze finally left LJ's hands—which he sure as fuck didn't remove from the soft hips of the woman in front of him—and landed on his daughter.

"What the hell are you doing, Dad? Why are you even here?" She was nearly vibrating with frustration beneath LJ's hands.

"Step away from him, Holly."

She blew out a long breath and shook her head, but she didn't move away. In fact, she leaned the slightest bit back, which bumped her directly into LJ's chest. The moment their bodies connected, some of the tension leached out of her. LJ couldn't help himself. Blame it on the same devil that gave Holly those great tits. He gave her hip a slow, sensual squeeze. When her father's eyes narrowed in on the action, LJ smirked.

"No, Dad. I'm not going to step away." Her voice held a slight tremor despite the strength of her words.

"Need us up there, LJ?" Screw called from below.

"Nah, brother. I got this. Hang tight, I'll be down in five."

"Dad, this is LJ. He's my next-door neighbor, and a…friend," she said.

"Holly," the sheriff said in a voice that was almost pleading. "Don't do this. You have no idea—"

"Dad, LJ is the guy who kindly helped me carry a million boxes up all those stairs the other night. He's been a complete gentleman since I met him."

LJ bit back a bark of laughter. Good to know he'd been a gentleman in his actions. Had she been privy to what was going on in his head or with the relationship between his fist and his cock while thinking of her last night, she might amend that statement.

"Look, Sheriff, I don't know what's going on here,"— whopper of a lie. He knew exactly what was going on. New sheriff hated the fuck out of bikers and was losing his shit over his daughter living next to one. And associating with one. Being touched by one. What would the guy do if he knew his daughter was gonna be fucked by one sooner rather than later?—"but I got shit to do, and it sounds like your daughter has plans as well. So why don't we just move alo—"

"Shut the fuck up."

"Dad!" Holly threw her hands in the air and pulled out of LJ's grasp, marching toward her father. "You need to stop this," she hissed under her breath when she was inches from him. "Now, I have a date to get to, and LJ seems to have plans as well. Since he hasn't done a single thing to warrant a police visit, I think you should let him pass by. You still haven't told me why you're here." Red tinged her cheeks whether from embarrassment or anger, LJ couldn't tell. Probably a bit of both.

Finally, the sheriff's attention shifted from LJ to his daughter. LJ held his ground, hands on his own hips now that Holly's weren't available.

"Came to see if you needed a ride to the restaurant."

It was probably wise if LJ did not snort at that moment, so thank fuck Holly did it for him. "Well, Dad, since it's been almost a decade since I was fifteen, I'll have to pass." She cast an apologetic look over her shoulder right before linking her arm through her father's. "Tell you what, though. I'd love an escort to my car." As she stepped forward, she gently tugged on her pop's arm in a sort of *come with* gesture.

The sheriff didn't budge. "Go on, honey. Have fun with Richard tonight. Just gonna have a quick chat with your neighbor, before I head on home to your mother."

Holly opened her mouth, but LJ gave her a quick shake of his head. Sexy as it was watching her get all steamed up, he didn't need her fighting his battles, and he sure as fuck didn't need anyone saving him from the small-town sheriff.

She nodded once in his direction, that biteable lower lip back between her teeth before walking toward the stairs.

"Let's get a few things straight, shall we?" The sheriff asked, closing the distance between them.

LJ smirked. "Sure thing, Sheriff. What's on your mind?"

"Sheriff Coleman is gone. That means whatever bullshit backdoor deals you had running with him are also gone. Money doesn't turn my head or make me hard. But you know what does?"

"Fucking someone who ain't your wife?"

"Nah, what turns me on more than anything is watching the scum of the earth rot away in prison. And there's no one lower than bikers, in my opinion."

LJ wrapped his hands around the rungs of the railing behind him to keep from lunging forward and slugging the arrogant son of a bitch who had the power to make life very uncomfortable for his club.

With a chuckle, as though he knew what the restraint was costing LJ, the sheriff turned and strolled toward the stairs. "Stay the fuck away from my daughter, asshole. She's way too clean for your kind of filth. Be seeing ya."

Little Jack

In his mind, LJ started to count. A little trick a therapist had taught him to keep from lashing out or losing his sense of reality. Focus on the numbers. Stay in the moment. By the time he hit thirty-seven, the sheriff's motor was running, and he was pulling out of the parking lot, ignoring the slurs yelled from LJ's brothers.

He jogged down the stairs to his waiting bike.

"You good, brother?" Screw asked, slapping him on the back.

"Yeah, no worries." A lie if he ever told one.

Nothing irked him more than being treated like trash. He'd served his country for years as a special forces operator. He'd saved lives, earned a purple heart, and was honorably discharged after a mission that left him scarred on the inside and outside.

To be looked at like a piece of garbage who was seconds away from raping and murdering the sheriff's daughter chapped his fucking ass.

With a laugh, Mav said, "You're about as shitty a liar as they come, Little Jack." Then he grinned. "Speaking of coming. Let's get you plastered and find a willing mouth to give you a good suck tonight. Yeah?"

With a grunt, LJ started his bike. As luck would have it, his dick had no interest in any mouth beside the one he'd been drooling over five minutes ago.

Goddamn fuckin' shame is what that was. A nice kick in the nuts. A woman walks right out of his dirty fantasies and into the apartment next door only to turn out to be the daughter of the cop who's fucking with his club.

Just his fucking luck.

CHAPTER SIX

"And let me tell you, we were so goddammed wasted," Richard —Rick as he'd requested she call him—said with a hearty laugh right before guzzling nearly half his wine glass in one long gulp.

What she found most impressive about this date so far was a toss-up between the magic trick in which he'd made three generous glasses of wine disappear in a span of thirty minutes, or how he'd told four stories in the same amount of time all containing the sentence, "We were so wasted."

Don't get her wrong; Holly liked to have fun as much as the next girl, but really? Did this guy enjoy anything besides getting sloppy with his fraternity brothers turned thirty-year-old *bros*?

"I'm talking could barely tell up from down smashed." He shook his head and chuckled. "Good fucking times, Holly. Good fucking times."

"Mm-hmm." Holly swallowed a mouthful of her wine. Sure, the irony wasn't lost on her. Here she was, bored out of her mind with his verbal diarrhea aka reminiscing about days he could only partially remember thanks to booze, and it was driving her to suck back the alcohol much as she imagined he did on a regular basis.

But, come on, a girl couldn't be expected to listen to this guy droll on without a little something to lube her ears.

Rick fell silent for a blessed moment, as though lost in the fantastic memories of his glory days. Shame to be only thirty and have his best times already behind him. Holly used the quiet to study him. He wasn't an unattractive man. Nicely muscled, nothing model-worthy, but certainly no slouch. A neatly pressed charcoal button-up with dark wash jeans. Hair styled almost too well. And none of the antipasto appetizer they'd shared gleamed at her from between his teeth.

He just wasn't for her. And whether that realization came about strictly because her father was pushing their connection or because she really had no interest, who knew? Wasn't worth overanalyzing. Not when this first date would probably be their last.

"Shit," he said with a bit of a self-deprecating laugh. "Where was I going with that story?"

Uhh, straight down the toilet?

Thankfully, Holly had only made it to the bottom of her first glass of wine, so the insensitive thought stayed in her head. "Um, not sure, but I've been meaning to ask how you like working for my dad so far." She winced as soon as the sentence had been uttered.

Seriously?

That's the best conversation starter she could muster? A question about his working relationship with her father? A father she was furious with at the moment. God, this date was about as exciting as waiting in line at the DMV.

Rick puffed out his chest, proud-peacock style. "Really enjoying it so far. I gotta tell you, Holly, your father has an impressive resume. He did some great work in Tampa before moving here. Working under Coleman was all right, but your father's ideals and work ethic fall much more in line with my own." His eyes practically glowed with adoration for her father. Now, every girl wanted a potential significant other to get along with her parents, but the hero-worship radiating off Rick was perhaps a bit too much. Didn't speak well for a relationship if the guy was more enamored with the girl's father than the girl.

Just as Holly went to ask exactly which *ideals* he was referring to, Rick tilted his head and gave her an almost boyish smile. "Want to know my favorite thing about working for your father?"

She snagged a sausage stuffed olive off the artfully arranged platter and said, "What's that?" right before popping it into her mouth. Delicious. So far, the food was the highlight of the date.

"Getting to sample all of the amazing treats you're constantly bringing by. If you offered me a million bucks right here and now, I couldn't pick a favorite. Thought it was those pumpkin scones, but then you brought brownies, and those fudgy coffee-ball things—man, those were unreal."

With a laugh, Holly said, "The espresso truffles."

"God, yes." His eyes rolled heavenward, and he let out a little moan.

Holly giggled as heat flooded her face. If Rick had been looking for a way to butter her up, he'd found it. Sure, she was a woman, and loved hearing she looked hot in a dress, or her hair looked nice, or someone admired her shoes, but compliment her pastries, and she'd pretty much bow at their feet.

Maybe she'd been too harsh on the guy. Judging him before getting to know him solely based on the sad fact this date had been a parental set-up wasn't exactly giving the guy a fair shot. And if she were honest with herself, she was probably extra critical after the LJ debacle earlier in the evening.

Ugh. The moment she'd slid behind the wheel of her car, she'd promised herself the mortifying incident wouldn't be thought of again until the date was over, and she was home. Alone.

But there she was, recalling the hatred on her father's face. Hatred directed at the first man who'd stirred something in her in a long time.

A goddammed biker.

LJ had seemed like such a good guy. Kind, helpful, funny, intelligent, and...hello, sexy as all get out. The total package.

Wrapped up in leather trimming and riding a Harley.

Basically, the antithesis of all her family stood for. While Holly might not have viewed the whole of bikers in as harsh a light as the rest of her tribe, she wasn't naïve enough to overlook the one-percenter patch on LJ's cut. Nor was she stupid enough to pretend that patch didn't mean trouble of the illegal variety. Plus, a life spent hearing about the evils of bikers had had an effect on her. She'd be lying if she said a little prickle of fear hadn't skittered up her spine when she'd finally noticed LJ's cut.

Joy's killer had been a biker. And though, as a twelve-year-old, she hadn't believed it was the MC who murdered her twin, what the hell did she really know? She'd been twelve. Once evidence had been found proving Curly was the murderer, her father tore that club apart, limb from limb, finding any and everything he could arrest the group for. Without the leadership of their behind-bars president, the club crumbled in under a year.

Last she'd heard, the vice president of that club was serving twenty years for a slew of crimes, and anyone who'd managed to escape her father's wrath had scattered in the wind.

Holly groaned. Why, oh, why did LJ have to be a biker?

"You okay?"

"Oh, uh, yeah, sure. I'm great." As she racked her brain for *something* interesting to discuss, their salt-and-pepper haired waiter dressed in black slacks with a silky black vest over a maroon oxford shirt arrived, balancing their oversize plates on his outstretched arm.

"Lobster ravioli for the lady," he said as he presented her plate with a flourish. The tantalizing scent of butter and cream chased away her impending foul mood. Man, it smelled like nirvana on a plate. "And the short rib *tagliatelle* for the gentleman. Anyone care for some fresh parmesan?"

"Uh, yes me. Definitely me," Holly said, practically bouncing in her seat.

"I like a girl who isn't afraid to eat," Rick said as he waved away the offer of cheese.

Their waiter winced and cast Holly a sympathetic look. God, how she hated when men said that dreaded phrase. It was one thing to say it to a twiggy girl who had a racing metabolism, but to say it to a girl constantly fighting to lose those extra ten pounds? Okay, fine, fifteen. Yeah, he might as well have said, "You're a little overweight, but I don't mind."

"That's me," she said, with a little more bite than she'd meant. "The girl who loves to eat."

"Can I get a refill on my wine?" Rick asked the waiter.

Seriously? He was gonna drink more? Holly resisted the urge to roll her eyes and sent a prayer of thanks to the heavens for having the foresight to meet him at the restaurant in her own car. No matter how lame LJ thought it was.

Must not think about LJ.

The rest of their meal went fine. Holly managed to be pleasant, Rick was pleasant enough, the food was outstanding, but not a single spark ignited between them. Not even a sparklet. Rick didn't commit any major dating faux pas, but he didn't wow her by any means, either. This relationship was pretty much doomed to stay at the acquaintance level. Holly wasn't even sure they'd make it to the friend zone.

After paying for their dinner, Rick stood and nearly toppled his chair. Looked like he had indeed committed one faux pas, getting smashed on date one. He caught himself with a chuckle and reached for her arm, more to steady himself than to guide her toward the door.

"You going to be okay to drive yourself home there, buddy?" Holly asked as she slowed her pace to match his stagger.

With a grunt, he slid his arm around her waist. Had he not seemed to need the stability to remain upright, Holly would have wormed her way out from his touch. "Pretty sure I'd have to arrest myself if I tried to drive out of here." He laughed then like he'd told the funniest joke in the world.

"Right," she said with a phony chuckle as she pushed the door to the outside open. "How about I give you a ride home?"

Exactly the scenario she'd been hoping to avoid. End of night awkwardness. Though maybe he was too hammered to notice.

"How about we head to your place instead. Have a nightcap." With a move she'd have thought he was too drunk to pull off, Rick spun and crowded her against the wall. The leering stare he gave her confirmed nightcap was code for sex.

Not happening in this or any other lifetime.

"Oh, uh, I uh, have a super early meeting tomorrow." True, but it was also true that had Rick been someone she was interested in, someone like say...LJ, she might have taken him up on the offer. It'd been a *reeeally* long time since she'd gotten laid.

Dammit. There LJ was again. Popping in all over her date.

"How early?" Rick ran his nose up the side of her cheek. Poor schmuck probably thought it was some kind of sexy caress, but unfortunately, he overshot the pressure in his drunken state and pretty much mashed his nose against her face.

"Too early to stay up much longer." Holly bent her knees and ducked under his arm. "But I'm more than happy to drop you at home before I head to my apartment." She shot a quick glance to the sky in anticipation of the lightning strike. She'd take him because it was the right thing to do but "more than happy" was an outright lie.

He straightened and ran his hand down his chest. "Nah. Got some buddies waiting on me at the bar next door. Gonna head on over there."

Holly's jaw dropped. So, he'd made a backup plan in case she wouldn't sleep with him? One that included getting further smashed and probably finding some equally sloppy girl to fall for his lack of charm and take him home.

Lovely.

"Had fun tonight, Holly. I'll call you, and we can make plans for next weekend."

She nearly snorted. "You do that," she muttered.

"Huh?" he asked, glassy-eyed and swaying.

"Just said I had a good time too. Have fun with your friends."

Thirty seconds later, she was behind the wheel of her vehicle and cruising home, happy to be alone and done with the date. If only all problems were that easy to wiggle out of.

Such as the problem of not being able to say no to a request from her father. Either of her parents, really. "No," she said out loud to the image in her rearview mirror. "See, it's easy? You need to learn to tell your parents no. You're twenty-freakin'-four for God's sake."

The drive home took about fifteen minutes. As soon as she stepped into the apartment, she kicked off her heels and stuffed her aching feet into fuzzy slippers.

"Hi, baby boy," she said to Biscuit as he sidled over with his leash dangling from his giant mouth. Holly chuckled. "You trying to tell me something, B?" She clipped the leash on his collar and headed back out. After a quick doggy leg lift, the pair was trudging back up the stairs.

Downside to a dog and a second-floor apartment. Many trips up and down the stairs.

Holly came to a stop outside her unit, but her attention was fully trained on LJ's closed door. It was then she remembered they'd made plans for the following evening. Friendly plans, a party with his friends, but seeing as how she now knew that party was probably a biker party, she needed to beg off. The epic fit her father would throw if she was caught at an MC party might cause an earthquake. Then there was the fact she was absolutely terrified at the prospect of walking into a biker den. The stories her father had told throughout the years made those parties sound like sin personified and not in a good way. Drugs, orgies, violence, the works.

Not for her.

There was just one problem. If he opened that door and invited her in, she'd be alone with LJ, at night, after a terrible date where she was feeling slightly vulnerable, unsexy, and lonely. A dangerous combination when presented with a man who'd been responsible for at least three sex dreams that week.

"Should I knock, B?" she asked the dog who just stared at her with soulful eyes. Holly sighed. "You're no help." After another few seconds of mental back and forth, she stepped in front of LJ's door and knocked twice. Might as well rip off the Band-Aid. The alternative consisted of hiding under the covers when he came to collect her tomorrow night, and that would just make her look like a bitch.

It didn't take long before the sound of LJ's heavy footsteps approaching the door had her heart racing. This was a mistake. Her breathing kicked up in anticipation of seeing him, and she swore her nipples puckered, but was too afraid to look down at the thin fabric of her dress. How could just the thought of seeing a man send her body into such a tailspin?

The door swung open and there he appeared, filling—completely filling—the space with his oversize body. Wearing a pair of faded black sweats hanging low on his hips, the V-line all women drooled over stood out. Inches above that sexy V extended a set of ripping abs Holly had only ever seen in magazines and movies.

"You need something, sugar, or you just wanting to look at a real man after spending a few hours with Dicky?" One eyebrow rose, and he lifted both arms, gripping the top of the door frame.

"How'd you know—?

"Who your date was with? I might be a piece of shit biker, but I'm not stupid. Figured out your pops set you up with his asshole deputy, Richard Schwartz."

Jesus, was it normal to find a man's armpit hair a turn on? Because Holly swore to God, LJ's armpits were sexier than any part of any other man she'd dated.

She blinked and literally peeled her dry mouth apart. Her face burned. There was no bluffing her way out of this. He'd caught her staring and totally zoning out. What had he said? Something about knowing she went out with Rick? Time to steer this conversation in another direction so she and Biscuit could return to their apartment.

Alone.

"I, uh, just wanted to talk to you for a minute if that's okay." Thank God for Biscuit's leash giving her something to hold in her hands or she'd be wringing them for sure. Being under LJ's intense focus would make a girl sweat on a good day, but now, when he was clearly pissed off, she had to fight the urge to turn tail and flee.

The light in his eyes dimmed, but he stepped back and waved her in. Biscuit bounded forward as though LJ's invitation was the best thing that'd happened to him in months.

"Hey, boy," LJ said, crouching down to the dog's level. He gave her baby a scratch behind the ears then patted his massive head. The sight of the big dog being loved on by the even bigger man had Holly's stomach fluttering.

She stepped into the apartment but didn't walk farther than the foyer. Seemed safer to avoid getting comfortable. Just get in, cancel their plans, get out and home to her cold and empty bed.

The click of the closing door had LJ's head lifting. His hot gaze landed on her once again. One corner of his mouth quirked. "Take a load off, buddy," he said to Biscuit, who flopped down and rolled to his back right there in the middle of LJ's hallway as though he owned the place. Of course, LJ obliged the beast and gave him a hearty belly rub.

"Traitor," she muttered.

LJ rose and in three steps, had the fifteen feet of distance separating them closed. Holly sucked in a breath as the aroma of sawdust, soap, and something spicy…whisky, maybe, assaulted her. Whatever the scent, on him the combination nearly drove her into some sex-crazed trance. She took a step back.

Space, she needed space.

To think, to avoid touching all those muscles, to keep from throwing herself at him. Her back collided with the door. So much for the safety of the foyer.

LJ continued to advance until he had her pinned against the door, much as Rick had her crowded against the restaurant's exterior not long ago. Only this time, her heart was racing, her chest heaving, and her freakin' panties were damp as her body nearly begged for his attention.

He leaned down until his breath wafted across her ear. "How was your date?"

CHAPTER SEVEN

She trembled. Actually fucking trembled as he spoke against her ear. The urge to capture that lobe between his teeth and give it a good tug before sliding his mouth down to the fluttering pulse point at the base of her neck almost tempted him beyond restraint.

"It was f-fine," she said on a breathy exhale.

Fine. She came back alone before ten on a Friday night. Unless they'd had a quick fuck in her car—and he'd bet his entire life savings against that having happened—the date sucked.

"You let ol' Dicky touch you?"

She'd closed her eyes at some point, but they popped open at his question. The pretty blue had deepened to near navy. "What? No!" She shook her head. "Wait. That is none of your business." Her hands landed on his bare chest as though to shove him back, but the moment her skin touched his, electricity shot straight to his groin. There was no doubt in his mind Holly felt it too.

She gasped, and her eyes shot wide before she wrenched her hands back and fisted them at her sides.

Goddamn, they'd burn the fucking complex down if they ever got between the sheets.

"Look," Holly said, seeming to gather strength with a strong inhale. "I came here to tell you I can't go out with you tomorrow." She wouldn't make eye contact, focusing instead on something off to the side.

Little Jack

The surge of anger and resentment came on so fast, LJ was powerless to stop it from spewing from his mouth. "Aww, don't want to piss off Daddy?" he said as he shoved away from the door.

Holly remained where he'd corralled her, plastered against his door wide-eyed and a little scared, if he wasn't mistaken.

Good, she should be fucking scared, because despite her verbal rejection, LJ was certain if he shoved his hand up that sinful as fuck dress, he'd encounter all sorts of creamy goodness. And not a drop of it would be residual arousal from her date with Dicky.

"N-no," she said even though they both knew it was a lie. "I just remembered I had something going on tomorrow night. That's all."

Another lie, this one so flimsy he could crush it with one hand.

"At least have the stones to tell me the truth, sugar," LJ said with a harsh chuckle.

Still against his door, looking innocent despite the sexy dress, Holly swallowed. LJ pressed his tongue to the roof of his mouth to stifle the urge to lick her throat. "I just don't think it's a good idea. You know, for us to start…anything."

Well, she was right on that account. Getting entangled with her was the worst fucking idea he'd had in years, but it was too goddamned late. His cock wanted inside her with a force he hadn't felt in ages, and at some point, it would happen. Chemistry like theirs couldn't be ignored.

Riots were started, battles were fought, and lives were lost all to slake lust not half as powerful as their connection.

LJ stalked back to her and placed his palms on either side of her head. "You think this will go away if you ignore it? If you deny it and pretend it doesn't exist?"

Her large tits rose and fell as she breathed with force. "I-ignore what?"

A smirk curled his lips and turned into a full-on grin as Holly's gaze zeroed in on his mouth.

"Tell me you don't want me." He spoke just inches from her upturned mouth. "If I work that tight dress up over your curvy hips and ask you to spread your legs, tell me I won't find you wet and ready for me."

She sucked in a startled breath, and though she shook her head, she didn't speak to refute his claim.

Time to end this shit. LJ sure as fuck wasn't about to start something up with the daughter of a sheriff who wanted to tear his club apart. Screw had mentioned the idea of him getting close to Holly to work her for information, but that wasn't LJ's style.

"You better scurry home," he said as he finally gave in to temptation and licked along the column of her throat. Sweetness flooded his tongue, even more delicious than the treats she'd shared with him.

Holly whimpered.

"I'm sure you'd be a good fuck, sugar, but I want a woman in my bed. Not a child who can't go against Daddy's wishes."

This time her gasp was of shock and horror instead of desire. If she was going to hate him, reject him, it was going to be because he was a shit instead of her father having a hard-on for his club.

"LJ—"

He held up a hand. "Pretty sure you can find your way out. See you around, Biscuit," he said, bending to give the dog one last scratch before he put Holly out of his mind and headed down the hallway. As he walked away from her, her phone rang and LJ couldn't help the harsh laugh that left him. "Looks like Daddy's calling. Better get that before he sends someone to arrest me for talking to you."

A quick glance over his shoulder revealed her frowning at her phone as she silenced it. When she lifted her gaze, a mixture of red-faced mortification and disappointment stared back at him.

And damn if that look didn't have him feeling like shit. He forced himself to ignore the unwanted emotion and continue down the hallway. If all Holly saw when she looked at him was a good-for-nothing biker, then she could fuck right off. Nothing riled him more than being viewed only at surface level. She and her father knew jack shit about him and what he'd endured in his life, accomplished, fought for, and lost. Fuck them for seeing nothing but leather and motorcycle grease. And fuck them for judging him for it. His club was his fucking family, and he'd die to protect any one of them.

No matter how desperately his body wanted her, he didn't need someone in his life who looked at him with disgust. He got enough of that each time he glanced in the mirror.

He'd begged off after just a few hours out with his brothers earlier. Just couldn't jerk himself out of his mood. Didn't matter how many women Screw had paraded in front of LJ, his cock and his fucking brain only wanted Holly. Now he wished he'd let one of them suck him off, at least. He'd still be in a piss poor mood, but at least he wouldn't be hard as fuck.

Oh, who was he kidding? Holly had been in his apartment looking like a wet dream come to life. He could have had six orgasms before seeing her, and he'd still stiffen in an instant.

After stroking himself to completion in the shower, LJ collapsed into bed and let the allure of oblivion drag him under. At least in sleep he wouldn't have to relive the fear and unease on Holly's face. Or the devastation when he'd sent her away, because for all his righteous indignation, that look stuck in his mind, giving him the ridiculous urge to apologize to her.

"No. Stay back. I got this...What are you doing? I said, stay the fuck back. Nooo!" Heat from the blast traveled faster than the powerful wave of wind that launched LJ into the air. His body flew ten feet up and careened back toward the earth so fast he wasn't able to brace for impact. His heart pounded in an erratic rhythm, and though his body sped through the air, time seemed to slow in his mind. Seconds before he connected with the ground, LJ saw it. Mick's body charred and

burning. Unrecognizable save for the metal bracelet a village child had gifted him the previous week.

"Mick!" he screamed as his body slammed into the unforgiving ground, shattering in pain.

"Mick!" LJ screamed as his eyes popped open. His back spasmed, catching him in a grip of pain that nearly stole his breath. It was then reality set in. "Jesus, fuck," he mumbled as he ran a hand down his face, wiping sweat out of his eyes. The drops hit his vinyl floor with a splat. He was dripping wet, as usual.

Been a hot minute since he had a nightmare so violent, it tossed his ass out of the bed. The nightmares themselves were a weekly occurrence, sometimes even more frequently, but most of the time they consisted of waking in a cold sweat with a hammering heart, pounding head, and sick feeling in his gut. Not to mention a slew of traumatic memories running through his mind.

The anger and emotional charge of the evening had to be to blame. Hopefully, Holly hadn't heard him lose his shit through the paper-thin wall separating his place from hers. Last thing he needed was her pity. Or worse, to have her run over to make sure he hadn't hurt himself. Six-feet-six inches of near three-hundred-pound man had to shake a floor on impact.

A glance at the clock revealed it was shortly after five-thirty in the morning. Looked like he'd forgotten to set his alarm in the mess of the previous night. Maybe the nightmare was a good thing. Kept his ass from getting chewed out by his boss for oversleeping.

As he rested back against his nightstand to give himself a few minutes to calm, his phone buzzed above his head. Without looking, LJ reached up and snagged the thing off his nightstand. Rocket was calling. LJ frowned. Couldn't be good. His brother and boss only called this early if there was a complication at a job site or an even more daunting alternative, trouble with the club.

"Hey, brother, you good?" LJ answered slightly breathless from the nightmare.

"No. I'm not fucking good. I'm fucking fucked," Rocket shot back, his tone full of disgust.

Despite what was turning out to be a serious phone call, LJ couldn't help but chuckle. Wasn't often Rocket lost his shit. He was a master at keeping his emotions locked down tight. Came from years working both sanctioned and unsanctioned black ops missions.

"What's going on?" LJ asked.

"Your girl's fucking father, that's what's going on."

LJ grunted. Bad news traveled fast. "She's not my girl." He recalled the look on her face when he'd called her a child who couldn't say no to her daddy. "Not even close."

"What-the-fuck-ever. Sheriff assface has all our jobs on hold right now. You know that casino over in Cherokee, North Carolina? The one that was knocked off two nights ago?"

LJ grunted again. How could he not know? Every news station in Tennessee and North Carolina had run the story every hour on the hour since the robbery went down. Some lucky assholes made off with over two million dollars after a high stakes poker game ended. "Yeah, what about it?"

"Well, our good sheriff got an *anonymous* tip saying the money was buried at one of our fucking job sites."

LJ couldn't help it. He laughed long and hard. "This some kinda prank, boss?"

"Ain't fucking funny, asshole," Rocket snapped then his voice grew muffled as though he was holding his hand over the phone. "Sorry, baby, go back to sleep. I'll get off in a minute."

Chloe must have made some sort of raunchy comment about getting Rocket off because the low chuckle that floated through the phone was full of heat and need.

"Hey, brother, feel free to do what you gotta do. I don't mind listening for a bit while you take care of that gorgeous woman of yours. Just make sure the phone is near her, so I don't have to hear your animal grunts while you're fucking."

"You're a real hoot now that you're patched in and think we can't do shit to make your life hell anymore. Don't get too comfortable, brother."

LJ laughed. Of all the men he considered brothers, Rocket was the closest. "So this is really happening then? We got a new sheriff with a hard-on for our club, and he's willing to pull some dirty stunts to break us."

Rocket grunted. "Looks like it."

They both knew the tip was complete and utter bullshit. There was no buried money, hell that money was long gone, never to be found again. And the Handlers didn't deal in that kinda shit. Knocking off casinos and banks was way too risky a game. Getting busted with a few million in stolen cash meant long, hard time behind bars. But how the hell could the club prove they weren't involved?

They couldn't, which meant the sheriff was going to spend days combing through and tearing up each of Rocket's job sites until he was happy with the amount of fuckery he'd placed on him.

And all this happened the morning after the sheriff found out his little princess was living next to and being touched by a biker? No fucking coincidence there.

"Shit," LJ said, rising to his feet. He then wandered toward his kitchen where the coffee should be waiting in the pot, hot and fresh. "This is on me, brother. I'll see if there's a way I can fix it."

"Nah," Rocket responded. "This guy wants us, Jack. Starting to think he's willing to stoop damn low to get us. This ain't on you. Wasn't this, it'd be something else with this asshole. Don't you dare go down to the station to plead our case. Ain't giving him the satisfaction of knowing he got to us. We ride this shit out and come up with our own plan. Asshole has no idea who he's up against."

LJ hummed his agreement as Holly's face flashed before his eyes. He may be pissed at her, but she didn't deserve to be caught in a war between the cops and an outlaw MC. And that's what it would be. A war. Not the type they'd have if another club went after them, but a war just the same.

LJ hit the speaker button and placed the phone down next to him as he prepared his coffee and grabbed the last energy bar from the box. His heart rate had finally returned to normal. The distraction of club business helped. "Why do I have the feeling this is going to get ugly?"

"You and me both, brother," Rocket said. "You and me both. All right, listen, I called you before Cop, so I better go fill him in. He'll probably call church for later today even though it's Saturday."

Construction was frequently a six to seven day a week business that didn't seem to care if the rest of the world was off each weekend. "Okay, brother. Thanks for filling me in. I'll take care of calling the crews to cancel for today."

"Thanks, LJ. Put them on standby for the next few days too. No idea how long this shit is going to take to play out."

"You got it." He took a sip of his coffee and sighed when the warm liquid seemed to wake up sleeping nerve endings after just one hit of caffeine.

Just as he was about to hang up, Rocket spoke again. "Hey, you okay? Sounded off when you answered the phone."

"Eh, shitty night," LJ said with a shrug as though dreaming about his best friend's horrific death was no big deal.

Rocket knew otherwise. He was the only one who did. Copper was aware that LJ had PTSD on paper, but even their president didn't know the extent of it. They were coming up on the three-year anniversary of Mick's death. Wasn't uncommon for the nightmares to increase in frequency and intensity at this time of year. The freak-outs during the day too. And weren't those always a blast of fun wrapped up in panic and humiliation?

"Need to talk about it?" Rocket asked.

"Nope." Same standard offer and refusal of an ear they'd used on and off over the years.

With a snort, Rocket said, "You need to get yourself a steady woman, J. Best way to stave off a shitty dream is to roll over and fuck your woman."

Yeah, no chance in hell of that happening. All it took was one incident in which LJ lashed out and nearly strangled a girlfriend in his sleep to keep him from so much as dozing in a woman's presence. Poor girl had to wear a scarf for weeks due to bruising on her neck. She'd refused every attempt at an apology and basically told LJ to rot in hell.

Nope, now he got in, got down to business, and got the hell out before the condom hit the trash can. He wasn't willing to risk hurting someone or be treated as an abuser again.

"I'm good, thanks, Rocket. Don't need a steady woman to get what I want."

"I ain't just talking about fucking, Jack. But I think you know that. And I know exactly where you've been."

LJ slammed his coffee mug on the counter. Hot liquid sloshed over the sides, scalding his hand. "Shit!" he barked as he yanked his hand back and shook it out. "Then you know exactly why I ain't willing to risk falling asleep next to a woman."

"There are things that can help, brother."

"Fucking tried it all." He could practically see one of Rocket's eyebrows lift as though to say, *"Who you trying to fool?"*

"Okay, I'll quit with the psychobabble. Just know that I get it and I got two good ears should you need one."

This right here was the part of the MC someone like Holly, and especially someone like her father, would never understand. They were blinded by fears of criminal activity, violence, and rumors of wild parties full of illicit sex. But they had no idea what resided at the core of a club like the Handlers. Family. A brotherhood with bonds stronger than blood. Blood didn't mean shit in many cases. Just ask most of his brothers.

But it meant something to Holly, apparently. Because she was willing to let hers color her opinion of LJ before she'd even had a chance to form one for herself.

Well fuck her. And fuck her father too. That asshole had no idea what would come for him if he crossed the line with the club.

"Thanks, brother. I'll check in with you later." He disconnected the call and bit through half his protein bar in one bite.

As he chewed, he contemplated what the next few days would bring. Copper was the patriarch of their family. He had an ol' lady who was a damn good woman, and he was raising her kid as his own. Copper was levelheaded and fair, but come at his family?

Well, then the man would take on the devil himself.

Bring it, Sheriff Lane. Fucking bring it.

CHAPTER EIGHT

Why on earth had Holly suggested meeting with the owner of the town's only diner at six-thirty on a Saturday morning? Because she was out of her mind, that's why. Of course, she hadn't anticipated a sleepless night of drama before her big interview.

She'd tried to sound sophisticated during her initial phone call to the diner's owner, Toni, making it seem like she had a well thought out business plan and boatloads of experience. Some of that was even true, the business plan portion anyway. The experience? Well, she was working on that. She'd been baking since she could measure and had been to pastry school, so she had that kind of experience. Just none working in professional kitchens or bakeries.

Sounding classy and put together had flown out the window the moment Toni told her the diner opened at seven-thirty in the morning but she usually arrived at six-thirty and most of the staff at seven. For some reason, Holly had blurted out the ridiculous idea of meeting with her early in the morning, which only made her sound... "Desperate. You sounded desperate," Holly whispered to herself.

Though, truth be told, she was a little desperate to find a kitchen and get her online business off the ground. So at least she sounded the way she felt...right?

"Okay," she said aloud. "Get it together, girl." She opened the trunk of the ten-year-old Jetta she'd inherited from her parents and carefully picked up the box of pastry samples she'd prepared. "You're smart, you're not half bad with people, and you're a damn good baker. So what if you need to lose ten pounds. No one will care about that in this interview. You shouldn't have changed your outfit ten times. That first one was fine. Now you look like an overripe strawberry." She said looking down at the casual, short-sleeved red dress she'd worn. "Just go in, be charming, don't stutter, and don't fucking puke."

Oh, my God. She was rambling. Aloud and to herself.

"And now you've gone from seeming desperate to craz—"

"Excuse me?"

Holly yelped and spun around, bobbling the box. Thank God, she caught it before it landed on the ground. As it was, she probably upset some of the frosting. Damnit. Off to a good start.

"Uh, yes, hi." She turned as she spoke, coming to face a thin woman with short, jet black hair in a spiky style that would have looked ridiculous on Holly, but made this woman look like some combination of badass meets model.

"Are you Holly?"

And she was the diner's owner. Great. Off to a truly disastrous start. Getting caught by the owner talking to herself while rifling in her trunk couldn't be a positive way to start the meeting. She cleared her throat and stuck out a hand while balancing the bakery box on the other. "Yes, I am. And you must be Toni?"

"Actually, I'm Jazmine, Jazz."

Which it clearly stated on the woman's silver nametag. "Oh, right, sorry."

Jazz smiled a warm smile. "No worries. It was supposed to be Toni here this morning, but I think she may have overdone it last night and was having some trouble getting up." Jazz chuckled. "I volunteered to step in. Don't worry, I've done plenty of interviews for her before. Oh, I guess I should mention I'm the manager here."

"Ah, okay, then. How about we just pretend you didn't find me talking to myself like some kind of crazy person because I'm not. I'm only half crazy."

Jazz threw back her head and laughed. "Considering I was giving myself an out-loud pep talk about a personal matter in the car on the way over here this morning, I have no right to judge." She raised her arms as if surrendering. "Call it even?" Jazz lowered her hands, extending one toward Holly.

"Yes, ma'am, that sounds good to me." With a smile and a much more relaxed posture, Holly placed her hand in Jazz's. The handshake was firm but welcoming.

"Follow me inside. It should be just the two of us for the next half-hour-ish so we can sit in a booth and chat." She turned and started for the door, walking with confidence.

Oh, how Holly wished they could trade places, and she could be the one comfortable with her position in life instead of being a constant ball of stressed-out nerves hoping to find a rental location and get her business up and running.

As she trailed behind Jazz, Holly couldn't help but take in the contradicting picture the other woman presented. With a slew of silver studs in each ear, a bar through her eyebrows, spiky hair, and a colorful butterfly tattooed on the back of her neck, Jazz gave off a badass vibe from the neck up. Below the color bone, she could have been a stereotypical kindergarten teacher. Khaki pants appearing a size too big rested on the woman's slender hips. Her diner T-shirt also seemed to dwarf her small frame and a very conservative navy blue cardigan topped off the outfit. Maybe it was just the diner's uniform, but still, it made for an odd picture.

"Please tell me you have something in that box there that'll go well with the coffee I'm about to brew," Jazz said as she unlocked the first of three outer locks on the entrance door. After all the locks had been released, she pulled the door open and stepped aside for Holly to pass.

"Well, if you're into dessert at six-thirty in the morning, then yes, I have some fantastic things to go with that coffee."

"I'm a firm believer in no-limits eating. Bring on the sugar. You don't scare me, Miss Lane." She said with a smile.

Holly nearly snorted. She highly doubted Jazz indulged in sweets at any hour, let alone bright and early in the morning. A body like that wasn't maintained by eating cupcakes and cookies. Unless she was just one of those unnatural, evil women, who could eat whatever and whenever they wanted.

God, Holly hated those skinny bitches.

"Holly?"

Oh shit, she'd totally wandered off to thoughts of calling her potential landlord of sorts a skinny bitch. Not good.

"I'm sorry, I drifted for a second. What did you say?"

"No worries. Grab a booth, and I'll be back with coffee in a few minutes. I'm excited to see what you brought." The smile Jazz tossed her way seemed one hundred percent genuine, which had Holly feeling like a shit for thinking mean thoughts about the woman.

Once she'd settled in a booth, her bakery box awaiting its grand reveal, Holly used the quiet few moments to take in her surroundings. The place wasn't what she'd expected. Shameful as it was, she'd been prepared for a run-down, small-town diner with cracked pleather seats, greasy tables, and a sticky floor. What she got instead was a retro fifties vibe in a clean and well-maintained restaurant.

A black and white checkered floor spanned the entire building. Booths and table chairs were a cheerful teal with chrome legs and trim, while tabletops were a pale pink. A long counter ran the length of the building with at least fifteen stools for customers looking to eat at the breakfast bar. Hell, there was even a jukebox in the corner.

Holly would kill to work out of the kitchen in this adorable diner.

"Cute, isn't it?" Jazz asked as she emerged from the kitchen with a tray containing two steaming mugs and coffee fixings.

"This place is great."

Jazz beamed as she set the tray down. "Help yourself. There's cream, sugar, Splenda, and some cinnamon. Wasn't sure how you took it."

"Thanks," Holly said as she reached for a mug with one hand and four packets of Splenda with the other. Yeah, she liked her coffee tooth-achingly sweet.

"Toni's parents apparently ran a great place, but she's spruced it up some since she took over. We got that jukebox just last week. I found it at an estate sale, actually." Jazz blushed. "It's kind of a hobby of mine, estate sale shopping. Anyway…" She waved her hand as though moving on from the tangent. "Toni and I were both intrigued by your idea. Why don't you fill me in on what you're proposing?"

Ahh, down to business. Holly took a deep breath and forged ahead with the speech she'd practiced in front of the mirror no less than fifteen times over the past few days.

"I graduated pastry school about six months ago. At the time, I was renting a room in a sizable home with a pretty big kitchen. I used the space to begin a small online bakery. Mostly cupcake orders, some wedding cakes, pastries for small to medium-sized events. Those kinds of things. Now that I'm here, I'm in a tiny apartment with a bite-sized kitchen. I also happen to have a humungous dog, and it's not like I can keep him separate from the baking area of the apartment. My ultimate goal is to have a storefront bakery, but I just don't have the start-up capital for that right now. So, what many online bakers do is rent kitchen space from restaurants, churches, schools, those kinds of places. Someone"—must not think about LJ—"gave me Toni's contact information and told me the diner closes around two in the afternoon."

Jazmine remained quiet, though engaged if her occasional nodding and hums of agreement were any indication. When Holly finally paused to take a breath and mentally berate herself for rambling off script, Jazz spoke up. "That's right. We close for business at two and are usually cleaned and locked up tight by three. You're looking to rent kitchen time in the evenings?"

"Yes, that's correct. Time to prepare and fill my orders, and if it's at all possible, a small amount of refrigerator space to store the finished products. We're not talking thousands of orders here, I haven't even started yet."

"Well, it sounds like a great idea to me," Jazz said with a shrug as though Holly renting the space was a foregone conclusion. "Now that we've got that out of the way, let's get to the important stuff." She rubbed her palms together, her long slender fingers revealing multiple silver rings. "Whatcha got in that box?"

Holly blinked. "Uh, so…I mean…is that…um, I mean will you talk to Toni?"

With another wave of her hand, Jazz opened the box and inhaled. "No, she gave me full authority to decide, and I'm all for it. Why not? The space isn't in use at that time, it'd be ridiculous to turn you down. Oh, mamma, this smells so good."

Could it really be that easy? Jazz sure seemed to think so. She lifted her head and winked at Holly. "Tell me what all this yumminess is."

A huge smile broke out across Holly's face as waves and waves of tension dissipated from her body. She'd done it. She'd gotten the kitchen space to start up her business which meant she could start saving money for her storefront. Progress toward her dreams. If she'd been alone, she would have squealed and done a happy dance, but she managed to keep her ass in the seat.

"Um, okay, I have an assortment of goodies, some for breakfast and some dessert. Let's start with the a.m. stuff, shall we?"

"You hand it over, I'll eat it, but I want this one first," Jazz said, pointing to a cinnamon roll slathered in a generous dollop of cream cheese glaze.

"Okay, I'll just tell you what they all are. The one you're salivating over is a cinnamon roll." Holly pointed to another pastry. "That's an apple turnover, then a scone, a classic brownie, a white chocolate cupcake with Bailey's frosting, a slice of peach pie, and a piece of cream cheese pound cake."

Jazz just stared at her.

"What?" Holly said as nerves ran up and down her spine once again.

"Are you for real?"

Holly chuckled. "Maybe you should taste something before you ask me that. It could all be gross."

With a snort, Jazz picked up the cinnamon roll. "Somehow I doubt that," she said before opening her mouth wider than Holly would ever have guessed it could go and taking a gigantic bite of the gooey treat. "Oh. My. God," she said, mouth full as her eyes literally rolled upward. "You have got to be kidding me right now."

In an impressive feat of sugar tolerance, Jazz sampled each and every baked good, not hiding her enjoyment or praise one bit. The two talked between bites until they were laughing and working on their second cups of coffee.

"Holy shit, I just had the best freakin' idea ever." Jazz said in a near-shout as her spine straightened. She practically bounced in her seat. "Ready for this?"

The sudden jolt of animation from Jazz had Holly laughing. "I'm not sure…"

Jazz laughed right along with her. "I'd apologize, but this idea is too good not to be this excited. Our lead chef, Ernesto, does some baking. Biscuits, simple rolls, a few types of pie. He flat out hates it, and, I'll be honest, they are far from the strongest items on our menu."

"Okay…" Where was she going with this?

"What if, instead of charging you a rental fee, you paid for the space in baked goods?" Jazz's eyes shone with delight over her idea, which warmed Holly's insides. The offer wasn't made out of pity or some kind of obligation. It was a genuine enjoyment of Holly's food that had Jazz wanting to sell her baked goods in the restaurant.

Before Holly had a chance to respond to the request, Jazz plowed on. "Breakfast items would sell like crazy in here. So would cakes, pies, and pastries. We can move it all." Her nose wrinkled, drawing a snort and chuckle from Holly. "What do you think? You, Toni, and I can sit down and determine an agreed-upon amount of baked good for you to provide in exchange for the rental space. If we end up requiring more, we'll pay *you*."

So much had happened in the last five minutes, Holly's head spun. She needed a few minutes to process since, though Jazz's offer was incredible, it did throw a wrench in Holly's plans. She'd be increasing her budget for supplies and spending time on the diner's orders. But she wouldn't have a rent payment. And there was the free promotion. Having her items on the diner's menu daily would be an enormous marketing boost that wouldn't cost her a dollar beyond what they determined was fair compensation for use of the space.

"I think it sounds like an absolutely amazing idea!"

"Yes!" Jazz clapped her hands, and she did bounce in her seat.

What the hell. Holly let out a small squeal and bounced right along with Jazz.

"Hey, you said you're new in town, right?"

Holly reached in the box and snagged a hunk of the scone. "Yeah, only been here about ten days, but my parents live here too. They moved about three weeks ago," she said right before popping the delicious pumpkin spice concoction in her mouth. Damn, that paired so well with Jazz's strong coffee.

"You got any plans for tonight?" Jazz asked, mouth slightly stuffed with a giant bite of cinnamon roll. "I'm not even sorry

I'm talking with my mouth full. This is just too damn good to care."

Well, shit, what chef didn't love a compliment like that? "Nope, no plans. I'm officially a friendless loser."

"You have plans now." She rattled off her phone number. "Text me your address, and I'll pick you up tonight at nine. We'll go out. Dance a little. Drink a little. You can meet my crew. It'll be fun. Whatdaya say?"

As Holly pulled out her phone to enter Jazz's number, she noticed a slew of missed text messages and calls from her mother. Fourteen texts and three calls in all. She'd silenced her phone for this meeting, and immediately her mind went to the worst-case scenario. With her heart pounding out a rhythm of dread, she opened the text app. "Jesus," she muttered. The first text was a good morning note, asking Holly what she was up to today. From there, each grew more frantic as Holly hadn't answered until the final, and fourteenth said her mother was going to have her father send some officers to her apartment.

This was getting out of control

"You okay?" Jazz asked.

"Yes, sorry. Family drama. But, I say that sounds like a great plan for tonight. I sent my address." And it did sound like a fun night out. Holly desperately needed to get out and make some new girlfriends. Otherwise, she was doomed to spend every weekend being fixed up by her father. A shudder ran through her. No, thank you. One of those dates was plenty.

"Great! Just wear something you'd wear to any bar." Jazz said as the jangle of bells indicted the door was opening. "Staff's starting to arrive, so I need to get moving. I'll see you tonight."

"See ya." After leaving the diner, Holly immediately placed a call to her mother.

"Holly, finally!" her mom said by way of greeting, tears evident in her voice. "I've been beside myself. Your father has a patrol car swinging by your apartment now. Are you okay? Do you need help?"

Holly pinched the bridge of her nose as she leaned against her car. "I'm fine mom. I was just busy and couldn't answer the phone."

"Well, Holly, that can't happen again. You always have your cell phone on you, so I don't see why you can't just answer when I call or text."

Staring up at the early morning sky, Holly blew out a breath. This had to stop. Her mother's need to know where she was at all times had only grown worse with each passing year. It'd almost reached the point of pathologic.

"Mom, I'm an adult, and even though I carry a phone with me, there are going to be times I'm unable to answer it. You know this. Everyone knows this."

"Well, I—"

"Look, mom, I don't have time to get into this right now. I'm fine and have a packed day and plans tonight, so you probably won't hear from me again until tomorrow, maybe even Monday, okay?"

"What? No, please let me know when you get home tonight, so I can sleep."

Holly hung her head, the word no at the tip of her tongue, but she couldn't do it. She'd had to learn to live with the guilt of failing her sister, but couldn't handle knowing she was the reason her parents suffered at night. They'd been through enough. "I'll text, but that's it. I gotta go." After hanging up, she shook her head at her weakness. How many twenty-four-year olds who lived alone still needed to let their parents know when they arrived home?

She spent the afternoon hours working on a few ideas for breakfast pastries she had a feeling would be fantastic for the diner's menu. At least it seemed as though they would complement the menu items she'd found on the diner's website.

By seven, she was covered in flour, egg goo, and sugar. A good scrubbing took care of the mess both to her and her kitchen, then she spent the next ninety minutes fretting over what to wear and working on her hair and face. Most of the time, since she baked for a living, she spent the day in yoga pants and makeup-less. Since this was the first time she'd actually had plans—not made by her father—in an embarrassing amount of weeks, she went a little heavier on the makeup and considerably lower-cut on the clothing than she might have, had she actually had an active social life.

At five minutes to nine, she jogged down the steps to wait for Jazz.

"Damn, girl, you clean up nice!!" Jazz yelled from the window of a Dodge Camaro as she pulled into the parking lot. "With a rack like that, you're gonna be beating them off with a stick tonight."

Holly giggled as she ran to the passenger side door. "Thanks for coming to get me. Is this all right?" she asked, indicating the black skinny jeans and charcoal gray tank with a plunging V-neck.

"Uh, yeah, you look hot, sister." Jazz also had jeans on, a dark wash, with a long-sleeved purple top that didn't show so much as a hint of skin. "All right let's do this. I'm excited to introduce you to my girls. Toni will be there so you can finally meet her."

"Great." They chatted for the fifteen-minute drive until Jazz cut a hard left and got in a line of vehicles waiting to enter through a fifteen-foot security gate.

What the…

Two men stood on either side of the open gate, peeking into the windows of each car that passed, though it was mostly motorcycles making their way into what appeared to be a compound of some sort.

Oh, shit.

Mostly motorcycles…

Holly glanced at the men guarding the gate. They had cuts identical to the one worn by LJ.

Her blood ran cold, and she fought the urgent need to vomit.

Jazz had brought her to the Hell's Handlers clubhouse.

CHAPTER NINE

LJ tossed his fourth shot of tequila down his gullet and fought the need to shove the overeager Handlers' Honey off his arm. A horny club girl ready to rock and roll. He should be all over that shit. Meant he wouldn't have to search for someone to fuck that evening. And fucking someone random was precisely what he needed to get his mind off the forbidden fruit fucking with his head.

Too bad his dick had no interest in the painted-up stick figure with fake tits clinging to him. The girl probably ate nothing more than a lettuce leaf and a can of tuna on a good day. Who the hell wanted to fuck a bag of bones?

"You gonna let me find out firsthand if the rumor is true?" the Honey whispered in his ear, making sure to brush her sticky lips against the shell of his ear. What the hell was her name? Cindy? Cami? Carli, maybe? All LJ remembered was the drama she'd caused by becoming overly interested in Maverick. She'd tried to fuck things up for him and his ol' lady, and nearly got herself booted from the club. In fact, she'd taken her rejected ass and sulked somewhere for more than half a year. Guess she'd returned for more biker dick.

"Hasn't anyone ever told you it's not nice to gossip?" LJ said as he lifted his hand to Thunder, who was working the bar. After four shots of tequila in twenty minutes, his head was growing pleasantly fuzzy. Maybe with another three or four, he'd be too far gone to give a shit who he fucked, and he could take Carli up on her offer.

Yeah, he'd decided her name was Carli.

"Pretty sure every man wants us girls gossiping about how he has a ten-inch dick."

He grunted.

"And I've heard it's ten inches soft," she purred, pressing her firm tits into his arm. Too bad another set of tits had been dominating his thoughts for days, so much so Carli's barely registered.

"Shouldn't believe everything you hear." Okay, so he had a big dick. It wasn't a secret. Not since he'd fucked a mouthy girl from town over a year ago. The short-lived fling ended when he found out she'd snuck into his room at the clubhouse, taken a dick pic while he was sleeping, and sent it to her girlfriends. Next thing he knew, all the goddamn Honeys in the club were running on about his huge dick and how they couldn't wait until he patched in so they could have a run at it.

Not happening.

Sure, he needed to get his rocks off as often as any of his brothers, but he just had no interest in fucking some chick half his brothers' dicks had spent time in. Call him weird, but it just wasn't his thing.

"How about you take me upstairs and show me, so I don't have to rely on rumors?" Carli practically purred into his ear.

"Sorry, sweetheart, not tonight." He accepted the shot from Thunder, fist-bumped the blond prospect, then downed it as fast as he'd housed the others. Unfortunately, Carli didn't take the hint. Instead of leaving him the fuck alone, she wrapped her arms around his bicep and hung on.

"Jazzy!" came a high-pitched squeal from somewhere across the crowded clubhouse. Sounded like a very drunk Stephanie. "'Bout time you got here, bitch!" Oh yeah, Steph was toasted.

LJ chuckled as his gaze sought out the woman who'd been an honorary member of the ol' ladies club for the past year or so.

Ever since she began working for Zach's woman, Toni, Jazz had been a constant presence around the club. Far as LJ knew, she had no interest in becoming an ol' lady, no need to be a Honey, and hadn't fucked a single one of his brothers. Rare for a woman so frequently around the club members. She was a bit of a mystery, one his brother, Screw, seemed to have taken particular interest in.

After a few seconds, his gaze found her where she was weaving her way through the bodies to get to her girls. She turned, holding out her slender hand for a woman behind her, and the pair wormed through the rowdy bikers as one unit.

This was the first time since LJ met Jazz that she'd brought a friend to a party. As far as he knew, she had no contact with the people in Arizona, where she'd last been living, and didn't socialize much outside the club.

Curious as to who Jazz's friend was, LJ shifted his attention from the puzzling woman to the one trailing behind her.

The moment his gaze landed on that sleek waterfall of honey-blonde hair, his throat closed, and his brain shut the fuck down.

Holly was in his goddammed clubhouse. Jeans so tight they'd be a struggle to remove cupped her ass. Those plump globes twitched with each step. No surprise, his dick perked to life, throbbing to the beat of her fucking walk.

After turning him down flat because he was a biker and she was too fucking special to touch a biker—at least according to her daddy—she had the audacity to show up here, cleavage on display and in those goddamned boner-inducing jeans.

Un-fucking-real.

He kept his gaze on her as she and Jazz made their way to the cluster of ol' ladies. Jesus, how the hell did she even know Jazz? She was stiff as a board, walking woodenly with her eyes darting in every direction.

Looking for him? Or scanning every corner for an impending attack?

"She can join us. I don't mind." Carli's voice reminded him of her presence, or more the fact that she didn't leave after he'd dismissed her.

"Not interested, Carli. Already said that. Move on."

"That giant bulge you're sportin' says different." Some might find the near-whine in her voice sexy, but to him, it was nails on a chalkboard.

He grunted. "That ain't for you."

Jazz and Holly reached the ol' ladies, and Jazz must have been introducing Holly around by the way she waved and nodded at each woman.

Still impersonating a boa constrictor, Carli pouted but didn't say anything else. He'd give her no more than two minutes before he removed her from his presence himself.

Jazz and Holly chatted with the ol' ladies for a moment before Jazz whispered in Holly's ear and pointed toward the bar. Holly's eyes grew wide, and he had a perfect view of those tempting lips mouthing the words "hell yes," before the two started for the bar.

Still scanning as she moved, Holly's gaze eventually landed on him. He wasn't hard to find since he stood at least a few inches above everyone except Copper. Her steps faltered, and she reached for Jazz to steady herself while her eyes grew saucer wide. Until they shifted to Carli, that is, then they narrowed, and her plum painted lips turned down.

LJ didn't bother going to her. He'd made an offer and was rejected. No point in beating that dead horse. "Get lost, Carli," he said, patience gone. This time he jerked his arm free and she finally got the message. The lost puppy dog look she cast his way as she walked backward from him was plain pitiful and not at all an action to make him change his mind.

Twenty minutes and another two shots later, LJ was done with this bullshit. He'd watched Holly and Jazz down a few drinks in the short time as man after man approached Holly and stared at her exposed cleavage. He hadn't been able to tear his gaze from it himself, but wasn't there some sort of finders keepers rule? He'd seen her first and was getting damn tired of watching his brothers drool over what somehow felt like his.

So, enough was enough. She was either going to cover those tits or leave. Simple drunken logic.

The trek to the opposite end of the bar took a solid five minutes since no less than three people interrupted him along the way. As he drew up behind Jazz, Holly's shiny mouth dropped open and she sputtered.

"What's wrong?" Jazz asked as she turned then looked up to him. "Oh, hey, LJ! I haven't seen you since your patch-in party. Congrats by the way. This is Hol—"

"Hey, Jazz, need to borrow your girl for a few minutes," he broke in as he wrapped his hand around Holly's wrist.

"What? No, I don't think so," Holly said, but she didn't fight him as he tugged her away from Jazz, who now wore a smirk.

"I'll find you later, girl." Laughing, Jazz wiggled her fingers at Holly who tossed her friend a scowl. "Or maybe I won't. If you're lucky." Jazz winked then turned, completely ignoring the desperate S.O.S. look Holly sent her.

Whatever Holly might think of him, Jazz was well aware her new friend would be perfectly safe in his company.

Without another word, LJ towed Holly down a darkened and deserted hallway leading to the exec member's offices. The rooms were strictly off-limits to anyone but their owners during a party. Holly put up a moderate amount of resistance. Not enough to make a scene, but enough for LJ to get the hint she wasn't thrilled by his caveman haul-off routine. Though it did her no good. He could lift her and toss her over his shoulder with one pinkie if he wanted and not a single soul in the place would rescue her, no matter how big a fit she threw. Hell, they'd whistle and cheer him on. Slap his back as he passed by.

The hallway was free of chatter since the rest of the club preferred to be out near the bar, but it wasn't quiet by any means. The heavy beat blaring from the speakers seemed to rattle the walls of the entire clubhouse. At some point, an eager couple would end up banging against one of the walls— probably Mav and Stephanie—but for now, he and Holly were the only two around.

The music drowned out the sound of Holly's ragged breathing, but as LJ stopped walking and caged her against the wall, he caught sight of her chest rising and falling much too fast. A dark part of him felt a small amount of pleasure at her unease. It'd heighten her senses, keep her on the edge.

"Your daddy know you're here?" he asked, forearms braced on the wall above her head. She had no choice but to crane her neck to see him in the dimly lit hallway. Being so much taller than her not only gave him a power advantage, it gave him a fucking spectacular birds-eye view of her plump cleavage. And man was it on display tonight.

Some of the fear evaporated from her gaze, replaced by the fire of annoyance. LJ hummed his approval. Anger was even sexier on her than the fear. "I didn't know where Jazz was taking me," she said through clenched teeth.

"Hmm. Yet you didn't leave when she showed up at the biker's den of sin, huh? You came strutting in here wearing jeans so fucking tight they look painted on that sexy ass, and a tiny top showing off your tits to every man in the room." Goddamn, she smelled incredible. Some kind of citrusy soap combined with something sweet. LJ would bet his life savings she'd spent the day baking.

"I d-didn't drive," she whispered. "I had no way to leave."

"Coulda called daddy."

Holly shook her head.

LJ knew shit about what went on when women gooped up their faces, but whatever Holly did to her eyes gave them this sultry, smoky dark look that could only be described as bedroom eyes. Naked-faced, she was downright gorgeous, but he'd be lying if he said this sexed-up version wasn't making his dick hard as well.

"Want to know what I think?" LJ asked as he traced one finger down the column of her neck.

She swallowed, as though her throat was following the trail of his hand. "W-what?"

"I think you wanted to come here. I think you wanted to get a little drunk. Get a little wild. See how the filthy half lives." Light as a feather, he stroked a fingertip over the swell of one partially exposed breast.

Holly let out a little gasp. The puff of air wasn't audible over the thrum of the music, but her glossy lips parted, and a small shudder ran through her. Though the lack of light made it difficult to see, LJ swore he could make out the pointed tips of her puckered nipples through the fabric of her dark tank. Helpless to do anything but find out if his suspicion was accurate, he brushed the back of his hand over one tit then the other.

Like little diamonds. "Tell me I'm wrong," he whispered as he bent so close, he could smell the tequila on her breath. Same drink preference as him. Why that made him even harder, he had no clue, but he was beginning to think Holly could sneeze and it'd turn him the fuck on. "Tell me you didn't want to come here and get dirtied up by a raunchy biker."

"Y-you're wrong." The protest was so weak, LJ chuckled.

"Liar," he said, one second before his mouth claimed hers.

For a moment, Holly remained stiff, forcing him to tease her sealed lips. He ran his tongue over the top one, then the bottom before nipping it with a sharp pressure. Apparently, little-miss-sugary-sweet liked a prick of pain because she let out a soft moan the second his teeth sank into that lip. LJ didn't waste one second plunging his tongue into her open mouth.

Tequila. Definitely tequila. And something sweet. Fuck, the woman tasted better than the most expensive liquor money could buy.

The stroke of his tongue against hers set her off. She let out a whimper and melted into him. Strong feminine arms came around his neck as Holly plastered those pillowy tits against him and dove into the kiss.

He'd been prepared to plunder, to steal her breath and make her suffer a little with a punishing kiss. The feelings of inadequacy she'd evoked in him combined with the rejection then the nightmare all came to a powerful head when she walked into his clubhouse looking like some kind of erotic goddess. But instead of a ferocious meeting of lips, tongue, and teeth, the kiss turned languid and exploratory.

They stroked against each other, testing angles and pressure, and repeating the moves which caused whimpers and moans. Holly parted her legs, allowing him to slip one of his between her thighs and damn if she didn't press that hot little denim-covered pussy right into the thick length of his quadricep.

LJ groaned as she rocked against him. The kiss remained slow, drugging, but the intensity increased until Holly ripped her mouth away and let out a long mewl. That sound, sexy as it was, shocked LJ out of his lust-filled stupor and back into the world where Holly thought he was scum of the earth and her father was on a mission to lock his ass up. And those he loved. The idea of Chloe or Toni or any of the ol' ladies watching as their men were carted off to prison was enough to shoot LJ's lust out of the sky until it crashed dead on the ground.

Even as her hungry mouth sought his again, he pried her arms from around his neck and anchored them to the wall at her sides. "I'm not going to be your little act of rebellion, sugar. Come find me when you figure your shit out."

With that, he pushed off the wall and stormed back down the hallway. As he made his way back to the party, his head pounded in time with the music. The tips of his fingers began to tingle and an invisible vise squeezed his chest tight.

Fuck.

Not now. This couldn't be happening.

Vision growing hazy, LJ paused at the bar and called out. "Thunder, give me the fucking bottle."

Little Jack

The prospect's eyes grew wide at the sight of him near losing his shit, but did as asked and handed the bottle of tequila across the bar. LJ grabbed it and continued straight on toward the stairs leading to the bedrooms. He had a small room he rarely made use of. Having his brothers and their women be privy to his screaming nightmares didn't top his list of fun times to be had.

Only two things worked to stave off an impending panic attack, or worse a dissociative episode as his shrink called it. First was the breathing and coping exercises the Navy appointed therapist gave him. Second was the bottle. One of those practices took time and so much mental effort, the struggle left him fatigued for hours. The other was too fucking easy and never failed, which was why LJ never, ever allowed himself to drink to cure the pain.

But tonight? Tonight was different. Tonight, he planned to polish off the tequlia and pass the fuck out. Consequences be damned.

As he motored toward the stairs, Carli stepped into his path. Her form wavered a bit in front of his eyes. "Get the fuck outta my way," he growled. With a yip, she hopped back a second before he'd have rammed into her.

Next to tequila-block him was Jazz. Hands on her slim hips, she raised an eyebrow. "Where the fuck is Holly?"

"Hallway," he barked. "Take her the fuck home, Jazz. She doesn't belong here." With that, he side-stepped around a gaping Jazz and took the stairs two at a time. Halfway up to the second floor, unable to draw in a full breath, he ripped the cap off the tequila and tossed it over his shoulder before taking a long, calming drink.

Fuck this day.

CHAPTER TEN

Eyes closed, Holly slumped against the wall and worked to get her erratic breathing under control. She held a hand over her heart as if she could manually slow the beat from a gallop to a steady trot.

What an asshole LJ turned out to be.

Twice. Twice in the last twenty-four hours, he'd crowded her against a wall and got her all worked up, only to drop some grenade of a comment then leave her all hot and bothered. And she'd fallen for it hook, line, and sinker both times.

She must seem like some kind of sex-starved bimbo to him.

Humiliation aside, Holly was just plain pissed to be left in a state of want yet again. Hell, maybe she *was* a sex-starved bimbo.

LJ was punishing her for everything that had happened since her father showed up last night.

Colossal asshole.

How had she thought him so kind those first few days?

"Holly?" Jazz's concerned voice floated down the hallway. "You okay?"

As she blew all the air out of her lungs, Holly nodded. "Yeah, I'm good."

Jazz's laugh was more of a grunt. "You're a shit liar, sweetie. Here."

Holly popped her eyes open to find her new friend holding out a tall shot glass. "You look like you could use this and then some. It's a double, so go easy."

Yes, a good drunk was exactly what Holly needed to forget the man who made her body sing and her mind scream. "Thank you," she said as she grabbed the shot glass and downed the entire content as though it was water instead of two mouthfuls of tequila.

"Damn," Jazz said with a chuckle. "I'm impressed. Shooting that much tequila at once takes commitment." She leaned against the wall next to Holly and took her hand. "I'm sorry, sweetie. Had I known there was bad blood between the two of you, I'd never have let him cart you off like that. I just thought it was some kind of foreplay. Don't worry though, I'm fully prepared to kick his giant ass into next week. Just say the word."

The image of Jazz trying to take on LJ, who could probably snap her in half with one twist of his wrist, finally dragged a smile out of Holly.

"That's better," Jazz said as she bumped Holly's shoulder with her own. "Wanna talk about it, or you want me to just take you home?"

Since Jazz had practically shoved her at LJ earlier and seemed right at home here in an outlaw MC's clubhouse, Holly assumed her loyalty ran deep and she'd side with the club as soon as she found out who Holly's father was. But as of now, Jazz remained the only friend Holly had in Townsend, and she desperately needed a girlfriend to confide all these swirling emotions to, so she took a chance. "LJ lives in the apartment next to me. We've only spent a little time together, but there seems to be a powerful...um...attraction between us."

Her cheeks heated. More than likely, she was the only person in the building who'd blush over the mention of sexual chemistry. Earlier, as she and Jazz had made their way from the entrance to the bar, Holly noticed no less than three couples going at it hot and heavy in various corners of the room, not to mention some seriously dirty dancing all around the place. Not quite the drunken orgy she'd expected, but certainly more than she'd witnessed in public anywhere else.

"But, um, I'm pretty sure LJ hates my guts even if he wants me, and I'm crazy conflicted about my feelings for him at this point. He seemed insanely nice when we first met, but last night and tonight he acted just plain shitty."

"Oh, fuck," Jazz said on an exhale. "You're the sheriff's daughter."

Holly's eyes widened and she met Jazz's gaze head-on. "What? How do you know that?"

She shrugged. "These dudes gossip worse than a bunch of high school chicks. They also think they're good at keeping shit from their women when they actually suck at it. Since I'm in with all the ol' ladies, I get the juicy gossip. And I hate to tell you girl, but the sexy baker who put LJ in a shit mood is today's main chatter."

"Wonderful." Holly thunked her head against the wall. Could this situation get any more fucked up? It was time to go. Maybe even time to find a new apartment. Living next door to an outlaw biker who she happened to want more than she'd ever wanted a guy was a recipe for disaster. Especially when she was supposed to hate him on sight, or at the very least fear him, but all she could think every time he was in her presence was how good he smelled, and how hot he looked. Unfortunately, now she could add how amazing his hands felt on her body to that list. God, the simple glide of one coarse fingertip over the top of her breast made her hotter than the entire sex act with her last boyfriend. How the hell was she supposed to function knowing all that lived only a few feet and some layers of drywall away, but she could never have it?

"Holly, I feel terrible. I've never been to LJ's place, so I had no idea he lived next to you. I'd never have asked you to come if I'd known what the situation was." Jazz sounded genuinely upset.

"Because you wouldn't have wanted to bring someone connected to the sheriff around your friends?" Holly turned her head until she met Jazz's gaze. An unfair question for sure. Jazz had been nothing but great since Holly met her. First with the job offer, then letting Holly tag along on her Saturday night plans, and now taking the time away from her real friends to talk Holly off the ledge. Even knowing all that, Holly had to find out for sure whether Jazz would turn her back on her now that she knew the connection to local law enforcement.

"No. I'm not like that. Most of the people here aren't. They won't judge you based on your family. Will they be wary until they learn whether you're a threat? Sure, but if you want to be here, want to be friends with the club, you won't be judged. Especially not by me. Trust me," she said with a self-deprecating laugh. "There is no one who understands fucked up family dynamics more than me. I'm the last one to throw stones. The glass of my house is so cheaply made, a cotton ball could shatter it."

Seemed Jazz had a story. Holly genuinely liked the other woman. Hopefully, this tentative friendship could continue to grow, and Jazz would one day get to the point where she felt comfortable confiding in Holly. For that to happen, she'd have to earn the other woman's trust. Best way to do that was to show vulnerability herself. "My relationship with my father is complicated. When I was a kid, he worked for years in the gang unit. Some of the shit he's seen and dealt with…" Holly shook her head. She wasn't ready to talk about Joy with her new friend. Too personal for such a new relationship.

After clearing her throat, Holly continued. "Anyway, his anger last night was more about me and our family's past than this club."

"I've only lived here about a year, but all the people associated with this club have become my family. If you give them a chance, LJ included, you'll find that there are some damn good men and women here. Now, come on, enough serious shit for the night." She grabbed Holly's hand and tugged. "If we're not going to leave, then it's time for some fun."

Twenty minutes and another shot later, Holly could admit to having a good time. Actually, a great time. Sure, about every forty-five seconds or so, she scanned the room for LJ, but other than that, she loved the women of the Hell's Handlers MC. They were funny, tough, sweet, and badass all in varying degrees.

And then there was Izzy. An absolutely gorgeous, tall woman with her hair in a long Dutch braid. She had the most adorable baby bump that appeared in contrast with her kick-ass personality. Izzy seemed awesome. The type of independent, sassy woman Holly only wished she could be. Until she decided to turn the conversation onto Holly herself.

"Okay," Izzy suddenly announced right after a woman named Stephanie had told an outrageous story about nearly getting caught having sex in public. "I'm just gonna put this right out there. Anybody have any objections?"

Seeing as she was pregnant, Izzy hadn't had a drop of alcohol. Same couldn't be said for the rest of the group of giggling women.

"No!" Shell, the MC president's ol' lady said with far too much exuberance. "Speak your truth, woman."

Izzy's face scrunched as she shook her head in Shell's direction before turning her attention on Holly. "Wasn't sure what to think of you once I found out your dad was the dick who keeps causing trouble for our men," Izzy said, staring straight at Holly. The rest of the women stopped dancing and fell silent. "But I fucking like you," she said with a scowl. "Fuck us over, and you'll answer to me. Get me?"

Holly's eyes widened at the same time Stephanie whistled.

"She's even scarier now that she's knocked up," Toni whispered.

"I'm not fucking scary," Izzy said with the scariest look on her face Holly had ever seen. "But LJ means a lot to all of us and preggers or not, I'll fuck you up if you mess with his head further."

The alcohol swirling in Holly's bloodstream made it hard to follow the conversation word for word. But the intensity of the emotion rolling off the frustrated Izzy? Yeah, Holly caught every ounce of that.

"I-I'm not here to—wait, what do you mean, mess with his head any further?" Holly looked from one ol' lady to the next. One of them would clue her in, right?

Wrong.

Instead, they just exchanged side-eyed looks with each other. Like they were trying to decide just how much info they could trust the sheriff's daughter with.

Shit!

Tears pricked the backs of Holly's eyes. It was long past time to leave this party and get back to her real life. She'd been crazy to start thinking she'd find friends here.

"Well, fuck," Izzy said with a roll of her eyes. "Don't go and get all cry baby on us. Makes us think you aren't going to run and tell the sheriff everything you saw tonight."

"I'm not," Holly immediately responded. "I wouldn't. Why would you think that?"

There went this tight-knit group again, communicating with their eyes. What the hell was going on?

"What?" She looked between the women who suddenly found the floor very interesting. All but Izzy. Clearly the most outspoken and ballsy of the bunch, Izzy cocked her head and kept her gaze on Holly.

"You don't know?"

Any pleasant buzz she'd achieved from the alcohol was quickly chased away by the frustration of being left in the dark about something everyone else seemed clued in on. "Don't know what? Someone just spill it already."

"Your dad has the entire sheriff's department coming after the club almost daily. The guys are being pulled over for bullshit while riding, our businesses are being shut down because your father has been getting anonymous tips about illegal activity, yet not a single thing has been found. I even had that prick Deputy Schwartz at my tattoo shop yesterday because supposedly three sets of parents came to complain I had tattooed their underage children." A furious scowl crossed her lips. "Fucking bullshit."

"Shit, Izzy," the redhead, Chloe, said. "Why didn't you tell us?"

Izzy shrugged. "Because it was bullshit and nothing came of it." Her attention came back to Holly. "You know he shut down every project LJ had running today?"

Holly's heart stuttered to a stop. The loud music faded until she could hear nothing but the sound of her own breathing and Izzy's words. "What do you mean?"

Chloe took over the story, sadness in her eyes. "My ol' man is Rocket. He owns the construction company LJ works for. LJ is his lead project manager. Right now, they have four separate sites running simultaneously. More than usual, so they're pushing it hard to finish everything on time, so pretty much someone was working at each site today even though it's the weekend. Anyway, the sheriff's office halted all work for the entire day, maybe even more, because they supposedly got a tip about the missing money from that casino robbery being stashed at one of the Hell's Handlers construction sites."

Holly's stomach rolled, the tequila sloshing around like the sea in a storm.

"Of course, they didn't find shit," Izzy said with heat in her voice. "Because our men aren't fucking bank robbers."

Oh, God. She pressed a hand to her stomach. Did her father do this because of her? Was this his fucked up way of warning LJ away from her? No wonder the man wanted nothing to do with her. Guilt pressed down on her shoulders, hard.

"I have to talk to LJ," she said, voice hoarse.

And tomorrow, she needed to have a difficult conversation with her father. Holly refused to be used as a pawn by the sheriff's department to funnel information on men she knew nothing about. Nor would she be used in the opposite way to provide the MC with police tidbits. No matter how hot LJ made her or how nice these women were.

"Upstairs," Izzy said indicating the staircase with a tilt of her gorgeous head. "Fourth door on the left."

"Is he, um, will he…"

A smile curled Izzy's lips for the first time since this conversation started. But it wasn't a reassuring grin; it had a more sinister quality. "Will he be up there fucking one of the Honeys?" She shrugged. "Guess you'll find out, won't you? You've got some sex-rumpled hair and your lipstick's all gone. How worked up did you get him?"

Pretty damn worked up if he felt even half of what she did when they kissed. With trembling legs, Holly nodded to the group of women who were clearly more family than friends before turning away. She'd taken three steps when a hand closed around her wrist.

"He's alone, I promise," Jazz whispered. "Just LJ and a bottle of tequila that's probably working its way toward empty by now."

"Thanks," Holly whispered to her new friend.

As she climbed the stairs, her head spun, and her stomach threatened to expel everything she'd consumed that day, which was pretty much alcohol and pastries. Great combination.

The short walk from the top of the staircase to LJs door seemed to pass far too quickly. She hadn't had enough time to prepare what she planned to say. Hell, she didn't even know what she wanted to say. All she knew was the thought of LJ's livelihood being threatened because her father discovered their quasi-friendship was sickening.

Without giving her swirling mind a chance to talk her out of it, she raised a hand and knocked on LJ's door.

"'S open," came the slightly slurred reply.

Holly willed her hand to stop shaking, but it was a wasted effort. With unsteady fingers, she opened LJ's door and stepped through.

"Fuck me," LJ said on a groan as she stepped into his line of sight.

He lay sprawled out on his bed, shirtless, with an unzipped pair of jeans. His boots lay scattered haphazardly next to the bed. A half-full bottle of tequila rested against his side. Holly swallowed around a thick throat. He looked beyond sexy. All those rolling muscles and ink spread out on display. Like he was lying there just waiting for her to climb on and ride him.

"We need to talk," she said.

He grunted. "We could skip the talk and just fuck."

"It's tempting," Holly said, some hidden inner vixen taking over her tongue. "Really tempting." This time she whispered the words. Holly had slept with a handful of men, not a crazy number, but she'd never been the aggressor. Never put herself out there and asked for it. Something about their chemistry seemed significant to her. As though indulging in LJ would somehow alter the course of her life. Could she really pass the experience by?

"But?" His voice made her jump.

Holly shored up her courage. "But you've left me hanging twice now. I don't want a third strike."

He sat straight up, grabbing the bottle with his left hand. Gaze dead-locked with hers, he rose and stalked toward her. Once he was close enough she had to look up, an advantage he seemed to enjoy, he spoke. "Your father is gunning for my club."

"I didn't know." She couldn't have torn her gaze away if the building exploded around her. His hazel eyes seemed greener tonight. Flecks of gold sparkled through them drawing her in. "The girls told me tonight. I had no idea that was happening, and I'm so sorry he messed with your work today."

"But you know why he hates bikers." Holly was eye level with the hard expanse of his broad chest. Resisting the urge to probe the muscles was proving more difficult by the second. Would his inked skin feel hot beneath her hands? His chest was free of hair, but a fuzzy brown trail ran down from his belly button and disappeared into his jeans, just begging her to follow the path.

"I know why he hates bikers."

Her father wasn't a bad guy, and certainly wasn't a dirty cop, but his loathing of motorcycle clubs ran so deep, Holly wasn't sure he'd ever approve of any of the men in this MC. But he was a fair man and a dedicated officer, so if the Handlers proved they weren't a threat to the people of Townsend, her father would back off. She was sure of it.

LJ brushed her hair from her shoulders until it all hung down her back. She shivered as his coarse fingertips grazed her skin. He didn't ask another question, but Holly felt the need to explain at least a little bit. "He's dealt with some biker clubs in the past that have been...bad."

"Bad?"

"My—my sister was kidnapped and murdered nearly thirteen years ago. The man who killed her was the president of a one-percenter motorcycle club." Each word felt like a knife cut to her soul.

"She why you wear this?" He asked, fingering the best friend charm resting against her chest. The one she never took off. If she had any hope of keeping her wits about her, the man needed to stop touching her. Never before had she had such a strong physical reaction to a man. The moment his callused fingertip grazed her skin, all good sense flew right out of her head.

"I'm sorry that happened to you." His intense and concerned gaze had her believing he meant the words. He leaned down until she could smell the tequila on his breath. "So now you think all bikers are murderers?"

What did she think? With him so close, Holly could barely breathe, let alone get her brain cells in gear. Part of her wanted to say yes. To fall into the repetitive pattern she'd followed her whole life. The one where she let her parents dictate her thinking, but, as she stared into LJ's eyes, she couldn't do that. "No. I don't."

"Your father does."

"Yes."

"So now what?" He stayed close, his hands landing on her hips as his nose trailed up her neck.

Now I run!

That'd be the sensible thing. The safe choice. Were anyone in her family to find out about this, they'd be horrified. It'd be seen as the ultimate betrayal to her twin sister and her parents. But Joy was different. Joy grabbed life with both hands. Her best friend charm felt warm where it rested against her skin. Though she knew it was crazy, Holly often felt that heat in times where she needed advice, craved guidance. She'd always viewed it as Joy's way of checking in on Holly's life. A life she'd promised her twin she'd live for the both of them.

So instead of walking away, she turned her face, so her lips were inches from LJ's. "Now you touch me," she whispered.

LJ lifted his hand, circling it around her throat in a light hold that had her pulse speeding up and her panties dampening. "I won't leave you hanging this time," he whispered against her lips. "You'll come so fucking hard they'll hear you over the music downstairs. You want that?"

His grip on her throat increased just enough to let her feel his power. Power he'd promised to use to pleasure her, not harm her. Her entire body trembled with his little squeeze. The skimpy thong she'd worn to bolster her confidence was soaked straight through. Hell, her jeans even felt wet.

She was more turned on than she'd even been in her life.

Falling into bed with LJ might make her a reckless woman, but walking away from her first taste of true ecstasy would make her a fool for sure.

Decision made, she finally let her hands have what they'd been itching for. Pressing her palms flat to his chest, she absorbed the feeling of those rock-hard pecs. Damn, the man was powerfully built. His strength an affirmation of life. And for one night at least, Holly was all about living life to the fullest.

"Like your hands on me, sugar, but I need an answer."

Holly gazed up into his smoldering eyes. "I promise you're not an act of rebellion. And I'll never betray your trust," she whispered. "I just really want you to make me come."

With that, she grabbed the back of his head and pulled him in.

CHAPTER ELEVEN

Shit, LJ just found the third thing to soothe his soul and chase away his demons. Holly's fucking delicious mouth. That dark, sweet cavern was more potent than the alcohol and far more pleasurable than any fucking mental exercise his shrink doled out.

Getting tangled with the sheriff's daughter had to be the worst fucking idea he'd ever had, but it no longer seemed to matter. The choice had been made. Might as well reap the benefits before the piper came 'round to collect.

"Fuck, you're so goddamned sweet," he said before ravaging her mouth.

Holly moaned and rubbed against him like a cat in fucking heat.

He could have spent hours feasting on her mouth, but those tits had been torturing him for the past few weeks. It was high time for a taste. Without breaking the kiss, he worked the fitted tank top up until it rested over her tits. His hands immediately went to them, encountering the soft scratch of very thin lace. Shit, no wonder her hard nipples were visible through the tank. This thing barely offered an ounce of coverage.

After a few moments of fondling her tits, testing their weight, plucking her nipples and fucking loving the desperate whimpers she made against his mouth, he pulled the lace cups down.

Ending the kiss felt like it might kill him, but knowing what was in store for his mouth made it well worth the sacrifice.

LJ ripped away from her lips and stared at her tits, panting hard. "Fuck," he whispered before bending his head and lifting one handful to his mouth. He didn't tease, didn't ease her into it, just latched on to her tight nipple with a fierce suction.

Holly let out a strangled sound as her hands landed on his head. But she didn't push him away or balk at the rough treatment. No, her nails scored his scalp, and she held tight as though she'd die if he stopped sucking her.

He kept at her with harsh pulls of his mouth and intermittent swipes of his tongue. As she'd done earlier in the evening, she widened her stance and tried to grind against his thigh. LJ would have chuckled if he wasn't so lost in desire. His girl needed some relief, now. Too bad for her, he was going to make her wait for it.

"LJ," she said on a gasp as he finally released her nipple. The heat of her pussy seared his thigh, straight through his jeans. God, she'd be blistering once he finally got inside. Kissing his way across to her other breast, he spoke against her silky skin. "Hope you don't think this is a one-shot deal, sugar. No way in fucking hell am I going to be satisfied with just one taste of these gorgeous tits. I'm too on edge to give them the proper attention tonight, but next time. Next time, I'll do right by them."

"Jesus," she whispered as a shudder ran through her. "You're going to kill me."

He gave the neglected tit a quick, hard suck and her nails scratched his scalp. Hissing as the bite of pain spiked through his bloodstream, he took a step back.

Mussed hair, swollen lips, and glazed eyes stared up at him. Framed by her bunched tank on top and her bra below, those gorgeous tits hung wet from his mouth with nipples a deep red from the attention.

"Take your jeans off then lie on the edge of the bed. I'm not done tasting yet."

"Oh, fuck," she whispered. Her hand went to her top.

"No," he bit out. "Leave it. I love the way it makes your tits look."

Her face flamed. "They look ridiculous like this."

"They look sexy as fuck. Leave it. Pants off. Hurry. I'm hungry."

Now, the red in her cheeks seemed more from heat than embarrassment. She obeyed, wiggling those generous hips out of her skintight jeans in a move that nearly made him come in his pants. Next time he'd be watching that from the rear view.

Her panties were totally useless, an aqua thong that couldn't possibly contain her arousal. The thing matched her bra and looked dark from her wetness. "Holly," he rasped out as his cock leaked into his own underwear.

She met his gaze, though it seemed to take effort. "I'm not exactly built like most of those girls downstairs."

"The Honeys?" He snorted. "Those scrawny bitches aren't worth a second of your time, sugar. You're built like you walked straight from my dirtiest fantasies, Holly. Curvy hips, big soft tits, and an ass I've jerked off to thoughts of every fucking night since I've met you."

"S-seriously?"

"Dead serious, sugar. Now get on the fucking bed for me."

The compliments seemed to bolster her confidence. Something they'd need to work on, because the woman had a traffic-stopping body. She should strut into any and every room, head held high, letting those rounded hips sway to their full potential while rocking outfits that showed off her tits and legs. Instead, she felt the need to issue a disclaimer.

By the time he was done with her, she'd be in love with her own body.

Holly straightened her shoulders, then turned giving him a prime view of her ass split by the fucking string of her thong. LJ let out a tortured groan which had Holly peeking over her shoulder with a playful smirk.

That's it, sugar. Tease me with that gorgeous body.

When she reached the bed, Holly faced him again, then sat on the edge of the mattress. She bit her lower lip, then slowly leaned back until her elbows held her in a semi-reclined position.

In two long strides, LJ stood directly in front of her. "Spread your legs."

Holly's breath caught, but she did as he asked, parting those creamy thighs wide enough his large body could fit between them. And that's exactly where he put it.

Attention fixed on the dark swath of fabric barely covering her pussy, LJ dropped to his knees between her legs. He placed one large hand on the inside of each of her thighs, eliciting a hiss from Holly as though he'd seared her skin. Still staring at her core, he pressed her legs even wider.

Holly remained on her elbows, watching every move he made with desire-filled eyes.

"You ready to come on my tongue?"

Her head moved up and down. "So ready," she whispered.

"Don't have to ask if you're wet." He'd thought that comment would make her blush again, but whatever spike in ego she'd gained earlier remained.

"No," she said. "You don't. Pretty sure you'd have to be blind to miss how soaked my panties are."

Goddamn, the woman was something when she owned her sexuality.

"Lie flat. Want to feel those kitten claws on my scalp again. Can't do that if you're propping yourself up."

Holly did as he asked, and he rewarded her by slowly kissing his way up her thigh. When he reached her sex, he slid his finger over the wet panel of her thong. Over and over, LJ teased her opening, rimming it with feather-light touches that had to be driving her mad.

He purposefully ignored her clit. Within seconds, he had Holly squirming on the bed, fists opening and closing at her sides.

Her hips jerked as she tried to get him to do something. Increase the pressure, enter her, finger her clit. None of that was going to happen until—"LJ, please"—there it was. Until she begged.

"Please what, sugar?"

"Please, stop torturing me. I need more."

The scent of her arousal was far more intoxicating than the tequila he'd indulged in earlier. He hooked a finger under her thong and dragged it to the side, exposing her glistening pussy. "More, like this?" he asked right before tonguing her clit.

Holly squeaked in surprise, then her hands landed on his head. Someone once told him he was nuts for keeping his head shaved. Said women wouldn't have anything to grab while he was eating them out. Clearly, that fucker never had a woman's nails piercing his scalp as they writhed in pleasure.

Sexiest fucking feeling.

Holly wasn't shy about taking what she wanted from his hungry mouth. She held his head firmly between her hands and rubbed her clit against his tongue as much as he was stroking his tongue against her.

As he'd suspected, she was sweet as sugar and twice as addicting.

LJ gave her clit a light scrape with his teeth, smiling as she jolted in response. He lapped at her, licking up all the juice that coated her sex and thighs. After he'd gotten his taste, he shoved his tongue straight into her pussy and went to town fucking her with it.

Holly screamed and thrust against his face, nearly stealing his air.

"Shit, LJ. You're so good at this. Oh, my God." She moaned, whimpered, and called out to her God often.

"Tell me how good," he demanded as he slid his hands under her ass. The flesh of her cheeks overfilled his hands. Squeezing the softness had more precum leaking from his cock.

"I've never…"

He sucked her clit between his lips, stroking his tongue over the nub at the same time.

"Jesus, it's never been like this," she said on a rush of air. "Not even close. Shit, LJ, I'm going to come already."

Fuck yes. "Give it to me, sugar. Come all over my face."

She groaned. "Like I have a choice."

LJ chuckled against her. Damn, he liked this girl. He just barely grazed her clit with his teeth at the same time he shoved two fingers in her tight channel. Three quick pumps and a little more suction to her clit, then Holly's back bowed, and she screamed out her orgasm.

It went on for a while, the intense clasping of her pussy around his fingers. His eyes were going to cross from the pressure on his dick once he finally got inside her. That was if he didn't bust a nut in his jeans like a fucking fourteen-year-old.

"Now that was an orgasm," Holly said with a slight slur to her voice as though she was the one who'd drunk three-quarters of a bottle of tequila.

LJ glanced up her body. Both hands still rested on his head, lightly stroking along his scalp. The tender gesture soothed the previous sting of her nails, something he doubted she was even aware she'd done. Watching her eyes bug in surprise when he showed her the marks would be something to look forward to. Those eyes were currently closed, with a dream smile curling her lips.

Yeah, he'd given her a good one. "I aim to please, sug—"

A loud pounding on the door had a yelp coming from Holly as she scrambled to right her top. "Zip it up, brother, we got pigs in the pen," Zach's voice said through the door.

"What?" Holly squeaked, face scrunched in confusion. She'd managed to tuck her tits back where they'd been, but her bare lower half was still spread eagle around LJ's body.

"Cops are here, babe," came Zach's reply.

LJ met Holly's horrified gaze. She shook her head. "No. LJ, no. This wasn't—I had nothing to do with this. Swear it on my life. Hell, I swear it on Biscuit's life. I wouldn't…I didn't."

As though a bucket of ice-cold water had been poured over him, his dick wilted and so did the feelings of strong affection he'd been feeling until five seconds ago. Shit. Had he been so fucking stupid as to fall for a ploy by the cops? Did the sheriff's daughter let him tongue fuck her as part of some fucked up scheme?

"Her pops ain't here," Zach said, though the door was still closed.

"Move the fuck along, Z. We'll be right down," LJ called out as he stood.

Holly's hands trembled as she fumbled her way into her jeans.

He felt hollow, sick to his stomach over the extreme roller coaster of emotions he'd been on in the past ninety minutes, hell, the past two days. "Hurry it the fuck up, Holly."

"I'm ready," she said five seconds later as she shoved her feet back into her heels. She reached for the door, but LJ slapped a hand against it, holding it closed and making her jump.

"Swear to God," he whispered in her ear from behind. "You even think about crying rape, I'll—"

"What?" Holly spun and shoved him back with surprising strength. "How dare you? You know what? Fuck you, LJ!" She turned back, yanked the door open and stomped down the hallway with such force, LJ was surprised one of those spiky heels didn't snap in half. He was also relieved she didn't use the thing as a weapon to unman him.

They were the last couple to make it downstairs. Someone had killed the music, and all chatter had died. Men and women stood or sat around with varying degrees of hatred written across their faces. Each exit was manned by two cops and another five or so positioned themselves throughout the clubhouse. Where the fuck did all these cops come from? Townsend didn't have this many on their entire police force. Was the sheriff deputizing any asshole that walked in his office?

"We have reason to believe there is a stash of money in this building from a robbery earlier in the week."

"Jesus fucking Christ," Maverick called out. "This bullshit again? Think I'd be drinking this bottom-shelf shit if I had money from a casino robbery laying around?" he said as he held up his glass. Stephanie, his former-FBI ol' lady, rolled her eyes and shoved his arm down before whispering something in his ear that had him kissing her.

From next to LJ, Holly gasped. His blood went from a slow simmer to a complete boil in milliseconds. Fucking great, now she thought they were fucking masked bank robbers, straight out of Hollywood. Not five minutes ago, he'd had his face buried between her legs and would have gladly spent the entire night there. Now he couldn't stand the fucking sight of her judgment and disgust.

He took a step away from her. Just being in her energy space was intolerable.

"If you're a member of the club or in a relationship with a member of the club, you stay. If you're just here for the party you are free to leave after an officer does a quick personal scan on your way out," Schwartz said.

The urge to wipe that fucking king-shit smirk off the deputy's face with one hard punch was almost more than LJ could resist. Schwartz said something to one of the other officers then laughed. He was fucking loving this.

"This is bullshit," Holly whispered.

What? He stared down at her. Mouth flat, eyes narrowed, she stood with her arms folded and plumping those delicious tits. She didn't seem to notice she'd propped those beauties sky high. Her sexy body vibrated with...anger?

"Seriously, LJ," she said as though he hadn't been sending her hate vibes for the past ten minutes. "This is complete bullshit. Look at him." She gestured toward Schwartz. "This isn't real police work. This is him being an ass and getting his rocks off on a Saturday night because he's bored and doesn't have a woman."

LJ blinked. Holly grew more worked up by the second. Those pretty eyes shot fire in Dicky's direction. That wasn't faked indignation. She was furious on his behalf, on his club's behalf.

Shit. He'd gotten it wrong. Holly hadn't lied, or conned him, or used her body to manipulate. She was just as blown away by this raid as he was.

"Who the fuck is talking? Did I not make myself clear when I said to shut the fuck up?" Dick walked in LJ and Holly's direction. "I got plenty of room in a cell downtown for anyone who can't keep their trap shut for ten min—Holly?"

The shock in Dicky's voice was music to LJ's ears, and he bit his lip to keep from cracking up. The high was short-lived.

"Are you all right, Holly?" he asked, stepping closer, his face drawn in what LJ could only assume was concern. As though he was worried about Holly's safety. Maybe worried some bikers had dragged her here by the hair and that's why it had that post-fucked wildness about it.

Nope, Dicky, that's one hundred percent post-tongue-fucking hair.

Schwartz placed his palm on Holly's bare shoulder, and LJ saw red. He started to reach out and yank her out of the fucker's grip, but Rocket caught his gaze and shook his head once.

Fuck.

Would Holly even choose him, or would she shrink from his touch? He'd been a shit to her since Zach knocked on the door. Doubted her, snapped at her, embarrassed her. Wouldn't surprise him at all if she told him to fuck off and begged Dicky to whisk her away.

Wouldn't surprise him, but it would fucking gut him. And there wasn't a damn thing he could do about it because his safe haven was swarming with cops.

The room wasn't as silent as it had been a few moments ago as the people only there for the party started to leave.

LJ sucked in a breath, and it caught somewhere in his chest.

Shit. There it went. Starting again. Fucking twice in one night. He tried a second time to inhale, but the air didn't make it past his throat, which got tighter and narrower by the second. Sweat broke out across his forehead. Black dotted his vision. Schwartz's words grew muffled, as though the cop spoke from the opposite end of a long tunnel, thanks to the rushing in LJ's ears.

"Let's get you out of here, okay, Holly? Has anyone threatened you? Hurt you?" Schwartz asked Holly as he stroked a hand down her arm.

LJ's nostrils flared. He tried to speak, to tell Dicky to get his clammy fucking hands off her, but all that came out was a strangled wheeze.

Helplessness did it every fucking time. And he'd never been more helpless than he was standing there while some bastard had his hands on his woman.

Not that she was his woman.

Fuck.

Holly cast a glance in his direction, and her brows immediately drew down. Dicky didn't seem to notice LJ was seconds away from totally losing his shit. And no one wanted that to happen.

In the next instant, soft skin brushed against LJ's palm. Holly stepped closer and slipped her hand into his. Her entire right side pressed against his left as she let her weight rest on him.

"No, Deputy Schwartz, I have not been harmed, or threatened, or scared in any way. It was my choice to come here tonight. As it is my choice to stay now."

Immediately the grip of panic began to abate, and LJ became able to engage his brain enough to employ a technique his therapist had taught him. He absorbed the feeling of Holly's smaller hand. Drew in the scent of vanilla and sugar that always seemed to hover around her in a cloud of sweetness, and he leaned slightly into the pressure from her body. All things real and tangible he used to ground him in reality. To keep his mind from running off into the past and losing his grip on the world.

"Holly, you can't be serious right now. Your father—"

"Has no say in who I hang out with or what I do in my spare time, Rick. I'm an adult. I can pick my own friends. And I'll stick around until you clear the club because it's laughable that you think they're hiding hidden money from a casino robbery." She gave LJ's hand a squeeze, and the pinch of her grip further helped lessen the anxiety. How the fuck did she manage with one touch what he'd been fighting for years to accomplish on his own?

A few murmurs of appreciation came from his brothers while all the ol' ladies smiled at Holly. She'd stood up for LJ, for his family even though she had to have questions. And even though he'd been an ass to her. There was no way Holly could be fully comfortable with the club, not after what she'd admitted about her family's past. Something warm fired low in LJ's gut.

She was a good woman.

And a sexy woman.

LJ freed his hand then circled his arm around her shoulders, anchoring her to his side. The increased contact chased away the final tingles of anxiety. He was back in the game.

"Go on, Dicky," he said before he dropped a kiss on the top of Holly's head. The scent of vanilla surrounded him. "Do whatcha gotta do. Finish wasting taxpayer money while we watch you make a fool of yourself and come up empty handed."

Schwartz sent a pleading look Holly's way, but she stood firm at LJ's side. In fact, she even wrapped her arm around his waist. Or as much around his much larger form as she could reach. God, he didn't deserve her touch after the way he'd doubted her motivations and actions. But he was going to take it, revel in it, and beg for more as soon as Dicky got his fucking mug out of their faces.

The cops spent nearly ninety minutes fucking up the clubhouse. With big shitty grins on their faces they dumped desk drawers, ransacked bedrooms, and made a general mess all in the name of search and seizure, which, yes, they had a fucking warrant for. Lord knows who sucked a judge's dick for that bogus warrant.

In the end, of course, they found nothing, but they'd done a bang-up job of ruining everyone's weekend. Sunday would be spent cleaning until their backs ached. By the time the cops had wrapped up their search, the only people who remained were the few members of the MC who'd planned to spend the night in the clubhouse. Copper asked everyone to return bright and early for clean-up duty. A few of his brothers snagged Honeys before retiring to their disorderly rooms, but in general, the mood had been killed.

The very second the last officer disappeared through the exit, Holly turned to LJ with a stricken expression. "LJ, I swear—"

He slid both hands into her hair and silenced her with a hard kiss. For long moments he ignored the whoops and whistles of one of his brothers—probably fucking Maverick—as LJ held her where he wanted her and plundered her mouth.

When he finally drew back, Holly's eyes were glazed and her lips wet and swollen. "I was an asshole. I'm fucking sorry," he said.

"Don't do it again," she whispered, giving him a lopsided grin.

He chuckled. "Hate to say it, sugar, but if we're gonna start something here, you need to know I'm probably gonna fuck up again before too long."

Her gaze met his, serious and heated. "We're starting something?" she asked.

As he lowered his mouth back to hers, he whispered, "I fucking hope so."

CHAPTER TWELVE

Tuesday found Holly sipping wine and planning items for the diner's menu with Toni and Jazz from a very plush couch in Toni's home.

"I think we've got a stellar plan, ladies." Toni wore a huge grin as she did a little wiggle dance from the cushion next to Holly.

Jazz, who sat perched on the edge of a recliner, laughed. "Excited much?"

"Oh, my God, I'm beyond excited," Toni replied. Her light brown hair hung from high on her head in a lopsided ponytail. Yoga pants and what had to be one of her ol' man's *Ripped* T-shirts completed the comfy outfit. If Holly wasn't mistaken, *Ripped* was the name of the gym Zach owned.

"Come casual," she'd said. "Actually, less than casual. Wear what you'd wear for a solo Netflix date with your couch."

"Seriously, Holly, you have no idea how long I've wanted to implement something like this. More and more, we get customers popping in on their way to work who don't have time to sit and eat but want a coffee to go and something they can take to eat for the road. This will do wonders for business. Mine and yours."

The pleasure Toni's words evoked had Holly beaming. She felt seconds from bursting into a glittery explosion of happiness.

Who wouldn't love being praised for their life's passion? "Okay, so next Monday will be our maiden voyage?"

"Does that work for you?" Jazz asked. She wore similar pants to Toni, only hers had an intricate neon purple pattern in a stripe down the sides. As usual, a crew neck long-sleeved T-shirt covered her top. Did any of the other girls in their group notice Jazz wore those long-sleeved tees like a uniform? September in Tennessee wasn't exactly cold, yet she'd worn a similar shirt each time Holly had met up with her. Even when they partied at the clubhouse.

"That's perfect for me. Gives me time to test a few new ideas out."

"Okay," Toni said as she reached for one of the peanut butter brownies Holly had brought along. "I worked out today, so don't judge me for eating two of these. Enough shop talk. I want to hear what's going on with you and LJ, Holly."

"Oooh yes!" Jazz said as her eyes lit. "I've been dying to know what the deal is there. Spill, girlfriend." She rubbed her hands together as though about to dive into a juicy steak.

"Oh, well, uh..." Did Holly really want to talk about the strange quasi-*thing* she had going on with LJ? She'd already jumped off the ledge where he was concerned, now she'd taken a job working at a diner deeply connected to the MC. Confiding in these women would only strengthen their budding friendships. Did she want that? Okay, yes, she did. But *should* she want that? No. Not at all. Her family would never understand. They'd think her disloyal to Joy's memory, though Joy would probably be the first one hanging out at the clubhouse, were she alive today. But she wasn't alive, and her death had been caused by an outlaw MC member.

It was so complicated, her head throbbed.

"Here." Toni refilled Holly's wineglass with a mischievous grin. "Suck this down, then tell us. Whatever you say won't leave this room. Promise, girl." She crossed her finger in an X over her heart. "Gashes before 'stashes."

"Ugh," Jazz wrinkled her nose. "Next time go with chicks before dicks."

"Huh, that is a little less offensive, isn't it?" Toni said as she crossed her legs and tilted her head as though she had all night to wait for Holly to spill her guts.

Holly heaved a sigh before swallowing a huge gulp of her drink. The flavor of the expensive vintage barely registered. She'd already committed the ultimate sin by pursuing her connection to LJ. So...in for a penny, in for a pound. A sentiment that would be oh, so comforting when her mother cried and her father blew a gasket over this. "Okay, fine, but you promise to keep it quiet?" She'd tell her parents when *she* was ready. Not when small-town gossip took the choice from her.

"You got it," Toni said.

"Promise." Jazz said.

"That's not enough. Put a hand on the plate of brownies."

With a giggle, Toni said, "What? Why?"

"Shh, just do it."

Also chuckling, Jazz scooted to the edge of the recliner and leaned forward, placing her hand on the large platter of brownies which was resting on Toni's coffee table.

Both women looked to Toni, who rolled her eyes but followed suit. Holly's hand joined her new friends'.

"Wait," Toni said. "Why are you doing it too, Holly?"

With a shrug, Holly said, "I didn't want to be left out."

That had both Jazz and Toni cracking up.

"Okay," Holly said then cleared her throat. "Let's get serious for a second. Repeat after me: I solemnly swear..."

"I solemnly swear..." Toni and Jazz parroted.

"To keep my trap shut..."

"To keep my trap shut..."

"No matter how much I want to gossip and share Holly's business."

They repeated the sentence.

"If I break this vow..."

"If I break this vow…"

"May I never have a brownie again."

"What?" Toni practically shrieked. "That's harsh!"

"May I never have brownies again," Jazz said. "Say it, Toni."

With a huff, Toni said, "Fine. May I never eat a brownie again. Happy?"

"Very," said Holly as she smiled. "Okay, me and LJ. We met the night I moved into my apartment. LJ literally ran into me as I was carrying stuff up the stairs. He helped me unpack my car and bring a bunch of heavy boxes to the apartment where it turned out he was my next-door neighbor."

"We know this part. Get to the sexy times." Toni said, refilling her own glass, then passing the bottle to Jazz.

"How do you know there were sexy times?"

"Uhh, have you seen the man? Pretty sure no woman alive could resist all those muscles and that sexy bald head. And oooh the beard!" Jazz said with a dramatic shiver that quickly turned into a frown as a scant amount of wine poured into her glass. "You bitch!" With puppy dog eyes and a pathetic pout, she turned her attention to Toni.

"Keep your panties on. There's another bottle in the kitchen."

Jazz hopped up. "Wait until I get back to finish the story. Unless you're just telling stuff I know. Then you can say it. And please, bitch, you only wish I'd take these panties off for you." As she walked to the kitchen, she gave a little butt shimmy.

Holly couldn't keep the grin off her face. These women were the best. Kind, welcoming, fun, hilarious, a good time all around. Meeting them, befriending them helped ease some of her fear and uncertainty about the MC. Would these women, these strong, independent women tie themselves to the club if it was full of rapists, murderers, and drug runners? Holly just couldn't picture it. None of them seemed abused or poorly treated. In fact, from what she saw at the party, the men of the Hell's Handlers MC treated their women better than most.

"Okay, I'm back," Jazz announced as she walked in the room with a full glass and a new bottle of wine. "Continue."

"Oh, thank you for the permission." Holly smirked at her new friend. "Okay, so LJ and I met a few times and had some instant, sparks-flying chemistry." Her face heated as she admitted. "I'm pretty sure I've never had such a strong and immediate attraction to anyone before. Uh, the night before the party at the clubhouse, he invited me to go, but my dad showed up and kinda killed the moment."

Toni snorted. "Yeah, that would do it. Sheriff dad popping in on a one-percenter trying to get with his daughter." With a wince, she shook her head. "Don't envy you that one."

"Yeah, it wasn't pretty. Anyway, I canceled the date, or whatever it was supposed to be. Then Jazz asked me to hang out Saturday night, and I ended up at the clubhouse anyway."

"Oh, my God," Jazz said, wide-eyed and hand over her mouth.

"I can see you laughing behind your hand."

"I'm sorry." This time her giggle broke free. "It's just, now I get why you were so freaked out about going to the clubhouse."

That and the fact part of her seriously wondered if she'd make it out of an outlaw MC's lair alive, which she was now ashamed to admit. Especially sitting in the home of one of the members.

"Yeah, you could say it was awkward. But, anyway, we had words at the party then we…"

"Had sex?" Toni asked with a toothy smile. "Please tell me you had sex."

"Uhh, you realize we're talking about Holly having sex, not you, right?" Jazz asked.

Toni waved the hand holding her wine glass. "Please, if I had any more sex, my brain would dissolve."

"Rub it in why don't you," Jazz mumbled into her glass.

"We didn't have sex-sex. We had…other sex."

"Did you come?" Toni asked.

"Um, yes," Holly answered in a squeak.

"Good enough," Jazz said. "Did he come?"

With the heat wafting off her face, it had to be cherry-red. "Nope. Zach knocked on the door to tell us the cops had arrived before we got to that part."

"Ohh, poor LJ," Jazz said.

"Right!" Holly said after taking another sip. "That's what I thought, and believe me, I was more than willing to pay that debt. But here's the kicker, after the police left, LJ dragged me out back where we made out against the building for a while, then, when I thought we'd head to his room, he passed me off to you, Jazz, and that was that. As you know since you took me home, I just went to my apartment. Alone. What the hell?"

She'd been left confused and feeling rejected as she slipped into her lonely bed. Had it been the raid? Did Schwartz's obnoxious behavior serve as an in-his-face reminder of her close connection to law enforcement? That fact hadn't seemed to bother him earlier in the night when he had his head buried between her legs, but then again, his club hadn't been turned upside down by the cops at that point.

How would this ever work? She'd been delusional to think she could sustain any kind of relationship with LJ, purely physical or otherwise. This had disaster written all over it in big block letters made by a permanent Sharpie.

"Hmm," Jazz said as she tapped her chin with a black painted nail. "That's interesting. I can tell you this, that man wants you. It was clear in the way he stalked you with his hungry eyes all night long, so don't go thinking that's the problem."

"So, what? I'd get it if he wanted a mash and dash, but the guy didn't even get so much as a hand in his pants. And I was more than willing. I'd even go so far as to say I was eager to pick up where we left off."

Both women broke out into fits of giggles. Jazz laughed so hard her wine sloshed to the top of her glass. "Oh, shit," she said as she set it down. "First this one says 'gashes before staches.'"

She jerked her thumb in Toni's direction. "And now, did you just say mash and dash?"

"Oh, yeah, I guess so. Saw it in a Facebook post." She waved it away. "We're getting off topic. The moral of this story is that LJ and I aren't a thing. I was rejected, big time." She lifted her glass to her lips only to remain dry-mouthed. Ugh, why was her wine glass empty already?

"I don't know about that. He's pretty hush-hush about his... let's call them rendezvous," Toni said.

Jazz nodded and grabbed her glass again. "He is. Never really hooks up with anyone around the clubhouse that I've seen. Only that one girl who started spreading rumors about the size of his dick." She wagged her eyebrows. "All good things, I promise. Maybe he just doesn't like to get busy in the clubhouse."

Holly frowned. They had a perfectly good apartment—two of them—just a short ride away. And he had no problem going down on her in his room at the clubhouse. "Maybe." She flopped back onto the couch. "Let's talk about something besides my pathetic love life, please."

The sound of a door opening was followed quickly by Zach's, "Hey, sexy lady! Good news is your man's home. Bad news is I had some stray dogs follow me from the gym."

"Fuck you, man," came the laughing reply.

Jazz snapped straight in her seat as her face blanched.

Holly leaned her forearms on her knees. "You okay?"

"What? Oh yeah, I'm fine. It's nothing. Just—"

"Well hot damn. Hit the fucking jackpot tonight. Brownies and my girl." Screw strode into the room. He wasn't nearly as big as LJ, and probably an inch shorter than Zach, but the man's confident swagger made him the biggest man in the room.

"Screw," Jazz finished.

Screw grabbed a brownie and took a bite, moaning while he walked straight for Jazz. All three men wore jeans and their Handler's cuts, but LJ and Zach had T-shirts under theirs where

Screw had what appeared to be a white wife-beater. The man was jacked and didn't seem shy about letting everyone know it.

Holly's eyebrows rose. "Did he call you his girl?" she mouthed to Jazz who rolled her eyes and shook her head.

"Don't ask," was mouthed back to her.

"Damn, I missed you today, baby," Zach said right before he pulled Toni to her feet and into a scorching kiss complete with ass fondling.

Rather than gawk like some kind of creeper, Holly looked away and right into the eyes of LJ.

Why the hell did he have to look so damn delicious? The freaking T-shirt he wore seemed seconds away from splitting in two from the strain of keeping his bulging muscles covered. With a bandana around his head, his beard recently trimmed, and a freshly showered smell, Holly was in danger of spontaneously combusting.

"Oh, uh, hey," she said, rubbing her suddenly damp palms on her sweatpants.

Damn, her sex was so slick she could give lessons to lube.

He walked straight to her and slipped his arms under hers. One quick yank and she was flush against his body. "Hey, sugar," he said. "Gonna give me a taste of all that sweetness?"

Huh? He wanted to kiss her? Hello, mixed signals flying in from every angle. He must have seen the confusion on her face because he said, "We'll talk later," then gave her a quick but dizzying kiss.

Okay, so we're talking later.

After he fried her circuits with his lips, LJ sat on the couch and pulled her onto his lap. For a moment, she remained stiff, then decided, fuck it. She had a hot man wanting to kiss her, touch her, and hang out with her. This was something to enjoy, not overanalyze. Obsessing could come later.

On the opposite end of the couch, Zach and Toni sat much as she and LJ did with Toni on Zach's lap except he kept trying to sneak his hands under his woman's shirt only to have them slapped away by a giggling Toni.

Then there was Jazz and Screw, the duo Holly couldn't help but gawk at. Screw had pulled Jazz onto his lap as well, but Holly's new friend sat rigid as a statue.

"You ladies working on adding some of Holly's stuff to the menu?" Zach asked as he nuzzled his nose in the crook of Toni's neck.

LJ gave her waist a squeeze, almost as though he was proud of her new job. But that was ridiculous. Why the hell would he care?

"Actually," Toni said, shooting a raised eyebrow in Jazz's direction. Jazz just shook her head and finally settled back against Screw. He whispered something in her ear that had her relaxing even further. "We decided to create a To-Go option for customers who don't have time to linger in the mornings. We're going to turn part of the counter into a quick-grab section. This way, people heading to work can stop and grab a coffee and a pastry on the run. Holly's going to work that portion of the counter and we'll have an assortment of baked goods each day. What do you think?"

"Shit, babe, I think that sounds like a fucking great idea." With Toni still on his lap, Zach reached forward and snagged a brownie. After taking a giant bite, he said, "And if the breakfast shit is half as good as this, they'll be lined up around the building."

The concept was a simple one. Holly running a breakfast-to-go counter. It wasn't her restaurant, hadn't been her idea, wasn't even her completely choosing the menu, yet her blood zinged, and excitement had her practically hopping up to do a happy dance. Best part of the entire thing was the diner would pay for all the supplies and ingredients and Holly would make a regular paycheck plus have access to the diner for her online customers.

Resting his head on her shoulder, LJ whispered. "That's fucking great news, sugar."

"Thanks."

"What do you say we get out of here and go celebrate?"

"Yeah?" Butterflies took flight in her stomach. When he looked at her like that, with a heavy-lidded hunger, she felt like a school girl with a mega crush. All giddy with anticipation.

"Yeah. We'll steal a bottle of wine from Z and Toni, then take a ride into the mountains. Bet you haven't had a chance to check out some of the overlooks yet, have you?"

Parking at a scenic overlook with LJ? High school Holly would have died and gone to heaven, had she known what was in store for adult Holly. A pack of rabid wildebeests couldn't keep her away. "Let's do it."

LJ kissed her, a little longer and deeper this time, until she clung to the open flaps of his cut rather than melt into a pile of goo. After he ended it, he stood and set her on the couch before sweet-talking Toni into a bottle of wine.

"Hey, Hol! *Yoohoo*, you're not allowed to be fuck drunk after one kiss," Screw said, making her jump.

"Huh?" Holly blinked at the four people staring at her.

The four people who were also snickering.

Whatever. "Maybe you shouldn't judge 'till you've been kissed by LJ." And what lethal kisses they were.

With a snort, Screw gave her a wink. "I've tried, but he always turns me down."

Huh? Holly shot a look to Jazz who just pursed her lips.

From the coffee table in front of her, Holly's phone buzzed. Her father's name appeared on the screen and just like that the wine soured in her stomach.

Dad: We need to chat. You home?

Oh, God, they so needed to chat. Ever since the night of her date with Schwartz, Holly had been avoiding both her parents. What the hell was she supposed to say? They had to have found out she was at the clubhouse party during the raid. Schwartz wouldn't have kept that tidbit to himself. Which meant they had to be flipping out.

And that meant at some point, Holly was going to have to make a choice. Stay on the path they'd laid out for her as she'd been doing since she was twelve. Allow them to hold her back from experiencing life, though that was never their intention. They only wanted to keep her safe. Or for the first time in her life, stand on her own two feet and chase after something *she* wanted. Even if that broke out of the safe little box her parents trapped her in. Problem was, asserting her independence came with a heaping side order of guilt. Even without the wrench of LJ in the mix, knowing she'd be causing her parents sleepless nights and serious stress ate away at her. There had to be a middle ground where they didn't try to control her but weren't constantly afraid of receiving a phone call about her death.

Holly: Out with friends. Lunch tomorrow?

Dad: What friends? Need me to send a patrol car to follow you home?

Hell no!

Holly: No! DO NOT DO THAT!

Dad: You're safe?

Holly: Of course. Diner tomorrow at 12?

The three bubbles appeared then disappeared three times before he finally agreed and said goodbye. Yeah, decision made, they needed boundaries. She'd have died if a patrol car showed up to escort her the five miles to her home like she was some untrustworthy kid. She'd just have to work her ass off to make them see her point of view.

LJ returned, holding up a bottle of red, two plastic cups, and wearing a grin. "Ready?"

"Let's do it."

"What's wrong?" His arms dropped to his side. "You okay?"

"Yeah, just making plans for an uncomfortable conversation with my father tomorrow."

"Ooh, girl, I don't envy you that one." Jazz said. She shot a scowl at Screw who had rubbed his nose along the shell of her ear. "Hands off, Screwball. Follow the rules. I'm only sitting here because I'd feel bad making you sit on the floor."

"Rules?" Screw kissed her cheek. "I haven't heard of this word before."

"Yeah, no shit," Jazz grumbled.

Their banter was just what Holly needed to shake off the impending conversation with her father. She stood. "Thanks for everything, Toni, Jazz. I can't tell you how excited I am to start working with you ladies."

"Please, I'm the one who should be thanking you. You're about to do wonderful things for my business." Toni stood and hugged Holly, as did Jazz. After promises to get together before their debut Monday, Holly followed LJ to the door. One last goodbye over her shoulder revealed Jazz hadn't returned to Screw's lap but took the spot on the couch vacated by Holly and LJ.

If Screw's frown was any indication, he wasn't thrilled with the development.

Interesting.

"You ready to get that sweet ass on the back of my bike?" LJ asked as he stored the wine and cups in his saddlebags after wrapping them in a T-shirt.

"Your bike? I've never been on one."

Well, once when she was a kid, but that didn't count.

"Figured." He grabbed her hand and pulled her against his body. The man was huge and he didn't give anywhere. Every part of his body was just so freakin' hard. "I'm excited to be the man who pops your cherry."

Huh? That ship sailed long—oh, right, the bike.

He kissed her, those firm lips and that skilled tongue wreaking havoc on her ability to rationalize.

"Okay," she said in a dreamy voice.

At this rate, the man could get her to rob banks and steal from little old ladies just with the power of his kiss. As it was, his lips had the power to make her forget the fact that the only other man to get her on a motorcycle ended up murdering her sister.

CHAPTER THIRTEEN

LJ hadn't been a lifelong motorcycle enthusiast like many of his brothers. In fact, the first time he so much as sat his ass on a bike hadn't been until he'd left the military. Rocket introduced him to the high of riding on two wheels a few weeks after they started working together. In the years since that eye-opening first ride, he'd sure as hell made up for lost time and missed miles.

Freedom. That's what he'd experienced the first time he flew through the mountain roads on Rocket's spare bike. Back then, his head had been fucked up far worse than it was now. Nightmares had plagued every sleep he'd dared to slumber, and the daytime hadn't been much better. Panic attacks and frequent loss of time and reality were constants in his life. To this day, he swore riding his motorcycle was worth more than any qualified therapist.

The peace, the freedom from four boxy walls. It allowed him time to get shit straight in his head and plod on another day. Without it, who knew what drastic measures he might have taken in those early days, when bitterness and anger clogged his thinking.

As much as he loved riding solo, and he fucking loved it, his favorite activity turned out to be infinitely better with Holly behind him. Shit, having a woman he genuinely liked clinging to him, those big soft tits cushioned against his back as they cruised to a destination where they would no doubt be unable to keep their hands off each other?

Fucking heaven.

"I freakin' love this!" Holly yelled as he followed the curve of the mountain road. She gasped. "Oh, my God! That view…"

Yeah, it was something to see. Especially now, as twilight faded to night and the sun slipped behind the mountains.

LJ slowed to a roll while pulling off to the scenic overlook. This spot wasn't an official tourist overlook, more a clearing he spotted a few years ago when his head had been a jumble of fucked thoughts. A quiet, peaceful stretch of the Smokies overlooking the picturesque towns below.

A place to soothe the mind and ease the soul. Two necessities in LJ's world and a place he bet Holly would love.

"Can I get down?" Holly asked the moment his boots hit the ground.

After cutting the engine, he glanced over his shoulder at the excitement written across her fresh, makeup-free face. "Sure, sugar. Need help with the helmet?"

"Nah, I got it." She wiggled a few times, her tits and the heat between her thighs rubbing all over him. LJ bit back a groan as his dick hardened. "See?" She hopped off the bike and held out the helmet like some kind of offering.

"I see." He took the helmet and hung it from the handlebars. As he watched her practically skip off, he was helpless to do anything but stare. Even in ratty workout pants and an old T-shirt, the woman was hot. Smokin' hot.

LJ swung his leg over the bike then strode to her. Standing with her back to him, she had her arms folded across her chest and her gaze fixed on the mesmerizing view. As he came up behind her, he wrapped his arms around her middle. Man, did she fit well there, snuggled against his perking dick.

"LJ, this is incredible," she said in a soft voice as she gazed at the twinkling lights of the towns hundreds, even thousands of feet below.

Rather than take in the gorgeous scenery, he stared down at the woman enjoying it. "Yeah, it sure as fuck is."

She tilted her head up and back. "You're not looking. How do you know it's beautiful?" Her pink tongue came out and swiped along her bottom lip. That move alone had his cock twitching with need.

"Trust me, nothing out here is more beautiful than what I'm looking at right now."

"LJ…" she said, breathless.

"No bullshit, Holly, I like you. Really fucking like you. I like your sass. I like your sweetness. I like how you try to take care of everyone you know by bringing them treats."

Her lips curved. Fucking spellbinding mouth.

"I also like this body. Fuck, do I like your body." As he spoke, he ran his hands over her hips, her ass, her sides. "All these sexy curves." Then he stroked up until he cupped her large tits. They filled his hands to the brim, and he groaned as he gave them a sensual squeeze. "And these tits. Goddamn, woman, these tits were made for my hands." He bent and nipped her ear while rubbing his thumbs over her hardened nipples. "And my mouth."

Her eyes fell shut, mouth tipped up as though waiting for his kiss. And who was he to turn down that unspoken request? Still teasing her nipples, he captured her lips in a kiss that began soft and exploratory but ramped up to warp speed the second she whimpered into his mouth.

Fuck, that needy little noise drove him out of his mind. Through her T-shirt and thin bra, he pinched her nipples, and she arched her back with a sharp cry. Their lips separated only long enough for the shout to escape before he fused them again and devoured her like a man who hadn't eaten in a week.

Holly's ass ground against his erection, nearly bringing him to his knees. His cock was so hard, LJ's head spun from the lack of blood flow.

A little rumble that sounded a whole lot like frustration erupted from Holly's throat, causing LJ to chuckle. With quick movements, he spun her, grabbed handfuls of her ass and hauled her up his body. Before he even had her in position, her legs circled his back, crossing at the ankles.

"Better?" he asked, finding her mouth yet again.

"So much better." Now she could rub against his cock all she wanted, giving her some relief from the sharp arousal. At least he assumed she felt as desperate for release as he did.

"God, LJ, you're so strong." Her head fell back, and he took immediate advantage, running his tongue up the side of her neck.

"Wait until you feel all that power fucking into you, baby." He kissed the underside of her chin, then down to her collar bone where he sucked at the junction of her neck and shoulder.

"Yesss," Holly hissed.

"Need to get this fucking shirt off you." He growled as he tried to hold her and remove her tee at the same time.

He cursed when the top got stuck between them, drawing a giggle from Holly. "You can put me down, big guy," she said.

"Fuck that." In a feat of clothes-removing magic, he managed to keep her in his arms and riding his cock through his jeans while he worked the shirt up her body. Together, they yanked it up and off her shoulders. He did the same with her bra, not bothering to unclasp it, just jerking it up and off her body which had Holly laughing. For a million bucks, LJ couldn't have said where either garment landed. He was too busy taking in the sight of the creamy breasts that had become his new obsession.

Starving for another taste of her, LJ went straight for broke, sucking a puckered nipple into his mouth. Holly moaned as she jolted in his arms. "Jesus, that feels incredible. Please don't stop."

Mouth full, he grunted. She was certifiable if she thought he planned to stop sucking her anytime soon. But he did need to give the other side some well-deserved attention. He released her, chuckling at her small whine as he stared at the shiny, wet nipple. When he blew on it, Holly shivered and yelped.

Fuck, she was perfect. So voluptuous. So responsive.

"Please, LJ," she said, one hand nudging his shoulder as though to guide him to her other tit.

So greedy.

"I'm on it, sugar," he said before scraping his teeth over her nipple one last time. Then he kissed down the side of her breast and across her chest where his mouth landed on a warm piece of metal.

The moment his lips touched the charm he'd inquired about the night before, Holly froze, but she didn't stay immobile for long.

"Stop!" she yelled as she shoved his shoulders, flailing like he was trying to mug her instead of make her come. "Put me down!" A note of hysteria rang clear in her voice. "Now, LJ. Put me down now!"

"Christ, Holly, what the fuck?" He had a feeling if he didn't let her go, she'd be clawing his eyes out in a matter of seconds. Shit, if he'd pushed her too far, scared her, or God forbid, hurt her, he'd fucking lose it.

He released her immediately but didn't just dump her on the ground. Instead, he set her down, grimacing as her thrashing thigh made contact with his erection. Once he was convinced she wouldn't land on her ass, he let go.

Holly sprung back as though she'd been electrocuted by his touch. Breathing as though she'd just run a marathon with her hand clasped around her necklace, Holly stared at him, horror in her gaze.

"Shit," she said as she lifted a hand to brush her wild hair out of her face. "I'm sorry. Oh, God, I'm so sorry. I've never...I just totally freaked on you. Oh, my God, what did I do?" she whispered more to herself than to him. "I screwed this up, didn't I?"

No, she hadn't, and that right there was LJ's biggest indication that he liked this girl way more than a quick fuck in the woods. Had she been any other woman he'd have nodded, tossed her the shirt she'd shed, given her a ride home, and peaced the fuck out. Then he'd have lost her number. Instead, after a heavy sigh, he said, "No, but I'm pretty sure we should be talking instead of fucking tonight."

WHAT HAVE I done?

Holly stared at LJ's broad retreating back as he turned and made his way toward the motorcycle. She was an idiot. Hands down the stupidest woman in Tennessee, the US if she was honest. Who the hell went berserk during a hot and heavy make-out session like that? All because he'd touched the necklace she only taken off twice in twelve years, and then it was only for a few seconds to replace a corroded chain.

What the hell must he think of her now? Her brother, Danny, had once called a woman he'd broken up with *crazy pussy*. At the time, she'd told him he was a pig for the crude description, but now she wondered if it didn't make perfect sense. Was she crazy pussy in LJ's eyes? A girl he'd messed around with who turned out to be psycho? She wouldn't be surprised if he hopped on his bike and peeled out, leaving her half-naked in the woods.

Shit! I'm half-naked.

Holly scanned the ground for her T-shirt. Didn't take her more than a few seconds to find it, but the damn black bra was much harder to locate.

Screw it. She'd survive without it. She lifted the shirt to wiggle back into it as she peeked at LJ from the corner of her eye. The moment she caught sight of him spreading a soft-looking red blanket in front of the bike, she froze. Instead of shrugging into the shirt, she clasped it to her chest.

"W-what are you doing?" she asked as he made his way back to her. The sun had all but disappeared since they arrived, shrouding them in an intimate cloud of darkness. Well illuminated by the headlight of his bike, the blanket he'd set up looked nothing short of romantic. The bottle of wine he'd borrowed from Zach and Toni lay alongside the plastic cups on the blanket in the quiet woods with the breathtaking view.

"I went about this the wrong way," he said, extending a hand to her.

For a second, Holly stared at the outstretched palm as she battled an internal war.

Take it, her irrational and starry-eyed side said. Her body, too. Really, her body practically begged her to go with him.

Don't you dare, her logical, parent-loving, guilt-bearing side screamed.

He sighed. "We should have sat down and talked first. Especially after what happened last night. I meant what I said, Holly. I like *you*. Not just your body."

You're not just a fuck.

The words he didn't voice were louder than the words he said. God, this would have been so much easier to do the night of the party, right after he left her hot and bothered in the hallway of the clubhouse. For those thirty minutes or so she'd thought he was an asshole. She could have walked away then. Not now when he worked to give her what she needed.

Clearly, she'd become quite proficient at lying to herself because if she could have walked away last night, she would have. Instead, she'd tracked him to his room and let him go down on her. Let him and loved it. Then she agreed they were a thing. And now that he was acting like the sweetest man on earth, she was having second thoughts.

She needed some serious help.

As she looked into those warm hazel eyes, Holly once again fell under his spell. She placed her hand in his and let him guide her to the blanket. LJ sat with his legs curled under his left side. Some inexplicable need to be close to him took over, so she knelt near him, her knees brushing his thigh. It was at that point she realized she still held her shirt to her chest, so she slipped it over her head.

"Well, that's just mean," LJ said, making her laugh. The light comment worked to get her out of her head and broke the thick tension in the air.

"Sorry, but I'm not talking to you while my boobs are hanging out. Especially not with that spotlight from your motorcycle on me."

He chuckled. "Wine?"

"Yes. Fill it to the brim." Anything that promised to relax her.

Another chuckle and he did as she asked, handing her a very full glass of the stolen wine. Silence fell between them, not necessarily awkward, but not quite as comfortable as it should have been.

Thanks to her and her little brain explosion a few moments ago.

Holly gulped a mouthful of wine then sighed. "So...you probably want to know what that was all about."

"Did I hurt you?" he asked in a more serious tone than she'd heard from him to date.

"What?" Her forehead scrunched.

"Or scare you?"

She shook her head. "What are you talking about?"

After blowing out a breath, LJ said, "Nothing. Just checking."

Holly took four large swallows of her wine. Liquid courage could only help her at this point. Even if she got drunk and acted a fool, nothing could top the mortification of making the man who'd been bringing her such intense pleasure worry he'd hurt her.

"You said you liked me. Really liked me." She spoke in a low voice. "I'm not fishing, I just..." She shrugged.

He nodded and opened his mouth, but she held up a hand. "Wait, let me keep going before I chicken out." When he nodded again, she continued, closing her eyes. Somehow this was easier to say without seeing his patient, compassionate expression. "LJ,

I like you just as much. And not just all those hard, sexy, muscles —though they are stellar." Her eyes opened and she sought his gaze. He deserved that much from her after the way he'd been so amazing post-Holly-freak-out. "I'm drawn to everything about you. How you make me feel safe and protected, your kindness and generosity, the way you are with your brothers and their women. All of it." The light in her eyes dimmed. "But—"

"But it's fucked from the start." He respected her space, not touching her, and she wanted to beg for his hands. How unfair was that? Ask for his comfort while telling him they'd never work.

With a sigh, Holly nodded and turned her head, taking in the beauty of the space. The sprawling mountains should have captured her full attention, but too much weighed on her mind. Her hand came up to clasp the charm once again. "My sister who was killed, the one I t-told you about?" Just the mention of Joy brought a fresh surge of grief.

"Mm-hmm," LJ said as he curled an arm around her waist and hauled her even closer. They sat facing each other, Holly on his left side with their thighs pressed together.

"She wasn't just my sister. She was m-my twin. My identical twin," she said as she averted her gaze. Saying the words took too much of her reserves. She might not have the strength to fight her connection to LJ and tell the gut-wrenching story at the same time.

But LJ seemed to have other plans. "Fuck," he said as he cupped her cheek, turning her face toward his. "I'm so sorry that happened to you, sugar."

She found herself trapped by the emotion in his eyes. Not pity, but genuine sorrow for her pain.

"You said it was a biker?"

Words failed her, so she nodded.

LJ slid a finger under the chain of her necklace, fishing it out of her shirt. Once it lay outside her T-shirt, he stroked the pad of his finger over it. Holly gasped. As insane as it sounded, the moment felt incredibly significant. As though he was meeting her sister and earning her approval. Tears filled Holly's eyes, but she blinked them away, determined to see this as an experience that bonded them, instead of just as a reliving of her grief.

"Tell me about her," he said.

Holly couldn't help but smile a wobbly grin as she thought of her sister this time. "She was...she was the best friend a girl could ask for. So different from me even though we looked exactly the same. Joy was bold, outgoing, liked to push the envelope. Where I always wanted to spend my weekends baking and experimenting in the kitchen, she spent her time talking me into breaking the rules and riding our bikes all over town. She'd spend her allowance money before she'd earned it where I saved it for months to by whatever kitchen item I'd had my eye on. She was boy crazy and just plain fun to be around. Just a burst of happy energy. She really did her name justice."

LJ smoothed his thumb over her lips, then caressed her cheek with his palm. "Sounds like you girls were the perfect complement to each other."

As she spoke, Holly fiddled with a patch on his cut that symbolized his time in the military. "We were. Two halves of a whole." And she'd been missing half of her heart for twelve years.

"Will you tell me what happened?"

She lifted her cup and took another few hefty gulps. Only a small amount of wine remained, so—*screw it*—she sucked back the rest then set the cup down next to the blanket. "She asked me to ride our bikes to the mall, which was just a few miles away. We weren't allowed to, but Joy had talked me into it more than once. That day, though, I didn't go. I had something in the oven, and I didn't think we'd make it back before our dad got home from work, so I turned her down." The memories of that absolutely horrifying day caused a reaction almost as sharp as though it were yesterday instead of twelve years ago. Her stomach cramped, and she started to shudder.

"Shhh," LJ said as he wrapped his arms around her and pulled her into his lap. He now sat cross-legged with her cradled against him. "You can stop, sugar."

His strong arms and clean, soapy scent surrounded her like a protective bubble, making the pain recede a bit. "It's okay. I want to tell you."

"All right. Take your time." He stroked his large palm up and down her back in a hypnotic pattern.

"S-she never made it home." Holly exhaled. Would the devastating memory of the moment she realized Joy wasn't coming back ever fade in intensity? Part of her hoped not. That sharp, painful reminder was so much less than Joy had suffered and kept Holly from ever forgetting how she let her sister down. "For about ten days straight, my father and his department searched night and day almost without rest. Finally, they found her on some property owned by the MC. She'd been strangled and dumped behind a building as though—" God, this was the hardest part. To think of or talk about. "As though she was t-trash." The tears that she'd been battling finally won out and Holly buried her face in LJ's chest as she let them flow. After this night, the man was going to run so fast he'd leave skid marks.

"Fuck, sugar, I can't believe you even gave me the time of day once you realized I was in a club."

With a huffed laugh into his chest, Holly said, "I harnessed Joy. Her wild heart and adventurous spirit. She wouldn't judge one book by the cover of another."

"Fuck, Holly, you're fucking wrecking me."

If she had her choice, she'd never leave the comfort of his arms. They could just stay right here, tangled up in each other forever. "Want to know something weird?" she said, resting her cheek against his chest. The strong, steady thump of his heart might become her new favorite sound.

"What's that?"

"About six months before Joy was killed, I was riding my bike home from my friend's house as fast as my legs would move because I was going to be super late and in serious trouble. My tire hit a rock, and I ended up soaring over the handlebars."

LJ winced. "Ouch."

"Oh yeah, hurt like a mother." She shuddered at the memory of tearing the skin of her knees, elbows, and palms. "So, there I was, lying in the middle of the street with bloodied knees and elbows, but an intact head thanks to the helmet I always gave my parents a hard time about."

LJ chuckled. He played with her hair, and even though the evening had taken a severe turn, Holly wanted to purr at the delightful sensation of having this man pet her.

"Anyway, a motorcycle pulled up next to where I was lying in the road, and this big guy with long, curly hair and an MC cut hopped off his bike and helped me up. He called me Little Miss and told me to climb on the back of his bike and said he'd give me a ride home. God, was I terrified. All my life I'd heard that the MC was full of sex-crazed maniacs who basically did drugs and had orgies all day long before going out and murdering innocent people."

When LJ snorted, Holly said, "You laugh, but I'm only exaggerating a tiny bit. Anyway, it was get on the bike or hobble the mile and a half home with knees that stung like a bitch. I can still remember the exact moment I realized the pain in my arms and knees outweighed my fear. And you want to know what?"

"What, sugar?"

"He couldn't have been nicer to me. He delivered me home safe and sound exactly two minutes before my dad walked in the door. And the next morning, my bike was in the driveway with a brand-new tire and a note that said *Thank you for trusting me, Little Miss*." She rubbed a hand over the left side of her chest where a familiar ache had formed. "For the longest time, I really didn't think he did it."

"But?"

She shrugged. "But he was convicted. And my family was one hundred percent convinced the right man was behind bars. After a while, it was just easier to go along with their thinking. And, I guess, eventually I started to believe it myself."

Once again, neither of them spoke, but this time the silence was much more comfortable. Finally, Holly said, "I should have gone with her to the mall."

"Oh, baby," LJ said, grasping her shoulders and pushing her back to stare straight in her eyes. "That kind of thinking is nothing but toxic. Trust me, Holly, you can spend a lifetime playing what if and swimming in guilt and the only outcome will be you drowning. It won't change the past, but it will poison your mind. Nothing about the night your sister disappeared is on you. You hear me? Nothing."

He spoke with such vehemence, such bone-deep understanding, Holly's focus shifted from her own heartbreaking past to LJ. "Has that happened to you? The drowning in guilt?"

His expression dulled, but he nodded once. "You don't survive multiple deployments without coming home with some kind of guilt."

Holly wanted to ask more, craved to know everything about him, but he'd spoken with a finality that had her thinking he wouldn't talk about it anymore. Plus, after spilling her own guts, she felt wrung out emotionally; not ready to dive right into another intense conversation. Hopefully another time. Because if this conversation had done anything for her, it'd made her realize she was fighting a losing battle in the war to keep her feelings away from LJ. "I don't think you or your club are like the biker who killed my sister. I can recognize the difference, LJ. It's clear as day."

"But your family?"

And there was the heart of her internal struggle. "They're never going to accept this. Even a friendship between us isn't going to work. It's not the kind of thing that will grow on them with time. They won't tolerate it while disapproving behind our backs. They'll be outwardly hostile." She wanted to shake some sense into them. Clear the corrosion from their minds and force them to see how good LJ and his brothers were at their core.

"You're close to them?"

Her laugh sounded harsh and uncaring, but how could she describe her relationship with her parents? "They love me. I know they love me, but their love has become a noose around my neck. My parents are petrified of something happening to me, so they are very involved in my life. I can't go anywhere or do anything without them needing a full play by play and detailed itinerary. And the crazy thing is, I can empathize. I remember in vivid, gut-wrenching detail their reactions after we heard Joy's body had been found. It nearly destroyed them and what's left of their lives would be demolished if something were to happen to me. I know we don't have a healthy relationship, but…" She shrugged, out of words to justify her allowing them so much influence in her life.

"They're holding you back, smothering you, and you let them because of what they went through."

"Yes. But I'm working on it. Getting my own apartment was the first step. Working with Toni and Jazz is the second."

"And choosing a man they hate, is that the third?"

Her eyes widened. Did he really think that? "No. No, LJ, no. I —God, how do I say this right? I like you. I want you. And both of those things were true before I knew you were in the MC. I'm not choosing a man they disapprove of. I'm just not letting their disapproval run me off who I choose."

And in that moment, giving this thing with LJ a fair shot became vital. Not just because the man was smokin' hot and had brought her more pleasure in the past few days than anyone she'd been with to date, but because *she* genuinely wanted to spend time with him both in and out of bed.

He was her choice, and if she passed by the first guy *she'd* been sincerely interested in for years, she might as well move back home, marry who they picked for her, and spend the rest of her life checking in with her parents five times a day.

Little Jack

Hopefully, she'd have the guts to spell it all out for her father tomorrow at lunch.

CHAPTER FOURTEEN

Under normal circumstances, LJ wouldn't give two shits if a woman wanted to get back at her parents by fucking him. Hell, she could send them a video mid-fuck for all he cared. Getting involved beyond tension relief had never been his goal, so who the hell cared if some chick's parents thought he was the scum of the earth?

But in this case, he'd found himself holding his breath like some kind of love-sick chump while he waited for Holly's answer.

And it hadn't disappointed.

I'm not choosing a man they disapprove of. I'm just not letting their disapproval run me off who I choose.

Those words had his cock filling once again, but more than that, an unfamiliar feeling of warmth developed in his chest and bloomed outward. Yes, he wanted to climb on and fuck her until she screamed, but he also wanted to check in and make sure she was okay. The woman had just flayed her past wide-open and left it bleeding on the ground. Ripping off her clothes and being impaled by his dick might not be her first order of business. With all she'd relived, he wouldn't blame her if she wanted to dive under the blanket they sat on and hide for the next week.

"So," he said, tracing a finger over her jaw and down to her collar bone where he stroked back and forth. "What now?" His admiration for her had only strengthened as she spoke of her past. She'd asked if he knew guilt. Fuck, did he ever. For years, it had ruled his empty life. Now it only came to him in the dead of night, ripping him from the comfort of sleep and reminding him of what'd he'd lost. Though he'd downplayed it by about a million times, that shared negative emotion bonded them in a deep way.

Holly met his gaze, and he'd be blind if he didn't notice the desire deepening her blue irises. "Now, I'm hoping we can try that again, but without my freak out this time." Her face turned an absolutely adorable shade of pink as though she couldn't believe she'd been so forward. "If that's what you still want, I mean."

With a chuckle, LJ caught the hem of her T-shirt. "If I want?" She nodded once.

"Baby, we shot way past want the first night I met you."

"Show me," she whispered as she climbed off his lap and sat on her heels.

Fuck yes.

With his cock now throbbing, LJ rose to his feet on the blanket, keeping his eyes on the gorgeous woman who knelt before him. Slowly, as though he had all the time in the world despite the rushing of blood in his veins, LJ bent to unlace his boots.

"Let me," Holly said, batting his hands away. She worked quickly despite unsteady hands as she loosened the laces. Once able, he toed off the boots, kicking them beyond the blanket.

Next, his hands went to the button of his jeans. One flick of his wrist and it popped open. Holly's heated gaze followed his every move, seemingly transfixed by what he was about to unveil. One shove of the denim had it pooling at his ankles. He paused, mouth kicked up in a half-smirk until Holly finally looked up at him and nodded.

After he'd obliged her by stepping out of the pooled denim, she zeroed in on the sizable bulge behind the fabric of his light gray boxer briefs.

"May I?" he asked with a smirk after it became apparent she couldn't do anything but sit there gawking.

"Please," she squeaked, cheeks a rosy red.

LJ hooked his thumbs in the side of his boxer briefs, then drew them all the way down and stepped out. His cock sprang out, then bounced back up toward his stomach. Thank God he was finally free of the tight fucking fabric. When he returned to his full height, Holly's eyes nearly fell out of her head.

"Um, you're...uh...wow!"

LJ threw back his head and let out a laugh. God, she was too fucking cute. "Shit, sugar, you're good for my self-esteem."

"Pretty sure all you gotta do is take a peek down your shorts and your self-esteem will skyrocket, big boy," she grumbled.

"Holly?"

"Y-yes?"

He gazed down at her, still crouched at his feet. "Don't be nervous. I'm about to crawl out of my skin with how much I want you." He pointed to his very large, very *hard* dick. "Case in point."

He could practically see the war between shyness and need battling it out for supremacy in her mind. Finally, after a few moments of indecision, Holly rose high on her knees and scooted the foot or so to get to him. She smoothed her palm over the weeping head of his dick then down the underside, where she circled the base as though testing the size and feel of him.

LJ hissed at the initial contact then groaned as Holly gave him a long, slow tug. When she licked her lips, it was all he could do to keep from grabbing her jaw and holding it open for a vigorous mouth fucking. "You gonna suck my cock, sugar?"

She nodded. With her T-shirt once again off and the light from the bike illuminating them, he had a perfect view of the hardened points of her tits. God, she wanted this as much as he did. He bet if he reached between her legs, she'd be fucking soaked. Part of him almost passed on the blow job in favor of diving between those lush thighs, but then her curious tongue came out and licked under the head of his cock and LJ couldn't have stopped her if the world was ending.

"You taste good," she whispered. LJ groaned. How could three mere words make his eyes roll back into his head even more than the feel of her eager mouth? With a slightly timid smile, Holly parted her lips and surrounded the head of his cock. The initial scorching hot pull of Holly's mouth nearly brought LJ to his knees. He fisted her hair, aware on some level the grip was too tight, but he couldn't get his fingers to open. Releasing her head meant she could pull away and he might actually die if she stopped.

"Fuck, baby," he said as the suction increased. She'd taken as much of him down her throat as she could tolerate, which wasn't his entire length, but given his admittedly impressive size, was pretty damn stellar.

More than enough to wreck him.

At his groan, she let him slide nearly out of her mouth before diving back down his dick. Once, twice. On the third pass, he couldn't help it—the need to fuck was too great—his hips punched forward of their own accord causing him to bump the back of her throat. He shouted as Holly gagged, the reflexive closing of her throat muscles strangling the tip of him in a heated grip of ecstasy.

Just as he was about to pull back to give her a breather, Holly grabbed his ass and held him deep in her throat, swallowing. There went that same massage to the head of his dick as when she gagged. He almost shot his load right there. Beads of sweat rolled down his face as he fought the impending orgasm by recalling the upcoming week's work schedule. The technique would only be effective for so long, especially with her hungry mouth still devouring him.

As incredible as that mouth felt, LJ needed to come in her pussy this first time. He just needed that full body connection. Mark her deep inside even though he'd be unloading in a condom.

Forcing himself to release her head, he cupped her jaw and held her still while he slid out of her lips. Wet from her mouth and as hard as fucking ever, his dick slapped against his stomach, spreading her saliva. For some reason, he fucking loved that, only wishing it was wetness from a different part of your body.

"Wh—"

"Want inside your pussy, sugar. Need to feel it all around me."

"Oh." Her mouth formed the perfect O shape that mimicked her round eyes.

"How about you get those pants off and let me feel how much you liked sucking my cock?"

While nodding, Holly scrambled to her feet and shimmied out of her workout pants and panties at the same time. When she was naked, she stepped right up to him, molding her body to his.

LJ kissed her, enjoying the desperate way she clung to his shoulders and wrapped a leg around the back of his thighs. Her hips moved against his leg as though she'd do anything to fulfill the need. And that just wouldn't do.

"I got you, baby," he murmured against her mouth as he dove two fingers between her legs into the drenched folds.

"LJ," Holly cried as her hands curled into his biceps and her head fell against his chest.

"Jack," he countered as he swept an arm under her leg, lifting her off the ground then lowering them to the blanket. "When we're like this, I'm Jack."

"Jack," Holly said, but it sounded more like a plea. A long shudder ran through her. She was close.

His hand never left her sex, stroking inside with confident swipes of his fingers. Holly rocked her pelvis like she was eager for more. After searching for his pants with his left hand, he dug around in his pocket until he found the foil packet he'd been carrying since the day after he fucking met her. No way in hell was he going to miss an opportunity to fuck her because he'd forgotten the rubber. Sitting on his ass with his knees bent, he tore the packet open and sheathed his cock. Then he reclined back on his elbows. From somewhere under the blanket, a rock gouged into his back. Not that he minded. If anyone was going to have Mother Nature digging into them, it'd be him. He'd die before risking her silky smooth skin to the harsh forest floor.

Besides, if all went according to plan, he'd be feeling nothing but euphoria in a matter of minutes. "C'mere, sugar," he ordered as he watched Holly watching him. Her lower lip rested between her teeth, and she looked so adorably uncertain he wanted to promise her the fucking world.

"LJ," she started but stopped at his raised eyebrow. "Jack, I can't...the light." Her hands lifted in a gesture of helplessness before she crossed her arms over her chest.

Jesus. Insecurity? Really? Holly was hands down the sexiest fucking woman he'd ever laid eyes on and she was insecure about riding him? Looked like he had some work to do. "Give me your hand," he said in a near bark.

Holly jumped and extended her right hand on impulse. With a grin, he curled it around his wrapped cock. "Feel how hard that fucker is?"

She tilted her head, a half-smile on her lips. "I feel it. Just like I felt it in my mouth."

LJ groaned and closed his fist around hers, applying just the right amount of pressure to his needy cock. He loved that about her. The combination of shyness and sass. It kept him guessing. With a wink, he cupped one of her breasts and thumbed her nipple. Holly's eyes fell closed as she whimpered.

"Every inch of me is hard for one reason and one reason only, sugar. Because I want inside your body. I don't know why you're feeling shy or timid right now, but I will tell you with one hundred percent honesty that I think you're the sexiest woman I've ever laid my goddammed eyes on. So please, put me out of my misery and let me see you as you climb up on my cock."

His words seemed to do the trick. A small smile curled Holly's lips, and she leaned forward, bracing her hands on his chest. Then she swung one leg over his stomach until she fully straddled him, her ass and that slippery pussy flush against his abs. In a move that shocked him and had him shouting her name, she rubbed that drenched pussy up and down the ridges of his stomach.

With her fingers curling into his pecs, Holly's full tits hung heavy toward his face, the pebbled nipples calling to him. "This better?"

"Fuck yes." He did a half sit up and captured one stiff bud between his lips, giving it a hard suck. Holly cried out in pleasure. "Have I mentioned how much I love your tits?" he said, his lips brushing her wet nipple.

She giggled. "Once or twice."

"Good."

"Can I take that ride now, Jack?"

"Fuck, yeah, baby." Christ, his name sounded good on her lips.

Sweet Holly had been taken over by a sexy siren. Radiating new-found confidence that hopefully came from the knowledge she was desperately wanted, Holly shimmied down his body. She rubbed her drenched pussy over his cock and the heat nearly blistered him.

Little tease.

If tomorrow her father decided to kill him, it will have all been worth it for this moment right here. Wrapping her small hand around his cock, Holly positioned him at her entrance where she hovered over him. As she began to sink down, she caught her lower lip between her teeth. LJ made a mental note to bite that same lip later on.

With a high-pitched squeak, her eyes widened as the tip of his shaft disappeared inside her. With the way her pussy grasped him, he had to be stretching her to the max.

"Fuck me, you're tight." His back arched as fiery pleasure shot up his spine. The movement pushed his dick deeper into Holly, who gasped.

"Jack, oh, my God, Jack, you're huge."

"You got it, baby. Keep working yourself on that big cock. You can take it all. That pussy was made to swallow my whole cock." LJ clenched his fists at his sides, curling his blunt nails into his palms.

As he spoke, her pussy softened around his length, and Holly inched even farther onto him. Look at that, his sweet little baker liked herself some dirty talk. He grinned. "You like that, huh? Like it when I tell you how good you're taking my cock?"

"Y-yes, I like it."

Shit, he wished he had a camera to capture this moment forever. Holly naked and flushed above him with his cock more than halfway in her. Her hair, wild as it slipped out of the ponytail, and those blue eyes like a stormy fucking sea. An image he would get off to for years to come.

The moment he bottomed out inside her, Holly froze with her mouth open in wonderment.

"Damn, baby, I'm all in. You good?" His heart pounded like a stampede of elephants and sweat ran down the sides of his face. Keeping himself in check was a workout and a half.

"So good, Jack. So full. I've never been this full."

"Damn right, I fill you best." He gripped the soft flesh of her hips, rocking her on his cock. "Ride, baby."

LJ couldn't help the feeling of being on top of the fucking world. More than just physically, the knowledge he'd been the one to put that goddammed awed look on her face with his cock had him wanting to pound his chest and holler out the victory. Instead, he let his gaze connect with hers as he absorbed the sensation of the tightest pussy he'd ever been inside.

But what snared him more than her pussy working him toward orgasm was the hit of emotion that slammed into him the moment their eyes met. It was the kind of connection men had been writing about for years. That can't-live-without-you gut-punch that had people throwing caution to the wind and diving headfirst into a woman that could turn their world upside down.

LJ had never been happier to view the world from the bottom up.

HOLLY COULD BARELY breathe as she stretched to accommodate LJ—Jack's—girth. She hadn't been putting him on or working to fluff his ego when she'd said he was huge. The man was extremely well hung, to the point that he stretched her right to that delicious limit of pleasure and pain where her body wanted to sing with bliss.

She'd been nervous, worried about the extra pounds she could never seem to lose bouncing and jiggling as she rode him. Curse of being a baker and sampling pastries all day. But, with a few well-placed words and a smoldering look, he'd settled her mind and ramped her desire so high she no longer cared what imperfections he'd discover.

There was something more here. Something greater than the incredible sensations starting in her core and shooting out through all the cells in her body, and it was the intense magnetic pull that kept her eyes fixated on his. She wanted to look away from the intense intimacy that would only complicate things to an unbearable degree, but that was impossible. Neither her mind nor her body would allow her to break the connection.

Instead of taking the smart route and treating him like a hookup, Holly threaded her fingers through his and raised his arms over his head. The position didn't make him nearly as vulnerable as it looked since her strength was no match for his, but it showed a level of trust and submission she'd have never expected from him.

It also gave him unfettered access to her breasts, which he took full advantage of. With a low moan, Holly drew her hips up then sank down on him once again.

His back arched and her breast slipped from between his lips. "Christ, I've never felt something so fucking good."

Still holding his hands against the woodsy ground, she began to rock on him, tentatively at first until she got her rhythm, but the moment her clit ground against his pelvis, all bets were off. All shyness and insecurity flew out the window as she went to town, riding him like a jockey gunning for first place, except she was racing toward an orgasm that promised to curl her hair.

Her heavy tits, which she'd despised for years for the annoyance of their size, swayed with wild bounces as she ramped up her efforts. LJ seemed transfixed by them, and before long, he freed his hands from her grasp and grabbed one breast, kneading the soft flesh. As his palm rotated over her nipple, a sharp jolt of pleasure shot straight to her clit. As though by reflex, she ground her clit against his pelvis and cried out at the intensity of ecstasy.

"That's it, baby, take what you need. Be greedy as fuck. Wanna feel you come all over me. Goddamn, you're so fucking beautiful."

The breath caught in Holly's lungs as he stared at her. What she saw in his expression had her fighting the fleeting urge to cover herself. Not her body; he'd made his appreciation for her form quite obvious, but her heart. Because at that moment, she swore he could see straight to her soul and she'd never felt more vulnerable. Never felt more connected to another person in a way that was vital to her survival. Except for Joy, and this connection, while so different, felt just as significant.

The hand on Holly's hip tightened, his strong fingers curling into the flesh in a way that might leave marks. Never one to be into that kind of rough possession before, Holly couldn't help the surge of delight she felt at the idea of seeing evidence of his desire in the mirror tomorrow morning.

LJ lifted his hips and pulled her forward at the same time, slamming deep into her with more force than she'd been able to achieve on her own.

Holly moaned and arched her back. "Jack," she cried. Her head whipped side to side as she careened toward a looming eruption that was bound to be bigger than anything she'd experienced. She'd completely lost control of her body. A flash of fear shot through her as the magnitude of what barreled toward her set in. "It's gonna, oh, God, it's gonna be so big, Jack."

"Fuck, baby, for me too." His voice sounded strained, as though he was speaking through a hand wrapped around his throat. "You're fucking strangling my cock. Let it take you, sugar," he rasped.

Holly shook her head. "It's too much. Too big."

"It's fucking perfect, baby. Let it take you. I'll meet you on the other side." All of a sudden, she felt his talented fingers strumming her clit and fighting it became impossible.

The assurance of him sticking around to catch her set her free and she moaned long and loud. Then, a violent tremor started in her fatigued thighs and ricocheted through her body. Her head fell back on her shoulders so hard; she was forced to brace her hands on his legs or collapse backward. Her nails pricked his skin seeming to ramp him up, if the shout of, "Fuck yes," was any indication.

The rising swell finally pulled her under making Holly scream into the quiet night. She quivered, grinding her pussy on him in an almost desperate attempt to draw out the orgasm. Her internal muscles clamped down, enhancing the incredible fullness beyond what she'd thought possible.

LJ shouted and let out a harsh curse as his body jerked on the blanket. His eyes flew wide as his neck arched, corded and bulging as he gritted his teeth. After another gravelly shout, he surged up, burying his face between her breasts as his arms banded around her back in a vice grip.

They stayed that way as the last of the tension seeped from Holly's bones, and her cries turned to whimpers. She had to admit she was glad his face was blocked from her view. The strength of the release left her feeling wide-open emotionally.

Too exposed, too vulnerable, and too exhausted to protect her heart.

The sheriff's daughter falling for the outlaw…

God, she was so screwed.

CHAPTER FIFTEEN

LJ had just come so hard, he felt as though his brain had exploded straight out through the top of his skull. Something about this experience had been different than any sexual encounter before it, and LJ was terrified he knew the reason why.

Because he felt connected to Holly on a level that went far deeper than naked bodies and shouts of completion. She'd wormed her way under his skin and dangerously close to that beating organ on the left side of his chest. The one he'd easily turned off in the past but seemed to be at the mercy of this time around. Holly's love for her sister, her devotion to her parents despite the way they unintentionally shadowed her light. Even the guilt she lived with drew him because he understood it far better than he'd probably ever admit to her.

And that made him quite the fucking coward. Holly had exposed her bleeding soul for him, and he wasn't willing or able to return the gesture. Nor was he able to take her home after she'd blown his mind and hold her through the night.

He should have tossed her on the back of his bike and taken her home the moment she shouted for him to stop earlier. Instead, he selfishly took from this sweet and generous woman without being able to give back in equal measure.

With his face still pressed between her tits and his arms holding her in an unbreakable bind, LJ inhaled Holly's sweet vanilla scent. Every few seconds an aftershock shook her body and made a soft whimper escape her lips. As though she was a delectable dessert, LJ licked the side of her tit. Fuck, even her sweat tasted sugary. He did it again and again until he was kissing back and forth between the sides of her tits with wet, open-mouthed, unsophisticated kisses. He couldn't get enough of the uniquely Holly flavor and given the opportunity, he just might consume her.

She stroked her soft hands over the smooth expanse of his scalp, eventually pulling his head back. With dazed eyes and a satisfied, almost goofy grin, she kissed him. Christ, he could live off her intoxicating mouth.

When Holly finally pulled her mouth free of his, the slightly shy smile she gave him had him chuckling.

She shrugged as though realizing acting bashful now was futile. "Well," she said as she tilted her head. "I think it's safe to say you rocked my world."

"Right back at you, sugar," he said as he rubbed his hands up and down her damp back. "Are you cold?"

"No," she said as she shook her head. "I'm not sure I could ever feel cold again."

Jesus, she slayed him. Keeping his arms around her, LJ leaned back and brought them both to lie on the blanket. Midway, he slipped out of her, making Holly gasp then frown in a near pout.

"Don't like it any more than you do, gorgeous," he said before nipping at that protruded lip. "I'd be the happiest man alive if I could just live in your pussy."

Now sprawled out across his chest, Holly wrinkled her nose. "That's kinda gross and kinda the nicest thing any man has ever said to me all at once."

With a laugh, he pressed her head to his chest. They stayed that way, snuggled up and enjoying the quiet night air until Holly began to giggle. The sound quickly morphed into full-on belly laugh that had her entire body shaking against his. If she wasn't careful, all that wriggling would have him hard and ready to fuck again in minutes.

"You care to share with the rest of the class?" he asked as he reached down and pinched her exposed ass.

Holly yelped, slapping his chest. "I just had sex outside in the woods." She propped a forearm on his chest and lifted her head. "Not just sex, but the best sex ever. Outside."

With a roll of his eyes, he flicked a finger over her nose. "Yeah, sugar, I'm pretty aware of that. You know, since I'm the dude you had sex with."

That had her racked with giggles all over again. "You don't get it. I'm like a total light-off, keep-my-shirt-on, kinda girl."

He snorted as he said, "Shut the fuck up."

She tweaked his nipple, and the sharp sensation made him grunt. "I'm serious. If someone had told me yesterday that I'd be having sex outside all exposed to the world, I'd have had them committed. You must have done some kinda voodoo on me, mister." As she spoke, she played with his nipple.

"You're the one who needs to be committed. I swear to fuck your body was created from my fucking fantasies, sugar. I'm making a rule, right here and now. We are a lights-on, all-articles-of-clothing-off kinda couple. Got it?"

A beaming smile lit her face, whether it was the compliments or the fact that he'd thrown the word couple out there, LJ was afraid to ask.

"You know what? I'm gonna say okay to that."

He winked. "Wouldn't a taken any other answer."

Feeling happier than he had in years, LJ pressed her back down to his chest. Once again they fell quiet until the post-fuck fatigue kicked in and LJ's eyelids began to droop.

Time to go.

He'd already let this go too far, and if they stayed this way much longer, he'd be drifting off and who the fuck knew what would happen after that.

"You ready to head out, sugar?" He patted her ass.

"What? Huh?" she asked in a slurred voice that indicated she'd been passed out.

"I know what you said earlier, but you gotta be getting cold by now. Plus, I should be getting you home."

"Oh." She shimmied off his body until she sat at his side, rubbing her sleep heavy eyes. "Yeah." She shivered then huffed out a laugh. "Okay, yeah it's getting pretty chilly now."

LJ peeled off the condom, knotted it, then shoved it in his back pocket. Not much else to do with it out there. Then he stood, gathered his clothes and a little something extra to keep as a souvenir.

Hunting around on her knees, Holly found her clothes as well. After her bra and T-shirt were back in place, she stood with her workout pants in hand and a frown on her face as she still scanned the ground. "Okay," she finally said. "There's a chance I can't find my panties."

LJ laughed, which had her head lifting. "What's so funny?" she asked, hands on her hips. Then she said, "Oh screw it," and stepped into her sweatpants sans panties.

Standing about five feet from her, LJ couldn't keep the smirk off his face.

"What? What's so funny? Am I missing something?"

LJ tapped the front right pocket of his jeans which bulged more than his left.

"I don't get it." Then her eyes bugged. "Please tell me you don't have my panties in there."

"Sure as fuck do, sugar." He patted the pocket again. "And they're mine now."

"LJ!" she shrieked as she dove for him, trying to shove her hand into his pocket. "They aren't even sexy panties! They're like my everyday, slumming around the house panties. You cannot keep them."

He was laughing so hard, he could barely stand, and Holly nearly managed to worm her sneaky fingers into his pocket, so he bent his knees and hoisted her up and over his shoulder.

"Oh, my God, seriously, LJ?"

Damn, he just might carry her around like this all the time. Her rounded ass was just inches from his face and so damn enticing he just had to smack a palm over a cheek covered by those fitted workout pants. When she yelped, he did it again then left his hand there, fingers spread over as much surface area as he could touch. "Serious as fuck, babe. Don't give a shit what kinda panties you had on. Don't care if they're your *slumming* panties or your goddammed Sunday best. They're fucking soaked with how much you wanted me. I'm keeping them."

"Ugh," she growled. "Fine, but maybe next time I'm wearing some sexy thong or something we can swap it out."

She was so much fucking fun. When the hell had LJ ever had this good a time just being with another person? "It's a deal as long as they're as wet as these."

"Don't have to worry about that," she mumbled. "I pretty much say your name and my panties are soaked."

And there went his cock, waking up once again. The fucker should have been on life support, but all this talk of Holly's arousal was all it took to have him wanting her again. "Shit, sugar, I like you."

She didn't say anything else as he carried her over to the bike, then set her down. Once he'd stowed the blanket, the rest of the wine, and the cups, they climbed on the bike and started back home. The weight of Holly on his back was heavier this time, indicating her exhaustion.

When they reached the apartment complex and he killed the engine, she didn't so much as twitch. "You alive back there?" he asked as he removed his helmet.

"Mmm, we back already? That was too fast."

"We're back."

Holly climbed down from the bike, removed her helmet and hung it on the handlebar as he'd shown her earlier. Hand in hand, they walked up to the second floor. As they reached her door, LJ pressed her back against it and kissed her. He needed one last taste to get him through the night without her.

She moaned into his mouth as her tongue played with his. "Fucking loved tonight, Holly," he whispered against her lips. "Can't wait for more."

Eyes closed, she smiled. "Me too. You coming i—"

He kissed her again, brief this time, but hard. "I'll see you tomorrow, okay?"

Holly blinked her eyes open. "What?" Confusion had her eyebrows drawing down. "Tomorrow?"

God, he was a fucker. Sending her into an empty apartment after all they'd shared. After all *she'd* shared with him. Of course she'd be confused. She'd probably curse him all throughout the night. And she wouldn't be alone in that. He'd be cursing himself to fucking hell and back.

"Yeah, beautiful, tomorrow." After dropping one last quick kiss to her forehead, he turned and slipped inside his apartment without another backward glance. If he saw the disappointment in her eyes, he'd be tempted to say fuck it and follow her into her bed.

And that would no doubt end in disaster. So instead, he walked straight to his room, shucked his jeans, and slipped between the covers all alone.

And when he woke three hours later on the floor, covered in a sheen of sweat and thrashing so hard, he bruised his wrist on the nightstand, he knew he'd made the right decision.

No matter how much Holly might end up hating him at some point, at least she wouldn't be the one with bruises.

CHAPTER SIXTEEN

The following morning, fifteen minutes before she was supposed to meet with her father, Holly dropped into a booth at the diner. Beneath the table, her foot bounced as though her heel had been rigged with a spring. Up above, she drummed her fingers on the gleaming tabletop.

"I was gonna offer you some of this coffee, but I think you're jittery enough. What gives, girl?"

Holly looked up to find Jazz standing next to her booth, coffeepot in one hand, the other propped on her hip. She wore a denim skirt and a long-sleeved diner T-shirt. "Hey, Jazz, you serving today or am I just special?" She shot her friend a grin.

With a laugh, Jazz slipped into the seat opposite Holly. "How about we go with a little bit of both. Shell had to run out early. Beth's preschool called saying she had a slight fever." She flipped over the white porcelain cup, then filled it with coffee.

"Aww, poor kiddo."

"Yeah, she's a sweetie." Jazz set the coffee pot on the table. "So, you wanna tell me why you're all buzzing with stressed-out energy over here?"

Holly forced her restless arms and legs to calm. Problem was, now she noticed the rapid beating of her heart and the twist of nerves in her gut. "I'm meeting my dad here in a few minutes. First time I've talked to him since my date with Deputy Schwartz."

"Well, all my other tables are happily munching away, so how about I sit and distract you for a few minutes, so you don't ruin your manicure before the good sheriff gets here?" With a raised brow, she stared pointedly at Holly's hands.

Whoops. She flattened her palms on the table, staring at the poor thumbnail she just destroyed with her teeth. "That sounds like a good plan. How about you distract me by telling me what the hell is going on with you and Screw." She poured cream into her coffee from the small silver pitcher, then snagged a few sugar packets.

"Ugh." Jazz's head whacked back against the high cushioned booth. "It's simple, really. Screw is a man-whore. Like the biggest I've ever met. I consistently refuse to sleep with him, so now I've become his favorite challenge."

Holly frowned. "Is he really that bad? Seems like he's really into you. At least from what I've seen."

"He's not." Jazz's voice grew flat as she shook her head. "I'm probably the only one who's turned him down in years. Look, I'm not blind. The guy is gorgeous. Sex in jeans. But he sleeps with anyone and everyone he encounters. Men, women, two at a time, three at a time, the man collects fucks like some people collect coins."

"He's bisexual? That's unusual in the biker community, isn't it?" She'd always pictured bikers as bigoted brutes who had a narrow-minded view of the world.

Jazz shrugged then snagged Holly's coffee cup. "You mind?"

"Go for it, sister."

After taking a sip, she leaned her head back against the booth again. "Not sure what he'd label himself, if anything. And I suppose some clubs are more backward and close-minded, but any I've been around have always been chill that way. Anyway, it's not about who Screw sleeps with, I couldn't give a shit about that, it's about how many. I'm not interested in being a notch on his bedpost. There are so many marks on that thing already, it can't be structurally sound. I'm too old to be used and discarded no matter how good I'm sure the sex would be. Or how long it's been since I've gotten any. Which, by the way, is a very pathetic amount of time."

Holly chuckled. "I hear that, girl. It had been quite a while for me as well. You said any club you've been around. Have you been connected to other clubs before?"

The light in Jazz's eyes dimmed, and Holly immediately wanted to take the question back. She hadn't meant to remind her friend of something painful or unpleasant.

"Just one," Jazz said, voice low. "Before I came here." She cleared her throat, clearly eager for a subject change, so Holly let her have it. "So, you said, it *had* been a while for you. Does that mean…" Jazz waggled her eyebrows up and down.

Holly's face heated and she giggled like a freakin' schoolgirl instead of the grown woman she was supposed to be. Just as she opened her mouth to spill the beans a, "Good morning, ladies," came from over her head.

She glanced up into the familiar face of her father. At once, her stomach cramped, and the urge to flee the diner hit her hard. Dread was the only word she could think of to describe her thoughts about the upcoming conversation. "Hey, Dad," she said, inwardly cursing at how timid her voice sounded. If she was going to do this, she needed to grow some lady-balls and just do it.

"Hey, sweetie."

"Sheriff," Jazz said as she rose from the booth. "Care for some coffee?"

With a nod, he took the seat Jazz had vacated. "Yes, please."

After filling the sheriff's coffee cup, Jazz said, "I'll give you two a few seconds to look at the menu." Bending down, she gave Holly an awkward one-armed hug in the booth. "You got this, girl," she whispered.

"Thanks, Jazz."

With a smile, Jazz moved on to check if her other tables needed anything.

Little Jack

"Friend of yours?" her father asked. He wore his uniform, looking distinguished, though tired if the dark circles under his eyes were a tell.

"Yes, I'd say we're quickly becoming good friends. She's great."

"That's good, honey. Glad you're meeting people."

She almost laughed out loud. He'd be singing a different tune if he knew how close Jazz was to all the members of the MC. With a heavy sigh, she sipped her coffee. Scanning the menu wasn't necessary; she already knew she wanted the cinnamon roll waffles, but that left her without anything to focus her attention on.

Thankfully, her father seemed to need a few moments to decide what he wanted to eat. Gave her a bit of time to study him where he sat across from her. Dressed in his uniform, he made an intimidating presence. Her father was a handsome man. At fifty-two, he'd only just begun to gray. For his entire life, or at least her entire life, he'd always been a gym-goer, keeping himself in great shape for his position as a police officer was a matter of pride for him. That hadn't changed after he promoted to detective, and now sheriff. He still had the physique of a much younger man.

Over the years, she'd seen him in uniform countless times, but not as much since he'd been a detective. Now that he was back to wearing a uniform daily, he looked so much more official. Actually, after Joy's funeral, she hadn't seen him in it for more than five years. The first time he'd worn it after that dreadful day, Holly had nearly thrown up at the sight of it. The outfit brought her right back to the day she had to see her sister's dead body.

Holly forced down a swallow of coffee that had suddenly soured in her mouth. Now, the uniform represented a different kind of heartbreak. It was a constant visual reminder that he'd never accept LJ in her life. That she was about to hurt two people

171

who loved her and had already been through so freaking much. She pushed away her coffee cup.

With guilt filling her, she wasn't positive she'd be able to stomach a bite of food.

"Okay, I've decided," he announced.

Jazz returned, and they placed their orders. Once she was off again, and their menus were gone, there wasn't anything to focus on but her father and her guilt.

"Holly, I'd like to apologize for the other night."

Her jaw dropped and she gaped across the booth. Her father sat, staring down into his black coffee. Never in a million years had she expected an apology. Her eyes closed as she took a breath. The apology should have made her feel better. Should have been exactly what she wanted, but instead it only drove the knife deeper into her heart. He was stepping out of character for her and, she was about to gut him. "Thank you, Dad. For saying that," she said around an arid throat.

Hands around his mug, he glanced up. "I can admit when I'm wrong, Hols. And my reaction was wrong. Over the top. I just…" He sighed and rubbed a hand down his face, pausing to scratch his chin. "I just saw that biker so close to you and I lost it. I know I've talked to you over the years about how dangerous these motorcycle clubs are, but, honey, you just don't know until you see it just how downright evil they can be."

Holly swallowed a painful lump in her throat. "LJ's a good guy, Dad. He's helped me out a lot since I moved in. Never been anything but a gentleman." A dirty-talking, sex god of a gentleman, but they could skip that part. "He's been a good f-friend." Saying the word in relation to LJ made her want to vomit. She could never be just friends with him. Not after last night.

His head moved from right to left. "Honey, he's not. You've always been sweet. Always seen the best in people, which is wonderful, but there's a downside to that as well. It makes you naïve, vulnerable to being used and manipulated. It happened to your sister, and it can happen to you. Just because LJ helped you carry some boxes, doesn't make him a good guy."

"Dad—" The mention of Joy had her heart clenching. But it wasn't the same. Her sister had been a twelve-year-old, unable to make adult choices. And that was the heart of their problem right there. Her parents still saw her at that age.

He held up a hand. "No, Holly, let me finish. That club is an outlaw club. Do you know what that means?"

Her stomach rolled as she nodded. "Yes. I know what it means."

"Pretty much by definition, it means they're criminals, honey. They are not good men. None of them. Do you understand?"

"Sure, Dad." There she went again, taking the easy way out instead of standing up for what she believed. What she wanted. That kind of behavior had to stop. Otherwise, she'd blink and be forty years old, stuck in a miserable marriage because she'd attached herself to someone her father chose. The last two men she'd dated, one for almost a year back in college, had been his choice. Both fizzled out long before she'd gotten the guts to end the relationships. "Look, Dad—"

"One sec, Holly, let me finish. I think you should find a new apartment."

She gasped. "What? No! I love that pla—"

That annoying hand lifted again, and she bit back a growl. Would he ever let her speak?

"My office is ramping up our efforts to shut down the MC. The man who held this position before me was crooked as can be. I'm not sure what perks he got, money or something else, but he turned a blind eye to the illegal activities of those damn bikers for as long as he was in office. No more. My goal is to have the MC disbanded and as many of those criminals in jail as possible by the end of the year."

Her hands began to shake. Slipping them under her thighs squashed the tremor out of them, but it did nothing to quell the internal quiver that began with her father's words. "D-dad," she said.

Be firm, Holly.

"Dad, I'm not sure you should be telling me this."

His eyes narrowed, assessing her. "Why not?" When she didn't answer right away, he slapped his palms on the table. "Why the hell not, Holly?"

Her face flamed as she felt the eyes of every customer in the diner shift to them. A quick glance at the counter revealed Jazz looking at her with concern. But she winked and gave Holly a nod. She could do this. She *had* to do this. "B-because I've become friends with many of the women, girlfriends of the club members. They're great people, Dad," she rushed on to say. "Not like clubs you've dealt with in the past."

He snorted and shook his head. "God, Holly, you're so naïve. What's it going to take to get you to realize how dangerous these people are? Your sister's murder clearly wasn't enough. Do you need to lose someone else you love?"

She gasped as pain lanced her heart. How dare he use that against her in such a callous manner? "Dad! I can't believe you said that to me." The words came out as a strangled whisper. Losing Joy had torn her apart. And while it had nearly killed her parents as well, and she'd always been sympathetic to that, something about their relationship had to change. Because it wasn't healthy.

But he didn't seem to be listening or paying attention to her distress. "I didn't want to believe it when one of my deputies told me, but you were at the party the other night, weren't you?" he asked.

Now or never. Holly swallowed. "I was." The words sounded hollow, much as she felt deep in her heart now that he'd speared it.

Jazz appeared at the side of their booth, coffeepot in hand. "Your food will be out in a few. Either of you ready for a refill…" One look at the fierce scowl on the sheriff's face had Jazz's eyes bugging. She glanced between Holly and her father. "You know what? I'm gonna give you another minute." As she backed away she mouthed the words, "You got this," to Holly while giving a discreet thumbs up at her side.

See? Good people. Genuinely good at their core.

"Dad, I'm seeing LJ," Holly blurted the moment Jazz stepped out of earshot. She held her breath, watching the play of emotions across her father's face. Anger, sadness, disbelief.

Hurt.

She swallowed, forcing herself to keep her head high and meet the displeasure in his gaze head-on. As he waited for a response, she gripped the edge of the booth for dear life. Shame threatened to consume her, but she fought it because she couldn't let her guilt win this time as it did every time.

With each second that ticked by, the tension mounted until it grew to a near physical presence at the table.

Shit. Maybe she shouldn't have said anything. Maybe she jumped the gun. Sure, she and LJ had talked about seeing each other again, but what did that even mean? Could she call him her boyfriend? Probably not. The man seemed to freak at the thought of spending the entire night with her. She sure as hell wasn't his ol' lady, whatever that meant. Here she was telling her father about a relationship that barely existed.

Why?

Was she just clinging to the idea of LJ to assert the independence she should have claimed ages ago? Was LJ right? Was this just an act of rebellion? Her thoughts spiraled until Holly completely doubted the wisdom of every word she'd just uttered.

"This is going to break your mother's heart."

He knew just what to say to ratchet up the guilt. Holly steeled her spine, remaining upright while her insides were crumbling to dust. Blinking back tears, she opened her mouth to speak but found it dry as the desert.

"I won't stop gunning for them, Holly. If this whole little announcement is to try and convince me to stop investigating the club, you wasted your time. That club is full of evil mean and foolish doormat women who are nothing more than a piece of property."

Holly almost laughed out loud. Clearly, her father had yet to meet Izzy. It shamed her to admit she'd love to watch him call her a doormat to her face.

"Dad, you may have come across clubs like that in the past, but this one—"

"What? Is different?" He laughed. "Please tell me you didn't fall for that line of bullshit. I'm going after the club, Holly. Mark my word, by the end of the year that clubhouse will be nothing but an abandoned building in the woods. I just hope you don't get caught in the fallout."

So do I.

Her father stood, and her heart sank. "I'm not hungry anymore," he said.

"So this is how it's gonna be? You won't even share a meal with me?"

"I'm not going to tell your mother about this. You can do that yourself. I won't be the one to break her heart." He turned, took two steps and froze. Standing not ten feet from the table, gaze locked on Holly, was LJ.

A shiver skittered down her spine. She'd be lying through her teeth if she didn't admit the sight of him watching her with such intensity sent a dark thrill through her. That look promised sensual delights she'd grown to crave since meeting LJ.

Her father strode forward, resting his hand on the pistol hanging from his belt. A hush fell over the diner. The weight of every nosy gaze in the place fell heavy on her shoulders. When her dad reached LJ's side, he whispered something to the man who made her heart skip a beat.

Other than a hardening of his eyes, LJ didn't react to her father's words. He stayed steady and strong as he focused on her. "You have a good day, Sheriff," he finally said as he walked forward. The jangle of bells five seconds later indicated her father had left the diner.

Without paying a lick of attention to another soul in the diner, LJ veered straight for her table. Instead of taking the spot vacated by her father, he slipped into the booth next to her.

"Hey," he said.

"Hey. What did he—"

"It doesn't matter." LJ captured her chin between his thumb and forefinger. "This here is what matters," he whispered before giving her a kiss sweeter than any he'd given her so far. Her body went haywire, nerves dancing with pleasure. But it was her heart that bloomed with a dangerous happiness.

After one last soft kiss to her lips, LJ settled one arm across her shoulders while signaling for Jazz to come get his order. "What'd you get, sugar?"

Just like that, her internal turmoil quieted. "Is it too late in the day for me to get waffles? Because that's what I ordered."

With a snort, LJ said, "Fuck no. You had them yet? They're fucking great. I'll get 'em too."

He dropped a kiss on top of her head. Holly smiled as she settled into the crook of his arm. As his warmth, his scent, and his strength surrounded her, it'd be so easy to slip fully under his spell.

But just as she was about to release the conversation with her father to the universe, his words rang through her head.

God, Holly, you're so naïve.

Was she? Was she doomed to crash and burn in embarrassment when it turned out her father was right, and the MC disbanded due to arrests of all its members?

The thought was sobering. Enough to make her second guess recent choices.

She glanced up at LJ who was waving one of his brothers over. One arm still around her shoulders, his eyes sparkled. The club brother said something Holly failed to hear. LJ threw his head back and laughed. The sound had Holly smiling. Full of happiness, lightness, and humor. She refused to believe this man had an evil core.

The tension with her father would blow over. It had to. They were family, and a close one at that. With time, he'd see how well LJ and his club treated Holly. LJ might never be her father's favorite person, but they'd get through it. And her whole family would be better off with a new and healthier dynamic.

God, Holly, you're so naïve.

Only time would tell. Something about the big man next to her made it impossible to walk away, no matter the risk.

CHAPTER SEVENTEEN

"Are you sure you're okay with me borrowing your truck?" Holly asked LJ for what had to be the tenth time that morning.

He rolled his eyes. Clearly, Holly was the one who wasn't entirely okay with borrowing his truck. "Sugar, what did I say the other million times you asked?"

"You said, 'what's mine is yours, sugar, so stop fucking asking,'" Holly said, mimicking his much deeper voice.

LJ laughed. "That's right. So, stop fucking asking. Here." He handed her one of the homemade donuts she'd brought over. "Stuff this in your face so you can't ask again."

"Pfft." Holly stuck her tongue out at him, which had him laughing again, but she passed on the donut. "I just didn't want to assume anything, and I've never driven a truck that big. You're under no obligation to let me borrow it."

It was Saturday morning, and Holly planned to swing by the diner to iron out some kinks in their To-Go plan. She'd mentioned wanting to make sure she had the register down, all the display cases ready, and to get a feel for the flow of the place. Working there would be a totally different vibe than eating as a paying customer. Or so Toni, Jazz, and Holly had informed LJ when he pouted and asked why he couldn't have Holly for the entire day.

"Assume away, woman. Seriously, you want something just ask for it. I'll give it to you, every time." And he would. If it was in his power to give, it was hers.

Except for one thing. A night spent in his arms. That gift wasn't his to give.

She bit her lower lip then opened her mouth as though she was going to say something. LJ waited, but she must have changed her mind because she shook her head and slipped a diner T-shirt on. Teal, like the rest of the staff wore. A denim skirt and Chuck Taylors topped off her outfit. She looked, young, fresh, and totally fuckable. Which he'd just done about ten minutes ago. And every chance he'd gotten over the past few days.

"Well, thank you, LJ. I'll take good care of it. Her? Does your truck have a name?" She shot him a saucy wink.

"Funny." He snagged her around the waist and playfully got her in a headlock. Holly made everything fun. The simple act of getting dressed turned into playtime, which often turned into sexy time. Case in point.

"LJ!" she squealed once she realized she couldn't escape his hold.

Keeping her trapped against him, he snuck a hand under the T-shirt and up to her tits. One finger slipped down into the cup of her bra and stroked her nipple. It beaded for him like a well-trained pup.

"LJ." This time his name was a breathy sigh.

"Tell me you get it, sugar. Tell me you get that I'll give you anything. Do anything to make you happy." With one blunt fingernail, he scraped over her nipple now rock hard from the attention.

She shuddered against him, that delectable ass cradling his dick in exactly the right way to make him hard. "LJ, I have to go."

"I know. Tell me first." He gently bit her neck.

"You'd do anything for me. Get a-anything I n-need."

"That's right." He kissed the top of her head. "Now don't crash my truck or I'll be forced to punish you. All night long." As the teasing words fell out of his mouth, he tensed. All night long wasn't possible. Would she call him out on it?

Thankfully, she seemed blissfully unaware of his slip up. She shuddered again, this time with an accompanying groan as he released her. "You realize now I'm going to drive straight into the first stop sign I come across."

With a laugh, LJ swatted her ass. God, he loved the way that thing jiggled for him.

"Thanks," she said as she grabbed the keys off his counter. "The towing company should be by in about an hour. Hopefully whatever is wrong with my hunk of junk car will be an easy and not too expensive fix."

"Sugar, I told you I have a brother who could look at it."

She held up her hand, and the urge to suck those fingers into his mouth hit him hard. "I know, but I need to do this myself. I can't rely on you for everything, LJ. I can stand on my own two feet and get my own car fixed."

In case you're not there in the future.

The unspoken sentence wasn't necessary. Between her father's hard-on for the MC and LJ's refusal to spend the night with her, how could he blame her for keeping some emotional distance? The question shone in her eyes frequently, in fact, just as he was telling her he'd do anything for her, he saw it.

She wanted to know why he kissed her and sent her off to her own bed the last four nights. Alone. After blowing each other's minds. But she hadn't asked. Too sweet and probably too worried to rock the damn boat.

"Okay, I'm out." She strode over to him, rose on tip-toes, and presented those glossy lips for a kiss.

LJ gave her a peck. Or at least he intended to, but the second their lips touched, he couldn't resist plunging in for more. His tongue invaded her mouth, swallowing down her moan, and inhaling the minty flavor of the toothpaste she'd borrowed. His actions were a weak compensation for the inability to spend an entire night with her. As though he could kiss her into believing his feelings and intent.

"Wow," Holly said, taking a step back. With her hair a little more mussed than it had been a few minutes ago, she had that just fucked look about her. "A girl could get used to that kind of goodbye."

She took a step, nearly fell on her face, then laughed when LJ caught her under her arms. "You made me weak in the knees, Jack." After winking at him, she made her way to the door.

"Come on, bud," LJ said to Biscuit who'd flopped on the floor in the kitchen and watched the scene unfold, as was his typical MO. "Let's make sure mommy gets out okay."

With a giant yawn, the mastiff climbed to his feet and lumbered after LJ. They stood side by side on the balcony in front of the apartments, gazing down at the parking lot below.

Holly climbed into LJ's massive pick-up with a scrunched brow. He hadn't been kidding when he told her he was happy to lend her the truck while her car was laid up. But now, seeing her frown at the backup camera, he couldn't help but have doubts. Well, she'd have to learn how to drive the beast some time or another and baptism by fire seemed the quickest way to go.

After navigating out of the parking spot and successfully avoiding taking out the cars on either side of her, Holly waved and gifted him with a triumphant smile.

"Inside, buddy," LJ said to the dog with a pat on his head.

Biscuit looked up at him and whined. "Come on, you big baby. Mommy will be back in a few hours." What he didn't say was how much he got that whine. Part of him wanted to join in the pitiful song. Once back in LJ's apartment, Biscuit plopped down next to the couch. Though he'd seen it at least a hundred times by now, LJ never failed to feel envy of the pooch's ability to fall asleep in under two seconds and stay in that state no matter what occurred around him.

For a few hours, LJ puttered around his apartment, completing tasks he'd been putting off since spending all his spare time with Holly. He washed some clothes, wrote up a few estimates for construction projects, and was about to chill with a Netflix binge when there was a knock on the door.

With a deep bark, Biscuit lumbered up and loafed over to greet the guest. Or guests. Copper, Rocket, and Zach stood outside his door. "Shit, did I forget we had something today?"

Copper chuckled and rubbed Biscuit's head. The dog immediately stopped barking and practically purred at the attention.

Worst guard dog ever.

"Nah, brother," Copper said. "You're good. Just had some shit to run by you. Sorry for busting in unannounced."

"Ain't a thing. Come on in. Want a beer?"

"Hell yes," Zach said while Rocket and Copper both nodded.

As he went to the fridge to grab four beers, LJ took a moment to shake off his nerves at the arrival of his president and half of the MC's executive board. Even though he'd been affiliated with the club for nearly sixteen months, he was the baby brother. A brand-new patch. While he respected the hell out of Copper and considered the man fair and levelheaded as a president, LJ was acutely aware Copper could make his life a living hell if he so desired.

Two long-necks dangling from each hand, he returned to the small living room, made even tinier by the presence of three additional huge men. Biscuit had returned to his spot next to the couch, snoozing once again. At least someone managed to be anxiety-free.

"What's up, Prez?" LJ asked as he handed out the beer, then tossed Copper a bottle opener.

"Shell received a letter today. Delivered by a courier, all official and shit." He popped the cap off his beer then took a long sip, seeming to need to get a handle on his frustration.

LJ raised an eyebrow. "What kind of letter?"

"It was a certified letter, made out to Shell, signed by a judge."

LJ accepted the bottle opener from Rocket after his brother opened his beer. "What did it say?"

"It was an official denial of the permits we need for the charity run. It clearly stated if we ignored the edict and organized the event anyway, we'd be subject to fines and possible arrest."

"You're fucking kidding me," LJ said, but none of the men appeared remotely jokey. "What a shit fucking move."

"Tell me about it," Zach said. "Fucking charity run for fucking children. It's a low fucking blow."

"We're not giving a shit, right? We're still putting it on?"

Copper nodded. "Yes, but we need to brainstorm some ideas so we can do this without risk of arrest. If it were just me, I wouldn't give a shit, but I ain't putting Shell at risk of being locked up."

With a snort, LJ, said, "Bet she had some choice words about that."

Zach and Rocket snickered while Copper rolled his eyes. "Don't feel comfortable repeating it with kids in the room." He glanced at Biscuit.

LJ laughed. Copper was officially the worst at curbing his language around Shell's daughter, Beth. The four-year-old spitfire called him out on it daily. "What do you need from me?"

The apartment grew silent except for the gentle rumble of Biscuit's snore. A ripple of unease crawled up LJ's spine.

Fuck.

Something was up.

Copper stroked his bearded chin. "You've been hanging with the sheriff's daughter."

And now the unease turned to straight-up dread.

"I have…" Suddenly this visit felt more like an ambush.

The sigh that left Copper was heavy with the weight of running the club. Being the head of the tight-knit group couldn't be easy on a good day, now throw in an overeager sheriff gunning for them, and it was a shock the man was as calm as he appeared. The men he led, the brothers in the club, were a family. And Copper took his role as head of the family deathly seriously. Which meant he suffered when his family was under attack.

Suffered and turned near feral in his desire to protect his family.

And that's why LJ knew the next words out of his prez's mouth were going to suck.

"The sheriff doesn't have any skeletons in his closet. At least none we've found yet. Sure, he's spent his career destroying clubs like ours, but it was all above board."

"Bullshit," LJ said. "He's been harassing us with drummed-up claims. There's no way he didn't pull the same shit or worse throughout his career."

With a nod, Copper said, "I agree. He's just covered his tracks well. Which brings us back to you. And his daughter." As Copper let that weighted statement hang in the air, he studied LJ. So did Zach and Rocket.

He felt like a bug under a microscope. One headed for a good squashing.

"Where's shit at with her?" Copper asked, then shook his head. Before LJ had a chance to answer, he spoke again. "Fuck it, I ain't beatin' around the bush. Need to know if you're willing to pump her for information."

"Bet he's pumping her for something," Zach muttered.

"You trying to be fucking Maverick now?" Copper asked with a scowl, but his chest rippled with restrained laughter.

Zach shrugged. "Sorry. Too good to pass up."

As was typical, Rocket remained quiet through the exchange. His silence shouldn't ever be mistaken for apathy or stupidity, however. His intense gaze studied LJ. The entire time, LJ's stomach was rolling and his mind was reeling as he struggled to come up with a way to refuse the first favor his president ever asked of him.

Until that very moment, he'd have said Copper could ask anything of him and he'd do it without hesitation. He respected his president enough to trust in his leadership without question.

But now? Faced with the possibility of betraying Holly? Now he was well and truly fucked. It'd be over. Whatever he and Holly were to each other would end the moment she found out he was using her for information. And could she even provide it? Shit with her father wasn't exactly roses at the moment, all because of the club.

Christ, what kind of fucker would he be to ask her to remedy her relationship with her father—which was only strained because of him—only to turn around and use that repaired relationship to betray her?

"Well, I guess that answers that," Copper said. It was hard to tell because of the thickness of his beard, but LJ swore his prez smirked.

"What?"

Zach snorted. "You've been quiet for about four minutes with this look of panic on your face. Guessing you're trying to figure out how to hand over a big fat fucking no."

Goddammit. "No," LJ said. "I'm just—"

Copper held up a hand. "Relax. I ain't gonna force you to do shit." He sighed and stroked his beard. "It was an idea I had to float. Wasn't sure how you felt about her. If you guys were just fucking and shit…" He shrugged then gave LJ a shit-eating grin. "Didn't know you were falling for this chick."

"What? No. No falling. Just hanging out." Falling for her? Ridiculous. He liked her, liked fucking her. End of story.

Liar.

Rocked barked out a laugh. So nice of him to finally join the conversation. LJ flipped him off.

"Look, I saw a potential opportunity. I'd be a shit president if I didn't at least see where your head was about this girl. I ain't gonna press you to do shit, LJ. You've got nothing to prove to me. You spent fifteen months earning my respect and proving your loyalty to my club. This ain't some kinda test. That shit is over. You're patched, you're a brother, and you're free to speak your mind. I'll tell you right now, had someone asked me to manipulate and use Shell, I'd have told them to go fuck themselves, president or not."

"Prez, this thing with Holly ain't like you and Shell." Shell had a man she could count on to keep her warm throughout the night. Shell had a man she could lie next to without fear of being attacked while she slept. Holly would never receive either of those assurances from him. No matter the desire or strength of his feelings, the relationship was doomed from the start.

"We'll see," Copper said.

Rocket caught his gaze. Of course, he didn't say anything, but he nodded once. Solidarity. Understanding. Rocket had demons, hell, so did his woman, maybe even more than Rocket himself. He knew what it was to suffer from the demons in his head.

LJ started to speak again but was cut short by the jangle of his phone.

Holly. He peeked at the time before answering. She'd been out about four hours and should have been on her way home. Jesus, he'd teased her about the truck, but had been confident she'd handle it just fine.

If she'd been in an accident when he could have just driven her…

"Hey, sugar. What's up?"

"Um, LJ?" she asked in a voice so small, he strained to make her out. His spine straightened, and he made eye contact with Copper. His three brothers snapped to attention, prepared to jump in and help in any way.

"What's wrong, Holly?"

"Um, could you come get me? And bring the registration paperwork for your gun…if you have it." If it's registered was the unspoken statement.

Of course, it was fucking registered. He was an outlaw MC member. Driving around with an unregistered gun would give every cop in a ten-mile radius a boner. "Where are you?" he asked as he marched toward the door to retrieve his boots.

"I've got my work truck," Rocket said. "You can ride with me."

Good. This way he could drive Holly back in his own truck.

"Um, I got pulled over. And when they searched the car, they found the gun and the cop wants to press charges since I don't have papers for it."

What the fuck? "Why the fuck did they search the car? Why the fuck were you pulled over? Did you tell 'em who your dad is?"

"Uh," she said, and it grew even more difficult to hear her. As though she spoke extra low to keep someone from overhearing. "Can you just hurry, please? I'm on the highway halfway between the diner and our apartments."

"Be there in five. Hold on, baby."

"Thank you," she said but it sounded more like a choked sob. The stark relief had him moving even faster. Had she thought he wouldn't come for her? Shit. He had some serious work to do to get her to understand how much she meant to him. Even if this couldn't end in happily ever after.

"Cops harassing her?"

"Sounds like it. Let's roll." He didn't bother waiting for his bothers or even locking his fucking door. LJ ran down the steps and jogged toward Rocket's truck.

Copper and Zach mounted their bikes. "We're right behind you," Copper said.

And even though his nerves were stretched thin, LJ felt the power of his brotherhood behind him. Didn't matter in the least that he'd turned down Copper's request. They had his back and would work this shit out.

One way or another.

CHAPTER EIGHTEEN

Five minutes earlier, Holly accelerated onto the highway with the cheesiest grin on her face. She glanced at her phone, lying on the passenger seat. It'd be so easy to call LJ and tell him how amazing her practice run had gone. How much Toni, Jazz, and all the employees at the diner loved what she'd made. And they had. Holly had never received so many compliments in her life. If she'd stayed there much longer, her head wouldn't have been able to fit in LJ's truck.

But no, she'd tell him when she saw him in person. Attaching LJ to every victory or milestone in her life was a fool's errand. One likely to end in crying fits every time something good happened to her in the future once he wasn't there to share in it any longer.

Instead of calling him, she had a private celebration in her mind. Monday was going to rock. Two more days and she'd be gainfully employed doing what she loved.

The shrill whoop of a siren startled her out of her musings. She peeked in her rearview mirror, scanning for the source. Hopefully, she had enough time to shift lanes before she found herself blocking their way. A police vehicle flew down the highway quickly approaching her in the left lane, so Holly switched to the right.

The cop followed suit, then they pulled up, hot on her tail.

So close Holly could see the officer waving her over.

Holly frowned at the mirror then returned her attention to the road. On her next check, the cop hadn't moved. He whooped his siren again and flashed his lights this time, again waving her over.

"Me?" Holly asked out loud as though someone would answer. "You're pulling *me* over? What the hell?"

Before easing up on the gas, she glanced at the speedometer which read an even sixty miles per hour. Okay, so the speed limit was fifty-five, but wasn't there a five-mile-per-hour margin of error in these cases?

Her heart lodged in her throat as she moved her foot to the gas. Even with two cops in her immediate family, Holly had always been terrified by the prospect of being pulled over. The one other time it had happened, she'd been a sweating, stammering mess by the time the officer had knocked on her window. Barely able to speak around her nerves, he'd thought she was wasted and demanded a breathalyzer, which she'd passed with flying colors and a hefty dose of mortification.

"Take a breath, girl," she whispered. "Relax. Hands on the wheel." She did as she advised herself, sitting with her hands at ten and two and staring straight ahead. Despite anticipating it, the rap on the window had her jumping out of her skin.

She depressed the window control. "Yes, officer?" He looked familiar, though she hadn't officially met him. If she remembered correctly, he was one of the cops present during the raid on the clubhouse.

"Well, you don't look like a Jack Olsen." The slim officer with a bushy blond mustache and a wicked southern drawl tucked his thumbs through his belt loops and rocked back on his heels. "You're a might bit prettier, I imagine. Though you never can tell these days with people switchin' genders left and right. Ran the plates as I was pullin' ya over. Says this here vehicle belongs to a Jack Olsen."

What. The. Hell. Did this guy seriously say that bigoted garbage to her? She took a breath and pushed it aside. They weren't there to discuss his social views or hers, just the ownership of the vehicle. "Um, yes, this truck is Jack's. He's my —" *Well shit, what was he? He's my fuck buddy* probably wouldn't be the wisest phrase to blurt out. *He's my friend with benefits?* "He's my boyfriend," she said.

Kinda.

Close enough for today.

"Boyfriend, huh?" The officer, actually the sheriff's deputy, said with a smug grin. "If that's what ya wanna call it, guess ya got the right." He propped his hip on the side of her car, folding his arms as though he planned to linger.

"Um, excuse me?" she asked.

The deputy, Higgins, his name tag read, leaned down until his face was level with her open window. "It's okay, darlin', ain't no judgment from me. Lived in this town a while now. Those Handlers always seem to have plenty of 'girlfriends'"—he dared to use air quotes—"hangin' 'round the club. Now here's the thang, ma'am. Some of those girlfriends have been known to cause drama. You know, stir up some trouble when their 'boyfriend' gets a new 'girlfriend.' Maybe ya decided to teach Mr. Jack Olsen a lesson by takin' his truck on a little joy ride."

If the man crooked his fingers in midair one more time, Holly was going to reach out and snap them off. Okay, she never would, but the fantasy took some of the sting out of being subtly called a whore and a thief.

After taking a calming breath, Holly looked at the officer. "My car wouldn't start his morning. Jack, my air-quote-free boyfriend, lent me his truck so I could get to and from work. If you'd like, I can call him, and he can verify my story."

"Hmm, how about ya just hand on over yer license, the registration, and insurance card."

"Sure. My license is in my purse and the other items are in the glove box. May I retrieve them?"

"Wouldn'ta asked for 'em if I didn't want you to get 'em," he said with a laugh that raked down Holly's back like metal scraping concrete.

Her nerves went haywire as she fished her wallet out of her purse. "Here's this." She handed it through the window, willing her hand not to shake.

"Purdy," he said. "Though you're even better lookin' in real life." He winked.

"Um, uh, thanks."

His focus wasn't on her license. In fact, he'd barely glanced at the thing. Instead, he zeroed in on her breasts, though they were fully hidden by her T-shirt. Goosebumps rose along her arms and the back of her neck. Not the good kind, either. Not the kind she got when LJ kissed her neck or whispered in her ear. No, these were warning goosebumps. Basically, an internal alarm system or creeper alert.

"Going to grab the registration now." She leaned over the center console and reached for the glove box. It was a stretch. The truck was just so damn big. Her shirt rode up in the back. A high-pitched whistle pierced the air making her jaw drop.

He did not just whistle at her, scumbag style...

Finally, after nearly dislocating her shoulder, she reached the latch and opened the glove box.

Out tumbled a shiny black pistol. Holly knew her way around a gun. A girl didn't grow up with a cop father and not learn to shoot, hell, she even had one locked in a small safe under her bed, but she hadn't been prepared for this one and recoiled as though it were a snake instead of a weapon.

"Hands on the wheel, now!" Higgins shouted as he drew his own weapon and aimed it at her through the window.

A rushing waterfall sounded in her ears. Higgins continued to yell, but the words didn't register.

Finally, after staring through the windshield for long seconds, the deputy's screams broke through her haze. "Last time I'm gonna say it. Get out of the vehicle. Now." He reached inside and pulled the lever, opening the door.

"It's not my gun! I didn't even know it was there. I haven't touched it and I'm not going to." She lifted her hands by her ears and used her foot to push the door open. Slowly, so as not to spook the deputy, she slipped out of the car.

"Is the gun registered?"

Was it? How the hell would she know, but damn she sure hoped it was. "It's not mine. I don't know anything about it. I didn't even know it was in there. Please, you can call LJ—Jack. I'm sure he'll straighten this up."

With his weapon still trained on her, he said, "Move around to the front of the vehicle. Face the windshield. Palms flat on the hood."

Why the hell wasn't he listening to a thing she said? "Um, I don't want to name drop or anything, but my father—"

"Oh, I know who your daddy is, Holly." He maneuvered his slim body around the car. "What's your daddy think about you whoring yourself out to the MC?"

Heat from the hood of LJ's truck, singed her hands, though it wasn't nearly as hot as her face. If she turned to mortification in the dictionary, she was pretty sure she'd find a picture of a woman standing in this very position. The posture had her feeling exposed despite being fully clothed. She was vulnerable. Unable to fully take in her surroundings and protect herself.

"I've removed the weapon from the vehicle."

Holly jumped as he appeared next to her.

"Gotta pat you down. Need to make sure you don't have any other surprise weapons on your person."

"I don't. I told you, that's not my—oh!" His hands landed heavy on her shoulders. He stroked straight down her back then up her sides. The journey of his hands seemed more like a caress than a search for contraband.

Holly stiffened. What the hell was she supposed to do? She couldn't say, "Excuse me, officer, you're touching me too intimately, please lighten it up." Could she? Would that land her in even hotter water?

Nausea swirled in her stomach as she clenched her teeth, squeezed her eyes shut and prepared to endure the unprofessional search.

Then his hands came around her sides, up and over her breasts where he paused and squeezed. Holly shrieked and jerked back. The situation had gone from slightly over the line to so far past it; the damn thing disappeared from view.

"Stop! You can't do this!" Holly tried to turn, but his hand pushed like a lead weight on her back, smashing her flat against the car's hood once again. Only this time, she landed hard and with an "oof."

To anyone passing by at fifty-five plus miles per hour, the scene appeared as though an officer was subduing a resisting perp.

"Hold still until I finish," he said as his hands roamed once again. His hands stroked over her ass, down her legs and back up. He stepped closer. The ridge of what could only be an erection pressed against her ass.

Tears burned in her eyes. The one hope she clung to like a lifeline was the fact they were in public. He couldn't rape her on the side of the road with cars driving by. Some Good Samaritan would notice and stop to help.

Right?

Finally, after what seemed like hours, he finally released her. Holly let out a shuddered breath. She was too terrified to be relieved at that point. Just because his wandering hands were no longer on her, she wasn't out of danger yet. As long as she remained in his presence, she couldn't relax.

"Well, ma'am," he continued as though he hadn't molested her. "You may stand up."

Holly straightened, wincing at the discomfort in her hip where he'd slammed it into the car. She turned and forced herself to meet his gaze instead of curling into a ball on the ground like she wanted.

Higgins was still close, too close and the sick twist in her gut intensified.

"You're in some trouble, as I see it," he said as he folded his arms. "Now, we got a couple options. I can slap some cuffs on you, toss you in the back of my vehicle, and haul you into the station. Be pretty embarrassin' for your daddy, dontcha think?"

"It's not my gun."

He shrugged and grinned a creepy smile like he knew he held all the cards and she was fucked. "Don't matter. You were drivin'. Makes you captain of this here ship. As captain, you're responsible for everythin' happenin' on the ship, even if it ain't your ship."

The cinnamon roll—all right *rolls*—she'd eaten about an hour ago tried to make a reappearance, but Holly forced the sick feeling down. "What's the, uh, what's the second option?" she asked, barely able to get the sour words past her mouth.

Because without asking, she knew.

"Well, the second option is you sit in the front seat of the car instead."

"W-what?" She shook her head. "I don't, um, I don't understand."

His grin grew sinister. "Not much to it." He grabbed his junk and gave it a solid heft. "You sit in the front seat of my cruiser and let me know how much you appreciate me not dragging you in on a weapons charge."

Holly gagged as her stomach lurched violently.

"M-my father—"

"Cares more about takin' out the MC than anything else. Trust me on that one, darlin'."

God. Was it true? Would her father care more about his hatred for bikers than his daughter being abused by one of his own? Two weeks ago, she'd have said no. Now...no, she refused to think it. The sheriff-father card was her only card left, and she'd play it to the max.

"You willing to risk it?" she asked, forcing strength she didn't feel into her voice. "Because it's sexual assault. You're a cop, you know that. Blackmailing me for a blowjob in your car is assault. You willing to put your job and your freedom on the line because you think my dad will overlook that shit? Trust me, he won't."

For the first time since he lured her out of the truck, Higgins focused his attention on something besides her body. He shifted and tapped his fingers against his pant leg.

A nervous habit?

Was his arrogance finally waning?

"Look," she said, holding out her hand. "Just hand me my phone. I'll call LJ, he'll bring whatever paperwork you need to see about the gun. Then we'll all just be on our way and forget the last few minutes."

Higgins cocked his head and smiled that spine-chilling smile again. Shit, she was fucked. He saw straight through her false bravado and posturing. "You know what, darlin'?" he asked. "I'm gonna give you this one." He held out her phone.

Of course, he held it close to his body, so she had to walk into his personal space to retrieve it. As her hand closed around the case, he held it firm. "And I'm gonna give it a few weeks. Figure by that point, your daddy will have arrested one or two of the Handlers. Whet his appetite. And he'll be starving for more. Pretty sure he won't give a fuck what any of us do by then. Guess you better watch your speed from now on, huh? This might turn out differently next time." He winked.

Good thing he'd removed the gun from LJ's glove box because for the first time in her life, Holly found herself willing and able to harm another human being to the point of death. Higgins was a disgusting asshole with a God complex. Like being a sheriff's deputy in small-town Tennessee made him some kind of higher power.

She walked a good fifteen steps away from him. Being so close to him had her skin crawling with imaginary bugs. Even with some distance, the chill that had settled in her bones didn't dissipate.

Holly wrapped one arm around her midsection and used the free hand to dial LJ. Man, oh man, this was not going to go well. If she could think of any possible way to keep him from finding out what Higgins proposed, she just might go that route. But LJ would know. She was shit at hiding her emotions.

With a sigh, she connected the call and lifted the phone to her ear.

"Hey, sugar. What's up?"

Shit. Here's goes nothing.

CHAPTER NINETEEN

Rocket slowed to a stop behind the police cruiser parked on the side of the highway, lights flashing. This song and dance with the cops wasn't any of the Handlers' first rodeo, so Copper drove a few more feet and pulled in front of LJ's truck, flanking the officer and Holly. Gave them a little advantage.

Holly and the deputy both stood between the cars. Holly had her arms wrapped around her midsection as though she was hugging herself. She swayed back and forth.

Something was wrong. Something beyond a simple mix-up over the ownership of a pistol. Higgins, a little fucking Schwartz wannabe waited with his ass propped on the trunk of his cruiser, legs crossed at the ankle as though he was waiting for coffee at Starbucks, not anticipating an encounter with an outlaw.

Higgins wasn't the shittiest cop on the force, but he ranked up there. An arrogant misogynist who fancied himself more important than his actual station in life, he'd been a complete asshole to Shell when she was involved in a minor fender-bender about a year ago. Hopefully Copper would let LJ handle this. If he got off his bike, the prez might lose his shit on Higgins.

Holly finally looked up and straight at him. The change in her would have been obvious to a blind man. Her face softened, her shoulders relaxed, and the tension seemed to pour out of her in waves. What the fuck had happened?

Nothing good.

LJ pushed the door open and started out of the truck only to be held back by Rocket's hand on his arm.

"Hold the fuck on," Rocket said.

"What?" That came out way harsher than intended. Luckily Rocket wasn't the type to take offense easily.

"You're too fucking hot right now. You can't go charging out there snarling like a fucking grizzly bear. You're trying to help your woman, not get your ass locked up. Tossing your giant ass in jail would be the highlight of that fucker's shitty life. Simmer down. Hear me?"

LJ braced his palms on the dash as he blew out a breath. His gaze remained locked on Holly. "I hear you. Thanks for looking out for me."

Rocket chuckled. "Always brother."

"I find out he hurt her, though…"

"I'll hold the fucker down for you," Rocket said.

LJ nodded. "Good deal." With a renewed sense of calm, or at least somewhat calmer, LJ opened the door.

Party time.

As LJ stepped out of the truck, Higgins' hand fell to his weapon. Out the corner of his eye, LJ saw Holly tense. He hated to pull his attention off her but ignoring the man with the gun might not be a smart idea. Thankfully, Copper and Zach remained on their bikes, though LJ had no doubt they'd jump the fuck in if shit went downhill.

"That's far enough," Higgins said as LJ approached. He held up the truck registration Holly had handed over. "Your real name Jack Olsen?"

"That's me. There a reason you're harassing my woman?" About ten feet separated them.

"Keep your hands where I can see them," Higgins barked as though LJ was about to reach for a hidden firearm. His voice dripped with hatred and disgust.

Feeling's mutual, buddy.

"I was just reaching for my wallet so I can show you my weapon registration and we can all be on our way."

Higgins wrinkled his nose, making that bushy pornstashe move. "Go ahead."

Keeping one hand in the air, LJ reached around for the wallet he kept in his back pocket with the other. "Can you tell me why you pulled her over?"

"Speeding," Higgins said with a smirk in her direction.

Holly had yet to say a word. She stood off to the side, hugging herself. She appeared small, fragile. And that was fucking unacceptable.

"Speeding?" LJ said as though shocked. "You got a lead foot I'm not aware of, sugar? 'Cuz the last few times I drove with you, it was granny-speed all the way."

Holly narrowed her eyes at him. Finally, a reaction beyond the blank stare.

She held up her ticket. "Five miles over, according to Deputy Higgins."

LJ snorted. "This some kinda fucking joke?"

"Nope," Higgins replied with a grin LJ wanted to ram his fist into. "It's dangerous to drive too fast, Jack. Gotta keep the citizens of Townsend safe from reckless drivers."

Christ, this guy was a smug asshole.

"You put your hands on my woman, Higgins?"

Tension grew to near combustible.

"Gun fell out of the glove box when she opened it, Jack Olsen. She was driving the truck of a known criminal affiliate." He shrugged like he didn't give two shits. "How was I supposed to know she was your woman? Just assumed she was a who—"

"Shut your fucking mouth."

"LJ?" Holly's shaky voice jerked his attention away from the cop whose death was imminent. She had tears in her eyes. Christ, the sight gutted him.

"Yeah, sugar."

"Can we just go, now? Please."

LJ stalked forward, ignoring the way Higgins' fingers tightened on the handle of his pistol. He held the registration card out for the cop to see. "We fucking done here?"

Higgins tilted his head and rubbed his chin as though studying the card, but his attention strayed over LJ's shoulder to Holly. No way did the motherfucker give one shit about the gun, who owned it, and whether or not it was legal. All he wanted was to harass the fucking club.

"Guess we're done. I'll tell you like I told your woman. She needs to watch herself over the next few weeks. We're gonna be dialin' up the pressure on your club. Being the sheriff's daughter won't be a get out of jail free card."

"Sugar?" LJ called without taking his attention off Higgins. "We're good to go. Hop in the truck. I'll be thirty seconds."

Holly remained silent for a beat, then said, "Please hurry. I really want to go home."

After he heard the truck door slam shut, LJ took another step closer to Higgins. He had a good six inches on the guy and at least sixty pounds of bulk. It'd be so easy to wrap his hand around the man's throat and give a good fucking squeeze.

So damn tempting. Instead, he said, "I find out you laid one hand on my woman, you'll learn exactly what the Handlers are all about."

Higgins raised an eyebrow. "Didn't think even you were dumb enough to threaten an officer of the law."

LJ glanced around. "No witnesses."

"Huh, guess not." Higgins tilted his head. "Just like there were no witnesses when I was here with your woman."

With a growl, LJ stepped forward. Higgins was a dead man.

"LJ! Your woman is waiting on you." Copper's booming brogue might have just prevented a murder.

"Aww, Daddy says it's time to go. Better listen."

Fuck this. He was done. He'd be behind bars if he took this fucker's bait and Copper was right, Holly's needs trumped Higgins. LJ turned, stuffing his weapons registration card in his back pocket. He nodded to Rocket who pulled out onto the highway. Copper would most likely stick around until both Higgins and LJ had gone.

Didn't fucking matter that Higgins still had his gun. He marched to the truck with two goals in mind. Get Holly as far away from this spot as fast as possible and find out what the fuck happened.

In that order.

He hauled himself into his massive truck with the ease someone only his size could pull off. With a two-fingered salute for Copper and Zach, he drove off. But not toward home. Their apartments didn't need to be tainted by whatever went down today. Hopefully, they could talk it out, then leave it in the past.

After about two minutes of silence, Holly said, "LJ, I—"

"Not yet."

He cast her a quick glance to find her watching him with wary eyes while she gnawed on her lower lip. Dammit. Freaking her out hadn't been the goal. He just needed a few minutes to get his shit locked down before they spoke.

For the rest of the fifteen-minute drive, neither made a sound. He should say something, comfort her in some way, but he was too on edge to offer anything more than time to think. As he pulled off to the side of the road, Holly gasped.

So, she recognized the overlook as the place he'd first had her. Hopefully, the positive memories of that night would outweigh whatever shit she was about to tell him. He put the truck in park, rolled the windows down halfway, then killed the engine. They turned to face each other at the same time.

"I'm okay, LJ," Holly said. "I can see this whole incident really upset you—"

"You being harassed by the cops and nearly arrested because I didn't think to remove the weapon from my car? Yeah, it fucking upsets me."

Her jaw dropped. "You're not blaming yourself for this, are you?" When he didn't respond, she said, "LJ that's crazy! That

Higgins guy is just a straight-up asshole. You aren't responsible for his actions in any way."

They'd have to agree to disagree on that one. Goddamn, why hadn't he just bulldozed over her desire to rely on herself and driven her to the damn diner? She'd been out there on the side of the road, unprotected. And once LJ had shown up? He still couldn't do anything without getting his ass tossed in jail. Goddamn fucking helpless. The worst state for him to be in. He blew out a breath. "Tell me what happened."

"You have to promise me you won't flip out, okay?"

"I make no such promise."

"LJ!" She scoffed. "Come on."

Instead of answering her, he captured her face between his mitts and gave her a kiss. Probably the sweetest kiss he'd ever given her. No exploring tongues or plans to escalate. Just lips pressed together in comfort. "Shoulda done that the second I saw you," he whispered as he pressed his forehead to hers. "My mistake. I'll try not to lose it. Okay, baby?"

Holly sighed and closed her eyes. "Damn you, LJ for being so sweet." Another sigh. "Like he said, he pulled me over for going a few miles above the limit."

He smiled. Though loosening her tongue hadn't been the purpose of that kiss, he'd be lying if he wasn't thrilled for the side benefit.

Her eyes remained closed. "He was your basic jerk at first. Suggesting I was some angry club whore who hijacked your car. A woman scorned kind of thing, I guess. I tried to explain we were…more than that." She shrugged. "He either didn't buy it or didn't care. You know what happened when he asked for the registration and insurance."

"Fuck, I'm so sorry, Holly. That damn gun's been in there since the day I bought the truck. Swear I've never taken it out once. Never even crossed my mind to warn you about it."

"LJ, you are not to blame here. He should have just let me call you straight away. You could have let him know I didn't steal your car and offered to show the gun registration card. Higgins had other plans though."

"He made you get out."

"Yes. And…" She swallowed and averted her gaze. "He said he had to search me after he removed the gun. So, he made me bend over the hood of the car with my palms down while he removed the gun."

She rubbed her fingertips over her palms again and again as though still feeling the heat of the car on her skin.

"And he searched you?" LJ asked, trying to make his voice sound soothing despite his anger quickly heating to the boiling point.

Holly lifted her gaze. "He searched me."

"He cross a line?"

She nodded, water pooling in the corners of her eyes.

"Where?" He didn't sound soothing anymore.

"Um," Holly cleared her throat. "A lotta wandering hands on my butt, all over my back, and my b-breasts." Her voice dropped so low on that last word, he barely heard her.

"Anything else?"

"Yes."

"Fucking hell." LJ dragged a hand down his face.

"LJ, I'm fine. Just a little shaken up."

"Good for fucking you," he barked. "I'm about as far from fine as it gets, so tell me the goddamn rest."

Her mouth opened and closed a few times.

God, he was such a piece of shit. "I'm sorry, sugar. I'm not mad at you, I promise."

"I know," she said in a small voice that only made him hate himself more. "Okay, I'm just gonna spit the rest of it out. He pressed against me while I was bent over the car, and he was quite obviously hard. Then he told me I had two options. Ride to the station in the back of his car or sit in the front and show my appreciation for not being arrested."

Little Jack

"Jesus fucking Christ!" LJ roared as he slammed his open palm into the dashboard.

It came on fast. Faster than he could ever recall. One minute he sat in the truck, listening to Holly, and the next...tingling fingers, hazy vision, chest tightness, it all slammed into him with the force of a wrecking ball.

And then, nothing.

He never even had a chance to warn Holly.

CHAPTER TWENTY

One second Holly had been recounting the humiliating events of the past hour and the next she was staring in shock as LJ completely disappeared.

In his place was a man gripping the steering wheel so hard all color leeched out of his hands. A man who wouldn't have noticed if the world exploded around him. He breathed like an elephant sat on his chest. Choked, gasping breaths that couldn't have been effective at providing oxygen. His pupils had blown so wide, they eclipsed the hazel she loved so much, but what disturbed her most was the blank, lights-on-nobody's-home stare he cast out the windshield.

"LJ?" she asked. What the hell was happening to him? Was he sick? Having a heart attack? Stroking out? His entire body began to shake and the breathing she'd thought sounded so atrocious seconds ago now had the added horror of a high-pitched whistling. "LJ!" she yelled this time.

Nothing. No response whatsoever. Just as she pulled her phone out to dial the emergency responders, LJ emitted the most gut-wrenching whimper she'd ever heard. It was then, the light bulb went on, and Holly realized he was deep in a severe panic attack.

She dropped the phone and scooted along the bench until her front was pressed up against his side. His big body shook so violently, she had a hard time grabbing him, but with a little effort managed to hold his face between her hands much as he did when he'd kissed her.

God, was that only a few minutes ago? Seemed like days.

"LJ," she said in a soft, loving tone. "Baby, come back to me. You're okay. You're safe. I'm safe. No one is hurt." Was she acting ridiculous? Holly had no clue what to do for someone in this state. Maybe she should have called nine-one-one. The story she'd told him had triggered something horrifying in his mind. Maybe if she reassured him she was unharmed and not in any danger, he'd return to her.

She stroked his cheek and beard, repeating nonsense over and over. How they were safe, how strong she thought he was, how she loved his hands and mouth on her, how amazing his club brothers and their women were. Anything to break him out of the grip of the attack.

Nothing seemed to work. He trembled and struggled to breathe for long minutes. Sweat poured down his ashen face. His hands were fisted so tight, he was at risk for cutting his palms with his fingernails.

Just as Holly was about to give up and call for help, she looked into his eyes. His pupils had returned to a normal size and for the first time since he'd lost control, his gaze shifted to her.

"Keep talking," he said in a rasp that sounded like someone had taken a cheese grater to his vocal cords. "Keep touching me."

Holly didn't care how shitty he sounded; relief nearly had her sobbing. He was back or working his way back.

"Want to hear a funny story?" she asked as she ran her hands over his chest then up his arms. Since she hadn't been expecting an answer, she just plowed ahead when he remained silent. "You know I grew up outside of Tampa, Florida. We didn't travel much, or ever, when I was little, so my sister Joy and I really had no experience with cold weather. Neither of us saw snow until we were ten, I think." Thoughts of her sister always brought a combination pang of sadness and burst of happiness. Why this story came to mind, she had no idea. Maybe it was Joy, lending help and approval of the man Holly felt the driving need to comfort.

Thank you, Joy.

Always looking out for her, even in death.

She swallowed around a lump in her throat and forced down the ache. This moment was about LJ and what he needed from her. "A-anyway, we had this big old freezer in our garage. You know the kind that serial killers stuff their victims into in the movies?"

He didn't speak, but the tiny jerk of his chin was a victory she'd gladly claim.

"Joy was always so much more extroverted and daring than I was. I was the goodie two-shoes, and she was born to be the rebel. So, one day, I think we were about nine, if I remember correctly, she decided we should have a competition to see who could tough out cold weather the longest. It was close to Christmas and still shorts weather in Florida. I was always reluctant to follow along with Joy's crazy plans but did it anyway." Holly chuckled. Man, the trouble they'd gotten into. "She was my twin, you know? I'd have followed her anywhere and vice versa."

She cleared her throat as memories both sad and so damn wonderful bombarded her. "Back to the story. We grabbed our sleeping bags and stuffed ourselves in the freezer. Thankfully at the last second, I thought to prop the lid open. My mom found us about fifteen minutes later, blue-lipped, teeth chattering, and shivering our little butts off, but both too damn stubborn to admit defeat. My parents made us clean the whole garage for that one."

As she shook her head at herself, LJ chuckled, and Holly could no longer keep the tears at bay. She threw her arms around him and held on for dear life. His tree-trunk arms came around her and his heavy body sagged as though too fatigued to even remain upright. He tucked his face into the crook of her neck. Holly kept one hand around him and held the back of his head against her with the other. As she held him, she took steadying breaths and controlled her tears. Last thing he needed was to see her weeping and feel even worse than he obviously did.

"Welcome back," she whispered into his damp neck. "You scared me."

"I'm sorry, Holly. Christ, I'm so fucking sorry." His words were heavy with shame. "I'd hoped to never let you see me like that." He pulled out of her arms and stared through the window, completely avoiding her gaze.

Her heart broke for the damaged man who worked so hard to keep everyone in his life from seeing his pain. "Come on," she said as she rubbed his shoulder. What she really wanted to do was force him to look at her, but she had no idea how hard to push. "Let's go home. We'll talk about it there. I'm driving, and if you argue with me, I'll never bake for you again."

That had a heartier laugh coming from him, and he finally turned shame-filled eyes her way. That was something they had to work on. He never needed to hide anything from her. She wouldn't pity him or think less of him for the internal battles he fought.

"Most women threaten to withhold sex. You threaten to take away my sugar fix."

Holly snorted. "That's because I'm not stupid. Withholding sex punishes me as well as you." She winked, then climbed down from the mountain of a truck. LJ scooted along the bench seat, taking her spot. She made a fool of herself climbing back into the truck in the most ungraceful way possible, but LJ didn't seem to notice.

"I'm fucked up, Holly. Too fucked up for this." He shook his head then stared out the window once again. "Fucking loser," he whispered to his reflection.

Holly's fingers shook as she shifted the car into gear then grabbed his hand. "If I ever hear that kind of garbage from your mouth again, not only will I withhold the treats, I'll make you watch me eat your share."

Without turning, he shook his head, but considering his state, she took it as a small victory. They had a lot to discuss. Holly only hoped their budding connection held up to this first test because she wasn't ready to let go of LJ. This man who'd come to her rescue. This man who'd been so affected by her experience, he succumbed to a fight she hadn't been aware he struggled with.

After she pulled into the lot at their apartment complex, Holly parked the monstrous truck next to LJ's bike. Seeing as how it was her first day driving the thing, she figured the slightly off-kilter park job was good enough.

LJ, however, didn't react. He just sat still, staring out the windshield, probably not seeing a thing.

"LJ?" Holly said. "We're home." She stroked a hand up and down his arm. "Let's head on up."

Still nothing. His lack of response no longer frightened her as it had when he'd been mid panic attack. He blinked, and breathed in a slow, steady pattern, but just seemed lost in whatever self-hatred he'd begun to engage in.

Holly frowned. "LJ, I'm beat." And a little sore from being slammed against the hood of his truck, but she wasn't about to tell him that. "How about we lounge on the couch and watch something mindless for the rest of the day?"

He turned to her then. "Let's get you inside," he said, and got moving. After he hopped out of the truck, he came around to her side.

God, this man. As soon as she mentioned a slight amount of fatigue, he forgot his own troubles and mobilized to help her.

Hand in hand, they walked up the stairs and into LJ's apartment. Biscuit greeted them with licks and a wagging tail before plopping right back down on the extra-large dog bed LJ had purchased for his furry buddy.

"Are you hungry? Thirsty?" LJ asked her.

"Nah, just want to veg if that's okay."

"Sounds perfect."

They moved to the couch, and LJ flipped the TV to some cooking show Holly would have normally been all over, but this subdued LJ had her so thrown, she couldn't think of anything but drawing him out of the mental hole he'd crawled into.

From the outside, they looked like any couple cuddled up on the couch, enjoying a lazy Saturday afternoon. He wrapped his long arm securely around her. Holly's head rested on his chest, legs draped over his lap. But neither spoke, and LJ seemed to be as lost in thought as she was.

After about twenty minutes of pretending to watch the TV, Holly reached her limit. "LJ," she finally said, peering up at him. "We need to talk about what happened earlier. Both with Deputy Higgins and in the car afterward."

He muted the TV then gazed down at her. "We can definitely revisit what happened with Higgins, but as for the other…" He shrugged. "It's nothing. Just lost my temper over what happened to you."

Holly straightened but didn't move from her spot half on his lap. "That wasn't a loss of temper. Screaming, punching the wall, throwing a vase…those are things people do when they lose their tempers. Being unable to breathe, shaking, and basically blacking out seems like signs of a severe panic attack."

He shrugged then turned the sound back on the TV. "Don't know what to tell you. Just know how fucking pissed Higgins made me."

There he went, burrowing back into his mind and blocking her out. As hard as he tried to appear unaffected and nonchalant, his eyes reflected the pain and even worse, shame. He was so damn ashamed she'd seen him in that state. Any other time, being shut out in this manner would sting, but LJ's reaction only made her more determined to draw him out.

She wanted him. Wanted to be with him on good days and the shitty ones. She'd take LJ any and every way she could get the man.

And it was time to prove that in a way he'd find impossible to resist, even after all that had happened today.

Holly stood, stripping her diner T-shirt over her head. Left in only a sunny yellow push-up bra, she took two steps forward until she stood between his spread legs. Then she lost the bra as well. LJ's eyes widened and his nostrils flared. With his height, it'd be so easy for him to lean forward and taste her.

Both fists curled on his thighs as though he was fighting a battle to touch her. That wouldn't work. She wanted his hands all over her, erasing the disgusting touch she'd endured from Higgins.

"Fuck me, LJ," she said, eliciting a rumble from him.

He shook his head. "No, Holly, not now. Not like this. You're sore. You're bruised for fuck's sake," he said, pointing to a purple mark where her hip peeked out from her jeans.

"I'm fine, LJ. Pretty sure a good, hard orgasm will cure any soreness I might be experiencing."

His knuckles blanched. "I'm riding the line right now, sugar. Trust me, you don't want me this way. I'll be rough as fuck."

Holly's heart rate skyrocketed, and she soaked her panties. That was exactly how she wanted him. Hard enough to erase both their memories of the day. Right before his eyes, her nipples hardened to points nearly painful with need. With his gaze locked on her breasts, there was no way he missed it. No way the effect his words had went unnoticed.

A war waged in his eyes. One Holly vowed to win.

Something somewhere along the line had damaged this big beautiful man, and Holly couldn't stem the desire to wrap him in her arms and promise nothing would hurt him ever again.

But she couldn't do that, because someone was gunning for his family and she had no idea what the outcome would be.

CHAPTER TWENTY-ONE

If he made it through the next five minutes without succumbing to the most tempting offer he'd ever been given, LJ should be nominated for sainthood.

Holly stood before him with those juicy tits just two feet from his mouth. All he had to do was lean forward, take one in between his lips, and he knew, he just knew all the shit of the day would wash away.

He also knew he'd lose control in a different way and have Holly bent over the couch stuffed full of his thick cock while he pounded her like some kind of wild beast. "Holly, please," he said on a groan. "You keep pushing this, and it's gonna go somewhere you're not prepared for."

One blonde eyebrow rose, and she propped a hand on her luscious hip, cocking it to the side. Of fucking course it made her tits jiggle and nearly had him shooting his load without so much as a whiff of air against his cock. The damn thing screamed to be set free, so goddamned hard, it nearly punched its way out of his jeans.

Her coy smile only made his dick harder. "Oh, I think *it's* going to go exactly where I want it to," she said as she slid her hand down the front of her jeans.

Where the hell had this seductress come from and what had she done with his sweet Holly?

"He fucking bruised you, Holly. Put his goddamn filthy hands on you." With each word he spoke the need to erase the other man's touch from her body grew stronger. He wanted to fuck her so hard, the memory of any man before him, or promise of any after him would cease to exist. He wanted her screaming his name until her voice grew raw and her world consisted of nothing but his hands, his cock, his mouth.

And it'd be the same for him. Hell, she'd already eclipsed any woman he'd ever had. She did that the first time he kissed her.

"Which is exactly why I need your touch. Need you filling me up. Make it all go away, LJ." She coasted her hands back up her body, cupping her tits. They overflowed her hands and made his mouth water. "Take me, LJ. I'm yours."

Even after what she'd witnessed in the car, she not only wanted him, she demanded him. "For fuck's sake," he whispered, staring up at the ceiling. "Give me fucking strength."

"You already have strength. More than your fair share. And I love when you use it on me—oh!"

His arm snaked out, curling around her waist and dragging her forward in one swift move. Before Holly had the chance to react, his mouth was full of her gorgeous tits. He kissed, sucked, licked, and bit until she was a quivering mess in his arms. Her hands gripped his head, guiding him from left to right, wherever her need was greatest.

"Please, LJ," she said on a moan.

Christ, she tasted so good.

"Fuck," he said. He sunk his teeth into the flesh of her tit, hard. "Beg me again."

She gasped. "Oh, my God. Please. Please. Please. Forget the rest, and just fuck me. As hard as you warned me you would. Please, LJ, just go crazy."

So much for fucking sainthood.

LJ shot to his feet so fast, he almost knocked Holly clear over. Instead, he snagged her around the waist and dragged her toward the end of the couch. Standing behind her, he grabbed her hair and yanked her head to the side. The curve of her neck was a particularly sensitive spot for her, and her reaction to his tongue dragging up the column of her throat didn't disappoint.

She moaned and ground her ass against his cock. He sucked on her pulse point hard enough he'd be seeing the evidence for days while working her tits with hard tugs and rolls. Her skin felt like silk beneath his rough fucking fingers. Way too lovely for the likes of him.

But she said she wanted it. And she said she wanted it down and fucking dirty. Without ceremony, he unbuttoned her jeans and yanked them down with her panties. Not that he didn't fucking love to see her ass in whatever sexy panties she had on, but they were just in his way at the moment. With a hand at the center of her back, he gently shoved her forward until her upper body flopped over the arm of his plush couch. "Only one man gets to bend you the fuck over and have you." He ran his hands wherever he could reach. Her back, her ass, her sides. His touch was heavy as he stroked over her, dragging her skin along by his fingers. Last thing he wanted was to hurt her, but he couldn't be fucking gentle if his life depended on it. "Only my touch matters. I'm the only one allowed to see you or feel you like this. I fucking promise, Holly, that shit won't happen again. Memorize this touch, because it's the only one you get to feel."

Until she came to her senses and walked away from the fucking mess he was.

Holly trembled, hands propping her up on the couch. "Yesss," she hissed. "Just you, LJ."

He took one step back, removed his own jeans and boxer briefs. Once naked, he took in the sight of his woman, ass up, pussy drenched, waiting to be filled.

Christ, Holly should be required to greet him like this whenever he came home.

"Last chance to bail, sugar. Shit's about to get real."

"Jack, fuck me alrea—" He slammed into her to the hilt. "Oh, fuck!" she cried.

He was too big to be tunneling into her like that, but the warmth, heat, and near punishing clench of her pussy snapped the last thread of his control and he couldn't summon the brainpower to check in with her. He hammered her with brutal force. Gripping the soft flesh of her hips as though she'd disappear if he didn't hold as tight as possible, he thought of nothing but filling her to the brim with his cum.

Condom be fucking damned.

He'd flood her then watch it drip like a stamp of ownership.

Holly whimpered with every violent thrust. The tiny part of his brain that remained rational worried it was too much until she shouted, "Yes, LJ. Fuck me harder than you've ever fucked before."

Jesus Christ, this woman was perfect.

Loud smacks reverberated through the room each time their hips met. Holly fisted the cushion of his couch and used it to propel her body backward with every powerful jerk of his hips.

Nothing had ever felt this fucking good.

Holly was so wet, her juices ran down his thigh. Fuck, he was never showering again. His balls ached with the need to come, but he fought it for as long as possible.

"More, LJ," Holly practically screamed. "Give me more. Give me all of you."

Goddamn, this woman was going to destroy him. He grabbed her shoulder with one hand and fucked into her with choppy, ruthless strokes completely lacking finesse. She took every single one and begged for more.

"Fuck, sugar, you take me so fucking good. So fucking tight."

All of a sudden, Holly's back arched, and she screamed his name so loud they must have heard her back at the clubhouse. LJ could have been dead, and watching Holly go off like that would have still sent him spiraling into an orgasm so intense his vision blanked.

"Jesus fuck, Holly," he screamed as pleasure ripped through him, tearing down any and every defense he'd ever built. This woman fucking owned him.

He held her ass flush against his body, his cock buried deep as they floated down from the high. Once Holly's arms gave out and she sagged into the couch, he pressed open-mouthed kisses along the curve of her back. She was slick with perspiration and salty on his tongue.

With a sigh, he rested his head between her shoulder blades. The position couldn't be the most comfortable for her, but he suddenly found himself unable to meet her eyes. At least this way he wouldn't be forced to. It was time. Not only had she bared her soul to him, she'd witnessed him at his very worst and didn't so much as hesitate to comfort him at a time he should have been soothing her. She was an incredible woman and deserved to know why he reacted as he had in the truck.

"I was a Navy SEAL for four years," he said against her back.

Holly sucked in a breath. "What? I had no idea. I knew you served, but how did I not know that?"

"I don't talk about it much." He licked a bead of sweat from her back.

"You have PTSD," she said, and it wasn't a question.

"I do."

Beneath him, Holly wiggled. There went his reprieve. He stood, taking her with him and moved them to the couch. Holly lay sprawled on top of him with her chin resting on her stacked hands.

He couldn't meet her gaze; instead keeping his focus on the unmoving ceiling fan above. Despite how cowardly a move, he just couldn't stomach seeing pity in her gaze.

"Hey!"

The sharp bark of Holly's voice surprised him enough to have him looking at her.

Her narrowed gaze burned with intensity. Mouth set in a firm line, she peered into his soul for a moment. "You know it's nothing to be ashamed of, right? Please tell me you know that?"

He shrugged. Sure, he knew it with his rational brain—the fucking therapist he'd been ordered to see had mentioned it at least three times per session—but that never seemed to matter when he lost his shit in front of another person. And in front of a woman he wanted more than he was willing to admit?

Humiliation coming out his ass.

"I know."

"But knowing and living it are two different things, aren't they?"

Christ, she was amazing. So understanding and compassionate. The pity he'd feared?

Absent.

All he saw reflected at him was concern. Maybe a deeper emotion, but he refused to delve too far down that rabbit hole. Sure, he'd told her about his PTSD diagnosis, but he still had no plans of revealing the severity of his nightmares or ever subjecting her to a night sleeping next to him and his unpredictable behavior.

"So that's what happens?" Holly asked. "A panic attack like you had the car?"

He nodded and fingered a lock of her hair. "It's called a dissociative episode. I basically shut down, kinda disappear into my mind while simultaneously having a panic attack. I never remember what I do, or say, or how I act." Same with the dreams. They were just another form of the disassociation. A more severe, frightening form because he tended to lash out violently.

Holly's forehead wrinkled as she nodded. She appeared to really be taking in what he said and letting it rattle around in her brain. "And today's episode was triggered by what happened with Higgins?"

LJ blew out a breath. As much as he dreaded speaking of his emotional issues, the burn of embarrassment wasn't as strong as it had been the few other times he'd opened up. Holly's presence and supportive reaction made all the difference. The feel of her soft, sated body draped all over him kept him grounded and able to continue talking. "Sort of. The Navy had me see a therapist for a while." He huffed out a laugh. "Fuck, I hated it."

She gave him a small smile.

"But it did help. Helplessness seems to be my trigger. Like today, he fucking touched you, propositioned you, threatened you, and I was completely helpless to do a goddammed thing because he could and would have tossed both our asses in jail. I'm a man of action and being hobbled like that fucks with my head." Talking about it again was enough to have his breathing growing ragged.

Holly pressed a kiss to his chest. "I think you're incredible," she whispered.

He snorted. Maybe she was the one who needed a therapist. Delusions such as finding him incredible couldn't be healthy.

"You're the one who's amazing, Holly. One of the things I learned to combat the panic and prevent a full-blown episode if I feel it coming on is to use my senses to ground myself in reality. So I focus on things I can smell, or see, or touch...you get the picture. If I hear a song playing, I sing the words. If something is cooking, I focus on the scent. And my breathing, I always try to concentrate on the in and out to regulate my breaths. Noticing things happening in real-time can help keep me from getting pulled under. You couldn't possibly know that, yet you had the instinct to touch me and talk to me."

He pulled one of her hands to his lips, pressing a lingering kiss to her palm "Your sweet voice and your soothing touch made all the difference, sugar. Wasn't the first time, either. The night that fucker Schwartz crashed the party at the clubhouse, I felt myself slipping. You grabbed my hand, and I focused on the feel of you. You're my lifeline, baby."

The admission should have terrified him, but instead, he felt lighter than he had in ages. As though he wasn't quite so alone in carrying his burdens. He still bore the biggest and ugliest of them, but having Holly in his corner bolstered him in a way he wouldn't have thought possible from a relationship.

Holly shimmied the rest of the way up his body until she ended up in the perfect position to kiss him. Which she did. Gentle and soothing. So in contrast to the wild way they came together moments ago. "Anytime, anywhere, LJ. You need me to be your rock, or to hold on to you, I'll drop everything and come running as fast as I possibly can. Day or night."

Day or night. She said it with a hint of knowledge. As though she'd begun to put two and two together and no longer questioned the fact he refused to spend the night with her. And once again, she accepted it.

Accepted him.

As is.

Fuck. He tangled his fingers in the back of her hair. "Nothing I've done in my life has led me to deserve you." Not an exaggeration. She was just so damn good. He didn't know a man alive deserving of all that was Holly. But he planned to hold onto her with two hands until she inevitably wised up.

"I don't believe that for one second," she whispered against his lips before she kissed him.

Considering the strength of the orgasm he'd had ten minutes ago, his cock should have been out of commission for the next week, but the press of Holly's lips against his was all it took to have him springing erect once again.

He held her against him by the back of her head, devouring her mouth until she moaned in need. Finally, she tugged against his hold. When she met his gaze, her eyes were dazed, lips shiny and swollen. "You hear me, LJ? I don't believe that garbage for one single second. By the time I'm done with you, you'll believe you're a good man."

Little Jack

Then she winked and squirmed her way down his body. A few seconds later, the blistering heat of her mouth surrounded his cock, and LJ gave himself over to her care.

CHAPTER TWENTY-TWO

"Door opens in five. You excited?" Jazz asked as she joined Holly in the diner's new To-Go section behind the counter.

"Does feeling like I'm about to vomit all over the food I spent hours creating mean I'm excited?" Holly asked as her stomach cramped. Jam-packed full of muffins, pastries, pies, and a few surprises Holly had worked on, the display case looked ready. More ready than Holly felt. After the roller-coaster ride Saturday turned out to be, she and LJ had laid low and hung out around their apartment Saturday evening and all day Sunday. After he'd realized he hadn't used a condom, and had a minor freak out, they'd had the birth control-STD test conversation. Both were clean, and she was protected, so a big sigh of relief had been breathed all around. Once that business was out of the way, they'd ordered an extra-large pizza and garlic knots and made it last for a day and a half. The mellow end to the weekend was the perfect way to round out the stressful beginning.

And it only served to make her fall in deeper with LJ. A place she was loving.

Jazz threw back her head and laughed. "Give it a half-hour, girl, and you'll have 'em lined up around the building."

Her biggest fear hadn't been customers disliking her food. Without bragging, she could honestly say all the items she'd prepared were delicious. She'd tested them on enough opinionated bikers and their women over the past week. No, lack of interest was her true concern. What if no more than a handful of customers strayed in during the five hours her counter would be open? Mortifying didn't even come close to describing how she'd feel. It would be a dream-crushing scenario.

"If you say so," she said, working to purge the negative thoughts.

"I do." Jazz slung a slender arm around Holly's shoulders. "Relax. The hard part is done. We came up with a great menu, marketed around town, and you baked your ass off. Now it's time to have fun and enjoy success."

Holly snorted. "I wish my ass would disappear with all this hard work."

"Hey! That's my woman's ass you're talking about. Happens to be one of my favorite parts of her body, so watch it."

Holly's jaw dropped. Before her stood LJ and a few of the guys he worked with at Rocket's company. "How…I didn't even hear the bell ring."

"Snuck in the back," LJ said as he leaned across the counter to give her a loud smooch. "Wanted to be your first customer." With a glance at his utility watch, he said, "This place officially opens in five…four…three…two…one…now! All right, woman, I'm ready for you to serve me," he said with a wink.

Holly chuckled. The bit of laughter came easier than speaking since he had her all choked up. The damn man was so good both to her and for her. If only he realized his worth. "Wh—" She cleared her throat, freeing the emotions lodged inside. "What can I get you, sir?"

"Oooh, sir, we may have to play with that bit more. Later." Another wink.

The guys he was with snickered while Holly's face heated. "Just tell me what you want," she said with a roll of her eyes, but inside, her core tightened with need. LJ was too damn sexy for his own good. And if he wanted her to call him sir a time or two? She could get down with that. She'd pretty much be on board with anything he wanted to try if he kept doling out the kind of orgasms she'd been experiencing.

"You sure you want me to say it out loud?"

Now her face was practically on fire. She was about to clarify with "Tell me what you want to eat," but that would only encourage him. Instead, she rolled her eyes and pretended to be more miffed than she was. In truth, seeing LJ playful and lighter made her heart sore. Hopefully, it came from their conversation Saturday night. She imagined carrying around such a heavy secret weighed down his soul.

"All right, give me a large coffee, black," he said as though she didn't know exactly how he took his coffee. He also ordered an assortment of muffins and pastries for the guys at the job site. The men with him ordered their own breakfast, and by the time she'd checked them out, three people waited in line behind LJ.

Holly couldn't hide her giddy smile.

"Kill it today, sugar," LJ said as he blew her a kiss across the counter.

Holly was riding such a high already, she didn't care who saw her, she grabbed the open edges of LJ's cut, yanked him forward, and laid one hell of a kiss on him over the counter. Of course, she ended up leaving herself dazed as well.

"Better not be sending all your fucking customers off that way," LJ said with a teasing growl. He winked and was gone, leaving her swooning.

The To-Go idea took off like it'd been shot out of a cannon. Not once in the three hours since opening did Holly have an interruption in the flow. Customers raved about her creations and promised to visit frequently, daily for some. She'd never made so much coffee in her life, and by ten-thirty when Jazz came to give her a much needed fifteen-minute break, she was more than ready for a hot minute of rest. Her fingers ached from hours of hitting the register buttons again and again, her feet screamed from the horrible kitten-heel shoe choice she'd gone with, and she'd burned herself no less than three times on the evil coffee machine. But she couldn't remember a time she'd felt so satisfied with a day's work and only a few hours had passed.

Just as she prepared to flee the counter, her mother appeared at the front of the line. "Mom!" Holly said on a gasp. "Wow, uh, hi. Can I get you anything?"

They hadn't spoken since the night of the Hell's Handlers party debacle. Holly had assumed her father requested her mom keep some distance until Holly either came to her senses or crashed and burned. While she'd be lying if she said she didn't enjoy the absence of her doting mother breathing down her neck, she'd also be lying if she said she didn't miss her. They'd gone from smothering to nothing in the blink of an eye. Somehow, they needed to learn to co-exist in the center zone.

Her mother perused the display cases and said, "I'd love a cappuccino and a banana crunch muffin, but I was also hoping to talk to you for a moment. Any chance you'll be taking a break soon?"

Holly shot a quick glance at Jazz who nodded. "Um, yeah, I was just about to take fifteen minutes. Wanna grab a booth, and I'll be there as soon as I hit the restroom?"

She took her time, giving herself a minute at the sink to gather her thoughts and anticipate what her mom would say. More likely than not, she came to plead a case for Holly's father. If she bad-mouthed LJ, Holly wasn't sure how she'd react, but she wouldn't stand for it. Not here, in her new place of business owned by the ol' lady of one of the Handlers.

As she left the restroom, she spotted her mother seated in a booth, picking at her muffin. Slender her whole life, Cynthia always seemed to be trying some new diet fad. Recently, low-carb had taken over their household so that poor muffin was liable to be ripped to shreds but never consumed.

"Hey, Mom," she said as she slid in the seat across the table.

"Holly," her mother replied with a warm smile. She reached across the table and laid her hand over Holly's. "I've missed you."

"Me too, Mom. I don't like it when there is tension between us."

Her mother sighed. "I know things between you and your father are strained right now…" With a sniff, she squeezed Holly's hands.

"Mom…" Her voice cracked as she tried to keep her own emotions in check.

"I'm sorry, honey." A tear spilled down Cynthia's perfectly made-up cheek. "But I can't bear the thought of losing another daughter. Holly, it would kill me."

Of course her mother was afraid of losing Holly. She'd already suffered the unimaginable pain of having a child murdered. She loved her mother, truly loved her. Both of her parents. And taking a step back from them had her popping Tums. But they couldn't go on this way. She couldn't keep denying her own desires and putting her own life on hold because of guilt. They had to meet her halfway. Had to learn how to live without constant fear of any and every bad thing happening to Holly.

This unexpected heavy conversation was taking more energy than Holly had after the busy morning on her feet. Why, oh why, hadn't she snagged herself a cup of coffee first? "Dad and I had an argument, mom. He doesn't approve of some of my choices. We'll work it out. Just give it some time."

By now, that one tear had descended into full-on crying. "Can't you just give us this one thing? Can't you just walk away from this boy? You just met him. Just this one thing, Holly. For us. So we don't lose you."

Rubbing her sweaty palms on her denim skirt, Holly blew out a breath. She stared at the table. Like a coward. But what would she see if she raised her gaze. Pleading, begging, fear? "I can't do that, Mom," she whispered. "I have to start making my own choices. I have to be allowed to fail and maybe even experience some pain along the way."

Even as they caused her stomach to hurt, the words had a freeing effect, and Holly finally found the strength to meet her mother's watery gaze.

"I know that you're an adult and you have every right to make your own choices, but...but, you have no idea how devastating it is to lose a child. No mother should have to go through that, and the thought of something happening to you now has your father and I obsessing over every decision you make. All we want is to keep you safe and protected at all times."

"I love you and dad, and I understand why you feel the need to keep me in a bubble, but I can't live there anymore." No, she didn't know what it was like to lose a child. Shattering would be how she'd guess such a loss would feel. But she did know the devastation of losing a sister. A twin. Basically, her other half. And she lost her before they had the chance to experience life together. Her parents seemed to forget that when consumed by their own grief. But Holly felt she handled the loss better than either of her parents ever had. They'd put her in therapy almost immediately after the funeral, but never took care of themselves in such a manner. Without a professional to help to move forward in a healthy way, they hadn't moved forward at all. They were stuck twelve years back in time.

And they were trying to keep her back there with them.

She flipped her palm and squeezed her mother's hand. "Mom, you can't protect me at all times like you could when I was a child. That's just not physically possible. I know it's hard to hear, but it's also important you understand reality. It's time for me to have control over my own life, make my own friends, and go where I want without feeling like I have to keep you and dad apprised of every decision I make. That includes my dating life."

Her mom's eyes dulled. "Holly," she began.

"Nuh-uh." Holly lifted a hand. "LJ is not up for discussion unless you are genuinely interested in learning about him as a person and my relationship with him. I will not have the conversation with you about the evils of motorcycle clubs or how dangerous you think he is."

Cynthia's lips compressed into a thin line. Clearly, she didn't approve of that mandate. But miracle of miracles, she didn't push it. "You need to talk to your father."

Holly nodded. "I will. When things cool down a little and when I'm ready. This disagreement is not as catastrophic as you think it is. Trust me, okay? We'll mend our fences."

Cynthia nodded but didn't crack a smile or light back up. "You're leaving me little choice, Holly."

"I know. And I'm sorry, but I think you and Dad will see this is better for all of us in the long run. I want you two to enjoy your lives as well. I want you to be free of constantly thinking about me and where I am, what I'm doing. You still have a lot of living to do, Mom. There's a lot of fun to be had out there." She gave her mom a tentative smile.

"Um, that kinda brings me to something else I wanted to ask you."

It was then Holly realized Cynthia had torn her napkin into a crumbly pile of shreds on the table. Was she that nervous? The thought had Holly's heart going out to her mom. Her goal here wasn't to make her mother uneasy or anxious, just gently assert some long-overdue independence. "Sure, Mom, what is it?"

"I got these tickets to see that country singer you like. Carrie Underwood."

Holly's mouth dropped open. "Seriously?"

For the first time since the conversation began, Cynthia smiled. "Yeah, it's in Knoxville in about a month." She wrung her hands, and now it was Holly's turn to reach across the table and comfort her mother. "I was hoping you'd come with me. A little mother-daughter thing. We can make a night of it and have breakfast with your brother while we're there."

"That sounds really nice, Mom. I'd love to." And she meant it. Severing ties with her family wouldn't bring her any contentment. Mending fences and moving forward with a healthier sense of boundaries would. Maybe this was the start of a new mother-daughter relationship where they could spend time together, enjoy each other's company and share their lives without the burden of guilt, and without Holly needing to tell her parents where she was at all times.

Cynthia beamed and clapped her hands together once. Interlacing her fingers, she pressed her joined hands to her chest. "Oh, Holly, I'm thrilled. We'll have so much fun." She pulled out her phone. "Let me text you the date, so you won't forget it."

"Good idea, with how busy this morning has been my brain will be fried by the time I get out of here." Fifteen minutes had flown by in an instant. Time to get back behind the counter.

"Maybe while we're there we can do some shopping or go to a day spa," she said without taking her attention off her phone.

A few seconds later, Holly's phone chimed.

With a squeal of delight, Cynthia stowed her cell in her oversize handbag. "This will be great Holly. I bet getting away for a day or two will give you a chance to get some perspective. With a clear mind and some space, you might see things in a different light."

Whomp, whomp, whomp. Holly's heart sank. So much for a new and healthier relationship.

With that little bomb, her mom stood, kissed Holly on the cheek, and practically floated out of the diner.

Left frowning, alone and hurt in the booth, Holly couldn't shake the feeling she'd been played.

Big time.

CHAPTER TWENTY-THREE

Three weeks from the day the diner began selling Holly's products, LJ found himself enjoying life more than he had in years.

And there was only one reason for it.

Holly.

He'd spent every spare waking hour with her in some form or another. They had dinner together nearly every night. He hit the diner on the way to work both for some sugar from Holly and some sugar from her oven. She'd swing by his job sites for lunch whenever her schedule allowed. They watched movies, rode his bike through the mountains, hung out at the clubhouse, and went on dates with the other couples in the MC.

And they fucked. As often and in as many ways as possible.

LJ had smiled more in the past month than he had in fucking years. And his brothers loved fucking busting his balls over it. Maybe if he didn't have the sexiest woman on earth burning up the sheets with him, he'd take offense to their constant ribbing, but fuck it. He was happy, his dick was happy, and Holly was fucking happy as well. Only two things kept their relationship from absolute perfection.

Holly's father and LJ's refusal to fall asleep in her presence. Each night, after exhausting each other for hours with brain-melting sex, they retired to their own beds. Not once had Holly breathed a word about it. No complaints, no whining about being rejected, no questions. But it had to be killing her. What woman would accept an arrangement like that long-term?

None he'd ever met.

Though he had an idea Holly suspected something, she still deserved to know why he left her each night. He was just too much of a pussy to admit his reasoning.

And Holly's father... Not much improvement on that front. She'd spoken with him a handful of times, but he hadn't come around. Nor had he halted his attack on the MC. Which brought them to Copper and Shell's new backyard for a cookout LJ assumed he was only invited to because of his connection to Holly. And while he trusted his president, he had no idea why the man requested his and Holly's presence at a barbecue-slash-meeting of the executive board.

"Damn, brother, your woman can fuckin' bake." Maverick said as he sat his ass in an Adirondack chair next to LJ's while rubbing his flat stomach. A fire crackled about ten feet away. Everyone who'd been invited sat around the fire, drinking beer and polishing off the Baileys cheesecake Holly had brought along.

"Tell me about it." He squeezed Holly's hip where she sat perched on his lap chatting with Chloe.

"What's that?" She and Chloe both looked at Maverick.

"Just telling your man what a rockstar you are when it comes to baking shit. Hey, Thunder," Mav said to the prospect sitting on his right. LJ had yet to figure out why Thunder was at this quasi-meeting too.

"'Sup, Mav?"

Mav handed his empty plate to Thunder. "Fork me over another slice." He turned back to Holly. "You're gonna make me fat, woman."

LJ snorted at the same time Holly's cheeks pinked and she giggled. "Glad you like it, but I'm pretty sure you could eat the whole thing and not gain an ounce."

"I get plenty exercise." Mav shot her a wink. "Hey," he said around a mouthful of cheesecake. "You guys hear Thunder hooked up with Carli?"

From across the fire, Izzy groaned. "Ohhh, Thunder, come on. You kissed my cheek, man. Now I gotta burn half my face off."

"What?" he said with his mouth full and face the picture of innocence. "I was tanked and horny, and she was there." He shrugged.

Holly leaned back against LJ's chest and asked, "Who's Carli?"

"She's a club whore who tried to stir up all kinds of drama when Steph and Mav got together," Shell said. "She had some misguided idea he was going to make her his ol' lady because he liked to...spend time with her." She sent a pointed look Maverick's way.

"Look, can I help it if my dick has the power to make women go crazy?"

Holly burst out laughing as the rest of the women groaned and rolled their eyes. Shell blew a raspberry and gave Mav a thumbs' down. "I thought she'd left town. Is she back?"

"She did, and she is," Thunder said. "Something about a sister being here."

"I gotta admit the woman had serious skills. Even if the devil sent her here from hell-o, baby!" Mav said as he suddenly noticed Stephanie standing over him with a significant frown. "You look so pretty tonight."

"Nice try," she said as she walked around his chair. With a bit of a sinister smile on her face—the kind LJ hoped to never see from Holly—Stephanie plopped down on Maverick's lap.

Hard.

Actually, it was less of a plop and more of a dropped-her-full-body-weight-on-him.

"Oh, fuck me, that hurt," Maverick said with a pitiful whimper as she no doubt landed on his dick.

"No," Steph said in a haughty tone. "I don't think I'll be doing that for a while."

LJ winced. Damn, he didn't envy the man. That couldn't have felt good. Not that Mav didn't have it coming.

"Nice, Steph," Izzy called out. "I've taught you well."

The rest of the women chuckled while the men winced in sympathy.

"Okay, everyone sufficiently fed, and good with their drink?" Copper suddenly asked. He'd been quiet throughout dinner, which did nothing to settle LJ's unease.

Shell, who sat curled up on Copper's lap, gave him an encouraging smile. Seemed none of the men wanted their women out of touching distance.

"I'm gonna let Thunder get started and let him tell you all what went down last night." As Copper spoke, he shifted his gaze around the room. Did it linger just a little too long on Holly, or was that LJ's imagination?

After draining his beer and dropping his empty plate to the grass, Thunder propped his forearms on his knees. His eyes shifted to Holly as well, and he had an almost apologetic half-smile.

What the hell had happened? By reflex, LJ tightened his arm around her waist as if he could protect her from whatever was coming.

"Sheriff arrested me last night."

Holly gasped, making Thunder wince. What the fuck was Copper thinking, inviting her here? She didn't need to hear any of this shit.

"Simmer down, LJ," Copper said. "I can see you starting to boil over there."

"It's okay, LJ," Holly whispered to him as she stroked his forearms where they lay across her waist. "It's reality. I know how complicated the mixing of my two worlds is."

"What the fuck did they arrest you for?" Jigsaw asked. He sat next to Izzy, their hands intertwined.

"Solicitation." Thunder waggled his eyebrows as though they weren't talking something serious, and he didn't give a shit about spending time behind bars. Which in all honesty, the guy probably didn't. "He caught me getting blown out in the alley behind the strip club."

"Lovely," Izzy muttered none too quietly.

The rest of the group, including Thunder, snickered. "Hey, what can I say, she saw me dance and couldn't keep her hands off me. I was hard, so…there you have it."

Holly wrinkled her nose.

"Anyway, I'd just finished my set when this chick came on hot and heavy. She dragged me out back and went to town. I hadn't even had time to grab my money from my g-string, so when she yanked it down dolla bills scattered all over the ground." He made a motion with his hands like he was scattering money all around.

"Oh, this story just gets classier and classier," Izzy said.

"He's a stripper?" Holly whispered.

LJ chuckled against her ear. "Yup."

She cocked her head. "Huh. Yeah, I guess I can see it. I bet that boy can move."

"Hey!" LJ tickled her side. "Don't you picture him in anything other than a fucking snowsuit."

"But no money changed hands for the act?" Zach asked.

"Nope." Thunder shrugged. "I've done it a handful of times. If a woman wants to pay me to fuck her, why the hell would I turn that down? Ya know?"

"You want a list of reasons?" Izzy asked.

Holly barked out a laugh then covered her mouth. "Sorry," she said behind her hand. "That was funny."

"Damn straight it was, sister." Izzy held her hand out for a high-five which Holly gladly gave. LJ stroked a hand up and down her back as she leaned far forward to reach Izzy. Pretty damn nice having a woman there with him. Of course, that nice feeling was about to be shot to shit.

"Anyway, I'm pretty sure it was some kind of set-up, because the cops came in hot and heavy like they fucking knew I'd be out there. Dragged me to the sheriff's office. I got handcuffs, fingerprints, the works. Took their sweet fucking time sorting it all out too. Had me in lock-up about fifteen hours. That shit sucks, man."

With a groan, Holly said, "Thunder, I'm—"

"Don't," Copper said in a tone so harsh, Holly jumped. Of course, she was gonna take this on herself, which was exactly why she shouldn't be there. LJ wanted to place his hands over her ears to keep her from hearing any of this shit.

Mouth agape, Holly stared at Copper.

"Look," he said. "It's no secret that your old man has it out for my club. Now, I wanna be fully above board with you because I can see how good you are for my brother." He glanced at LJ then focused back on Holly. "You deserve to hear what's going on from us instead of from some gossip."

Shame twisted LJ's insides. Maybe he should have put a little more faith in Copper.

"T-thank you," Holly said. Her rubbing his arm turned to gripping him with surprising strength.

"Also gotta tell you, I approached LJ to find out if he was willing to work you for information from your father a few weeks ago when you two first started up."

"Oh, Copper," Shell said with a groan as she smacked him on the chest. "Seriously?"

Holly stiffened so fast, she nearly jerked out of LJ's hold.

Christ, Copper was lucky LJ trusted him as much as he did. Because were he anyone else, LJ would have already pounded him into the ground.

"Don't get your panties in a wad, you two," Copper said, holding up his hands. "Holly, he flat out told me no. Didn't even give it a second of thought. Just want to put that out there because we are going to have to do something about this bullshit investigation. We've tried enduring it until it passed, but the fake claims and harassment have only escalated. Your pops is fucking up our businesses, and that needs to stop. But I want you to know, Holly, we won't use you against your pops or vice versa. None of us are above getting down and dirty to fight our battles, but we don't fuck with family. LJ is family and so are you by extension."

Holly hadn't relaxed her tense posture. Pride surged in LJ as she straightened her shoulders and looked Copper right in the eye. The six-foot-five, redheaded, bushy-bearded outlaw intimidated even the toughest of men. Something the MC counted on plenty of times to assert their position.

"Thank you," she said. "For being honest with me. I just have one question, and I hope you'll continue being honest with me."

Beneath the beard, Copper's lips quirked.

The man liked Holly. A lot. Not a requirement for LJ, but a definite bonus. Having his club's approval, especially the leader of that club, went a long way.

"Fair enough," Copper said. "Fire away, whisk."

All eyes fell to Holly who stood her fucking ground and didn't back down. Damn, she was something. "Are you planning to hurt him? My father."

As he inhaled a slow breath, Copper stroked his beard. The attention that had been on Holly shifted to him.

"Of course not," Shell said with a frown. Then she elbowed Copper. "Right, Copper?"

"You asked me not to lie, so here it is straight. No, I'm not going to hurt him and I'm not going to authorize anyone in my club to hurt him. Physically or otherwise. Now, were you not in the picture, we would definitely turn up the heat and try to make his life...uncomfortable. But you're here, and you mean something to LJ. And I'd be lying if I said I didn't fucking like you myself. You make a mean cheesecake. We are going to work through the club's lawyers to get the sheriff's office to back the fuck off."

"Okay," Holly said as she released a breath. "That's good. Thank you."

"I'm not done," Copper went on. "Since I promised honesty, I need this to end and soon. So the club is actively working to have certain officers removed from the police force. Schwartz and Higgins to name a few. We're hoping to get your pops to back off without jeopardizing his job, but I can't one hundred percent guarantee it."

LJ held his breath. The information share was more than LJ expected. Not great news, but a real fucking effort on Copper's part. If it weren't for Holly, the club would be moving in a very different direction in their efforts to get the target off their collective backs.

"All right," she said with a nod. "Not that it matters," she said with a breathy laugh, "but I can get behind that plan."

There went Copper's lips again. Quirking in a sort of half-smile. "It matters," he said.

"Uh," Holly said. "Did I hear you right? Did you call me whisk?"

"Sure did," Copper replied as he lifted his beer to his lips.

"Why?" Shell's forehead scrunched. "You could have picked a million better baking related nicknames, babe. LJ calls her sugar."

"Don't even think about it, prez," LJ said with a mock scowl that had Holly pressing a kiss to his cheek.

"Shit got all scrambled when she popped up in my club," Copper said.

For about five seconds, the crackling fire was the only sound. Izzy ended up being the first to lose it, but the rest of them followed shortly behind until everyone laughed like fools.

"Shit, Cop," Mav said. "Think we all needed that."

The conversation lightened after that. Tomorrow, in church, the patched members would work out a plan of action, but they could enjoy the rest of the night and the company before diving back into the heavy shit.

"Come on," LJ said, patting Holly's hip. "Grab a drink with me." He didn't give a fuck about a drink, but they could use a hot second alone. When they reached the house, which was a good sixty feet from the fire pit, LJ dragged Holly through the French doors.

They were the only two inside the quiet house unless Beth counted, but she'd been fast asleep upstairs for the past hour. Copper and Shell purchased the house about a month ago. At least three times the size of Shell and Beth's itty bitty two-bedroom home, she'd been in love with the place the moment she saw it. As for Copper, anything was better than living at the clubhouse as he'd done for a few years.

"This place is great," Holly said as they walked through the family room. "Shell did a fantastic job decorating. Seems like the perfect combination of the two of them, right?"

Um, what the hell did he know about decorating? "Sure?"

Holly laughed. "I'd describe it as mountain chic. The wood beams, the brick fireplace, and the dark cabinets, kinda remind me of Copper while the cozy furniture and pops of bright color are all Shell. They did a nice job merging their lives, is all I mean."

Well, he couldn't argue with that. "They did. They're a strong couple who's been through some unimaginable shit. I'll tell you about it sometime. Too deep for tonight."

"Thought we were grabbing drinks?" Holly asked, halfway to the kitchen, as LJ sat on the couch.

"In a minute." He snagged her hand and tugged her down next to him. "Wanted to check in first."

Beaming at him, Holly stretched up and kissed his mouth. She'd meant it to be short and sweet, but he needed more. As she started to pull back, he grabbed the base of her skull and held her close for a proper kiss.

"Dayum, LJ," Holly said as she panted and swiped her thumb over her lower lip. "You trying to get us caught going at it on our friends' couch? 'Cuz I'm thinking we might not be invited back."

Our friends.

It was fucking stupid how happy those two words made him. "Depends who walks in on us. If it's Mav, he'll just whip out his phone and start filming. Then we'll be in a legal battle over the rights to the media files after he uploads them to some home porn site and makes big money. And that just sounds like way too much work, so maybe you're right and I shouldn't kiss you like that again until we leave." He winked.

"Well, I didn't say that…" She rested her head on his shoulder.

"Where's your head at with everything Copper said tonight?"

She fell silent, and he gave her the moment to formulate her thoughts. Holly wasn't reactionary, which LJ appreciated. He spent his days with hot-headed assholes at the construction sites then even hotter-headed fuckers at the clubhouse. Coming home to someone even-keeled made for a nice end to each day.

Would be even nicer if he could wake to her as well.

"I'm struggling," Holly admitted. "Not so much with what Copper said. From his perspective, I get it. His family is being threatened and he needs the threat to go away. I'm sure if it wasn't for me, he'd be taking a different approach, but I greatly appreciate how he's trying to go a legal route instead of beating anyone bloody in the street."

Most likely Higgins would end up that way, but for now, that info was need-to-know. And Holly did not need to know it. What Higgins had coming was independent of the shit with the club. It was fucking personal.

"But?" He played with her hair, something that nearly made her purr every time.

"No but, not really. I just wish there was a way to break through to my father and get him to see your club isn't what he thinks. He's blinded by his hatred and living in the past." Holly sighed. "I worry he's going to cross a line he can't come back from."

The sheriff had been dancing on that line for weeks. At this point, with the number of Handlers who'd been pulled over for bullshit, the quantity of ridiculous searches of the clubhouse and places of business, the club had a straight-up claim for harassment. Most likely that was the route Copper would play, but he'd try to pin most of it on Schwartz and Higgins to keep Holly's father out of the fire. Best case scenario, the club's attorney could scare the sheriff straight with a hard lesson in the detriment of police harassment by making an example of two of the deputies.

"I just keep wondering if he's going to authorize one of his deputies to hurt one of you guys or something, and it's making me sick." Holly placed a hand over her stomach.

"Babe, you think there's one of us who couldn't take on any of those deputies?" Maybe a little levity would haul her out of the black hole she'd tumbled down.

"Imagine something like what happened to Thunder. Someone gets arrested on bullshit charges. What do they do? They make you lie face down and they cuff you."

"Sugar..."

"Do you know how vulnerable you are then? What if one of the deputies gets frustrated because their tactics aren't getting them anywhere?"

"Holly..."

"What if it's Maverick, and he runs that smart mouth of his and makes a deputy so angry that they flip out. What if—"

"Holly!" LJ yelled as he grabbed her shoulders and gave a gentle shake.

"Oh, my God." She covered her face with her hands. "I'm spiraling."

"Yeah," he said with a laugh. "You are."

"I don't want any of you guys to get h-hurt." Her breath hitched as she choked on a sob. "I'm sorry. I'm a mess."

Engulfing her in his arms, he held her tight to his chest. "Sugar, you're the most perfect mess I've ever met."

That finally got a small huff of laughter.

"None of us are going to get hurt. The men working for your father aren't stupid enough to risk jail time or losing their badges. Harassment is a hard claim to prove. All this shit they're pulling is child's play, and we can handle it. I promise you we'll all be okay."

"He's my dad," she said in the most defeated voice he'd ever heard. "I've already lost a sister." The words seemed like an apology for not cutting the man out of her life.

"I get it, babe. I really do. He's your blood. No one's gonna ask you to ax him from your life. I know it's a fucking mess right now, but we'll figure it out."

"We?"

Shit. He sucked. Was he so bad at this relationship thing she didn't even know he had her back? "Yeah, sugar, we."

"I like that."

So did he.

Too fucking much.

CHAPTER TWENTY-FOUR

"I'm dead serious, Holly. That motherfucker lays one hand on you, he so much as brushes a piece of lint off your shoulder, and I'll feed him his nuts before he has a chance to say biker cock. Jesus, I can't believe I'm allowing this."

Holly chuckled and rolled her eyes as she took the exit from the highway directed by her GPS. "I'm sorry," she said into the hands-free phone system as she coasted to a red stoplight. "Can't believe you're *allowing* this? And why the hell would Rick ever say biker cock?" The light turned green, and she hit the gas to drive the last few miles to Rick Schwartz's house.

"You know what I mean, sugar." LJ's voice turned to a whispered growl. Poker night at the clubhouse didn't allow for much privacy. "I don't like this. I don't trust him, and I don't like this. I wish you'd let me put a prospect on you tonight."

Holly had been floored when she won that argument. She'd thought for sure LJ would have had someone tailing her whether she wanted it or not, but he'd respected her wishes and skipped the chaperone if she promised to check in every half-hour. "I know you don't. Believe me, you've made it clear. But my mom called in tears, LJ. She was devastated she had to back out on this concert. It's all she's talked about for the past month. She sprained her ankle, what was I supposed to do?"

"Uh, say no when she told you she'd given her ticket to Dicky?"

Holly sighed. They'd had this exact same conversation six times in the ten hours since her mom called hysterical and heartbroken.

"Look, my dad—"

"Almost jizzed himself over the idea of you going on another date with that fuckwad?"

Holly wrinkled her nose as she made a left. "Um, could you maybe not use the word jizz in a sentence with my dad?" she said into the car's Bluetooth.

The line grew silent.

"Anyway, my dad actually got on the phone because she was crying so hard. It was the first time he's spoken more than two words to me in weeks. He told me himself how crushed my mom was she couldn't go with me. How she was supposed to have two daughters to spend time with, but one was stolen from her. How she wants us to be close and she's so devastated that she hurt herself. I just..."

I can't say no to them.

"I'm trying to build a new kind of relationship with them. Maybe this is the first step toward a more normal parent-child bond."

"I'm gonna say something you don't want to hear."

"Yikes, that doesn't sound good." Holly scanned the house numbers for seven-six-two-nine... There it was. After parking along the curb, she killed the engine but remained seated. "What is it?"

"Has it crossed your mind they might have planned this all along?"

"Ha! You mean she pretended to sprain her ankle, and getting me to go out with Rick is all part of some master matchmaking scheme?"

LJ didn't say anything.

"LJ, come on," she said, but the words tasted bitter. She opened her mouth again to tell him there was no way, but the argument died on her tongue. "Shit." Her shoulders sagged.

Had she been hoodwinked so easily? Would her parents have played her that way? Or was LJ turning into a conspiracy theorist?

"I'll come back. I'll make an excuse and go join the ladies for girls' night." She grabbed the key which was still in the ignition. Just as she went to turn the car on again, LJ's heavy exhale came through the line.

"Stay," he grumbled. "You're there. You've been so excited about that goddammed concert."

She really had been. And she was there... Maybe Rick would even spill some beans about the department's plan for the MC.

"He won't touch me, LJ. I have less interest in him than Jazz has about being one of Screw's conquests."

Finally, LJ laughed. Over the past month, Screw had dialed up the attempts to nail Jazz, and she'd pushed back just as hard.

"I know, sugar, and I trust you. But if that fucker so much as breathes too close to you—"

"Yeah, yeah, yeah, the ripping of nuts and the biker cock thing. I got it." She paused for a second. "I really am sorry, LJ. Please try to have fun tonight. It's killing me that you're so upset over this. Would it help if I told you I want him to be my date about as much as you want him to be my date?"

He grunted. "It would help if you told me you'd drop to your knees and suck my dick the moment you walk through the door."

"Done," Holly said with a grin, though LJ couldn't see it through the car's Bluetooth. Men were easy. Promises of sexual favors forgave a world of sin.

"Babe," he said, tone full of a warning that had her shivering in response. Yeah, he wasn't the only one that'd be getting off once she got home. For the life of her, she'd never imagined a scenario where she had no desire to go to a Carrie Underwood concert. The country star had been Holly's favorite singer for years. But that bitch better sing fast because this obligation could not be over fast enough.

"I have to go. I'm here," she said then winced at the silence from his end.

"All right," he finally said. "Sugar?" This time she heard the sincerity in his voice.

"Yeah?"

"I really don't want him to touch you."

"Neither do I, LJ. Promise it won't happen, okay? I already have a man. And he's more than enough man for me. In fact, there's probably enough of him for two women."

"No shit?" All of a sudden, he sounded like a kid on Christmas. "You looking to invite a friend to bed with us?"

"Goodbye, LJ," she said with an exaggerated sigh and a roll of her eyes.

His laugh was the only response she heard before disconnecting the call.

Holly stared at Schwartz's house. This thing with LJ had progressed to a place she absolutely loved, except for one giant elephant that walked into the room every damn night. The fact that LJ still hadn't spent an entire night with her. She hadn't pushed it, slightly nervous about bringing it up because she sensed his reasoning was more than the typical commitment-phobic guy nonsense. What frustrated her more than the lack of sleeping next to him was the fact he didn't seem comfortable even talking about it with her. That was a hard pill to swallow.

"All right," she said to no one. "Get out of your head, and let's get this over with."

Holly trudged up the driveway to the front stoop of Rick's surprisingly charming ranch-style house. With a brick façade and navy blue shutters around four front windows, the place had a cozy vibe to it. After a fortifying breath, Holly knocked on the blue door that matched the shutters.

"'S open! Come on in," came the muffled reply.

Holly pressed down on the lever, pushed the door open, and stepped into the foyer of Rick's house. First impression: the man needed to watch some HGTV. Bare white walls greeted her, no rug or mat on the worn linoleum floor, and a few unopened twelve-packs of beer stacked halfway down the hall. "Rick?"

"Yeah, babe, in the kitchen. Come straight to the end of the hall."

Holly winced at the endearment. When LJ called her babe, her insides turned to jelly. When the guys in the MC did it? She took it in stride. Actually, she liked it. It was sisterly in some way, which made no sense, but she rolled with it.

With Rick? Not so much. Seemed somehow…sleazy.

She walked down the sparse hallway until she entered the quintessential stereotype of a man's kitchen. Open pizza box on the black countertop. Empty beer bottles lined up near the trash can. A pristine oven that didn't look like it'd ever been used. A neon Blue Moon beer sign was the only decoration she'd seen so far. The monstrosity hung above an unvarnished round wood table with two chairs.

"Damn, woman, you sure can rock a pair of tight jeans."

Holly turned her head to the left and found Rick leaning against his small kitchen island. His eyes shone, and the tip of his nose practically glowed red. A beer bottle dangled from one hand with another six empties near the box of half-eaten pizza on the counter.

"Oh, uh, thanks." Was he on his seventh beer? No way. It was six on a Saturday evening, and he'd planned to be the driver to Knoxville.

He took an unsteady step away from the island and toward her. "Too bad you're giving all that away to a piece of trash."

At once, Holly's blood ran cold. He was drunk off his ass.

"Rick," she said with a shake of her head. "Can we please not do this? I came as a favor to my parents. I understand how awkward this is, but we're here, and we have the tickets, so let's just try to make a fun evening of it. Huh? I'll drive."

"Giving it to a fucking biker," he continued as though she hadn't spoken. "I don't get it." As he talked, he gestured with his hands, spilling a stream of beer onto his linoleum floor. The mess went completely unnoticed by him. "Just don't get it."

Could this get any more uncomfortable? "So, uh, how long have you lived here?"

Please accept the change of subject.

"Heard a rumor that Little Jack has a monster cock. That what you're looking for? A giant cock?"

What the hell? "You did not just ask me that. You know what, Rick, I know I made a promise to my father, but I don't think I can go through with this. I'm gonna head out."

She spun on her heel and started for the door at a rapid clip. Halfway to salvation, a hand clamped down on her wrist and yanked her back. She slammed into his chest, hard. Her momentum nearly toppled the wobbly man, and on instinct, she reached out to steady him.

Somehow, they ended up in reversed positions, with him now blocking her path to the door.

Shit.

"He thinks he's so fucking tough. They all do. Think they're untouchable. Well, they have no idea what's coming for them. No idea how your father is going to burn their club to the ground."

Holly's belly ached like her stomach acids were burning a hole straight through every layer of the organ. Now, when LJ asked, she'd have to tell him Rick touched her. That thought almost made her more nauseated than thinking of her father's scheme to take down the motorcycle club.

"Rick, I need to leave, and I think you need to stop drinking and lie down for a bit." Would he even remember this encounter in the morning? Would he wake wondering what the fuck happened and curious over the fact he couldn't recall a single moment of the concert?

"Sure, LJ's big," Rick went on, with a laugh. He tried to take a step closer to her but ended up listing too far to the right and careening into the wall. "He's a big motherfucker, but I bet he can't fight for shit. Bet I could fucking take him."

Take him where? What was going on? Holly could barely follow this conversation. Before she had the chance to respond, Rick jumped and somehow managed to land in a fighter's stance without falling flat on his face. "I could so fucking take him."

She'd landed herself in a scene straight out of a kung-fu movie.

Rick bounced on the balls of his feet then quickly air-punched through some kind of boxing combination. He had large hands and meaty fists. With each bounce, he inched closer to Holly until one fist whizzed by, way too close to her head. "Jesus, Rick. Watch where you're swinging those things! You almost took me out."

With a laugh, he continued to fight an invisible opponent with all the coordination of a jellyfish. After a few more punches, he lunged forward as he threw a jab with his left. His damn fist came within an inch of her nose. So close, Holly had to jerk back to avoid a bloody nose. "Rick, seriously!" she said, practically yelling this time. Something had to snap him out of his drunken biker hatred.

"I'd lay him out flat, Holly. Mark my word, that biker won't stand a chance against me."

"Rick!" she shouted. Another fist aiming for an invisible LJ came flying toward her face. Holly tried to dodge it, but Rick's aim and depth perception had been shot to shit a few beers ago. His fist connected with the tender cheekbone just below her right eye with the force of a Mack truck.

"Oh, ow!" Holly cried as pain made her face feel like it had exploded into a thousand pieces.

"Fuck!" Rick said. He lurched toward her and Holly wasn't able to stop him since she'd doubled over, cradling her throbbing face.

"Don't touch me," she screamed as he tried to lift her upper body. She wrenched away only to whack the back of her head against the wall. Fuck this night sucked a big one.

"I didn't mean it," Rick said, suddenly seeming almost sober. "Let me take a look."

"No!" She scurried past him, tears streaming down the right side of her face. Shit, the entire thing felt like it was growing by the second. "Please just stay right there." Sounded like she had a mouthful of cotton balls.

Finally, Rick respected her wishes and remained in his hallway, with his hands dangling at his sides and a stricken expression.

Holly tried to run, but each step jolted a shot of agony through her swollen cheek. Instead, she power-walked out the door, down the driveway, and to her car. She practically dove into the driver's seat then closed the door. Now she had to make the thirty-minute trip back to her house with one eye near swollen shut.

Then she had to face LJ.

The thought of it had her opening her door and vomiting onto the asphalt. Or maybe that was the pain, so intense she could barely think. Somehow, she had to find a way to drive, because there was no way in hell, she planned to remain parked outside Rick's house for more time than absolutely necessary

Holly closed her one functional eye and leaned back into her seat. After counting to twenty and breathing in and out as slow as possible, she reached up and unfolded the visor mirror.

"Oh shit," she breathed. Gruesome was too kind a word to describe the morbid state of her face. The swelling was epic. Her right eye was already rimmed with a deep, dark purple circle and puffed up like a bubble gum bubble. Purple bruising also mottled her jaw. It looked like she'd taken a massive beating instead of just one hard punch.

Her face needed ice. Unfortunately, it had to wait until she made it home because stopping somewhere wasn't an option.

Not with that face. LJ would be occupied with poker for the next few hours. Maybe she could shoot him a text claiming a stomachache. If she made it to bed before he returned home, she had a chance of postponing his impending detonation until tomorrow.

Took three tries, but Holly managed to get the keys in the ignition. Two seconds after the engine turned over, her gas light lit like Rudolph's nose.

"No," she whined. "No, no, no, no, no. This cannot be happening." Her little old Jetta had scary few miles between the empty light igniting and running out of gas. She'd never make it home without filling her tank.

Fighting tears, Holly navigated to the nearest gas station. Only one other car idled next to a pump, and she chose the farthest spot from them.

As she waited for the tank to fill, Holly kept her head down and hair curtaining her face. Wasn't much, but hopefully, it'd be enough to keep any other patrons who came upon her from noticing her face.

When the pump clicked off, Holly straightened and removed it from her car. Just as she was returning the nozzle to the rack, a voice from her right said, "Holly? Is that you?"

Shit, shit, shit.

A voice she recognized. Her stomach bottomed out. Faced with no other choice, Holly turned toward the newcomer. Bob Tanner, her parents' next-door neighbor stared at her, jaw hanging and eyes bugging.

"Oh, my God, Holly, are you okay?" The portly man who sported the same greasy combover all four times she'd met him took a step toward her.

Holly held a hand up between them. As best she could with the intact side of her face, she gave him a half-smile. Pain shot up her cheek, nearly bringing her to her knees. "Hi, Mr. Tanner. I apologize for the shock. Had an accident in my self-defense class." With a weak chuckle, she pointed to the mess of her cheek. "Took a hard elbow to the face. Guess I need a few more lessons."

The attempt at levity fell as flat as Mr. Tanner's compressed lips. The pity in his eyes told her he wasn't buying a single second of her pathetic cover story.

"Do you need medical attention?"

Did she? Maybe. All she knew was she hurt. Bad. And wanted nothing more than to crawl between her sheets and sleep the disaster of this night away. Preferably with LJ's strong body wrapping her in a protective cocoon of strength. But, of course, that was about as likely to happen as a herd of zebras stampeding out of Tanner's ass.

"No, sir, I'm, really okay. Please don't give it a second thought."

He opened his mouth as though to protest, then he shook his head. "All right. If you're sure. I'd get some ice on that as soon as possible though."

Ya think? Holly nodded and hummed her agreement. "Thank you, Mr. Tanner. You have a nice evening."

How long did she have before he was on the phone calling her father? Five minutes? Fewer? Maybe as few as two.

"You try to have a good one, too," Tanner said with a nod before turning toward the gas station's convenience store.

Once out of earshot, Holly let out a furious curse. Her legs started to tremble. Time to go before she went into full-on freak out mode.

She scrambled back into the car and peeled out of the gas station as fast as possible. The pain continued to intensify, almost faster than she could tolerate. With a swimming head, she white-knuckled the steering wheel and forced herself to remain focused on the road.

Fifteen core-rattling minutes later, Holly pulled into the apartment complex's lot. LJ's bike sat in its usual spot.

Shit.

Seven pm. What the hell was he doing home? Poker night should have lasted until ten at the earliest followed by drinking and general craziness. No way should he be home already.

Her phone chimed. Holly grabbed it from her purse.

Mom: Have a great time, honey. Text us when you're home.

With a harsh laugh, Holly jammed the phone back in her purse and left the car.

On the very tips of her toes, she climbed the steps to the second floor. Three goals dominated her mind. Ice, ibuprofen, and sleep.

Outside her door, she held her breath while trying to insert the key in the lock with quivering fingers and fucked up vision. If LJ heard her, it'd be game over. She needed the next few hours to fortify herself to face his inevitable fury. And to think of a way to keep him from committing murder.

The click of nails on the vinyl floor came from behind her closed door. Her furry welcome wagon. Since she couldn't fall asleep in LJ's arms, cuddling with her other man would have to do.

Biscuit whined.

"Shh, boy," Holly whispered as she missed again with the key. At the sound of her voice, Biscuit let out a deep woof. Followed by another. And another. "Shit, shit, shit! It's okay, buddy. I'm coming. Please be quiet."

Since the universe really seemed to have it in for her tonight, LJ's door opened, and he appeared. She couldn't see him since he was on her busted side, and she was staring at the ground.

"Sugar? What the hell are you doing home?"

"Uhh," Holly said, keeping her head down and quickly pulling her hair over her shoulder. "Not feeling well. Just gonna lie down. Don't come too close in case I'm contagious."

"Fuck that," he said, coming up behind her. His huge hands went to her shoulders, massaging until she wanted to purr despite the excruciating pain in her face. "Your hands are shaking, let me help."

As he reached around her with his left hand to take the key, he used his right to sweep her hair back over her shoulder.

Holly's heart stopped.

LJ's hand went to her forehead. "You don't feel feverish."

She couldn't stem the flinch as his fingertips grazed her cheek.

"What the..." LJ took a step back. "Holly, turn the fuck around." If his voice grew any frostier, icicles would dangle from his tongue.

Slowly, as though she was about to face her executioner—even though she had full confidence LJ would never hurt her—Holly turned. Knowing how the sight of her face would upset him gut her.

Once she faced him, she took a breath then lifted her head.

The eyes that stared back at her were the stormiest she'd ever seen. A shiver raced down her spine. At that moment, she had no doubt that LJ wouldn't have hesitated to kill Rick Schwartz in cold blood had the other man been in the vicinity.

CHAPTER TWENTY-FIVE

LJ's blood pounded in his ears like a tribal drum calling him to war. Every instinct he possessed was screaming at him to hunt down Schwartz and peel the man's skin from his body one inch at a time. Without a single detail, he was certain the cop was responsible for the destruction of his favorite face.

But one glance at the fat tear rolling down Holly's bruised cheek had him checking his own needs in favor of hers. He shifted his head side to side, cracking his neck. Schwartz could wait. The motherfucker would pay, but it didn't have to happen at that moment. Taking care of Holly needed to be priority number one.

In as level a voice as he could muster with rage simmering in his gut, he said, "Let me have the keys, sugar."

Without a word, she handed them over. Five seconds later, LJ scooped Holly into his arms and carried her straight to the sofa. She still didn't speak but rested the uninjured side of her face against his chest. With the force his heart was slamming into his ribs, she was in danger of getting bruises on that side of her face as well.

"LJ," she said as he lowered her to the couch. The word sounded slurred passing through her swollen lip.

He kissed the top of her head then the shell of her ear. "Shh," he whispered against her ear. "Let me get you some ice, pain medicine, and a drink. Then we'll talk."

"Thank you," she whispered. "For not freaking out."

He rested his forehead against hers. "It's taking a lot of effort not to lose my shit."

"I know. If it helps, it was about ninety percent an accident."

He held back a snort. Didn't matter the circumstances. Just mattered it happened. "Doesn't help. Want to kiss you so bad right now, but I'm terrified of hurting you."

With a one-sided smile, she brushed her lips against his lighter than the stroke of a feather. LJ groaned. The brief contact wasn't enough. His body was fired up, wanting and needing to know she was okay in the most primal way possible. But along with fucking Schwartz up, taking his woman would have to wait as well. "I'll be right back."

He took his time grabbing some ibuprofen from her medicine cabinet, filling a bag with ice, and pouring her a glass of wine. In that time, he also fired off a text to Rocket letting him know Holly had been hurt and he'd need to find someone to cover for him at work in the morning.

Rocket: I can be there in fifteen if you need me.

LJ: Don't have details yet. Good for tonight. Fill you in tomorrow. Might need to organize an ass-kicking.

Rocket: Anything. Any time.

When he returned to the den, Holly had her eyes closed, one hand resting on her stomach the other dangling toward the floor. LJ took a second to analyze the state of her injuries. Her right eye was swollen shut and so dark purple it was nearly black. Just below, her cheek was only a shade lighter and nearly as swollen. The right side of her mouth was puffed up as well.

How the fuck had this happened? Guilt hit him hard. He'd known, deep in his gut, he should have put a prospect on Holly for the evening. A fucking mistake that cost her dearly.

"I can feel you seething over there," she said.

"Sorry, beautiful. Wouldn't be a man if the sight of my woman injured didn't wreck me."

Her one eye popped open. "You'd still be a man, you just wouldn't be the incredible man you are."

Shit, this woman destroyed him.

"How bad is the pain?"

"Scale of one to ten?"

"Sure." LJ knelt next to the couch and gently placed the towel wrapped ice bag against her cheek. Her cringe felt like an actual slap.

"'Bout an eight out of ten right now. Was a nine for most of the drive home. Not sure the pain lessened. Think I'm just getting used to it. Ohhh, that ice feels so good."

"Leave it on a while. Want some meds too?"

"Yes. Hell yes," she said as she struggled to sit up straight.

"Woman…" LJ rolled his eyes as he set the wineglass and pain medicine on an end table. "Let me help you for fuck's sake."

He lifted her back, then handed off the pills and drink.

"Washing pain meds down with wine," she said with a chuckle. "That's poor-decision making one-oh-one right there."

LJ grunted. Watching her wince and groan as she moved had the need to pulverize Schwartz returning in full-force. Only way to keep it at bay would be to have Holly in his arms. "Hold on," he said as she went to lie back down.

"What's wrong?" She had the ice pressed against her face, hiding the worst of the damage.

"Nothing's wrong, beautiful. Just need to hold you." The maneuvering ended up being awkward as hell since he was trying hard not to jostle her, but he managed to wedge himself behind her on the couch. Once in position, he encouraged her to lie back and use his bicep as a pillow.

As she snuggled into him, Holly let out a sigh. "This feels so nice."

The surprise and appreciation in her voice had LJ feeling like shit. Of course, it felt nice to be held by her man or fuck buddy or whatever the hell he was. Despite weeks of fucking, eating together, hanging out alone and with his friends, this was the first time he'd held her in his arms like this. The risk of falling asleep was too great and weighed too heavily on his mind. Meanwhile, Holly probably assumed he just wasn't into her enough to just lie around cuddling her.

He was a grade-A prick.

"Yeah, baby, it is nice."

"I'm guessing you want to know what happened."

"You up for telling me, now?" Please let her be up for it because his mind would swirl with horrifying possibilities if he didn't get the real story.

"Yeah," she said.

"What'd you mean by mostly an accident?"

Eyes closed, Holly held the ice to her face. LJ stroked her hair over and over.

"He was drunk when I got there. Super drunk. Right from the moment I walked in his house, he was a complete jerk. Spouting off all kinds of shit about you and the club, and you and me."

"What kinda shit?"

Holly shook her head. He'd give her tonight, but tomorrow he wanted a word for word repeat of the conversation.

"It's all right. What happened next?"

"He started going off about not understanding why I'm with you, which somehow morphed into him being able to take you in a fight. He was stumbling around, swaying but decided to demonstrate his amazing boxing abilities. He started throwing all these wild punches in the air, but he was crazy close to me. I tried to dodge them all, but he got me once. Oh, my God, LJ, it hurt so bad. I had no idea one punch could hurt like that."

One punch to a woman from a man twice her size. Yeah, that would fucking hurt and fuck up a face, as it did.

"See," she said, voice growing thick. "Mostly an accident."

A grunt was the only response he could form. Mostly an accident made sense to his logical brain, but he didn't tend to think with that side of his brain when it came to Holly. Mostly an accident translated to a little bit not an accident which was un-fucking-acceptable. Even if he hadn't hit her, the fucker shouldn't have spouted off his fat mouth and shouldn't have been drunk off his ass when he was about to take out a woman. Especially LJ's woman.

Asshole had a bill to pay, and LJ couldn't wait to collect.

"I'm not sure why I'm so sleepy. It's not late at all."

"Adrenaline dump." Decision made, he said, "Sleep, sugar. I've got you and I'm not going anywhere." And he wasn't. It'd been a solid seven days since LJ had been plagued by any nightmares, so he was probably safe to doze for a few. Besides, chances were high he wouldn't sleep a wink, just stare at Holly and plot Schwartz's death.

THE LAST THING Holly remembered before falling asleep was the incredible sensation of being wrapped in LJ's strength. Warm, safe, comforted. Free to let her mind release the events of the night long enough to fall asleep. Him cuddling her had been just what she needed after learning just how vulnerable she was last night.

Waking, however, wasn't nearly as pleasant. It happened in an instant. No warning, no time to prepare. Holly was ripped from the cozy cocoon of sleep by an intense weight on her chest and a crushing pressure against her windpipe.

Her eyes flew open to find a stone-faced LJ flattening her with the full weight of his six-and-a-half-foot frame. One bulging forearm lay across her neck, compressing her airway with such great force, she couldn't draw in a breath.

"LJ," she mouthed. The only sound she expelled was a feeble squeak since there was no air behind the words.

Busted face forgotten, Holly immediately surged into survival mode. She thrashed, clawed at LJ's back, and tried to shove him off with her legs. Nothing worked, and every action only served to drain her reserves and increase the need for air. He had to be covered in bloody scratches as she could feel his skin gathering beneath her fingernails.

Panic began to take over, but Holly fought the terror for all she was worth. Above her, LJ's eyes darted in every direction, but he seemed completely unaware of his surroundings, or the fact she was grappling under him. With each passing second, she grew closer to passing out until darkness rimmed the edges of her vision.

He groaned, a tortured sound that had Holly's heart clenching despite her anxiety. Whatever nightmare had him prisoner, it was a chilling place to be. LJ jerked up slightly, staring at the white wall behind her couch as though he'd seen a ghost. The movement shifted his arm and finally allowed Holly to suck a breath.

"LJ," she screamed as loud as her ravaged voice would allow. A deep bark followed by the rapid click-clack of Biscuits nails sounded from somewhere in the apartment. Holly's bedroom probably, where the lazy dog had spent the night in her bed.

The moment LJ snapped back to reality, the awareness he'd hurt her would absolutely kill him, but he needed to wake up before one or both of them were seriously injured. "LJ please wake up! It's Holly. You're safe. I promise. You're safe."

She repeated the phrase again and again. His arm had returned to its position across her throat, but no longer held with pressure. Just a warning not to move. LJ continued to scan the room as though anticipating an enemy attack from any angle at any second.

Was he back in the Middle Eastern desert? Reliving the horrors he'd encountered while fighting overseas? The thought sent a twist of sadness through Holly. This was why he'd refused to sleep with her. Dread of this exact scenario was why he wouldn't so much as close his eyes in her presence. What a lonely way to go through life, terrified to let his guard down.

"LJ," she tried again, this time, making her voice as soothing and caring as possible despite the rasp. Instead of scratching, she smoothed her fingers over his back, flinching as she encountered wetness.

He blinked twice and stared down at her. Just as his expression morphed into one of abject horror, the door to Holly's apartment flew open with so much power, it smacked against the wall behind it.

Before either of them had a chance to process who had breached Holly's home, LJ was ripped off her. His scream of agony would ring through Holly's head for years to come. LJ fought like an animal, growling, kicking, and screaming as four uniformed police officers forced him face down on her floor.

"No!" Holly screamed as she launched off the couch only to be tackled back down. "No! Get off him!" Biscuit went crazy. Her loyal dog snarled and snapped at the officers, barking like mad at the men who'd entered her home without permission.

Whoever had restrained Holly seemed to misunderstand her freak out, probably assuming she was traumatized by the scene they discovered her and LJ in. Had someone heard her yelling at him and called the cops? Everything had happened so fast; she had no idea how long she'd been struggling under him.

And now she was fighting to get free of the officer with the same ferocity LJ fought with on the ground. He screamed something about diving for cover and tried to army-crawl away, but the four officers slammed him back down, making his head crack on the floor with a sickening thump. He was gone again, lost in a disassociate episode far worse than the last she'd witnessed.

"Let him go!" she yelled. "Get off of him."

Biscuit grabbed the pant leg of one of the officers, near his ankle, shaking it as though attempting to kill a rabbit.

"Get this fucking dog to stand down!" the officer cried.

Holly forced herself to stop struggling and try to make eye contact with the officer who was now dragging her away from the fray. "Please," she said in a much calmer voice. "Please let LJ go. He didn't do anything. He didn't hurt me. Please, I promise."

The officer snorted. "Your face says differently. So does your father. And the blood on your hands."

Her face. Jesus, in all the chaos, she'd completely forgotten about the ruin of her face. That's what the raid was about. Not the nightmare. That was just the icing on the cake. To walk into LJ on top of Holly while she tried to free herself.

"No! Please, you don't understand. Oh, my God, what are they doing to him?"

LJ continued to struggle on the ground, though he no longer appeared to be out of it. Now he was fully conscious, cursing, and fighting for his life. He had to be so confused. To be jerked into reality only to discover four men on top of him, screaming and holding him down. One of the officers reached into his utility belt and pulled out what looked like a small yellow gun. He shoved it into LJ's side and pulled the trigger. LJ's body jerked and he shouted in pain, but finally stopped struggling.

"What are they doing to him? Did they hurt him? Stop! LJ! Please make them stop," she begged the man holding her back.

"Miss Lane, I'm going to have to ask you to calm down," the officer who still held her around the waist said. "And you need to call off your dog before we are forced to subdue him." Biscuit was still in full-on protective mode, growling at anyone who went near him.

"Wait! Where are they taking him? Where is he going?"

"He's under arrest Miss Lane. Call off your dog!"

"What?" she screamed as the four officers guided a disoriented LJ out of the apartment. "No! Get him back here! This is fucking crazy!"

It was then she noticed her father standing near the door. He slapped one of the officers leading LJ on the back. Holly read, "Good work" on his lips.

"I want to speak to my father. Let me talk to my father." She started struggling again, kicking her legs out, so the officer was forced to hold her in midair. "Put me the fuck down!"

"Miss Lane," he stated, far calmer than she. "Call. Off. The. Dog."

"B-Biscuit," she finally said. Her dog immediately stopped barking and stared at his master. "It's okay, baby. Mommy's okay." A lie if she ever told one. "Come here, buddy." Biscuit trotted over to her, but he didn't stand down. Instead, he emitted a low growl at the officer with Holly.

The officer kept a hand on her arm but stepped farther away from her protective dog. She'd honestly believed Biscuit would have been useless in a situation where she needed protection. Clearly, she'd underestimated her gentle giant.

I'm going to need you to come down to the station to make a statement. Then we can formally press charges."

"Press charges?" She lifted an unsteady hand to her head, pushing the wild mane of her hair from her eyes. This couldn't be happening. Why wouldn't a single one of these assholes listen to her? "I don't want to press charges against LJ. Jesus, aren't you listening? He didn't do this." She finally jerked free of her captor and stood in her now quiet apartment where her father and two other officers were waiting for her to exit.

They each wore looks of pity. Like she was the battered woman, unwilling to take action against the man who'd hurt her. Well, fuck that. She was more than goddamned willing to tell the whole world who hurt her.

"Fine," she said, held high despite her face which now hurt like a bitch and her hands which were smeared with LJ's blood. "I'd love to come down to the station and press charges against the man who did this to my face," she said, pointing to herself.

She marched forward until she stood right in front of her father. He pulled her into a gentle hug. "Jesus, Holly. He's going to pay for this, okay? I promise that piece of shit biker won't lay a hand on you ever again. I'm throwing every charge I can possibly think of at him."

Holly stepped back and out of his embrace. "Can you please have one of your deputies find some pain medication for me?"

"Yes, of course." He gestured to one of the remaining officers. "Find her something to take for the pain."

Little Jack

"Great." She looked her father dead in the eye. "I don't want to be hindered by pain when I formally press charges against Richard Schwartz for what he did to my face."

CHAPTER TWENTY-SIX

Bile burned the back of LJ's throat as he sat in the interrogation room listening to the deputy recount the events of the morning. Someone had found him a T-shirt one size too small, and it stretched across his back, adhering to the dried blood from the scratches Holly had given him.

He'd hurt her. Fucking choked her. Did anyone here realize just how easily he could have killed her? Of course, they did. It's why they'd been dispatched to the house. Some neighbor of the sheriff saw his daughter's ravaged face and called him. Naturally, he'd assumed the guy Holly was seeing had been responsible for the abuse.

Fifteen hours ago, LJ would have lost his shit if he'd heard someone thought him capable of harming Holly. The notion had been inconceivable. Now? Well, now he sat silently in a sterile room with his hands cuffed to the table and his back stinging from Holly's brutal fight for survival. He'd declined any kind of counsel. Whatever they wanted to do to him, he deserved times ten.

"Nothing to say?" the deputy asked. The guy looked like he could have been Schwartz's long-lost cousin. Same high and tight haircut, same swinging-dick swagger, same smug grin. No doubt a bromance existed between the two.

Two assholes cut from the same motherfucking cloth.

LJ remained silent.

"So, all we've got outta you so far is that you don't remember hurting her because you were having a nightmare?" the deputy asked, humor lacing his tone. He'd introduced himself at some point, but LJ's brain was still a bit fuzzy. Something super generic like Smith or Jones…Brown. Deputy Brown.

"What's the matter?" Brown continued. "Boogieman come to you in your dreams? Tell you to hurt that sweet woman? Come on, man. We've heard all sorts of shit excuses from abusers like you. Dinner was cold, she looked at another man, she's always bitching…any shit to try and justify their barbaric behavior. But, a nightmare made you do it?" He laughed. "Now that's some funny shit."

Grinding his teeth together, LJ lifted his gaze. *Fuck my life.* And fuck this guy. The only reason he'd mentioned the nightmare was because he'd been so disoriented when he came out of it to find four large men pinning him to the ground, he'd fought like hell. After they'd tased him and he'd nearly pissed himself, he was wrung out with a foggy mind. He'd let the nightmare thing slip.

No one knew the extent of his nightmares. Not even the therapist he'd seen after being medically discharged from the military. Not a single soul knew how they plagued him. How he woke on the floor in a sweaty, confused panic at least once a week. But now this jackass knew some of it. And his judgmental response was the very reason LJ had kept his mouth shut and suffered in silence for years.

"What about the face? Nightmare make you crack her across the face too?"

Any other time, LJ would have had some choice fucking words for the deputy, but the choking incident was too dark a mark on his soul to be overlooked. The cops wanted to toss his ass in jail for a bit, fine. He fucking deserved it for being dumb enough to sleep next to Holly.

Actions had consequences, and this was his.

A commotion in the hallway had both LJ and Brown turning toward the open interrogation room door.

"Where the hell is he?" came Holly's frantic shout from somewhere in the building. "LJ? Where the fuck do you have him? I want him released immediately! Do you fucking hear me? This is bullshit!"

A muffled response LJ couldn't make out was followed by more fury from Holly. The woman swore more in the last twenty seconds than she had since he'd met her. Goddamn, he was so proud of her. Not taking shit, not being railroaded by the police or her father. He sure as hell didn't deserve her loyalty, but it made him fall just a little deeper anyway.

Too fucking bad. The morning's incident drove home the lack of future for him and Holly like nothing else could have. Didn't mean he couldn't appreciate her for the kick-ass woman she was.

Deputy Brown rose and stepped out of the room, leaving LJ alone, cuffed to the table. He hung his head as the weight of his actions settled deeper into his consciousness.

I hurt her.

"No! I will not fucking calm down. You see this?" Holly yelled, and LJ imagined her pointing to her black-and-blue face.

Had anyone gotten her any pain medication? Ice? Did they actually give a shit about the fact that her injury had to be throbbing like a bitch? Or were they all just hell-bent on locking up the biker?

"This was done by Deputy Schwartz last night. He was drunk off his ass and acting like a dipshit. It was mostly an accident, but still, something that never should have happened. I'm more than happy to sit down and give you all the damn details you want, but not until LJ is fucking released."

"Holly!" The sharp bite of her father's voice had LJ dropping his head. Fucking helpless to do anything but let this scene play out.

"LJ didn't do this, Dad," she said much softer. So much so, LJ had to strain to hear. "Please let him go. He wouldn't hurt me."

LJ squeezed his eyes shut. The pain in her voice hit him like knives carving into his skin. He focused on her words, the pitch and volume of her voice. He focused on the cold, heavy feeling of the cuffs around his wrists. The hard, unyielding metal of his seat. Anything and everything to keep him grounded in reality and not let the helplessness pull him back under.

"Holly," her father said back. "The way we found you—"

"Is none of your business," she fired back without hesitation.

If only LJ could see her instead of being chained up like a damn animal. She was so fucking strong, so fierce, marching in here and making demands on his behalf.

"Look, Dad, I'm telling you LJ did not hurt me. Not last night and not this morning. I'm not willing to discuss what you walked in on this morning, but I am willing to talk about what happened with Deputy Schwartz last night. However, I want LJ released first."

The building grew quiet. With no other options, LJ sat waiting for whatever came next. Deputy Brown never returned, but about fifteen minutes later, Holly's father entered the room. The sheriff shared those light blue eyes and the shape of his nose with his daughter, but that's where the resemblance ended. The rest of Holly's features must have come from her mother.

"She's sticking to her story. Says you didn't do this. Says it was Schwartz," the sheriff said.

LJ nodded. "It was."

The sheriff scoffed.

"You saying your daughter's a liar?"

Sheriff's nostrils flared, but he didn't take the bait. "Spoke with Schwartz a few moments ago. Poor guy is nursing the hangover from hell. Doesn't even remember seeing Holly last night."

"Convenient."

"The deputy is quite taken with my daughter. Has been since their first meeting. And instead of dating her, he's forced to sit back and watch her be with you. A biker. A loser heading nowhere in life but prison. A scumbag who couldn't be less deserving of her affection."

The words hit his battered soul like bullets, but LJ forced himself to ignore them for now. "You saying his actions are justified because he's pissed he didn't get the girl? That's your daughter he hit."

The sheriff's eyes widened and he took a step back. "No. No, of course not," he said with a shake of his slightly graying head. "Of course, it shouldn't have happened. But you have to admit you can understand the guy's need for a few drinks."

LJ stared at the man whose hatred for bikers ran so deep, he preferred a man who'd punched his daughter over the MC member who'd rather die than hurt her.

But he had hurt her. Unintentional, but then again, Schwartz hadn't purposefully harmed her either. "And if I'd been the one to get blitzed and fuck up Holly's face?"

The same blue eyes he loved so much on Holly stared at him with so much revulsion, it practically oozed from his sockets.

"Thought so."

How he could lose himself in those eyes on one person and despise them on another was a mystery.

As he stepped around the table, the sheriff said, "You're free to go." He unlocked the cuffs. "Deputy Brown will give you a ride home."

Not happening. "That's a hard pass. Spent about as much time with that douche bag as I can take. One of my brothers will be here by now."

"Brothers," the sheriff said with a scoff as though the concept was completely unfathomable.

As soon as the cuffs were off, LJ veered straight for the open door.

"Your club's done," the sheriff said from behind him.

LJ froze but didn't turn.

"It's only a matter of time."

"Whatever you say, old man." With a shake of his head, LJ took another step forward.

"If you care about her at all, you'll let her go before she's caught in the backlash."

They agreed on one thing, he had to let Holly go, only not for the reasons the sheriff wanted. What kind of future could they have if he couldn't even fall asleep next to her? A life of separate bedrooms and Holly waking in the night to the screams of LJ's haunting past?

He could have killed her. Easily.

Killed her.

The thought had his steps faltering as pain slammed into him. Shit, what the hell was he doing thinking in terms of a future? Years ago, he'd resigned himself to quick fucks and blowjobs from random women to take the edge off. Not even one-night stands since that implied sticking around for the night.

And it had been fine. LJ had been fine. He had his work and his brothers with plenty of willing women to step into the role he'd allow them to fill when the itch struck. Then Holly had to go and fuck it all up with her sweetness, and her irresistible body, and her warmth. Now, all he could think about was how she brought him those goddammed Nutella cupcakes at work. And how she called him every morning, the second she woke up. How well she got along with his brothers and their women. The way she curled her fingers into his ass and held him deep inside her even after they'd both come. And now, the way she fucking felt clinging to him in sleep.

"Stop at the desk on your way out," the sheriff called behind him. "There's some paperwork for you to sign."

Fuck that. LJ lifted his middle finger, strode straight past the geriatric manning the desk, and out the front door. The morning sun had warmed the air in the hour since he'd been dragged to the station.

"You okay, brother?" Rocket called from across the lot.

Relief shot through LJ at the sight of his bike ready and waiting for him.

"Ain't a thing," he replied as he crossed to where his Harley and his brother waited.

"Bullshit," Rocket said. Sunglasses blocked his eyes, but LJ bet they were dark with anger. "Are. You. Okay."

"They thought I hit her." Christ, those words made him want to tear something apart. Tear *someone* apart.

"Figured. Fucked as it is, figured they'd pin that shit on you. Holly stand by you?"

LJ nodded and rubbed his gritty eyes. "Yeah, she was… incredible. But it's more complicated than just that."

As was his way, Rocket sat silently on his bike, waiting for LJ to continue.

Throughout the two years he'd worked for Rocket, LJ had confided in his brother to a small extent. Though he had no desire to get into the weeds, LJ needed to unburden to someone. The lid would likely blow off his pressure cooker otherwise.

"Fell asleep with her for the first time. Almost made it through the whole night too. But I had the mother of all fucking nightmares. When I came around, I was face down on the floor with four fucking cops screaming in my face. Turns out, when they busted in, I was on top of Holly, choking her out." He shook his head. His heart felt shredded. When the hell had his heart become such a strong part of the equation?

"Fuck," was all Rocket said.

"Didn't remember a thing. Still don't. So now she's been clocked in the face and fucking choked all because of me. I gotta go, brother. Need to put an end to it."

"She want out?"

LJ shrugged. "Fuck if I know. Doesn't matter. Way it's gotta be."

"It matters, brother. Things are fucked right now, and shit got out of control, but it matters. A good woman, a woman like Holly, she won't leave because of that shit. She'll make you work through it and hang by your side the entire ride. You think you feel bad now?" He snorted. "Wait until she gets you talking. You'll feel like your insides were ripped out, beaten with a bat, and shoved back in all fucking lopsided. You'll wanna crawl in a hole and fucking die. But then you'll realize she hasn't left. She's still there, still holding you, still fucking you, still loving you. Then shit gets a little better. And the next day, a little better than that. Until one day, you realize you'd do anything, and I mean fucking anything to keep her tied to you. You'd rather die a million deaths than lose her. That's what the love of a good woman will do for you."

With wide eyes and a hanging jaw, LJ stared at the man he considered a brother. His words hit deep, digging down under LJ's fears and planting a small seed of hope. "Fuuuck, Rocket. Didn't know you could string that many words together at once."

Rocket flipped him off with a grunt. "Don't like to waste my air on bullshit. But I'll give it to you straight when it's important."

"Appreciate it, brother." He held a hand out toward Rocket.

With a rare smile, Rocket clasped LJ's hand and pulled him close, bumping their chests and slapping LJ on the back. "Need me to follow you home?" he asked when they pulled apart.

"Nah." LJ shook his head, shifting his gaze to the road leading home. The magnetic pull, the need to be in Holly's presence grew exponentially with each word spoken. Was she home? In pain? Worried? Angry? Christ, was she afraid? The notion of her having a legitimate fear of him after the morning's incident speared his heart. But it was a very real possibility. Something he deserved no matter how much it wounded him. Would she let him in, or would he arrive at a locked door and a barred heart? "Need the time to think a little. You head on home to your woman."

"Never gonna argue with that." They slapped hands again before Rocket said, "We're ready when you want to take care of Schwartz."

"Give me the day. I'll be by the clubhouse tomorrow."

Rocket nodded then fired up his bike. He rode off, leaving LJ alone, and he'd be lying if he said the silence wasn't welcome. With heaviness in his chest, he spent the ride home trying to come up with a plan of action, a battle plan of sorts for when he saw Holly. In the end, after many failed attempts at devising a speech, he gave up. Go with the flow was more his style. So he'd shoot from the hip once he saw her.

Each time his boots hit the ground, he inched one step closer to Holly. By the time he reached the second floor, LJ had himself worked the fuck up. Was Holly even home? Maybe she'd gone to her parents', or even her brother's to get away from the drama.

For the first time in his entire life, LJ had the urge to bury his head in the sand and hide. What came next had the power to wreck him.

Before knocking on her door, he needed to get out of the too-small T-shirt and shower the events of the past fifteen hours away. At least he could remove the physical evidence of what went down. The extra scars on his soul would remain forever.

As LJ turned the key and pushed his door open, a low whine greeted him. "What?" He stepped in only to be greeted by a forceful nose to the crotch. He patted the dog's big head, but his attention was elsewhere.

Standing in the middle of his foyer wearing nothing but one of his Handlers' T-shirts, with tears streaming down her bruised face was Holly. Despite red eyes, a discolored cheek, and the mess of her hair, she was the most gorgeous woman he'd ever laid eyes on.

They stared at each other across the ten feet that separated them. Biscuit seemed oblivious to the tension, wanting nothing more than a good scratch from LJ.

Little Jack

"I—" Holly swallowed as she closed her eyes. After a breath, she tried again. "I'm so sorry, LJ."

The absolute agony in her voice cracked his heart in two. "Jesus, Holly, say anything, *anything* to me besides an apology. Scream, tell me to fuck off, say you never want to see me again, but for fuck's sake don't tell me you're sorry for a goddammed thing."

CHAPTER TWENTY-SEVEN

Emotions radiated off LJ in such powerful waves, the feelings were practically visible. Stress, anger, fatigue, guilt, a whole host of negative thinking wafted Holly's way, and it had her heart sinking straight to the floor.

He was going to end it. She could feel it in her bones. The incident with his nightmare was fucking with his head, and he was going to cast her aside with some noble notion of keeping her safe from him.

Despite the fact her heart was splintering—something she refused to acknowledge because her heart wasn't supposed to have gotten involved here—Holly stepped forward and held out a hand. "Come on," she said. "Let's get cleaned up."

"Holly—"

"Not now, LJ, okay? I need a few moments to think about something other than the past day. Take a shower with me. We'll get cleaned up, then lie down and talk."

He watched her for a moment, eyes assessing as though waiting for her to break. She wouldn't, at least not until she'd made sure he was holding up.

LJ's whole body sagged and seemed to deflate like the air being let out of a balloon. With a nod, he put his palm against Holly's outstretched hand. For just one second, she closed her eyes and enjoyed the feeling of having his trust before she walked them both to LJ's un-frilly bathroom.

His shower was small, a replica of hers, only in reverse. The tiny space began to fill with steam only seconds after she cranked the water to steaming hot. "Turn around," Holly ordered.

Surprisingly, LJ obeyed. Holly slid her hands under the tight shirt, working it up his back. At mid-spine level, angry red scratches revealed themselves. She sucked in a breath as the fabric of the T-shirt stuck to the marks.

"It's all right," he said. "Just give it a good yank."

She peered around his body and met his gaze in the foggy mirror. "I'll hurt you."

A snort was the only response.

Holly gentled her touch as much as possible and took her time working the stuck shirt free of his mangled skin. Every few seconds, she had to give a firm tug to release the fabric. She flinched with each of those. Finally, the shirt made it up to his shoulders, and he took over removing it since she wasn't tall enough to reach up and over his head.

Long red lines marked his entire upper back and shoulder area. Evidence of how hard she'd been fighting to escape him earlier. Odd, as now all she wanted was to be so close to him they became one. She pressed a soft kiss to an unharmed patch of skin on his back, then rested her forehead against him. "I'm —"

"Don't say it." He turned around, cupping a hand against her sore cheek in a touch so gentle, it shouldn't have been possible from such a large man. "You're the one who's hurt. I should be taking care of you."

The past twenty-four hours had been such a roller coaster of emotions, Holly could barely process the dichotomy between the soaring highs and crushing lows. The loop-de-loops had her mind racing so fast, the rest of her couldn't keep up. "Let's take care of each other."

With a nod, LJ guided her into the shower stall, following directly behind. His big body took up so much of the space,

Holly ended up with her back against the wall opposite the spray.

The moment the water hit LJ's back, he let out a loud hiss that had Holly cringing. "I'm sorry," he said. "Didn't mean to hog all the hot water, just wanted to get this part over with."

Large hands landed on her shoulders, then LJ turned them until she was the one under the warm water. "It's fine," she said. "Turn around, let me see."

For a moment, he just watched her with an expression she couldn't read. Compressed lips, flat eyes, ticking jaw. Then he smoothed wet hair off her brow, gripped the back of her head and placed the gentlest of kisses on her forehead.

Thank God for the cascade of water as it hid the sheen of tears in her eyes.

LJ turned, bracing his hands high on the slippery wall.

"I'm just going to use my hands instead of a washcloth, okay?" she asked. "Feel like I can be gentler that way."

"Sure, sugar."

Holly grabbed the generic bottle of body wash from the small cutout shelf and squeezed a dollop onto her palms. With slow movements, she worked the gel into a later, taking a moment to enjoy the sight of his muscular back and shoulders. Even with the wounds, he was impressive. "Ready?"

"To have you put those hands all over me? Yeah, sugar, think I can handle it."

With one hand, Holly tested his response by rubbing over one of the scratches. When he didn't hiss again or jolt form the sting, she grew bolder and stroked her hands over his entire back, washing away the blood that had dried in streaks on his tanned skin.

"I don't think I messed up any of your tattoos," she said as the washing became more of a massage.

"I'm sure you didn't. Feels good, Hol," he said as she kneaded his shoulders like dough.

"You're so strong." And that power and muscle felt incredible beneath her palms.

"Product of the job. Lifting, swinging tools, carrying heavy shit."

"Hmm." She slid her hands around the front, washing his chest and abs. "You work out too though, don't you? I know you at least run a lot."

"Yeah, and I try to hit Zach's gym a few times a week. Been tough lately with my schedule."

By now most of the suds had rinsed away, but Holly continued running her hands over his skin as though washing him. She coasted her hands down to the front of LJ's thighs and back around to the very firm globes of his ass. God, the man could quit his job and become an underwear model any day of the week. He'd be a millionaire by the end of the month.

She took a step forward, plastering her wet front to his back as she skimmed around his body once again. This time, she circled her fingers around his cock and gave a long, slow squeeze.

Hard, just as she'd hoped. She stroked it, and LJ growled. Damn, that sound did things to her no other man had come close to. Part approval, part desire, part warning, the growl he emitted made her wet every time. With a confidence she'd gained since being with him, she jacked his cock in a hand-over-hand pattern. Wrapped in the circle of her arms, he tensed, the muscles she'd just been admiring rippling with restraint.

"You looking to get fucked, baby?" he asked in a ragged voice. Her man was near the edge.

A shiver undulated through her. "Don't know what you mean. I'm just making sure you're all nice and clean."

He chuckled. "Oh, baby, you wanna play, huh?"

Yes, God, yes, she wanted to play with him. Wanted to lose herself in the heat and passion they shared. It seemed the only thing possible to chase away the events of the past day.

Faster than should have been possible for such a big man in a tiny space, LJ spun. Holly squeaked as her back met the shower wall.

Those large, rough hands squeezed her breasts with a kneading motion much as she'd used on his shoulders seconds ago. Her eyes fell shut as pleasure replaced the pain and stress that had been present from the moment she stepped into Schwartz's home. She'd be lying if she didn't admit the fact that LJ loved her breasts so much thrilled her as much as his touch. There was a power in knowing she could make a man crazy with just her body.

A sharp jolt of pleasure had her eyes flying back open and her back arching off the wall as his thumb and forefingers pinched her nipples.

"Jack," she said, drawing it out in a raspy moan.

He wasn't gentle, twisting and pulling on the sensitive tips. Each tug sent a rush of need between her legs.

"Just returning the favor, sugar. Getting you all clean."

Somehow her brain engaged enough to process his words, and she chuckled. "How exactly are you getting me clean?"

"Do you give a fuck?"

He scraped his blunt nails over the tips of her nipples, making her cry out in pleasure. "No, absolutely no fucks given. Oh, shit. Please, Jack."

The grin he gave her as he stared down at her and continued to torture her nipples was positively wicked. "Please what, baby?"

"Please touch me." He was going to make her insane with need. With each passing second, the ache in her core grew in intensity. Her pussy practically spasmed with the need to be filled. To be pounded. To be fucked until she was screaming.

"Pretty sure I've been touching you for the last few minutes."

"Not enough." She groaned and shifted her legs until they straddled his thigh. Something, anything to give her the friction she needed.

"Oh, I see," he said, the grin turning playful. Such a welcome change to the strain written on his face since he'd woken up. "You want to be fucked, don't you sugar?"

"You already know this," Holly practically snarled as she worked her hips on his thigh. He pulled back, and this time she did growl.

LJ chuckled. "I do know it, baby. But I want to hear you say it. I want to hear how much you need my cock. How much your pretty pussy wants to be full of my dick. Wants to be fucked hard."

She was going to die if he didn't do all of that and soon. "Yes. Yes!" she said as he increased the pressure on her nipples. "All of that. Please, Jack, stop torturing me and fuck me."

"Yes, ma'am," he replied as his hands left her tits and grabbed her ass. He lifted as though she weighed nothing.

"LJ!" she yelped, banding her arms and legs around him. "Are you crazy? I'm way too—"

"Don't say it! Don't fucking say it."

She closed her mouth. She supposed she could keep it in. Didn't seem like he was struggling to hold her weight.

"Fuck, I want that mouth," he whispered against her lips now that they were lined up with his.

"Then take it."

"Your face." He released one ass cheek then shut off the water. Had she been alone, she'd have been shivering by now, but the heat radiating off LJ plus the strong desire flowing through her kept her well beyond heated.

"It's fine. I could be shot right now and I don't think I'd feel it. Kiss me, LJ."

He needed no other encouragement though his kiss was far more gentle than usual. They stood in the shower for a few moments, exploring each other's mouths before LJ ripped his away.

"Was gonna dry you off, take you to my bed, do you right, but I can't fucking wait any longer," he said as he stepped out of the shower.

"Thank God."

He grunted out a chuckle. The moment her ass hit the vanity counter, he surged into her.

"Oh, fuck!" she cried. He went deep, so deliciously deep. And with his size, he filled her until she squirmed. The forceful claiming was exactly what she needed.

"So good," he said as he began to thrust, hard. "So fucking hot and wet."

"Don't even think about stopping."

"Wouldn't dream of it, baby," he said, though his thrusts never faltered.

"More," she begged. "Harder, LJ."

He wasn't giving it to her gentle to begin with, but she needed something more. Something raw, near savage to erase her guilt and fears.

His fingers tightened on her ass, and even that made her moan in need. Everything he was doing ramped up her desire. On the next thrust, her ass slipped off the edge of the counter. "LJ!" she yelled as she waited to hit the floor.

But he didn't miss a beat. Still pumping his hips in and out of her, he carried them across his bedroom. Holly got with the program in no time and worked her hips, pretty much riding him while he walked.

He attacked her neck with deep, sucking kisses that were sure to leave even more marks on her skin. It was as though he was trying to replace what happened earlier with evidence of his desire and need.

Without releasing her or breaking their connection, he somehow managed to climb onto the bed and set her on her back. As he loomed over her, Holly couldn't help the heart-squeeze that meant she was falling in too deep.

"Ready?" he asked.

"Ready? For what?"

"To be fucked?"

"Umm...what have you been doing the past few minutes? What are you doing now—oh God," she whispered as he sat back on his heels, shifting inside her. The new position had her ass resting atop his thighs and legs splayed around him. Only the tip of his cock remained inside her. Smirk in place, he grabbed her ass and yanked her up his body, seating himself so deep inside her, she swore she'd feel him for hours afterward.

"Want me to repeat the question?" he asked as he rose to a high kneel.

Holly's upper back, shoulders, and head remained on the mattress, but that was it, the rest of her was suspended in the air by LJ's cock, and hands on her ass. Her groin muscles ached from the intense stretch of being spread so wide. "Wh-what question?" she asked as excitement shot through her.

This was going to be so good.

"Thought so." He winked and squeezed her ass in the second before he started fucking her like she'd never been fucked before. LJ put the full power of his huge thighs and rounded ass into every plunge. Over and over, he slammed into her.

The position rendered her helpless to do anything but submit to the brutal pounding. Before long, her mind blanked to anything but the intense pleasure of LJ's full power unleashed on her.

"Could watch those big tits bounce like that all goddamned day."

Their gazes met and a sly smile curled Holly's mouth. She cupped her breasts, which were swaying heavily with each thrust, then thumbed her nipples. LJ's focus left her face and lasered in on her breasts. His nostrils flared and she swore his lip curled.

"Go at 'em hard."

At that moment he could have asked her to start singing the National Anthem and she'd have belted out the tune. Anything to keep that look of fascination with her body on his face. She pinched her nipples.

"Christ, your pussy just clenched me like a vise. Roll 'em, baby. Let me see how much attention my girl's tits like."

Nearly out of her mind with pleasure, she did as he asked. The tips of her toes started to tingle, and it felt like electricity zinged through her body.

"That's it." His hands tightened on her ass. "Rub your clit. Need to feel you come around me."

Holly moaned as she moved one hand to her clit. She worked it with rough strokes as she spiraled closer and closer to orgasm. The rest of the world faded away as pleasure flooded every pore in Holly's body. Her pussy tightened on LJ's tunneling dick.

"That's it, baby. Get it, squeeze me."

"Oh, Jack," she cried as the orgasm slammed into her with punishing force. Her eyes screwed shut, and she let it overtake her. LJ kept the pace up, grunting and praising her. Just as she opened her eyes, he slammed home one last time, holding her tight again him. His back arched, exposing the corded muscles of his throat as he shouted through his own climax.

When the storm passed, LJ lowered her body to the bed. Their gazes locked.

She needed him to lie next to her, wrap her in those sturdy arms, and hold her as they slept, but she knew without asking that would never happen. After that morning, she'd be lucky if LJ blinked in her presence, let alone closed his eyes for a nap.

She saw it, the moment of change. Something shifted in his eyes. Now that the physical need had been slaked—at least for the moment—reality began to creep back in. Holly swallowed, pushing away the tremendous heartache that hovered right there.

"Don't do it," she whispered.

He tilted his head. "Don't do what?"

"Push me away." She held her breath. What a vulnerable position to be in. Splayed out naked before him, as he held her heart in his hand. Her body was safe. No fear there. But her heart?

"I don't have a choice, sugar."

Her heart was in grave danger.

CHAPTER TWENTY-EIGHT

LJ's body craved the slide into deep relaxation that followed an earth-shattering orgasm, but his mind had already jumped two steps ahead. Never would he put Holly at risk like he had that morning by letting down his guard and nodding off no matter how tempted he was to curl up next to her and let oblivion claim him.

"Not yet," she whispered. Wiggling, she propped herself onto her elbows.

Why did she have to go and make this difficult? With a sigh, he slipped from between her thighs and flopped down beside her. They both rolled to face each other, and he immediately stroked a hand over her hip. Asshole that he was, he couldn't keep from touching her even though he had every intention of severing their connection.

"Holly, I could have killed you this morning."

"That never would have happened." Her hand landed on his chest, drifting up and down. All he wanted to do was purr like a damn cat and give himself over to the gentle attention.

Instead, he captured her hand and held it palm to palm against his own. The size difference was laughable, with his mitt being almost twice the size of her hand. "Look how much bigger I am than you. I'm not being extreme here, Holly. I could have *hurt* you. I could have fucking killed you."

With a shake of her head, she frowned.

"You trying to tell me you weren't afraid this morning. There wasn't a single second where you felt fear for your life and safety while I had my whole fucking arm across your throat." As he spoke, he circled her neck with his free hand.

One squeeze is all it would take. Twenty, thirty seconds of no oxygen and she'd be out like a light. She was so much more fragile than he was. Why the hell had he let things progress so far? Now there would be a different kind of pain. An internal cut that never fully healed. For both of them.

Holly's eyes flared and there it was. Proof she couldn't hide. A tiny hint of fear despite her brave talk. She shifted her gaze way. "LJ—"

"I wish I could tell you this morning was an anomaly, that I had some crazy reaction to what Schwartz did to you and it set off an intense nightmare I couldn't break out of. But I can't say that. Because for the past few years I have at least one of those brutal fucking nightmares each week. I wake up angry, on the floor, ready to attack, with my heart pounding, covered in sweat, sometimes even screaming. Don't look at me like that."

"Like what?"

She needed to stop touching him, or he'd lose his resolve to walk out of that room and sleep on the couch. "Like you want to cry."

"What's wrong with me crying for you, LJ? I care about you. A lot. More than just about anyone else. And when you care for someone, you suffer when they do."

Why the fuck did she have to be so goddammed sweet?

A single tear slid from the corner of her eye, soaking into the pillow and stabbing into his heart. "Because I don't deserve it. Your tears or your caring." He swiped a thumb under her eye, capturing the next bead of moisture. "Please don't waste your tears on me."

"So this is why you leave me every night? This is why you won't even close your eyes in my presence? Why I'm always wondering what I d-did wrong and why you won't stay with me?" The little hitch in her voice nearly broke him.

Step one: remove his hands from her, but that task was proving to be impossible. With skin as soft as Holly's, any man would have trouble resisting a touch. Up and down the swell of her hip, he stroked. The contrast of his sun-tanned hands and forearms with a pale part of Holly she never allowed to see the sun looked gorgeous. So creamy and smooth just like the vanilla frosting she always smelled of.

"That's why. And that's why this has to end, Holly. I have no choice." Finally, he tore his hand from the lush skin of her hip only to stroke it over the column of her throat. "I have no memory of hurting you, Holly. I wasn't in my right mind. Wasn't present, but when the deputy told me what I did?" He pressed his forehead to hers. "Please let me walk away without a fight. I can't, won't put you at risk like that again, sugar."

"We can—"

His nose bumped hers as he pressed an index finger over her lips. "No, we can't just continue on as we were. Both of us know what will happen. We'll be tired one night, and we'll fuck until we pass out. Or we'll have a little too much to drink at the clubhouse, and we'll tell ourselves we're only going to close our eyes for a moment. Or we'll snuggle up on the couch with a movie and drift off before it ends."

"All of those things sound perfect," Holly whispered against his finger.

"Yeah, sugar," he rubbed her pink lips. "They do. Until halfway through the night, I attack you in some dissociative state where my mind is back in Afghanistan, and my body is here, fucking choking you to death."

"You won't…"

"I *did*."

Holly let out a heavy breath. What argument did she have? She knew he was right, even if she didn't like it. Her sense of self-preservation would win out in the end. It had to. That was human nature. Who would willingly put themselves in a relationship where their options were separate beds for life or risking their life?

"You said your mind was back in Afghanistan."

Of course, she picked up on that slip.

"Yeah."

"In your nightmares, are you reliving something?" With a shake of her head, she said, "I'm sorry. You don't have to tell me. I shouldn't have asked."

LJ stroked his thumb over her lips, still partially swollen from his earlier kisses. "It's all right. Yeah, I relive the last event of my military career. The incident that sent me home and had me medically separated. I've never talked about it. Not once. Not in all the years since. Not with my brothers. Not with my therapist."

"You don't have to now."

But maybe he did. Maybe if she knew the extent of how fucked in the head he was, she'd finally understand she was better off without him. Perhaps sharing his story would free her. Because he'd never get over it. Not fully. And she deserved a whole man, not a deadly shell.

"I told you I was special forces, a Navy SEAL. I deployed frequently and for varying amounts of time. Even before this final deployment, I'd been showing signs of PTSD. Extra jumpy, mild nightmares, some anger issues, things like that. What people don't understand is the mental strain of just being in a war zone. Even on days when nothing happened. Days so boring you'd count your eyelashes for entertainment, the possibility of a life and death situation was always there. Which meant the entire time, you're on edge, waiting, anticipating, hypervigilant. Even in sleep, part of you stays alert and ready for action. You have any idea how draining that is on a six-month deployment?" He shook his head. "Fucks you up."

"I can't even imagine the strength, the bravery it takes to do what you did, Jack."

With a snort, he said, "Not fishing for compliments here, sugar. Just telling it like it is."

"You still deserve to hear how incredible I think you are."

He wasn't touching that comment. "Anyway, on our last mission, we were helping an EOD team. They're the explosives guys. They were disarming an explosive device they'd discovered while traveling, and we were back up since we were the closest team around. Anyway, just as they'd given the all-clear, someone screamed about tripping a bomb we hadn't been aware of. The guy was running toward us at full speed, hollering about how we had to get the fuck outta there as fast as possible."

Holly began to fade into the background as LJ transported back to that last horrifying day in the Middle East. With each word he spoke, the weight of the memories increased until a crushing weight sat on his chest.

"Do you need to stop?" Holly asked as she kissed his chest. Just that one little touch of her lips grounded him in ways he wouldn't have thought possible.

"No. Don't need to stop." Now that he'd started, he just wanted the fucking poison out of his system. "My best friend, Mick, had been standing next to me, and like a fucking hero, he ran toward the guy instead of away. I have no idea what he was thinking. Maybe he thought he could get to him and help drag him out of the blast zone. I'll never know, and that's one of the things that haunts me to this day."

"Oh, Jack," she said. Yeah, she knew what was coming.

"I screamed at him to get his stupid ass back, but he didn't listen. The blast was huge, took out an entire building. I was thrown about fifteen feet from the force of it. Later, someone told me I was only in the air a few seconds, but fuck, Holly, it felt like hours. I witnessed it all. Mick's death is branded on every one of my fucking senses. I saw his black and charred body. Felt the heat as it scorched my skin. Heard his fucking screams of terror and anguish. Smelled his fucking melting flesh, and, fuck, if the goddammed smoke didn't coat my taste buds. I was helpless, so fucking helpless as I flew through the air and crashed down to a pile of broken bones."

"Helplessness," Holly whispered.

LJ pressed his thumb and forefinger to his eyes. Fuck if he would cry now. "Gets me every time. So, you see, sugar, I relive that shit in vivid detail during the night, and I lash the fuck out at anyone or anything near. I can't be trusted and I'm not sure that'll ever go away."

She grabbed his hand, pulled it from his face and pressed her lips to his fingertips. "What about talking to someone? Going to see a therapist? I can go with you." Her voice held a note of pleading.

Too sweet. Too goddammed sweet. "I've done it, sugar, for about two years. Learned some shit to deal with the panic attacks during the day, but it didn't do shit for the nightmares."

Of course, he hadn't told the therapist everything. He hadn't told anyone everything. Never uttered the words of the trauma that haunted him in the night.

All of a sudden, Holly shot straight up. "Oh, my God!" She spun, kneeling next to him. "I know someone. LJ, I know someone perfect."

"How? You've lived here for five minutes."

"He doesn't live here. He lives in Tampa."

"He? You fuck him?" He narrowed his eyes.

With a roll of her eyes, she swatted his chest. "Jesus, LJ, of course not. Will you listen for a minute?"

He made a show of zippering his lips closed and tossing away the key.

Holly snorted. "You're ridiculous. Okay, my brother's best friend growing up lived next door to us. His family went through some shit while he was in high school, and he eventually fell in with the wrong crowd."

"A one-percenter MC?" With a smirk, he raised an eyebrow.

"Ha, ha. Are you listening? This is serious LJ."

Ugh, he was an ass. Here she was, working to come up with an idea so they could not only be together, but he could finally have relief from the crippling nightmares. He placed a hand on her thigh. "Sorry, sugar. Keep going."

Shooting him a sassy smile, she said, "Thank you. Anyway, his name is Baxter but we call him Bax, and he spiraled out of control pretty fast. Drugs, fights, theft. Eventually, when he was eighteen, the cops picked him up on an auto theft charge. He was sentenced to ten years, served five."

"Shit."

"Yeah. When he came out, he was a different person. He was a man, but he'd made that transition while behind bars, which I imagine would scar anyone."

Sure would. Since prospecting, LJ had met plenty of guys who'd served hard time. Changed a man no matter their age, but to go from child to an adult in prison fucked men up more than most things.

"Anyway," she went on. "He turned his life around. Got a degree in psychology and works mostly but not exclusively with prisoners. I have a feeling you'd like him. My brother, Daniel, still keeps in touch with him pretty often, so I can get his number for you."

The thought of baring his soul to another stranger had LJ's gut rolling and his mind shooting up road blocks. He'd tried that route, sorta, and here he was after having practically killed his woman.

"LJ..." Holly's voice softened. "I know we have a lot of factors working against us. It's made us have to fight for each other when we should be in the easy blissful honeymoon phase. I'm not going to lie and tell you it won't crush me if you want to walk away, but I will understand if having to fight for this thing is too much too early."

She cupped his face between her palms. "But I like us, LJ, uphill battle and all. I need you to really hear me right now, okay?"

He nodded, captivated by the fierce expression on her face. "I'm listening, sugar."

"I'm willing to fight with everything I have. For you. For us. And I'm willing to wait to spend another night in your arms until you feel safe and ready. For as long as it takes, I'm willing and happy to do it if it means we're moving forward. It's not a sacrifice or a compromise, so don't use those as an argument." She winked then grew serious again. "But I can't fight alone. It just won't work. We'll end up resenting each other, and that would be so much worse than losing you now." She stopped talking to wipe at a tear that escaped.

A second one followed. This time LJ smoothed it away with his thumb. He heard her loud and clear. She'd stick around. She'd wait for him to get his shit together. She thought he was worth it—*they* were worth it.

But that meant he had to get that shit together. Which meant facing his issues, finally confronting and coming to terms with the most painful event of his life. The incident that left him emotionally crippled.

"This guy, the therapist, think we could make it work with him being long distance?" LJ finally asked.

Her eyes widened, and she shook her head as more tears rolled down her cheeks. This time though, he had a feeling they were tears of relief. "I'm sure he'd be willing to talk through FaceTime. I know he's done it before."

After taking a breath, LJ jumped off a cliff he'd promised he'd never scale again. "All right. Get me his number."

Before he had a chance to process what was happening, Holly threw her arms around him and knocked him back on the bed. "Thank you," she whispered in his ear right before smothering him with kisses all over his face.

"Jesus, sugar," he said as he stilled her movement with a grip on her hair. "I should be getting on my knees and thanking you. No one has ever cared as much as you. No one has ever wanted me like you do. There's just no one like you. My sugar."

Holly's throat rose and fell with the force of her swallow as her eyes glistened again. Instead of allowing the tears to fall this time, she said, "If you're gonna get on your knees, LJ, I can think of something better for you to do than thank me."

Quick as lightning, he flipped Holly to her back. "Don't need to be on my knees for that, baby." He kissed his way down her gorgeous body and straight to her sex, pressing her thighs wide as he went.

Surprisingly, he felt light deep inside. Not the dread he'd expected when he agreed to see a therapist. All owed to Holly. The amazing woman healed his soul one day at a time.

He circled her clit with his tongue, fucking loving the familiar prick of her nails on his scalp.

The least he could do for his woman in return was make her come until she passed out.

CHAPTER TWENTY-NINE

The weeks of working at the diner passed in the blink of an eye. By now, her face had healed, allowing her to feel confident in public once again. Holly adored every second spent behind that counter, from the constant stream of customers to the lively and enthusiastic staff, to the success of her menu. Even the two crotchety old regulars who sat at the counter spreading town gossip and bitching about anything and every aspect of their lives made her laugh on the regular. Both in their late seventies, the pair had been friends since grade school, and had been eating at the diner at least three days a week since Toni's parents opened the place over thirty years ago. Holly arrived and left work with a bounce in her step and a smile on her face each shift.

"Can I interest you in a muffin to go with that coffee, Mrs. Stokes?" Holly asked one of her favorite customers. A woman in her late-fifties who worked at the local library. She'd been by every weekday since Holly's counter opened. Five mornings a week, she made a production of only ordering a coffee. Once Holly offered her a muffin or a donut, she'd hem and haw about how she should stick to her diet. In the end, she left with a giant, warmed treat each morning. "Fresh out of the oven as of ten minutes ago."

"Oh, Holly Lane, you're hell on my diet," Mrs. Stokes said as she peered into the display case over the top of her light pink glasses. "You know, I didn't lose a pound last week? Not one pound." She clucked and shook her head. "I blame you." When she lifted her gaze, her eyes twinkled, and she winked. "Haven't tried the cinnamon streusel muffin yet."

"You got it," Holly said as she stifled her laugh.

Once Mrs. Stokes had been rung up and sent on her merry way, Holly took a breath. This ten-thirty to eleven am stretch tended to be the quietest thirty minutes of the morning. Too late for the breakfast crowd, too early for lunch. Gave Toni's staff a chance to rub their aching backs and reenergize for the next few hours.

While soaking up the calm for a few moments, Holly let her gaze wander to LJ's table as it often did when he came in to eat. He made a point to stop in every time she worked, even if it was only to grab a coffee on the run. Her heart never failed to flutter when the bell above the door jangled, and she looked up into his heated gaze. And her man never failed to leave her with a lip-lock that had her turning beet red at work. Today, he and Rocket had estimates to write up, so they'd decided on a late working breakfast.

LJ caught her staring as he always did when she gawked at him. The stud had some kind of radar alerting him when her eyes were on him, which was pretty much all the time. Come on, with a T-shirt hugging his muscles, face tight with concentration, and a pen tapping those lips she loved, the man was hot as hell. The wink he shot her way had her face heating at the memories of that morning and the way those lips made her scream out his name as she came. Good Lord, she'd never be able to show her face to the neighbors above or below her again.

The bell clanged, and Holly turned to greet the next customer. She tried to welcome each patron since she was the first employee they encountered walking through the door.

"Good morning," she said before she fully faced the entrance. "Welcome to—Dad!"

Her father marched in, uniform on, followed by three deputies. Each wore varying degrees of a scowl. The rigid set of her father's shoulders, combined with his piercing gaze, and lack of greeting let her know he wasn't here with a hankerin' for a scone.

This was business.

And that couldn't be good for Toni.

LJ was on his feet and cruising toward Holly before her father reached her counter.

"Thant's far enough," her father said, holding out his hand as LJ neared. LJ's mouth flattened but stopped about ten feet out.

Holly gripped the edge of the marble so hard her fingertips ached. "What's going on, Dad?" she asked as he approached.

Toni emerged from the kitchen, eyes narrowed, and lips compressed.

"You the owner, ma'am?" her father said to Toni, who'd worn a simple coral sheath dress. Most of the time, she dressed as casual as the rest of the employees, but she'd had an appointment earlier and had upped her game.

"Yes, Sheriff. Something I can help you with today?" As she spoke, Toni dried her hands on a bar towel. Most likely it was to keep her hands busy enough she wouldn't be tempted to flip Holly's father off or try to wring his neck. Neither of her hands appeared very wet to begin with.

"I'm gonna need to shut this place down for the day at least," her father said in a voice loud enough everyone in the diner could hear the announcement.

"The fuck?" LJ said, advancing two more steps.

Holly gasped, and Toni looked like she might scream.

"Dad," Holly started.

"Honey, please, this is between me and the proprietor of this establishment," he said without so much as a glance in her direction. His gaze focused on Toni except for every few seconds when he checked in on LJ out of his peripheral vision.

Holly's jaw nearly hit the floor. Never before had her dad dismissed her in such a flippant, unfeeling manner as though she was nothing more than a pesky fly. She risked a glance at LJ whose feet were spread, hands fisted at his sides as if preparing for a fight.

Concern number one centered around keeping LJ from having a panic attack. He'd completed three sessions with the therapist she'd recommended, and the results seemed to be positive, but three sessions didn't exactly equal a cure. She shot him what was supposed to be a reassuring smile.

Probably just looked like gas with the way her insides churned.

"All right, sheriff," Toni said as she lost the air of friendly ignorance. "You've made your spectacle in front of my customers. Got everyone all worked up and wondering what's going on. This will fuel the town's gossip for days. Now, state your business or let me go about mine."

You go girl.

God, if only Holly had balls half the size of Toni's, she could have wiggled out from under her parents' heavy thumbs years ago.

He handed a folded piece of paper over to Toni without another word.

Holly rolled her eyes. So this was how he planned to play it? Couldn't even make a bit of a concession for the fact his daughter stood five feet away.

Screw it.

"What's this about, Dad?" Holly asked as Toni unfolded the paper. Her friend's face went from mildly annoyed to infuriated in a matter of seconds. The diner remained quieter than ever before as every patron, employee, and cop stared in their direction.

Jesus, was that a smirk on her father's face?

"Apparently, I'm using the diner to traffic illegal narcotics," Toni said with a huff.

"Jesus fucking Christ, this is some rank bullshit," LJ said.

Holly laughed. It came out as a bark of shock and disbelief but quickly morphed into a full-on laugh. "You have got to be kidding me." She turned to her father. "Toni? Trafficking drugs?"

The sheriff wasn't laughing. "This isn't a joke at all, Holly. We arrested a low-level dealer yesterday who claimed he received his supply here."

"Then he's lying," Toni said as she tossed the papers to the counter. "Go ahead Sheriff, search the fuck outta my place. Waste your time and mine." With that, she stormed off to her office.

"Don't leave the building, ma'am," one of the deputies called.

"Wouldn't dream of it. I'm not going to miss out on the apology when you find jack shit," Toni called, but she was no longer within view.

"All right," the same deputy yelled, the one who'd interrogated LJ a few weeks ago. Deputy Brown. "If you work here, please stay. If you're a customer, I'm sorry to cut your meal short, but you need to vacate the premises immediately." He wandered farther into the diner, ushering customers toward the exit.

LJ didn't budge from where he stood sentry, neither did Rocket who'd joined him midway between their booth and Holly's counter. Though, as Brown passed by, LJ's nostrils flared, and he cracked his knuckles. Thankfully, LJ seemed to realize walking over to where Holly stood by her father would only antagonize the man and escalate a volatile situation, so he stayed put, but sent death rays her dad's way.

"Dad, Toni isn't some secret drug kingpin. I'm not sure who gave you this information, but it's not accurate. It's seriously ridiculous."

And please don't let it be made up by you as a way to screw with the MC's businesses.

"Your friend Toni has an ugly history, Holly. You think the best of people, always have, but that's a naïve way to go through life." He rested his palms on the counter and sent a pitying look her way. Not for the first time since he began his war on the MC, Holly noticed how unhealthy he looked. Pale with bags under his eyes and more rapidly graying hair. Was it their strained relationship taking a toll on his health? Or had he just forsaken caring for himself in favor of using all his time and energy to screw with the Handlers?

Normally, she'd have more sympathy for him, but after the incident with Schwartz, she'd reached her limit.

With an exaggerated roll of her eyes as though she were a huffy teen again, Holly threw her arms in the air. "Oh, come off it, Dad. I know all about Toni's history. Which is why I know she isn't dealing drugs. Toni was a young, dumb kid when she got into trouble. What? All of a sudden you're holding who people were as kids against them now? You should probably lock yourself up because I'm pretty sure you told me some stories about making a few shitty decisions yourself back in the day. Trust me, Toni is not that kid anymore. She's a fully-grown woman who has suffered over the decisions of her past. She's a business owner who helps kids in situations similar to the one she found herself in back in high school."

"Or she sells those kids drugs," her dad said in a mocking tone as though Holly were a moron.

Holly frowned. Did he truly believe that?

"Her *ol' man* is the enforcer for an outlaw MC, Holly." He sounded like he tasted something disgusting.

"So that's what this is all really about? Your constant attack on the Handlers? Dad, you need to give it up. This club isn't what you think."

By now, the few who remained in the diner had tuned into the father-daughter showdown. Holly was beyond caring. This had to stop before Copper decided he'd been patient enough and took a more aggressive approach. One that cost her father his job, landed him in the hospital, or worse.

Her dad leaned across the counter and got right in her face. "This is what I meant about you getting caught in the crossfire.

Here you are dating a criminal, working with criminals. Holly, you don't belong here. You're better than this."

"Fuck that," LJ muttered.

She opened and closed her mouth a few times before finally saying, "Better like who? Like Rick Schwartz who's a drunk asshole? Better than a man who encourages my dreams and allows me to be myself?" Her focus drifted to LJ, who was watching her. As their gazes met, his face softened though his stance remained rigid. "Better than a man who makes me feel safe and would never punch me in the face? Better than a man who treats me like I'm made of gold?"

Her father snorted and slapped his palm against the glass display case. "Encourages your dreams? You've given up on your dream. You've wanted to own a bakery since you were a child. Now you're working for someone else? Selling a few things at a counter. You seem like you're settling in here, not using it as a stepping stone to start your own place."

"Well—I..." Shit. He had her there. Working with Toni, Jazz, and the rest of the crew had been so much fun, over the past few weeks, Holly began to think of herself as a permanent fixture in the diner. Would that be so terrible? Life changed. She'd moved, made new friends, met a new man; only seemed fitting to create a new dream. Or at least an altered version of her original dream. Holly hadn't once viewed working with and for Toni as giving up until he'd uttered those words.

Now, they burned an uncomfortable hole in her brain.

Is that what she was doing? Giving up? Settling?

Her father must have taken her silence as agreement because he continued. "Come with me now, Holly and I can keep you out of all this. We can move on as a family, and this will just be a dark blip in your life."

A dark blip? What? These had been the best freakin' days of Holly's life. "Wha—" She lifted a hand to her temple as her head began to throb. "I don't...Dad, I've been so happy."

The smile he gave her was rife with pity. As though she was some dumb teenage girl who gave her virginity away to a football player under the bleachers and now realized how used she'd been. "Holly, it's not real happiness. It's infatuation, lust, rebellion, whatever you want to call it."

Her head swirled. "No, it's not."

"I admit we've been overprotective, your mother and I. You've never had the chance to go wild like most kids do. So you're doing it now, a few years too late. But these choices have consequences. Severe ones. Your sister paid the ultimate price for her poor decisions. The same could happen to you."

No.

Rebellion? Her relationship with LJ and friendship with the ol' ladies of the MC couldn't be described as rebellion. Could it? Had she channeled Joy a little too well?

Her mouth turned down.

"Holly," LJ said from across the room where the deputy had herded him and Rocket. "Don't listen to this bullshit. You know it's fucking garbage."

"Shut the fuck up!" her father roared. Out came his weapon. "Hands up mouth closed, or I'll drag you downtown. Again."

LJ seethed, smoke practically rising from his body. But what choice did he have? He lifted his hands, shut his mouth and stared at Holly with a look so imploring she nearly cried.

She'd been on cloud nine just a half-hour ago. Now, doubt, confusion, and fear dominated her emotions and had her questioning her every move.

"Here's how this is going to go, Holly. You have one chance to walk out the door with me." Her father cupped her face between his hands, keeping her attention on him. "One chance to save yourself from all of this. Otherwise, I'm washing my hands of you. You'll be lumped in with the rest of these losers. I won't be able to protect you when the entire club implodes. You'll be risking serious jail time. Make your choice."

She jerked out of his hold as everyone remaining in the diner went bananas. LJ ignored the order to keep quiet and threw more profanities at her father. Rocket went against his customary silence. Toni reemerged from her office to add her disbelief to the mix. Jazz exited the kitchen, escorted by one of the deputies. Her dad screamed at everyone to shut up, but no one listened.

All the sounds merged into one loud buzzing in Holly's head. Choose? Choose between her family and LJ? No, no, no. That wasn't possible. How had it come to this? Despite all the drama of the past few weeks, Holly had truly believed in her heart of hearts, she and her family would work out their issues and find a new common ground to exist on. Sure, she'd known their relationship would change and be strained for a while. But to be written out of their lives? Since Joy died, they'd drilled into her how petrified they'd become of her getting so much as a hangnail. Over and over she'd listened to them express how their lives would end should they lose her.

And now they were willing to toss her away? Did her mother feel the same? How was it possible?

She shook her head as her father's form blurred in her vision. Blood rushed in her ears. All of a sudden, she couldn't catch her breath. She pressed a hand to her chest as she stumbled backward, crashing into the coffee maker. God, was this how LJ felt in the midst of a panic attack? Out of control, confused, and terrified, unable to get his body to respond to commands?

How did someone choose between their family, their blood, and a man they…

Oh, God.

Her arms fell to her sides.

A man they loved.

An impossible decision with an outcome of intense pain no matter which side she chose.

How to make that choice?

"I don't know," she answered her internal question out loud.

She looked between her dad and LJ and back again at least four times, shaking her head while her eyes grew wetter and wetter with unshed tears. Then she closed them and just let the tears fall.

A hand cupped her elbow. "Come on, Holly."

Her father's soothing tone registered, but her brain wouldn't process what it meant for her. Feeling as though her mind had separated from her body, Holly allowed herself to be led outside and gently pushed down to the curb. She had no idea how long she sat there staring at nothing while her brain tried to process the past few moments.

Eventually, her father joined her. "You made the right choice, Holly."

What? Right choice? She hadn't made any choice. She'd sat there in a trance.

Holly forced her body to move and turned toward her father. His face was drawn in concern.

"I-I didn't make any choice, Dad." Her mouth felt sticky and dry.

He frowned. "But you came out with me. Holly, you're just upset, tired. You came out with me and left that all behind. You did good, honey. When you're ready, we'll head home to your mother. I'll call her to get some things from your apartment so you can stay with us until we find you a new place. A safe place."

A new apartment? No. She wasn't leaving LJ.

Holly blinked and looked around, suddenly realizing she was in fact out of the diner. Shit, she'd been so deep in Zombie mode, she'd allowed herself to be maneuvered. "LJ," she whispered as she looked over her shoulder at the building. He must be freaking out. "Where's LJ?"

"Who cares?"

"I care, Dad. I care about him very much. Where is he?" She searched right and left trying to catch sight of the man.

He shrugged. "Come on. Let's go home. Your mother has been worried sick about you."

Clarity hit her then like a ton of bricks. Her choice had been made. "Worried about me?" She laughed, and the high-pitched slightly hysterical sound would have terrified her had it come from someone else. "Worried enough to fabricate an injury and send me off to an asshole who hit me? Like you're worried enough to storm into my place of business and threaten to arrest me and my friends. Worried enough to haul the man I love into jail even though I was screaming at you to stop? You call that worry?"

"Love?" Her dad barked a bitter laugh. "Holly, you're a silly child who has no idea what love is. Now stop this tantrum and let's go."

"I'm not going anywhere with you. Not now, and apparently not ever, since you're the one who issued the ultimatum." She shot to her feet. "And I do know what love is. Even better, I know what it isn't. It isn't threats and stipulations. It isn't forcing someone to bend to your will. It isn't impossible choices and emotional blackmail. It's allowing the person you love to be who they are, flaws and all. It's supporting someone even if you don't understand or fully agree with their choice. It's encouraging someone's dreams and creating new dreams with them. It's all the things LJ gives me and everything I want to give to him. Now, if you'll excuse me, Sheriff, I need to get inside to the man I love. I'm sure your deputies have finished searching for something that doesn't exist."

Her legs trembled as she stomped to the diner's entrance. She kept her head held high despite the urge to curl up into a ball and grieve the loss of her family. Once LJ's arms closed around her, she could let the emotions fly free, but she'd be damned if her father saw her cry right now.

The bell jangled when she stepped through the door as though she were a hungry customer instead of an exiled daughter on the verge of a breakdown. She scanned the empty space. All the deputies had left at some point while she'd been zoned out. Jazz and Toni were the only two who remained, seated at a booth drinking coffee. Zach would probably be by any minute, storming in like a Tasmanian devil with the force of his outrage.

"Where's LJ?" she asked as she continued to look around. He must be in the back or maybe the bathroom. God, had he had a panic attack?

Jazz gave her a sympathetic smile. "Um, he's gone, Holly. I'm so sorry." She kept her hands wrapped around her coffee mug as though she needed the warmth to infuse into her bones.

Holly got that. She felt cold as well, chilled to the core.

She stopped walking. "Gone? What do you mean gone? Did he go back to work?"

Both women shook their heads. Toni looked over her shoulder at Holly. "I'm not sure where he went. When he saw you walk out with your father, he got the wrong impression. He assumed you'd made your choice."

This can't be happening. "I did make my choice. I chose him. I'll always choose him!" She closed the distance to their table.

With tears in her eyes, Jazz stood then wrapped Holly in a tight hug. "I'm so sorry honey, I tried to get him to stay, but he looked like he was close to snapping."

"Did he say anything?" Holly asked, the words muffled by Jazz's shoulder.

"Um...well..."

"Just say it." How much worse could she feel than she already did?

"Uh..." Jazz's voice dropped low. "He said, 'Fuck it. No chick's worth this shit.' Then he left."

Much worse.

Infinitely worse.

CHAPTER THIRTY

LJ hefted the sledgehammer over his cramping shoulder then let the thing fly. The steel head crashed into the brick with a satisfying crunch and a powerful reverberation through his bunched forearms.

He did it again.

And again.

And again, until the brick fireplace he'd been tasked with demolishing had been reduced to a pile of rubble and he was a sweaty, dusty, exhausted mess. He'd been pushing the limit over the past few days. Working himself to the bone. Having a weary, aching body to tend to at the end of the day helped keep his mind occupied and off a certain curvy blonde.

Okay, that was utter crap. Nothing took his mind off Holly, but busting his ass until he hurt like a motherfucker seemed fitting punishment for breaking his rule and getting in too deep with the woman.

"Looks like some good fucking stress relief."

"Huh?" LJ spun at Copper's statement. "Prez? What are you doing here? You need me for something?"

"Nah." Copper strode his large—almost as large as LJ's—body into the remnants of the house LJ and Rocket were remodeling. His heavy boots crunched over bits of broken tile and drywall as he made his way over. "Just checking in."

"What for?"

Copper raised a bushy red eyebrow. "Seriously?"

"Uh, yeah?" Sure, he'd been a bit tense the past few days, but he'd thought he'd been dealing with the split from Holly pretty well.

A lance of pain tore through his stomach. Shit, just the thought of her name had his gut in knots. There was a good chance he had a fucking ulcer.

"Let's see, Rocket called you a 'cranky fucker' at least a dozen times—today. Zach said you've been a fucking dickass all week. Izzy told me she almost ripped your nuts off twice. And Mav said if someone didn't shove an enema up your ass, he was gonna gut you with a switchblade to relieve the pressure."

Oookay, so he hadn't been hiding his shitty mood as well as he'd thought.

Message received.

"Sorry, prez, just dealing with some shit this week."

"Yeah, brother. Think we all solved that mystery. Holly." His president's eyes fucking sparkled. Was he enjoying this?

LJ grunted. Holly. Fuck he missed her like he'd miss a blown off limb. Which coincidentally was how he'd felt when she'd walked out of that diner at her father's side. Actually, it'd been worse than a lost limb. She'd ripped his fucking heart right out of his chest. It flopped to the floor and rolled out the door right after her.

Serious fucking pain.

Which led to the realization that he loved her.

He'd fallen the fuck in love with a woman.

Holly. A five-foot-five, walking wet dream who hardened his dick and inspired him to slay his own dragons with just one glance.

He fucking loved her, and she'd picked her family over him without so much as an apologetic backward glance in his direction.

"Heard she's called you a few times this week."

Another grunt. If Copper wanted more than an unintelligible sound, he needed to change the subject. Talk of Holly was off fucking limits. LJ swung the sledgehammer over his shoulder, preparing to take out the last of the remaining bricks.

"Also heard a few of the ol' ladies have tried to talk to you about her, but you shut 'em down before they got two words out. Hence Izzy's threats to your balls. Even my ol' lady kept me up last night telling me what an idiot you are."

With a sigh, LJ let the hammer fall to his side. "Look, Cop, no disrespect, I'm sorry I cut into your time with your woman, but is there a point to all this?"

Copper leaned against an exposed beam while he rubbed his chin. "Sure is. And you didn't cut into shit. How do you think I got her to shut up about you?"

He wasn't touching that one. "Well can you get to it already? I got shit to do here."

"Yeah, breaking shit to relieve your foul mood since you don't have a woman to fuck the sour outta you."

Jesus, Copper didn't pull any punches. "Way to hit me when I'm down, prez."

With a chuckle, Copper straightened. "Stop being a stubborn ass and fucking call the woman."

LJ lifted the hammer once again and this time slammed it down. The last of the remaining fireplace crumpled beneath the combined strength of LJ and the hammer. "Why the fuck would I do that? So I can hear her tell me how sorry she is? How much she cares for me, but her father is blood, and how can she walk away from that? How she'll always cherish our time together?" He snorted. "No fucking thanks."

With a laugh, Copper said, "Always cherish our time together? You watch too many movies, brother. No, you pull that giant hairless head out of your ass and call the woman because you owe it to her." He narrowed his eyes at LJ, that laser look telling him Copper knew more than he let on. Like he somehow knew Holly had been healing him, making him whole again.

How she'd been selfless and willing to stick by him despite his many issues.

Or so she'd said.

"You ever think maybe you jumped the gun? Left the diner too early? Ran and cut off communication prematurely?" Copper shot him a wicked grin as he kicked some bricks out of his way. "Hope that's all you do prematurely or else I'll hide Holly away from you myself."

"A joke, seriously?"

Copper shrugged. "Shit's too serious. You need to fucking chill."

Jumped the gun? What did that even mean? "You know something, Cop?"

Of course, he knew something. He had an ol' lady, and his ol' lady was all kinds of close with Holly and the other women. Gossip was a competitive sport to those ladies. Hence why he'd refused to speak with any of them about Holly all week.

"I might. Don't mean I'm gonna tell you shit." He fucking smirked, the asshole. "You need to unfuck your head and stop trying to sabotage yourself. If you can't do that, then you sure as fuck don't deserve that girl." He slapped the back of LJ's shoulder. "Church in three hours. Take a fuckin' break, brother. It's the weekend for Christ's sake. Go for a ride to clear your head."

Copper left as quietly as he came.

"Fuck it," he said out loud. Maybe Cop was right, and he needed to clear his head instead of tear shit down. Three hours was long enough to get a good ride in, shower, and make it to the clubhouse in time for church. After cleaning the demo mess and stowing his equipment in the portable shed on-site, he hopped on his bike.

For a solid hour, LJ cruised through the mountains, replaying every conversation with Holly that took place in the few days prior to her father throwing down the gauntlet. Maybe he'd missed something, some indication Holly wanted out. Some hint she wasn't happy with him or wanted to walk away.

He didn't come up with a damn thing. But what he did realize, was he may have fucked up in a major way. He'd practically begged Holly to walk away from him, and she'd flat out refused. She'd stuck by his side despite him being unable to make her any promises about the future.

As doubt regarding the way he'd ignored all contact from Holly over the past week set in, LJ pulled off to the side of the deserted country road. Christ, he never thought he'd be doing something like this. With a sigh, he pulled out his phone and dialed the number he'd memorized over the past week and change.

"Hey there, Jack. You need help?" came the greeting after just one ring. Bax had turned out to be opposite of every therapist LJ had ever encountered. Big, bearded, tatted, and with jet black hair that fell halfway down his back, the guy looked like he belonged on a bike next to LJ rather than a couch taking notes.

"Not the kind you mean, but I could use some if you have a few minutes." Each time they had a session via FaceTime, Bax had made LJ promise to call any time day or night if he was struggling.

This fucking counted.

"Think I mighta fucked shit up with Holly."

Instead of telling LJ that giving out relationship advice didn't exactly fall under his job description as a PTSD therapist, he asked, "How so?"

As he stared at the gorgeous Smoky Mountains rising through the clouds, LJ spilled his guts about everything that had happened at the diner that horrible day. "I was so fucking pissed when her father led her out of the diner. I shut her out. After she called and texted a few times, I blocked her number. Told our mutual friends not to mention her. And apparently, I've been a miserable fuck all week."

With a chuckle, Bax said, "Happens to the best of us, man."

"Had a visit from my club's president today. He said something I haven't been able to shake from my head."

"What's that?" A rustle of paper sounded in the background, similar to the sound that accompanied Bax flipping open a new page in his notebook. The guy was nothing if not a goddammed note-taker.

"Said I needed to stop sabotaging myself."

"Huh," Bax said. "And what—"

"Fuck, if you ask 'what that makes me feel,' I'm gonna lose my shit."

With a laugh, Bax said, "Have I asked you that once? Come on, buddy, think you know me better by now. I make it a point to never ask that question. I was gonna say what do you think he meant by that?"

LJ fell quiet, and as usual, Bax waited without prodding him along. The therapist always gave LJ the time he needed to formulate his thoughts. "Dunno," he said. "I've been out riding for an hour trying to come up with an answer."

"Mind if I take a stab at it?"

"Called you for a reason, didn't I?"

Bax grunted. The man really would fit in with LJ's brothers. "We've only been at this a short while, but we've crammed a lot of sessions in that time. You're doing well, LJ. Progressing. Digging through issues I know you'd rather peel your own skin off than examine. All for Holly. All for a chance at a life with her. A chance to sleep next to your woman at night."

"And?" None of this was new information. Somehow, LJ managed to keep his voice level though the mention of Holly's name and the image of himself wrapped around her all night had his heart squeezing with pain. Fuck, he missed her.

"And every inch of progress means you're closer to that reality. Which is scary as shit, especially given what happened the one time you fell asleep with her. You're running scared, and it's understandable and not at all unexpected."

A hawk flew overhead. The ultimate symbol of freedom. A feeling LJ only came close to capturing when he was on his bike. Or when he was inside Holly, watching her spiral into ecstasy. "But I want it. I want her and I want to be able to fucking sleep with her. It's all I can think about. Why would I purposefully fuck that up?"

"It's not purposeful," Bax said. "Not intentional, or even conscious. Think of it like a defense mechanism of your subconscious. Your mind is trying to protect itself from the very real anxiety and very real risk you'll soon have to take the next time you try to sleep with Holly. If she's not there, if you run from her, you don't have to take that risk. And there's no chance of failure."

And that, right there, hit the nail straight into the heart of the issue LJ hadn't even realized was an issue. But now it crashed down on him like that brick fireplace he'd torn apart. "Shit, Bax, what if I go through all this, what if I fucking spill my guts out to you for months and work on fixing all this shit only to hurt her one night? Isn't it better to let her go now than to give her hope and destroy us both later?"

"It's always a possibility, Jack."

"Well, fucking thanks. That's just what I needed to hear, asshole."

Not once had Bax seemed offended when LJ mouthed off to him. This time was no different. The other man just laughed and said, "Told you when we started this, I wouldn't blow smoke up your skirt, man. Gonna give it to you real. Now, by the time you and I both think you're ready to try again, the possibility of something happening will be minuscule. I can promise you that. You're making progress. You'll start having fewer and fewer nightmares. I've seen it many times."

LJ scrubbed a hand down his face. He had to get rolling if he wanted to make it to church on time. "I'm not sure I'd feel comfortable even giving it a shot unless I'd been nightmare free for at least three months." Never before had he gone that long.

Never had he gone longer than thirty days, and even that amount of time had only happened once or twice.

"I think setting a goal like that is a solid idea. Gives you something to strive for, a measurable count of success. So, let's go with that. You go nightmare free for ninety days, then you give yourself to your girl for the entire night. Sound good?"

LJ grunted. "Gotta get the girl back first, don't I?"

Another laugh. This guy was having too much fun on LJ's dime. "Yeah, guess that's kind of an integral part of the plan."

"Ninety days, Jesus. Think she'll go for it?"

"Brother, if you can manage to get her back, I know she will."

Right. Get back the woman he wasn't a hundred percent certain still wanted him.

Nothing to it.

First step in *Operation Get Holly Back* involved pulling his head out of his ass as Copper unsubtly suggested. He searched his contacts for someone he'd been ignoring almost as much as he'd shunned Holly the past few days.

"LJ?" Jazz answered, sounding shocked by his call.

"Hey, Jazzy. Can you do me a favor?"

"Maybe." The surprise was gone, and all that remained was sass and attitude. Another time it would have pissed him off, but his lips quirked. Holly had herself some good and loyal girlfriends.

"Need you to tell me, Jazz."

"Ahh," she said. "You mean you want to know what really happened last week? Not what your stupid man brain turned it into?"

"Something like that."

"Glad you finally woke the fuck up."

Leave it to Jazz to hand him his ass worse than Copper. "I'm wide awake, Jazzy."

"All right, then."

As she filled him in on what happened when Holly returned, LJ realized he didn't need anyone to hand him his ass. He'd kick his own ass halfway across the country for being such a dumb shit.

"Thanks, Jazz," he said when she finished her tale.

"What are you going to do?"

"I'm gonna get my fucking woman back," he said.

Then I'm gonna tell her I love her and make it so she never wants to leave.

CHAPTER THIRTY-ONE

Holly shouldn't have eaten that scone.

Or had the double shot of espresso.

For sure, she should have skipped the muffin she hadn't been remotely hungry for. Stress eating only worked if severe nausea wasn't likely to occur from said stress.

And Holly was so nauseated, she might never eat again.

As she stood outside the brick sheriff's station, she had to fight the urge to flee. Instead, she forced herself to pull the door open and step inside the quiet lobby.

"Oh, Holly, dear, how wonderful to see you! It's been a while," Marjorie said, all smiles and blissful ignorance as to the shambles of the father-daughter relationship between her boss and Holly.

"Hi, Mrs. B, uh, Marjorie. Great to see you too."

"There you go, dear, I knew you'd get it at some point." With a wink, she grabbed her oversize handbag and shuffled from behind her desk. "I'm running out to grab a late lunch. Been quiet around here today. Your father is in the conference room with a few of his deputies. Some hush-hush stuff going on in there. You can knock, though. He told me he'd always make time for you no matter what."

No matter what. Ha. What a joke.

"Thanks, Marjorie. Enjoy your lunch."

"Why, thank you, dear." Marjorie patted the side of Holly's arm as she passed. "Let your daddy know I'll be back in an hour."

"Will do."

Once she was alone in the front lobby, Holly let out a breath. Whether or not this was a mistake would be revealed shortly, but the pit in Holly's stomach didn't seem a positive way to begin. She hadn't spoken a word to either of her parents since the day her father raided diner.

She hadn't spoken to LJ either.

Difference was, she'd reached out to LJ a number of times where she'd been ignoring all communication from her family. Even her brother's calls weren't given an answer. She loved Daniel, but he was a cop like her father, and if he planned to try to soften her attitude toward her parents, she wanted no part of it.

Today was her Hail Mary pass. The one move she'd make to repair the damage before she accepted the fact that, yes, her parents planned to write her out of their lives. Over and over she'd rehearsed what she planned to say.

She loved them, respected them, and wanted to remain a part of their life. But she also loved LJ. And after she walked out of this office, she was tracking his tight ass down and getting him to hear her out. Then, if he still rejected her, she'd have to accept it, but at least she'd be able to say she'd given it her all. Her all and then some because she was prepared to get down and dirty to win this battle.

Hence the ultra-sexy underwear currently riding up her crack. That stuff may be successful at turning her man on, but dayum, it was uncomfortable as all get out.

Time to stop dawdling and get on with this miserable task.

As Holly walked toward the conference room, with about as much enthusiasm as if she were walking into Jury Duty, voices of the officers met her in the hallway.

"Shit, Sheriff, you really worked this from all angles, didn't you." The voice belonged to Schwartz.

Holly slowed and stifled a groan. Since the hellish night of the missed concert, she hadn't laid eyes on the man and didn't relish it now. If her task weren't so important, she'd bail and come back at a time the deputy was absent.

"I have," her father said. "It's time to move forward and start putting these bastards behind bars."

With a frown, Holly crept closer to the open conference room door. Was it wrong to eavesdrop? Sure, but that wasn't going to stop her. Not when she had a really good idea who the "bastards" were.

"You sure Marjorie's gone? No one left in the building?" That was Higgins. Apparently, this meeting was a gathering of reptiles.

"Yeah," Schwartz said. "Saw her car drive off a minute ago out that window."

"All right. Let's review the plan one more time," her dad said. A chair creaked and footsteps sounded in the room.

Holly's heart raced as she flattened herself against the wall. Like that would do anything if the men stepped into the hallway. She should leave. *Needed* to leave, but her feet were rooted to the ground, and her body froze as she waited for more.

"In exactly thirty minutes, dispatch is going to receive a phone call from a chick who was partying at the clubhouse last night," Schwartz said.

"What's 'er name again?" Higgins asked.

"Carli. She's some whore who used to hang around the club begging for scraps. Had dreams of being an ol' lady." Schwartz snorted as though the thought disgusted him. "Stupid girl learned a hard lesson about how little whores are valued."

All three men laughed.

All three.

Her father. Laughing at some poor woman's pathetic life situation. Despite the pain in her heart and the sickening feeling of betraying her blood, Holly pulled her phone from her purse. After silencing it, she opened the camera and pressed record.

"Anyway," Schwartz continued. "Five hundred bucks goes a long way in Carli's world and she was more than willing to do anything I wanted."

"You fuck 'er?" Higgins asked, and Holly nearly vomited.

No one said anything for a second then all three laughed again. She imagined Schwartz winking or making some kind of obscene gesture.

"Let's get serious for a second," her father said. "She was able to plant the drugs, right?"

Oh, my God. *Oh, my God.*

Plant the drugs?

This could not be happening.

Holly bit down on her lower lip, hard, to keep from screaming. A tiny whimper of pain escaped, and she clamped a hand over her mouth and held her breath. The men seemed completely oblivious to her presence. Tears streamed down her face, landing on the screen of her phone. She'd just recorded her father admitting he'd planted evidence to frame the Hell's Handlers.

"She did it, not sure how she managed to smuggle that much meth in when she was wearing next to nothing, but the woman pulled it off."

Higgins snorted. "Probably shoved it up 'er twat."

"Maybe," her dad said. "Who gives a fuck? The deed is done, and we'll find enough meth in enough places around that clubhouse to arrest a good handful of them. Enough to fuck up their businesses both legal and illegal for a while. Judge Milson is home today with his family. We can get a warrant signed five minutes after the whore calls it in."

Never once in her entire life had she heard her father refer to a woman as a whore. Even when he arrested prostitutes as a beat cop. What the hell happened to the man she grew up with?

His daughter was murdered by a biker.

"So what's Carli gonna say when she calls into dispatch?" Higgins asked.

With a laugh, Schwartz responded, "She's good, I'll give her that much. She's gonna be all weepy and say she met this guy, thought he was really fucking fun, partied with him. When he took her back to his room, she found the drugs in his bathroom. She's gonna act all heartbroken because she thought she'd finally met a good guy."

"Jesus," her dad said with a chuckle. "Like taking candy from a fucking baby."

"Where'd she plant it?" Higgins asked.

"Told her not to tell us. Can't have it looking too easy. This way, when we show up with a search warrant, we actually have to fucking search. Don't worry about being too careful with their shit, either," her dad said, and of course, the goons laughed.

Holly trembled as she took two silent steps back down the hall. Thirty minutes wasn't a lot of time to get to the clubhouse, let them know what was going on, and for the men to find the drugs. Just as she was about to pick up her pace, Schwartz spoke again.

"This is pretty fucking genius, Sheriff. How'd you think of it?"

Her dad snorted. "Ain't my first rodeo, boys."

Holly froze again. What? He'd done this before? Set someone up? Jesus, as bad as this was, she'd kinda hoped he'd just lost his mind over his biker hatred and acted out of character. But to know he'd been dirty before?

For a second, she worried she'd pass out if she heard much more, but how could she leave now? She tip-toed closer to the door once again.

"No shit?" Higgins asked.

"Yeah, back in Florida, there was an MC, real nasty fuckers. Legit drug dealers, weapons traffickers, prostitution, the works. They were slick, though. Couldn't pin a goddamned thing on them."

"So how'd you get 'em?"

Holly couldn't move, couldn't breathe, couldn't even blink. How'd he get them?

"About a week after my daughter was murdered, a drifter was arrested on a drunk and disorderly. We found my daughter's necklace in his pocket. Didn't take much to break the guy. He squealed after just a few whacks to the ribs. Confessed to my daughter's murder."

What?

But Curly had murdered Joy. Hadn't he? She'd been told that for the past twelve years…

Oh shit.

No.

No! He couldn't have.

"Oh man, if yer going where I think yer going with this, yer a fucking genius," Higgins said.

She could practically see the evil grin cross her father's face. "Bet you're ass I am. My partner and I kept the confession on the down-low. Destroyed the interrogation tapes. We got lucky with the drifter. Committed suicide before we could even take care of him ourselves. Didn't take much to plant my daughter's body on one of the MC's properties. Did something similar to what we're doing with Carli. Paid some cracked-out whore to sneak Joy's necklace into the clubhouse. She also took a few things from the clubhouse, which we planted with the body. Bing, bang, boom, irrefutable evidence. Guy's rotting away for life, and the MC fucking crumbled after that."

"Fuck," Schwartz said. "You're my fucking hero, Sheriff."

Holly stood in the hall, hand over her mouth and shaking her head. How was it even possible her entire world had imploded in a matter of seconds? With unsteady fingers, she ended the recording. If someone heard that, her father would spend the rest of his life behind bars. But how could she keep it to herself and still look in the mirror each morning? An innocent man was rotting behind bars for her sister's murder.

Disgusting.

"Twenty-five minutes," Higgins said. Then someone clapped their hands together once and rubbed them as though preparing to dig in to a delicious spread.

Twenty-five minutes. Not a lot of time. As quickly as she dared, Holly tiptoe-ran toward the exit. With soft hands, she pushed the door open, slipped out, then held it as it closed so it wouldn't make a sound. Once outside, she darted to her car. If they heard or saw her, she was screwed, so she circled her car around the building and left via the back exit. The maneuver avoided the conference room windows.

The moment she pulled out onto the highway, Holly floored the gas pedal. Her car shot forward, sputtered, then the speed began to drop.

"No, no, no!" she cried, slamming her palm on the steering wheel. "They said they fixed it! Shit!" She pulled off to the side of the road just in time for the car to utter a pitiful coughing noise and flat out die. Smoke drifted up from under the hood. Cars were not her thing; she knew next to nothing about them, so there wasn't even a point in looking under the hood.

"Fuuuck!" she screamed. "What do I do? What do I do?" All she knew was she needed to get to the clubhouse even if she had to jump on the hood of a passing vehicle.

Jazz. She could call Jazz.

Scrambling, she opened her phone. "Hey, girl," Jazz said after answering at the end of the first ring. "Aren't you supposed to be—"

"Jazz, my car broke down on Chestnut Hill Road. I need you to come get me right now and drive me to the clubhouse. I can't explain now, but it's one hundred and ten percent an emergency."

"Leaving the diner now." The clatter of Jazz's keys sounded in the background. "I'll be to you in less than three minutes. Just tell me if you're hurt."

"No. Not hurt."

Not physically anyway.

"Okay, I'm coming, girl. Hang tight." Jazz disconnected the call and Holly waited by her car. She couldn't stand still to save her life, so she paced. Something, anything to burn up the anxious energy shooting through her nervous system.

As promised, Jazz rolled up in two minutes and fifty-two seconds. Before the car had stopped, Holly had ripped the door open and hopped in. "Clubhouse, Jazz, ten minutes ago."

"Okay, hold on to your seat." She hit the gas so hard, Holly flew back into the seat, but it was exactly what they needed to get to the clubhouse in time.

"Girl, you're so tense, you look like you're gonna shatter if we hit a bump. Tell me what's going on?"

"M-my father, Schwartz, and Higgins are framing the club. They had someone plant drugs there last night. A lot of drugs. They'll be at the clubhouse to search in less than twenty minutes."

"Fuck." The car sped up.

The drive to the clubhouse took ten minutes, and that was with Jazz flying twenty over the speed limit the entire ride. "What if he won't speak to me?" Holly asked as Jazz pulled up to the gate.

She snorted. "He'll speak to you, trust me. He'll probably jump you the second you walk through the door. They're in church, by the way," Jazz said as the prospect guarding the gate waved her by.

"Oh great, so I get to bust in on all of them at once?"

"Least you only have to say it all one time."

"Small silver lining, I guess." She gnawed on her lip. The poor thing was going to need stitches at this point.

Jazz didn't bother pulling into a parking spot. She screeched the car to a stop as close as possible to the entrance. Both women ignored the gate prospect yelling at Jazz's driving. "Good luck, girl. I'll deal with the prospect and be right in."

"You're the best, Jazz." After a quick hug, Holly was out the door and rushing into the clubhouse. Too bad she hadn't had time to prepare what exactly she was going to say to the room full of intimidating men.

As she charged through the quiet bar area toward the chapel doors, Thunder yelled out, "Holly! They're in church! You can't go—"

"It's a fucking emergency," she screamed over her shoulder.

"Shit." Thunder's boots pounded after her, but she didn't stop.

She couldn't stop.

Not when she was under the gun to save the man she loved and his entire family.

CHAPTER THIRTY-TWO

LJ scowled at the clock on the wall for the tenth time since church began, fifteen minutes ago. Never had he wanted to escape his brothers like he did at that moment. Now that he'd finally spoken to Jazz and heard how devastated Holly had been after he pulled a disappearing act last week, he wanted nothing more than to go claim his woman. A few times, he'd almost shot her a text, but winning her back needed to be done in person.

"All right let's pipe the fuck down for a few minutes. Got some serious shit to go over with you." As he spoke, Copper glanced at LJ one too many times for his liking.

Shit. He'd put money on this having something to do with Holly's father.

"We got trouble?" Jigsaw asked.

Copper stroked his beard. "Not sure yet. Could be. Wanted to run my info by you guys and get your take." He flicked another look at LJ.

What the fuck?

"I've been looking into the death of Holly's sister."

LJ's spine straightened. "What the fuck?"

Holding up his hand, Copper said, "Hear me out, brother."

"All right." LJ stood down but didn't fucking relax. Copper didn't do shit willy nilly. If he thought this was necessary, there had to be a good reason for it.

"Guy serving time for the death of Joy Lane was a president of a one-percenter club down near Tampa. Goes by the handle Curly. Their club was into shit we ain't, but not fucking murdering little girls. Club's gone now. Lane tore it to fucking pieces after his daughter was killed. Anyway, Curly has maintained his innocence through the investigation, trial, and still, after twelve years of incarceration, swears he was set up." Another look in LJ's direction.

"Spit it out already, Cop," LJ said.

"I was able to speak with him at the prison. Says Sheriff Lane spent his career trying to take out the MC. After one too many failed attempts, this guy swears Lane framed him. Says he'd stake the life of any one of his men on it. Doesn't know how, but he's one hundred percent confident Lane is the man responsible for his arrest. Swears to fuck and back he didn't kill the girl."

"Oh fuck," LJ whispered.

"Fuck," Mav echoed. "Shit, Cop, this is a goddamn fucking mess. You believe him?"

This time, Copper locked gazes with LJ. "Don't know the guy for shit, but my gut tells me he's innocent. Whether the sheriff was the one who framed him, I can't be sure, but it's not ringing as out of the realm of possibility, is it?"

This was going to destroy Holly. Absolutely shatter what remained of her heart.

"You'll get her through it, brother," Rocket said, as he landed his hand on LJ's shoulder.

He looked up. "Sorry, didn't realize I'd spoken out loud."

"We got your back, brother," Zach said from across the table. "Your woman's too."

LJ grunted. "Pretty sure she ain't my woman right now."

"Eh," Mav said with a wave of his hand. "Details."

Leave it to Mav to finally have him cracking a smile.

"So, what do we d—"

The double doors leading to the chapel flew open, and as though he'd conjured her with his mind, there stood Holly.

Thunder ran up behind her a second later. "Shit! Fuck, Copper, I'm sorry. She ran past me. She's fucking fast." He shot Holly a dirty look, but she paid him no attention. Instead, her gaze shifted between LJ and Copper.

Her eyes were wide, frenzied and her chest rose and fell in a rapid clip. Could have been from running in there, but the way she was fiddling with the hem of her shirt led LJ to believe something was stressing her in a major way. Almost to the point of panic.

LJ stood. So did Copper. "What's wrong, Holly?"

Ahh, so his oh-shit meter shot off the charts as well.

"I—" She looked around the room then shook her head. In a strangled voice, she whispered, "My father will be here in about ten minutes with I don't know how much backup. He paid some woman named Carli to plant drugs in the clubhouse. I don't know where and I don't know how much, but I know it's enough to have you all arrested for intent to distribute." She spoke so fast the words rushed together.

LJ jumped to his feet. Jesus Christ, how had she found this out? Her father wouldn't have told her without serious motivation. "Sugar—" he started at the same time Copper barked, "Later, LJ. You said ten minutes?"

"Holly nodded. I'd say ten to fifteen by the time they get the warrant signed and get here."

Copper placed his palms flat on the table. He leaned forward and scanned each face in the room. "Get searching, men. Every fucking nook and cranny in this goddamned place. We start in the rooms of anyone who spent five seconds alone with Carli. Thunder?"

"On it," he said before jetting out the door, looking a little green around the gills.

"Get fucking moving!" Copper barked. The men jumped to their feet, and all fled the room. The sounds pounding of motorcycle boots across the floors rang out a thunderous crescendo.

Though he needed to help his brothers, LJ stayed rooted to his spot, eyes glued to Holly. She stared at him right back. God, he'd missed her. Even frazzled as fuck, she looked so damn beautiful.

"Holly," Copper said, breaking the spell.

"Y-yes?"

Fuck, LJ hated the uncertainty in her voice. As though she'd done something wrong by being related to the bastard.

"LJ needs to go search his room. If your father wants anyone to go down, it's him."

She gasped. "Yes. LJ, go please! You can't—it'll kill me if—" She swallowed and shook her head. "Please go. We'll talk later."

He didn't move.

"You're free to leave, Holly," Copper said.

What? LJ wanted to body slam his president. Holly couldn't leave. She belonged right there, tucked against his side where he could protect her.

Her forehead wrinkled.

"I'm sure you don't want to be here when this all goes down. Your father might not let you walk if he starts making arrests. You can go before they get here," Copper said.

Fuck. Good thing one of them maintained the ability to think straight. "He's right, Holly. You need to get the hell outta here."

Holly straightened her shoulders. Suddenly, the muscles of her face relaxed and she lost the tension in her spine. "I'm exactly where I'm supposed to be. Where I want to be. With you. So please go search your room because I'm going to be pissed off if I have to speak to you through bars tonight, when I spent a fortune on this skimpy as hell underwear for our make-up sex."

Hot damn!

Copper did a shitty job of covering his laugh with a cough as Holly's cheeks turned bright pink. A fucking stampede of wild elephants couldn't chase him away from that sexy promise. He rounded the table, stopping in front of his woman. "Wouldn't miss tonight for the world," he said before giving her a quick, hard kiss. "Wait for me at the bar. I'll be right back."

"Wait!" Holly cried as he stepped through the door. She darted over to him and grabbed the sides of his face, pulling him down to her. "I love you," she whispered in his ear, as though she might not get a chance to say it later. Then she kissed him stupid. "Now go find those drugs!" she said as she shoved him away.

Like some kind of lovesick pussy, LJ nearly floated up the fucking stairs. Holly loved him. And as soon as this clusterfuck of a day was over, he'd be giving those words right back to her.

With a lighter heart than he should have had given the circumstances, LJ began the search of his room with his minimally used closet. He rifled through his belongings as fast as possible while remaining thorough. Though he'd been staying at the clubhouse since things went sour with Holly, he hadn't been within spitting distance of Carli. The female snake didn't begin to tempt him and that was before he'd known she had the balls to betray the club. The fool would be lucky if Copper let her live until the next sunrise.

Of course, he'd have to be a free man to go after her. Fuck, Shell would be destroyed if Copper got himself locked up.

With a huff of frustration, he slammed the closet door closed. There went the good vibes.

Next, he ransacked his own dresser only to come up empty there as well. Nothing on the small bookshelf across from his bed either. Three minutes left if Holly's timeline was correct. Just as he was about to leave the room and check on his brothers' progress, his eyes fell to his bed.

Tightly made thanks to years in the Navy, there was no way she could have hidden something under the covers. Besides, he'd slept there, alone last night and would have noticed a brick of meth next to him. Yet something scratching at the back of his neck kept him from ignoring the bed. After stripping the sheets, he flipped the mattress, giving it a good once over.

"Well, I'll be a motherfucker," he whispered. Sure enough, something sharp had been used to slice a slit in the mattress.

When he stuck his fingers through the slash, he encountered a plastic bag. One good tug had the fucking drugs in LJ's hands

"Fuck, fuck, fuck," he whispered as he righted the mattress. Time being his enemy at the moment, he tossed the bedding on the mattress. When the cops came to search his room, they'd find a messy bed that looked like it'd been recently fucked in. And if they found the hole in the mattress? So fucking be it. There weren't any drugs to be found in there, so what the fuck could they bust him for? Destroying furniture?

Meth in hand, LJ jogged back downstairs and straight into the chapel. Holly, who of course hadn't waited by the bar as instructed, sat at the table, chewing her poor thumbnail to bits.

"Got it," LJ called out as he entered and walked straight to Holly. "Holy fuck balls."

"Yeah, what I said," Mav added.

Laid out on the table were four more gallon-sized bags, identical to the one LJ had found in his room. None of them weighed much, maybe a pound a piece, but there were fucking five.

Zach entered the room and let out a low whistle. "That's a lotta ice, boys," he said.

"How much you think?" Copper asked.

Zach bit the inside of his cheek as he scratched his chin. Then he picked up a bag. "We're talking a pound here. Could be a little over that. Shit, Cop, each of these bags could net up to twenty Gs. We're talking a hundred big ones. Carli musta brought this in over a few weeks. Someone sure wants to see us burn for this."

"I'm so sorry," Holly whispered.

LJ dropped in the seat next to her. "Shit, sugar, none of this is on you. You just saved our asses big time here."

"Not that I don't love a good schmoop fest," Mav said. "But we're working on borrowed time here. Sheriff's gonna be here any second. What the fuck do we do with this shit that now has our prints all over it?"

"Thunder!" Copper barked out.

The prospect snapped to attention. "Yeah, prez?"

"Here." Copper tossed him a black backpack. "Fill it and run it out to the box. There's a crowbar in the corner. Use it to pry the lid off the drain. Toss this shit in there and cover it back up. Stay down there until one of us comes for you."

"On it," he said as he stuffed the last of the packages in the backpack, then took off running.

"What's the box?" Holly asked with a quiver in her voice.

"You don't wanna know, sweetie," Mav said with a wink.

Holly looked to LJ. "It's basically an underground bunker the club uses to handle...sensitive issues."

"You're right, Mav, I didn't want to know." Holly dropped her head to the table with a groan. A few of the guys laughed and the tension relief couldn't have come at a better time. Just as LJ soothed his palm up Holly's spine, a loud banging sounded from the front door of the clubhouse. The kind of heavy-handed knock only made by one kind of person. A cop.

"Open the fuck up!" Schwartz shouted.

When no one made a move to welcome the cops into the building, the pounding continued followed by, "Coming in hot!"

The door flew open.

Bang, bang, bang.

The successive ear-ringing bursts were accompanied by blinding flashes of light and a cloud of smoke.

Holly screamed.

LJ tackled her to the ground, using his big body to keep her covered. All around him, men cursed and hit the ground as cops shouted for everyone to drop to their knees.

As he lay over Holly, the buzzin in LJ's ears grew to deafening. His fingertips began to tingle and the crushing band wrapped its way around his chest.

No, no, fucking no.

Not now.

Next came the shakes and a gasping breath that only meant one thing. Full-on panic was rushing in.

Just as his mind began to slip into that dark place, soft hands landed on his face. "Baby, you're okay. I'm okay. It was just a few flashbangs. Don't go anywhere. Stay with me. My father is here, and we gotta help your brothers, okay? I need you to concentrate on my voice and stay with me here, in the clubhouse. You're not in the Middle East. You're safe. Shit kinda sucks here now, but we got your whole family here with us."

As she spoke and caressed his cheeks, LJ's mind began to clear. Within seconds, the tingling disappeared, he was able to draw in a breath, and the noise in his head dulled to an annoying buzz. "I'm good, sugar," he whispered. "Not going anywhere unless you're right by my side."

"Line up! On your fucking knees. Hands behind your back," one of the officers yelled.

LJ pushed off Holly then extended a hand to her. After hauling her up, he spoke close to her ear. "Do what they say. Don't panic. No one will fucking touch you with all of us here. Okay?"

Saucer-eyed, Holly nodded. "O-okay."

"Just do what I do." He dropped to his knees next to Screw and interlaced his hands behind his back. After watching, Holly did the same. Her startled gasp had him glancing in the direction she stared.

Fucking Higgins was dragging Jazz out of the kitchen with about ten times the necessary force.

"Get your motherfucking dirty pig hands off her," Screw snarled as he began to get up.

Someone shoved him back to his knees with a, "Stay the fuck down, asshole." He was cuffed a second later.

Near purple-faced, Screw's nostrils flared, and his breath left in audible bursts as he fought the urge to buck the officer's orders.

"I'm okay, Screw," Jazz said in a low voice as she was pushed to her knees as well.

One of the officers went down the line, applying flexi cuffs to each and every man, or woman in the room. LJ could practically feel the fear wafting off Holly. "You holding up, sugar?" he asked low enough none of the cops heard.

"Yes. I'm good." Clearly a lie, but he admired her fucking guts.

"That's my girl."

Her lips twitched.

Of course, her father chose that moment to stroll in the room like the big swinging dick. "Listen up," he said. "Know all you shitheads think you're infallible, but we've finally got the proof we need to put you—" His gaze landed on Holly and his steps faltered. But then he rallied, clearing his throat. "To put many of you animals behind bars."

With a grin, he held up a folded piece of paper then walked it over to Copper. The fucker made a production of unfolding it and holding it in front of Copper's face as if to rub in the fact his hands were restrained. Sure seemed to love handing over warrants.

"I can't believe this is real," Holly whispered.

"Hang in, sugar. You're doin' great." Witnessing Holly's disbelief and despair cut LJ deep. The need to shield her, protect her from all this soul-crushing drama flared strong, but there he was, handcuffed like a chump.

Helpless.

The worst place for him to be.

Yet, he didn't have that suffocating sensation. He owed the thanks for that to the woman at his side. The amazing woman suffering because her father turned out to be a monster.

"Got a warrant to search this shithole," Lane said.

"Oh, come on," Holly muttered. "No matter what he thinks about the club, even he can't think this place is a shithole. It's fucking awesome."

Jesus, LJ couldn't help it, he barked out a harsh laugh.

"Something funny over there?" the sheriff asked

"Yeah," LJ said. "Your daughter, who you don't seem to give a shit about as she's handcuffed on her knees over here, she thinks our clubhouse is fucking awesome."

Snickers rose up from all of his brothers as well as looks of respect shot in Holly's direction. The sheriff's jaw ticked, and he appeared seconds away from cracking a filling.

"You're crazy," Holly whispered.

"Crazy about you."

"Cheesy too." Her giggle was near silent.

"Dispatch received a call from a woman who was here last night. She called in, distressed because she discovered an alarming quantity of drugs in the clubhouse. Poor girl came to have some fun and had no idea what she was walking into."

Poor girl? Carli? LJ nearly snorted. That conniving bitch had it coming to her.

"Game over, Copper," her father said, glaring down at the president. "I win." His tone grew gleeful.

"We'll see," Copper replied, cool as a fucking cucumber. With his shoulders straight, head high, and laser-focused eyes looking straight ahead, nothing about the man presented someone concerned for going to prison.

Her father's smile slipped a hair. "Start searching," he ordered, glancing over his shoulder at the band of officers milling about. "I want every inch of this place turned over. The drugs are here somewhere."

"That's what you think, asshole," Screw muttered.

LJ met the sheriff's gaze. He winked, letting the man know he wasn't remotely worried.

Until Holly's father shifted his gaze to her and started in their direction.

Then LJ grew very uneasy.

CHAPTER THIRTY-THREE

The past hour had been such a cyclone of mind games, Holly swore she'd wake from a nightmare at any time. She'd open her eyes to find herself tucked in her bed, all warm and cozy. Her father wouldn't be a dirty cop who framed an innocent man for murder and was trying to set up the man she loved as well.

But none of that happened. Instead, her stern-faced father drew to a stop in front of her. Despite the complete lack of humor in the situation Holly almost laughed. This was certainly a scenario she'd never imagined. Handcuffed on the ground, waiting to find out if her father would be sending her to prison. Sure, they'd found and removed a buttload of the planted drugs, but had they gotten it all? According to Zach, just one of those bags could cause serious trouble for the club.

Her insides trembled as her father burned her with a glare she'd seen him use many times in the past. One full of revulsion and loathing reserved for criminals.

And now her.

"Holly, once the drugs are recovered, you'll be transported to the county jail like everyone else here. We don't have enough space at our small station for the entire MC."

"I don't expect special treatment," she said, proud of the even keel of her voice. "I chose to be here like everyone else in this room."

"Your mother will never recover from this. You've broken her heart."

"*I* broke her heart?"

Beside her, LJ cleared his throat. They'd decided Holly shouldn't reveal what she knew about her father's and the deputies' scheme. At least not yet. Copper wanted to have the information so he could control the situation and planned to drop the bomb when he felt it was most beneficial for the club.

So instead of calling her father the nastiest names she could drum up, Holly bit her already abused lower lip so hard a metallic taste flooded her tongue.

"You realize your life is over?" Her dad cocked his head.

She straightened her spine despite the ache already forming between her shoulders from the unnatural position. Then she took a breath and allowed all her feelings for LJ to fill her heart. A grin took over her face. "I like to think my life is just beginning."

Her father grunted. "You might be right about that," he said. "Especially if you're referring to your life behind bars." He turned and walked over to the officers searching behind the bar.

Dismissed, just like that. Like she was nothing.

"Damn, woman," Screw muttered from the other side of LJ. "You're something else. If this dummy doesn't lock you down, let me know and I'll work his ass over for you." He bumped LJ's shoulder with his own.

Though Holly smiled at Screw's faux threat, LJ remained straight faced. "Consider her locked the fuck down," he said without tearing his gaze from her.

Holly's insides burst with delight.

"All righty then," Screw said. "Guess that takes care of that."

This time, neither she nor LJ paid him any attention.

"Holly Lane, you're fucking amazing."

The delight turned to elation.

"You all need to shut the fuck up," Schwartz yelled as he strode down the stairs.

Empty handed.

Holly let out a tiny sigh of relief. All around her, the men exchanged glances, their eyes sparking and most of them succeeding in hiding their smirks to various degrees.

Not Mav. He grinned like a loon. "No luck?" he asked.

"The fuck I just say?" Schwartz practically snarled.

Mav just chuckled and Holly had to admit the moment called for a good laugh. Seeing Schwartz knocked down a few pegs felt damn good.

The deputy marched straight over to her father and the two whispered back and forth. With each word spoken, her father's face pinched tighter.

Time crawled. What in reality was probably no more than a half-hour felt like ages. The longer the bones of her knees ground into the unforgiving floor, the more her legs ached. What started as an annoying discomfort morphed into a full-on pain traveling up both thighs. Then there was the tingling in her fingers and burning stretch in her shoulders.

"You okay, sugar?" LJ asked after she shifted one too many times.

"Right as rain."

He grunted. "How does a long soak in the tub followed by pizza and wine sound for later?" he whispered.

"Oh man, heavenly."

"All right gorgeous. It's a date." He winked down at her.

Despite the horrors of the day, knowing she'd be ending it with the man she loved helped soothe her. After days of no contact, she wanted to lock herself away with him for just as long to make up for the lost time. They whispered back and forth while the officer's attention was diverted and after a few moments, Holly caught onto the fact he was trying to distract her from the discomfort and help pass the time.

The wonderful man.

One by one, uniformed officers filtered back downstairs, unsuccessful in their search. When there were around ten to fifteen gathered in the bar area, Holly lost sight of her father. He seemed to be at the center of the group. But then he cursed, loud. And something crashed across the room.

Her breath caught in her lungs. Were things about to escalate? Her father set this whole charade up. What was to keep him from attacking one of the Handlers in anger? Where was the line?

With her nerves at about a nine out of ten, Holly's gaze darted between the group of men and Copper. The president still seemed completely unaffected by the events of the day. Had he even moved once since being cuffed? His knees had to be screaming by now, but once she thought about it, she hadn't noticed the man so much as blink.

A red-faced and sweaty Schwartz began uncuffing the men, one by one. Each had some sort of snarky comment for the deputy that had him bordering on purple, and seconds from detonation.

When he freed Maverick, the man hopped to his feet. "Well, this has been fun, boys, but I'm feeling a little unsatisfied. When my woman cuffs me, she usually goes to town on my dick." He patted his crotch. "Any takers?"

Holly gasped and LJ shook his head with a laugh.

"No?" Mav shrugged. "All right. This mean I'm free to go find my woman?"

Schwartz ignored him and moved on. As he released LJ, LJ whispered something to him that sounded scarily like, "I'm coming for you."

The moment everyone was free, the officers started filing back outside. Each resembled a man whose puppy had been kicked. Holly almost felt bad for the innocent ones dragged along in her father's fool's errand.

"Guess I won after all, huh?" Copper said, rubbing his hands together.

"Everyone get the fuck out," her dad yelled. "I want to talk to Copper alone."

When no one made a move to leave, Copper laughed. "You've concluded your business here, Sheriff. My men don't answer to you."

"We have shit to discuss." Her father couldn't stand still. He shifted and squirmed like a junkie coming down from a high.

Copper nodded as he folded his thick arms across his chest. "That we do."

What did the president have planned for her father now? Copper had promised he wouldn't physically go after him, but that was before everything they discovered today. Though she didn't want her father harmed, she couldn't honestly say she'd blame Copper if he decided to take aggressive action. Had Holly not happened to walk into the sheriff's station this afternoon, things would have turned out very differently for the club.

And that fell one hundred percent onto her father's dirty shoulders.

"Head on out, men," Copper said. "Holly, you and LJ okay to stay?"

"Uh, yes." She sounded like a squeaky mouse.

"Wouldn't miss this for the world, prez," LJ said.

"I want everyone back here tonight with their ol' ladies. We got some celebrating to do. Sheriff Lane is stepping down."

Holly sucked in a breath. While she stared on, stunned, the rest of the men cheered, then headed on out.

In just a few moments, only the four of them remained in the clubhouse. Though Copper hadn't informed her of what he planned to say, she just knew he was going to tell her dad what she'd overheard. Her heart pounded so hard, she felt it in her head as well as her chest.

Then the warm slide of LJ's palm against hers had her staring down as he interlaced their fingers. "It's going to be okay," he said, voice full of conviction. "You're going to be okay."

She nodded. "How did it come to this?" God, could she sound weaker and more pathetic? But she couldn't stop it. "My family is destroyed."

He cupped her chin, tilting her face up. "Then it's a damn good thing my family fucking loves you and is ready and willing to adopt you," he said right before placing a soft kiss on her lips.

God, she loved this man.

"Sit," Copper said, his voice like steel. The tables had turned, and the outlaw now held all the cards in this little power play. With his confident stance and commanding voice, the man was clearly in his comfort zone issuing the orders.

Her dad sat at a four-person table about fifteen feet from the bar. Holly couldn't stop staring at the man who'd protected her for most of her life. Who claimed to love her and want only what was best for her. The man who'd once been her hero was a stranger to her now. At the moment, Holly felt stunned and confused. As her brain struggled to process the new state of her life, one where her parents no longer played a role, she had to remind herself everything that happened today had been reality. No matter how fantastic it seemed.

"Sweetheart, you feel like sticking around or is this too much?" Copper asked.

"What?" Holly blinked and tore her attention away from her seething father. The man who just inquired about her wellbeing was so in contrast with the one who'd spoken to her father. Yet they were one and the same. Copper clearly had many layers to him. "I'll stay." She sat at the table across from her father. LJ immediately slipped into the seat next to her then pulled her chair so it was flush against his. The warm, solid arm he placed across her back kept her anxiety in check.

Now that the ball was in play, she had to see it through to the finish.

Maybe watching this unfold would provide some kind of closure before she was forced to move on with her life. But the moment she looked up into her father's face, her heart shattered. Nothing. No guilt, regret, remorse, or even love. Just pure black hatred for the two men flanking her at the table. Nothing mattered to this man beyond his hatred. It ruled his life.

Well, it would no longer rule hers.

Forget what Copper had to say, she had a few things of her own to get off her chest. Just as Copper opened his mouth to begin, Holly pulled her phone out of her back pocked and slapped it down on the table.

All three men whipped their heads in her direction, but she kept her gaze locked with her father's. With trembling fingers, she unlocked the phone. The recording from earlier still remained open from when she'd played it for the bikers earlier. Without a word—because what the hell could she say about it—Holly pressed play. Schwartz's voice filled the clubhouse.

Her father instantly paled. "You?" he said in disbelief. "You ran to them?" He started to stand. "You fucking betrayed me!" Both LJ and Copper's hands landed on his shoulders at the same time, shoving them back into his seat. For the first time, her father seemed to shrink before her eyes. As though he realized his chances of leaving the clubhouse of his own accord weren't great.

Now he was scared.

"Keep listening," she said. Who cared about his fear? What about the fear of the man rotting away behind bars for a murder he didn't commit?

No one spoke as the recording continued to play. Listening to her father admit to framing a man for murder hurt just as much the second time around. But some of the shock had faded, leaving room for sorrow. "Why?" she asked.

Her father tilted his head. "Because he was scum, Holly. His entire club was full of filth. Just like this one."

"But he didn't kill her!" A sob lodged in her throat as the pain of losing her twin rose to the surface as though a fresh wound.

"You don't think he killed others? What about all the kids who OD'd on the drugs he sold? Huh, Holly? Don't you think they deserve some justice?"

"Not this way!" Holly screamed as her emotions became too much to bear. It all crashed down around her at once. The loss of her sister. The betrayal by her father. The intense fear and anxiety she'd been experiencing all afternoon. The damn finally broke. "Not this way! You can't swap out one crime for another. You need proof, evidence!" She slapped her palms on the table. "A man is in jail for life. For his *entire* life because you lied! And you tried to do it again today. All for what? Hatred of a group of men you don't even know. I'm trying to understand it, but I just can't wrap my head around it. You're my father! I thought I knew you." Her voice broke. Oh, God, she was yelling, rambling, completely losing her shit, but the hole in her heart hurt so bad she couldn't stem the flow of words.

"Baby," LJ said. His strong arms encircled her, scooped her up off her chair, and settled her on his lap like she weighed nothing more than a paper doll. It was then she realized her cheeks were wet. "Shh, I've got you, sugar," he whispered in her ear. "I've always got you."

She nodded and buried her face in his neck. Looking at her father had just become too painful. LJ stroked his hand up and down her back over and over.

"I'm going to make this simple," Copper said. "Three conditions and I'll keep this recording quiet."

Holly gasped. Resting her cheek on LJ's chest, she watched the exchange between her father and Copper.

The president held up one long index finger. "You step down as sheriff." His middle finger popped up. "You leave town." The ring finger joined the other two. "None of us, and that includes Holly, ever hear from you again."

Her father's fists curled where they rested on the table, but he just nodded. What the hell else could he do? Copper had the power to destroy him.

"Same goes for Schwartz and Higgins. I so much as catch a whiff of one of you after today, this video will be in the hands of every news outlet in the country. Are we clear?"

"We're clear," her father said as though the words felt like a hot poker stabbing in his gut.

"Good. Get the fuck out of my home. Someone will be by your house tomorrow as well as Schwartz and Higgins to ensure you've left. Trust me, you don't want to fucking be there."

Her father stood. His gaze shifted to her and for a heartbeat the man she remembered reappeared, but then his eyes hardened, and he turned and strode out without another word.

It was over. Her family reduced to rubble.

Yet it all could have ended very differently.

"Copper," Holly said. The man gave her his intense attention. "Thank you."

He just nodded. She probably should have said more, explained herself better, or thanked him specifically for not killing or harming her father. Though she'd never ask, she had a feeling the outcome of this exchange would have been very different had it not been for her. Copper didn't strike her as a man who let his enemies walk away freely. But he did today.

For her.

"You're family, sweetheart," he said as he stood. "And family is fucking everything."

Holly snorted.

Clearly that meant something different to Copper than it did to her father.

LJ'S HEART BROKE for the woman in his arms.

His woman.

She sighed, wrapped her arms around him, and pressed her forehead to his chest. He just held her close. How did he comfort her when her own flesh and blood had tried to destroy her?

Copper gave him a chin lift then turned and strode away. Just before the prez disappeared into his office, LJ heard him on the phone. "Bring me fucking Carli," he said, probably to Zach, then he was out of sight.

Grateful for the privacy, LJ tugged on Holly's ponytail. The middle of the clubhouse probably wasn't the best place for what he wanted to say, but he had shit that couldn't wait.

Holly lifted her head and gazed into his eyes. The sadness in hers felt like a punch to the gut.

"I can't change what happened today, sugar. And I realize it's gotta be fucking with your head real bad. You take as much time as you need to get things straight in your mind. I'll be right here by your side the whole time, trying to make you smile, trying to make you laugh, trying to make each day a little better than the one before it. And of course, making you come as often as possible."

With each word he spoke, Holly's spirit seemed to lighten, but that last statement drew a laugh from her.

"LJ," she whispered,

"I know you feel like you lost your family today, but you didn't. Your family is here with me. And like Copper said, it's fucking everything."

"You're everything," Holly said. "I l—"

He covered her mouth. "It's my turn, sugar. I love you, Holly. And if you choose to be with me, choose my family, I will not be the only one who loves you. You'll have a huge group of brothers and sisters that will drive you crazy for the rest of your life."

She smiled and it lit his fucking world. "Can I say it now?"

He nodded.

"I love you, Jack. And I'm not going anywhere."

"Good. That means I don't have you chase you, sugar." He kissed her then, pouring everything he felt into it, especially the one promise he planned to use every ounce of energy working to fulfill.

One day soon, he'd hold her through the night. And it'd be the first of many. The first of every night moving forward with Holly by his side and in his arms.

EPILOGUE

"This was a mistake," Holly said aloud to the empty room. Well, not entirely empty. Biscuit tilted his head and let out a low whine.

"Don't judge me," she said to the dog.

Holly groaned. Who the hell had thought this was a good idea?

She did.

Oh yeah, and frickin' Maverick. Stephanie, too. Stephanie, who was now going to pay for her ol' man's damn idea. About a month ago, the two horndogs had asked Holly if she and LJ ever got a little frisky with some frosting. Her face had been hot as hell as she'd told them no, but the idea had stuck. And now...

After snagging her cell off the counter, Holly scrolled through the contacts until she found Stephanie's name. Her friend answered on the third ring.

"Hey, Holly! What's up?" Steph's bright voice greeted.

"This is all your fault. It's all your fault, and now I'm freaking out. Because of you." Oh, God, she sounded like a lunatic, which she probably looked like as well.

"What's my fault? Are you okay?" Steph's tone took on a level of worry.

"No, I'm not okay. I'm sitting on a barstool in my kitchen, naked, with frickin' frosting on my tits! What the hell was I thinking?"

The squeal that came through the line had Holly yanking the phone away from her ear. "Holy shit!" Stephanie yelled. "You did it? Maverick, come here! Holly did it! The frosting sex thing!"

"Shhh! Don't tell him!" Why would she tell Maverick? "Whatever happened to girl code?"

"Hey," Steph said, humor lacing her voice, "you're the one who said it was Mav who inspired you."

"Uhh, no I believe I said it was his stupid-ass idea that I'm now regretting. I'm gonna wipe this off and go get dressed. Thank you! Bye!"

"No, no, no! Wait! Don't do that." There was some muffled back and forth, then Mav's voice came through the phone.

"Hol? We got you on speaker. Don't you dare clean up!"

If the apocalypse could occur in the next five minutes, Holly would be indebted to the universe.

"What are the chances you'd be willing to shoot a selfie and send it my way?"

"Maverick," Stephanie said right before she giggled hysterically. The traitor.

"What's the chance you can survive twenty-four hours without your balls?" Holly fired back.

Mav fell silent.

"There you go. Chances are about the same. I need to go shower now."

"No!" They both yelled at the same time.

"Look, woman," Mav said. "LJ is gonna lose his fucking mind in the best way. I can promise you that with one hundred percent certainty. The man is gonna walk in, take one look at you and fucking pounce. So stop fucking overthinking. You're a goddess, and your man knows it. Put on your confidence panties and own your sexy shit!"

"What the hell are confidence panties?" Steph asked, muffled in the background.

"Well, shit, Maverick. Who knew you could be such an awesome motivational speaker?" All of a sudden, Holly felt foolish for feeling foolish. Mav was right. Never once had LJ given her any indication he found her body anything less than incredible. He was gonna love this.

"Uhh, I did." Mav said, and the sound of a smack filled Holly's ear.

"Ow! Shit, woman, you're gonna pay for that," Mav said, and the words were followed by more of Stephanie's giggles. This time with a husky quality to them.

Holly's cue to hang up. "Thanks, guys! Have a fun night."

"We will now that you got Mav all revved up," Steph said, but it quickly turned into a moan. "Knock 'em dead, girl!"

Gross. "Make good choices!" Holly yelled, and the last thing she heard before the line went dead was Maverick's bark of laughter.

All right. She could do this. She was sexy. She was confident. With a glance down at the vanilla frosting coating her nipples, Holly rolled her eyes.

She was ridiculous.

A quick swipe of the frosting followed by a taste had her lips quirking.

At least she tasted delicious.

And that's when the giggles started which abruptly stopped when LJ's key jangled in her lock. They'd maintained their individual apartments but exchanged keys months ago. Though they still hadn't spent a full night together, they spent almost every waking moment they weren't working in each other presence.

"Hol?" LJ yelled as he entered the apartment.

Biscuit let out a low woof then loafed off to greet his favorite person.

"Hey, bud," LJ said. "Where's your pretty mama?"

The description had Holly smiling as she took one last peek at herself. Fluffy white frosting topped each breast, and she'd even created a little triangle of frosting in her bikini area. She leaned one arm on the counter, spread her legs slightly, and tried for a smoldering expression.

"Sugar?" LJ called out. The clicking of Biscuit's nails signaled the duo's arrival in the kitchen seconds before they appeared in the doorway to the kitchen. "Holy fucking shit," he said as he came to a dead stop.

Holly smiled. The moment she saw the appreciation in his gaze, all nerves evaporated, and desire shot through the roof. "Hey," she said in a breathy voice she barely recognized. "Thought we might have dessert first tonight."

"You're a fucking genius," LJ said as he stripped off his shirt right there in the doorway. Next, he went to work on his boots. Last to go were the jeans. He straightened in all his super tall muscley glory. Damn, her man was a feast for the eyes.

"Going commando today?"

He winked. "Musta known I'd need quick access."

Holly threw back her head and laughed. LJ shot across the room in a second, his mouth kissing a trail up her exposed throat. "How the fuck did I get so lucky?" he whispered against her ear.

"You liked my baking," she said.

"Can I have my dessert now?"

"You can have whatever you want," she responded.

"Fuck yes." Then without any further words, LJ's mouth surrounded one of Holly's nipples, mouthful of frosting and all.

Her head dropped back, and she moaned as he sucked, then licked her entire breast clean. "Delicious," he whispered, making her smile. He moved to the other breast, taking his time now, to savor both the frosting and her skin. He slowly licked and nipped in circles until all that remained was a dollop of sticky sweetness on the tip of her nipple. Then he sucked it deep into his mouth.

Holly panted as bolts of lightning shot from her breast to her clit. This had been the best idea ever. Mav would be getting one hell of a Christmas present from her.

"Just when I thought you couldn't get any fucking sweeter," he said before pressing a kiss to her lips. "Now…" He dropped to his knees between her thighs. "For the rest of my treat." He grabbed her ass, pulling her so close to the edge of the barstool, she nearly fell off.

Holly yelped right before he licked through her pussy then over her mound, capturing more of the frosting.

"Fuck, that's good," he said. "Get comfy, baby, I'm gonna be here a while."

His tongue hit her clit, and her breath caught as her eyes fell closed. Okay, she owed Stephanie and Maverick a big tub of frosting. Clearly, the couple was onto something great here.

LJ LAY IN Holly's bed with his arms tight around her, his lips licking a path up her neck. After enjoying the best treat he'd ever eaten an hour ago, he'd bent Holly over the counter, spread some frosting over her ass and enjoyed himself a second helping. She'd returned the favor with a frosting-assisted blow job he'd never fucking forget.

They'd showered and decided to skip dinner, full from their sugar fest. With a sigh, Holly snuggled her back against him. If she kept fucking wiggling like that he'd be rock hard again in no time. But before he got carried away for the second time that night, he had something to tell her.

"Got a surprise for you, sugar."

Holly turned in his arms. "Oh, what is it?"

"Colin called me today," he said, referring to the lawyer who'd taken Curly's case pro bono. Hell, once it came out the man was innocent, attorneys were flying out of the woodwork for a crack at the case. It'd been tricky, releasing the information of Curly's innocence while keeping Holly's father out of jail, but Copper managed to pull it off. With some clever maneuvering, new evidence came to light in the case, namely the identity of the actual killer who'd killed himself in jail. The information made Holly's father and the force he'd been on look like bumbling idiots, but not criminals.

"The judge ruled today. As of three this afternoon Curly is a free man."

"Oh my God," Holly breathed. "It worked! He's out?"

"He's out."

"What's he gonna do?"

With a shrug, LJ said. "Not sure. I know Copper offered him a place in our club. He'd have to get used to a different kind of club life, but it could work."

"I think that's a great idea." Her smile took up her entire beautiful face. "I've been so nervous something would fall through, and he'd be forced to stay behind bars."

"It all worked out, baby. Thanks to you."

Holly snorted. "Thanks to Copper. He's the magician here."

After pressing a kiss to her forehead, LJ turned Holly back around and pulled her tight against him. "Just keep telling yourself that, Houdini."

She giggled then sighed, practically melting into him. LJ kissed her shoulder, cupped her breast, and let his eyes drift closed. The sugary scent of vanilla that meant Holly was nearby surrounded him as he began to slide into sleep.

It'd been a great fucking day all around. An hour before he'd heard the good news about Curly, Copper had called LJ into his office.

It was done. Schwartz and Higgins were both dead. The club had waited a while to go after them. Both men had left the sheriff's department and Townsend as ordered, but the club kept close tabs on them, as well as Holly's father. Her parents were now living in the Midwest. According to some digging Mav had done, Holly's father now worked as a mall security guard. Once Copper was confident no heat would land on the club, he'd ordered the two deputies' punishment. LJ had wanted to carry it out himself, but let Copper handle it his way. He wasn't certain, but he had an idea Rocket was the man to take them both out since he'd traveled a few times over the past month. Regardless, the fuckers were gone, Curly was free, and Holly was in his arms where he planned to keep her for the rest of his life.

"J-Jack?" Holly said, voice tinged with uncertainty.

He smiled, his heart so fucking full he could be a goddammed fairy tale character. "Yeah, sugar?"

"A-are you…um…are you—"

He tightened his hold on her. "Sure am, sugar." It'd been a solid ninety days since LJ had any kind of nightmare. He'd reached his target, and instead of being terrified of going to sleep next to his woman, all he felt was the peace of being exactly where he belonged.

Tonight and every night moving forward, he'd be sleeping all wrapped around Holly.

"I'm so proud of you," she whispered, voice thick with emotion. "I love you so much, Jack."

"God, I love you too, sugar."

They fell silent for a while. Neither slept though that had been the goal all these months. LJ just held her, enjoying the absence of anxiety. Loving that he could relax and fade into sleep at any point without fear of hurting the woman he loved.

"This is the best," Holly whispered after a few moments, her voice slurred with impending sleep.

"The fucking best," he said as his eyes grew too heavy to keep open.

Join my Facebook group, **Lilly's Ladies** for book previews, early cover reveals, contests and more!

Thank you so much for reading **Little Jack**. If you enjoyed it, please consider leaving a review on Goodreads or your favorite retailer.

Other books by Lilly Atlas

No Prisoners MC
Hook: A No Prisoners Novella
Striker
Jester
Acer
Lucky
Snake

Trident Ink
Escapades

Hell's Handlers MC
Zach
Maverick
Jigsaw
Copper
Rocket
Little Jack
❈ ❈ ❈

Join Lilly's mailing list for a **FREE** No Prisoners short story.

www.lillyatlas.com

About the Author

Lilly Atlas is an award-winning contemporary romance author. She's a proud Navy wife and mother of three spunky girls. Every time Lilly downloads a new eBook she expects her Kindle App to tell her it's exhausted and overworked, and to beg for some rest. Thankfully that hasn't happened yet so she can often be found absorbed in a good book.